The Collaborators

Originally published in French as *Ferdinaud Céline* by
Éditions Payot & Rivages, 1997
Copyright ©1997, 2002 by Éditions Payot & Rivages
Translation copyright © 2010 by Jordan Stump
First English translation, 2010

Library of Congress Cataloging-in-Publication Data

Siniac, Pierre.
[Ferdinaud Céline. English]
The collaborators : a novel / by Pierre Siniac ; translated by Jordan Stump.
p. cm.
ISBN 978-1-56478-579-4 (pbk. : alk. paper)
1. France--Fiction. I. Stump, Jordan, 1959- II. Title.
PQ2679.I54F4713 2010
843'.914--dc22
2009050630

Partially funded by the University of Illinois at Urbana-Champaign
and by a grant from the Illinois Arts Council, a state agency

Traduit avec le concours du Ministère français de la Culture –
Centre national du Livre

Translated with the support of the French Ministry of Culture –
Centre national du Livre

www.dalkeyarchive.com

Cover: design and composition by Danielle Dutton,
illustration by Nicholas Motte
Printed on permanent/durable acid-free paper
and bound in the United States of America

The Collaborators a novel by Pierre Siniac

translated by Jordan Stump

Dalkey Archive Press
Champaign / London

PART I Blood and Ink

1 Book Culture

Two men sat center stage on the *Book Culture* set that night, flanked by a panel of supporting guests culled from the world of fine writing: they were the two guests of honor, the stars of the show, the now-famed duo known as Dochin-Gastinel. Two names to be reckoned with, names with a ring to rival the illustrious Erckmann-Chatrian, Allain and Souvestre, or Boileau-Narcejac: the authors of *Dancing the Brown Java,* an epic novel published six weeks before, a sprawling panorama of the underside of Occupation-era Paris, a *roman à clef* ecstatically hailed by the critics as a great work of art, a book whose uncompromisingly new style had hit the literary world like a ton of bricks and shaken it to its very foundations, an event some compared to the appearance of Céline's *Journey* in 1932.

The short, thin one, his face drawn, his air drowsy, his eye ungleaming, was Dochin; the tall, fat one, a colossus reminiscent of the hulking brutes in Chaplin's early movies, was Gastinel. Heavy as lead weights, his hairy paws lay flat on his thighs, his bulbous knees stretching his gray pinstriped pants to the splitting point.

There was nothing writerly about their appearance, assuming that writers have some particular physiognomy; they brought to mind nothing so much as a couple of has-beens from some musty music-hall act.

In a few words, Eyebrows, the host, outlined the lives-to-date of these two authors who had so recently burst into literature's hallowed halls—or been pushed in, one might have thought, so reclusive they seemed, so standoffish. And yet, in a little over a month, their book had sold nearly 500,000 copies; the bookstores could hardly keep it in stock, and requests for translation rights were coming thick and fast.

Their demeanor studiously louche, the two partners nevertheless seemed entirely out of their depth. The fat one kept casting anxious glances at the glorious book lovingly cradled in Eyebrows's lap, the host occasionally picking it up and turning the pages in search of a sentence to cite . . .

". . . And for those viewers who don't know it yet—though there can't be many of you left—let us recall that Jean-Rémi Dochin . . ." Amiably, he interrupted himself: "I'll start with Dochin . . . I assume Gastinel won't mind . . ."

Gastinel cracked a wan smile, his glistening face like a deflating beach ball.

"Not at all. Dochin-Gastinel. D-G. Jean-Rémi gets top billing. And besides, we must honor our youngfolk . . . Theirs is the future . . . Jean-Rémi could almost be my son . . ."

"It's true," Eyebrows resumed. "Jean-Rémi Dochin was born in 1950, and you, Gastinel, in 1932."

"Thirty-two, the year of the *Journey*!" the leviathan exulted.

"I'm going through all this a bit quickly . . ." said the host. "I hope our good viewers won't mind. But before the show I promised Gastinel not to detain our honored guests too long; let me remind you that Jean-Rémi Dochin has only just been released from a private clinic. He's still feeling a bit drained, so we're very lucky he's agreed to come up from his home in the Limousin and tell us about his book. Never mind, though: we'll have another chance to talk soon enough, when volume two of *Brown Java* comes out, and then I promise to devote an entire show to our two novelists. For the moment, let's get back to the introductions. Dochin hails from Château-Gontier, in the Mayenne."

"Actually Rechangé, four miles from town," Dochin fussed.

Glancing through his index cards, Eyebrows went on to inform anyone who might not already know it that Jean-Rémi Dochin was born into a modest family of shopkeepers; he came up to Paris at age twenty-four, worked a series of insignificant jobs with no great success, then fell on hard times—living in the streets, begging for handouts, the old story. Eventually, thanks to the devotion of a major in the Salvation Army, he got back on his feet and penned a couple of minor works, one of them eventually published under a pseudonym, unnoticed by press and public alike. Not long after, he met Charles Gastinel, a former puppeteer possessed by the demon of literature, a great lover of poetry, an avid reader of Céline, Dostoevsky, and Gogol—thus embarking on a most fruitful collaboration, culminating in the fevered creation of *Dancing the Brown Java*, and, in the course of that great undertaking, who knows how many memorable arguments!

Eyebrows wanted to cut the introductions short and move on to the book itself, but Gastinel called him to heel:

"Don't forget our little agreement. Dochin and I think it vitally important not to spoil our novel's plot for your viewers. So if you don't mind, let's talk about the book's authors instead. In the end, I think that's what interests your audience the most. People want to see what the novelist looks like, get to know him, size him up . . . Mind you, I don't know why, since that has nothing to do with literature."

"Is that right? You think readers are more interested in writers than in their books?"

"I'm convinced of it. A lot of them, at least. Otherwise, why invite writers onto programs like yours? Why force them to go on display?"

"Well then, let's hear some more about our two authors' lives," said Eyebrows, conciliatory. "Tell us about yourself, Charles Gastinel . . ."

The rotund novelist had first seen the light of day in the Caux region of Normandy. His parents were tenant farmers; they perished in a movie-house fire in Dieppe, one terrible Sunday when Charles was only seven. Taken in by a Parisian uncle who ran a tripemonger's shop near the Porte de Pantin, the orphan spent the Occupation years in the capital. His adolescence was difficult; after his military service he struck out on his own, traveling the world, wherever fate took him. He was a svelte and comely lad in those days; it was only much later, nearing fifty, that he first noted a nascent pudginess that would soon evolve into outright obesity. Returning to Paris after his planet-wide peregrinations (from which, like most travelers, he'd learned little save that men are the same everywhere), still as impoverished as ever, Gastinel took over his uncle's tripe shop and married the daughter of the former cashier. Soon business began to fall off, the taxman came calling, and so he slipped into bankruptcy, like dozens of other Parisians each month. With four children to feed, assailed by a mountain of material difficulties, Gastinel, not unlike Gauguin, chose to ditch his old life; he abandoned his family, dreaming of throwing himself headlong into literature, yearning to take up the pen, convinced he had a book in him.

On the brink of beggary, desperate to escape poverty's clutches, he'd gone so far as to burglarize a jeweler's shop in Rouen. He was arrested almost immediately and got put away for two and a half years. Nonetheless, some good came of his time in the slammer, for there he met an aged Czech puppeteer who taught him the basics of his trade. On his release, he cashed in the gems stolen in Rouen—he'd found time to stow them away somewhere before his arrest—and with the proceeds established a rudimentary marionette theater: a simple wooden crate with a false bottom and fifty-some puppets. Transporting his gear in a little truck, he began putting on shows all over Paris, on playgrounds, at boarding schools, in orphanages and community centers. In summertime he set up shop in parks and gardens all around town, sometimes even on the beaches of Normandy. Things seemed to be working out, so he persevered, expanding his turf into the remotest provincial backwaters. He kept up the puppeteer act for eleven good years, earning a respectable living. But alas, all good things must come to an end. Spurred on by some niggling protein deficiency, Gastinel's weight began to balloon at an alarming rate; by 1984, now fifty-two years of age, he was frankly obese, almost elephantiasical. And this soon brought his puppeteer days to a close, for he now found himself impossibly cramped in the wooden shed that served as his theater—unable to give his buttock a scratch, should the need arise, and too closely confined to manipulate his marionettes. One Christmas day, making a final desperate attempt to put on his show, he reduced the multicolored shed to splinters—much to the delight of his young audience, who assumed this was all part of the act, and so shrieked with joy as he sat on the ground with the planks of his theater around him. Oh, how that laughter rang in his ears! Years and years later, it was resounding still!

Deeply discouraged, he sold off his equipment, his marionettes, and set out on his aimless travels once more. Back to hard times, panhandling, sleeping under bridges, his meager savings soon dwindling to nothing. Homeless at fifty-three, trudging endlessly through the streets of Paris, his misshapen body like some cruel caricature come to life.

And then, one fine day, he met up with an uncle he hadn't seen for many long years. This uncle had made a vast fortune in canned goods. A generous man, keen to the suffering of others, he offered his nephew a loan. The chance for a fresh start in life. Finally realizing a lifelong dream, Gastinel invested that capital in a little publishing venture, very modest, scarcely even what people might call a small press: popular literature, science fiction (and not the top-drawer stuff, either), vacation guides, comic books, porn . . .

Soon—let us remember that this was the "about the authors" version of the story, and so to be taken with a grain of salt, since it was almost pure fabrication—the publishing house started to founder, and Gastinel found himself back on the street. One more brief return to the world of meat, but this time in the provinces, humbly manning the scalding vat in the slaughterhouses of Vierzon. Once a puppeteer, then a publisher, and now back to offal and scrap! What a fall! Day after day spent slinging sides of beef over his massive shoulders. A number of legs of lamb having gone missing, he was soon shown the door; and so he returned to Paris, where he went straight back to the skids, the subway gratings, the whole down-and-out routine, peddling the homeless newspaper *Le Réverbère* on the boulevards, or at stoplights, sleeping on the quais of the Seine. Then—still according to the "life of the down-and-out author before he found fame" version—one February evening, beneath the Pont Mirabeau, he encountered a certain Dochin. Gastinel lay huddled on the cobblestones, bundled up in old newspapers to keep out the cold (his preference went to *Le Figaro* or *Paris-Turf*, whose pages are bigger), lost in a volume of

Apollinaire poems stolen from a secondhand dealer on the quais. Dochin had come there to sleep after being unceremoniously booted out of his dishwashing job in a restaurant on the Avenue Kennedy, where he'd had the bad fortune to break several plates (while slipping some good silverware into his pocket).

Little by little, knocking around from homeless shelter to soup kitchen, the two outcasts discovered they had certain tastes in common—in literature, politics, women, and food—and so, despite their considerable age difference, a warm friendship was born. Ending up in a Belleville squat, they embarked on a literary experiment that would eventually become the massive first volume—almost six hundred close-set pages—of *Dancing the Brown Java*. So many empty, pretentious novels (or thus, at least, the duo deemed them), generally penned by bourgeois writers (whereas they themselves came from the commonfolk, among whom nothing is ever phony), so many incompetent, often interchangeable books were published every year, to such great acclaim—"Why not us?" they'd asked themselves, and resolved to try their hand. Gastinel managed to pinch a typewriter from an employment agency, and so our two misfits, long used to tightening their belts while others stuffed their fat faces, buckled manfully down to work, typing by turns on the stolen machine.

This laudable attempt to pull themselves and each other up by their bootstraps—in an age when yearning to better one's less-than-ideal social condition generally means sitting around and wondering, "When is the government finally going to do something for *me*?," without lifting a finger—soon paid off. Success was theirs, virtually overnight. The press went wild. Fame and glory. Record sales figures. Their publisher in seventh heaven. Visibly so, in fact: he was there in the audience, beaming as his two darlings held forth, especially Gastinel, since Dochin—as if lost in some deep torpor—scarcely so much as opened his mouth.

Rather than submit their work to one of the major publishers, the two authors chose to bestow it on a virtually unknown little press—Le Papyrus, offices near the Porte d'Ivry, a low-rent outfit specializing in cheap study guides for backward schoolchildren and sentimental novels by literary nobodies—whose director, Euloge Malgodin, sixty-five, had had some hard knocks himself. It must also be said that, having little faith in their work, Gastinel and his accomplice were reluctant to approach the big wheels of the publishing world, lest they be brushed off with the usual humiliating "despite the genuine literary merits of your work, we regret that it does not fit our needs at the present time . . ." etc., etc.

But what does it matter why they chose Le Papyrus: Malgodin's was the right door to knock on. Six months after taking that perilous first step, these progenitors of a novel neither white-bread nor *noir* but in fact verdigris (as one critic put it, evoking the color of the German uniform), found themselves rich and famous, at the top of the heap, and now the guests of honor on *Book Culture*.

Eyebrows wasn't going to give up so easily: he was quite clearly aching to talk about the novel. Gastinel brushed him aside once more, then with a wrenching sigh agreed to say two or three words about their book after all. Not a syllable about the many collaborationist traitors teeming in its pages; no, he would speak only of the book's two innocents, two wonderfully fresh minor characters whom he seemed to favor above all the rest: Max and Mimile, two kids who popped up now and then in that dark journey through the grim, gloomy Paris of the Occupation. For Eyebrows's sake, he grudgingly offered up two or three little remarks—though without giving anything away: still that same maniacal insistence on not spoiling the plot—concerning this Max and this Mimile, after which, masterfully, as if he himself were moderating this mini-roundtable, the adipose wordsmith turned the conversation toward Occupation-era Paris in general: the roundups of the Jews, the restrictions, the long lines before sparsely stocked shops, the curfew, the hostage lists posted on the walls, the anonymous denunciations, the whole litany of daily sorrows from those four endless years. And not without reason, for that sinister, oppressive atmosphere served as a backdrop to the entire novel. A *roman à clef*, sometimes bitter and disturbing in tone, abounding in revelations that might be mere hearsay, of course, or simply inventions dreamed up by two over-imaginative novelists . . . But what talent in their recreation of an entire era! What vehemence! One episode after another, all purely fictive, of course, but nonetheless lifting a corner of the veil still cast over those events, events that some would, to this day, prefer to keep hidden—blithely suggesting that there was a great deal yet to be learned about that particularly dark period of French history.

Dochin, meanwhile, seemed closer to nodding off with each passing minute, as if unconcerned by these proceedings. He appeared to be having trouble following. When the camera turned to him, he remained tentative, fuzzy, rarely finishing the few sentences he deigned to fling out. Besides, like Gastinel, he loathed the glare of the spotlight. He nodded when his accomplice proclaimed that a writer worthy of the name should never exhibit himself, lest he dilute—or even completely erase—the enchantment of his book, assuming there is any. "Exactly like a puppeteer," Gastinel added. "And believe me, I know what I'm talking about. Imagine how disappointed the kiddies would be if the guy pulling the strings suddenly showed up himself on his own little stage!"

"On that subject," Eyebrows conceded, "some of your characters do make their way through this saga like clowns . . . even like marionettes . . . Indeed, I thought there was some real humor in this book . . . of a rather bitter sort, of course."

Then the host posed the quasi-ritualized question that always infuriated the two authors:

"How do you work, Dochin-Gastinel? It's difficult to imagine two writers sitting down to . . . How did Erckmann and Chatrian write their books? I must confess, I . . . There was also Boileau-Narcejac, not so long ago . . . I think it was Boileau who came up with the plot . . . and then they spent hours on the telephone . . . Jean-Rémi Dochin?"

"Hard to say," answered Dochin after a jaw-dislocating yawn, his eyes almost crossing, one thumb kneading a weak, indecisive chin, hairless and dull white as an andouillette or the skin on some bulldogs. "Let's see . . . Take the general idea of the book . . . Well, to tell you the truth . . ."

"We went over all that on the radio," Gastinel interrupted with a sort of groan, just this side of rude.

"As for . . . uh . . . the details of everyday life in Paris during the Occupation . . . well . . . Gastinel lived through all that, as a child," said Dochin. "So . . ."

"I was eight years old when the Germans came, in '40," the butcher-turned-puppeteer reminisced. "I remember like it was yesterday. I can still see them marching down the Rue de Flandre. My uncle and I were out delivering lambs' brains to the restaurants . . ."

Dochin shot him a disapproving glance. Hadn't he warned his partner not to dwell too long on his tripemonger past, lest he turn off five or six thousand well-bred potential readers who might have a hard time seeing any connection between the preparation and sale of offal and a work of literature deemed wholly pure and magisterial by a host of great critics whose unerring tastes were beyond question?

"And for everything else, you know, when we weren't using Charles's memories," Dochin resumed, "well, there's . . . uh . . . a lot of material out there . . . The newspapers from the time, for instance . . . And there were a lot of them in those days! . . . Also, my family used to talk about that stuff a lot, back home. I had an uncle in the Resistance. Bousquet's police turned him over to the Germans, and he died at Mauthausen. There's also . . . Um, what else? Diaries, too . . . For example, for the secret notebooks of Jean-Hérold Paquis, discovered in . . ."

As usual, Dochin was proving more than a little unfocused. This seemed to irritate some of the panelists sitting on either side of the duo, as well as the show's invited audience, visible in the background, many of them apparently drifting off to sleep while he spoke. Even Malgodin was looking fed up. Gastinel threw Dochin a withering glance, cut him off, and smoothly segued:

"The first thing we do, before we get started on a manuscript— and I should tell you, we're already hard at work on the next volume—is divide up the roles. And then, when the mood strikes us, we switch off. So-and-so many days for Jean-Rémi, such-and-such many days for me. Here's an example, from a chapter toward the end of the first third of the second volume, which we're working on now. I'm thinking of the scene where our two kids, Max and Mimile, are staying with a distant cousin of Lagardelle, Vichy's Labor Minister—we call him La Bardelle in the book—who raises hamsters in the Franche-Comté. Oh, and another one too, where Bibi Belles-Fesses, the favorite catamite of Mouzuy, who invented the bathtub torture used by the French Gestapo, prints up a batch of forged ration cards. So to bone up for those two episodes, I went off to the Indre-et-Loire and paid a call on the heirs of Luchaire, the director of the collaborationist paper *Les Nouveaux Temps*, where I received a charming welcome and ready access to all the newspaper's archives—there were suitcases full of them!—as well as a voluminous private correspondence from people in very high places at the time; meanwhile, back home in the Limousin, Jean-Rémi was writing up the episode where Coco Beau-Sourire, the Oriental danseuse secretly in love with Arno Breker, is kidnapped by Moudot, one of Bonny's right-hand men . . ."

None of this had even been written yet, Dochin knew . . . "But who cares?" he said to himself. Max and Mimile and the hamster farmer . . . Coco Beau-Sourire kidnapped by a heavy from the Rue Lauriston gang . . . and the rest . . . episodes that he, Dochin, had chosen for the sequel to their book . . . just a few quick little notes, for the moment, jotted down toward the end of his stay in the clinic, when his head was starting to clear. At his bedside, the blimp had skimmed through those sketches, congratulating the patient on finding the courage to work even as he lay stricken in his sickbed . . .

"Those scenes were written by Jean-Rémi," Gastinel added. "Will we keep them in the definitive draft of volume two? At this point, I can't say. But for the next part, the attempted murder of Otto Abetz (Otto Abesses in the novel)—a great mystery, that, unexplained to this day—well, there we switched roles: I took up the pen while Jean-Rémi headed for Ingolstadt to meet Knochen's grandson, a former Green Party leader who took a real beating in the Bavarian elections and went into the air-conditioning business, to see what he could worm out of him about certain secrets concerning his ancestor. You see?"

"What a bullshitter!" Dochin said to himself, awestruck by his partner's glibness. "Never even bats an eye!" Of course, not one word of this overview of their methods was true. Just like that stuff about the attack on Otto Abetz! Gastinel was making it up as he went along. They'd never so much as talked about using that in the second volume.

But the behemoth continued all the same, unstoppable:

"As for the secrets belatedly confided by the actor Lucien Coëdel to Lucienne Martin, the public-toilet attendant in the Gare du Nord, who claims to be Carbone's illegitimate daughter, secrets concerning a driver for the Avenue Foch Gestapo, who supposedly witnessed the execution of the Rosselli brothers at Bagnoles-de-l'Orne in 1938, well . . . That was back in the Occupation too, Coëdel was shooting *The Bellman* with Christian-Jacque at the time. Three years later, perhaps you remember, the poor man was mysteriously pushed from a night train. But anyway . . . where was I?"

Dochin looked on, wide-eyed. "Where does he come up with this stuff?" he wondered. No such thing had been written, no such thing had been discussed. "Actually, it's not a bad idea," he thought. "Might be worth using, it could almost be a chapter to itself. Let's keep that in mind."

"You're certainly a great deal more forthcoming about volume two, Gastinel," said Eyebrows with a smile. "But rest assured, we'll talk about all this again when that book comes out, and by then I'm sure Jean-Rémi Dochin will be fully recovered. But tell me: there's one thing I can't quite get my head around. The logistics of this kind of collaboration, sort of like a work for four hands . . . fine, I can understand that much. But still . . . Come on now! The style! The celebrated *little music* of your prose—pure genius, as all the critics are saying! Pardon me for putting it so bluntly, but how can that be the work of two people? How do you do it?"

"Let's just say I hold the score while Jean-Rémi blows into the instrument," Gastinel retorted with a great laugh.

"In any case, I don't know if your book is really a *roman à clef*," said Eyebrows. "But it's chock-full of gossip . . . sometimes rather venomous, I must say!"

"You think so?" asked Dochin.

"Often you seem to be dragging people's names through the mud purely for the fun of it . . . It's not hard to see who you're talking about, behind the false names . . ."

"Well after all, that's no crime," Gastinel argued. "Stirring shit up doesn't make it stink any worse."

"You're going to make enemies."

"All the better, we love a good fight. But it's true, we've made more than a few since our success. We've even had to turn some away—no room!"

"All these allusions to Monsieur X or Madame Y . . . people of some importance in those days . . . quite provocative, at times . . ."

"I don't see that at all," said Dochin. "You must be misreading."

"We never really attack anyone," said Gastinel. "Those are only . . . let's call them . . . gentle little swats."

"Yes, but forgive me . . . As I understand it from Euloge Malgodin, here with us tonight, there are going to be some much bigger revelations in volume two. It sounds like you've got a real broadside in store for us, something really explosive, a blistering barrage of inflammatory assertions . . . Am I wrong?"

"We'll see," said Gastinel, with an enigmatic air. "But yes, I'll grant you, we're building to a sort of crescendo . . ."

Observing the authors' growing impatience—and the audience's discomfort as the clearly exhausted Dochin succumbed to another fierce yawning fit—the host of the show thought this a good time to close the discussion. He lay *Dancing the Brown Java* on the book-strewn table in front of him—to Gastinel's apparent relief—then picked up another volume and turned toward the panel, each of whom, before (briefly, as time was almost up) detailing what-they-were-saying-or-trying-to-say in their own books, unanimously affirmed their admiration for Dochin-Gastinel's novel: so captivating, so blistering, so masterful in its descriptions, it's terrific!, it's tremendous!, so utterly new in its suggestivity, so irresistibly piquant in its paroxysmal sub-quintessenciation of the unsaid and the sub-experienced, in the neo-Brechtian parody of the context and the underlying depths of the style. And then it was time for one last set of questions, the standard end-of-show ritual:

"Gastinel, what's your favorite sound?"

"A hard-boiled egg being cracked against an old tin-topped bar—a reminder of my many years of poverty. Bleak years indeed, but without them I would never have found the words necessary to write, with Jean-Rémi, our dear *Brown Java*."

"Jean-Rémi Dochin, what historical figure would you like to see on a bank note?"

"A couple like us. Like those two plumbers: Jacob on the recto, Delafon on the verso. Or maybe those elevator guys: Roux on one side, Combaluzier on the other."

A few convivial *ha ha!*s erupted in the studio, albeit unaccompanied by knee-slapping.

"Charles Gastinel, what would you like God to say to you when you reach the gates of Heaven?"

"That'll do."

2   The Blow-Up

Emerging from the studio after the broadcast, Dochin and Gastinel downed a quick drink with their publisher and his assistant, then climbed into the blimp's Mercedes E280 and headed for a bistro on the Montagne Sainte-Geneviève, one of the puppeteer's regular haunts, where they ordered his favorite dish: *tête de veau* swimming in *sauce ravigote* and surrounded by parsleyed new potatoes, another four or five pounds for Gastinel's massive body.

The evening went peacefully by. They lingered a while at their table, nibbling slices of plum tart, picking their teeth, belching, smoking cigars. Only later, near one in the morning, as the pair made their way through the tangle of streets surrounding the Panthéon, did Dochin finally give vent to his fury:

"Okay, in the restaurant I kept quiet . . . there were people around, including two or three assholes with their girlfriends who looked like they recognized us, they must have watched that damn show . . . I kept quiet, but I wanted to ask if you were proud of yourself, you piece of shit!"

"What's the matter? What's up with you? We had some good grub, a nice smoke, our publisher's eyes were twinkling all through the show, and now that we're alone in the dark Monsieur finally decides to open his big mouth?"

The two writers had stopped in the very middle of the Place du Panthéon, deserted on this chilly late October night.

"Scum! Bastard! Thug!" Dochin shot back, suddenly beside himself with rage.

"Keep it down, pal. People will think we're a couple of bums who had one aperitif too many back at the soup kitchen. Just like old times for you—or maybe not so old . . . eh, my dumpster-diving friend? So Monsieur's decided to throw a fit, has he? Not surprising, the way you were sucking down the Bourgueil back in the restaurant. They do have mineral water in those joints, you know. All you have to do is ask."

"I should have talked," Dochin raged, almost sobbing, an impotent grimace contorting his features. "Right there in front of all those dumb-asses watching us on their stupid TVs!"

"Oh, I see. Bravo. Spill the beans in public, is that your idea?"

"I should have howled it, roared it . . ."

"Come on, let's get going. You'll wake up Jean Moulin and his bunkmates in the Panthéon if you keep yelling like that."

The blimp grabbed Dochin by his jacket and pulled him along. Like fleeing rats, they slipped into a little side street—Rue d'Ulm, an egghead hangout—and slinked away.

"Let's drag our sorry asses down this way, I parked the heap by the old Cinémathèque . . ."

"I should have shouted it, bellowed it . . . I should have told them all: there's only one author, Jean-Rémi Dochin. And the other one, Monsieur Gastinel, is a big, fat piece of shit!"

"Well now, that's a fine how-do-you-do! You didn't kick like this back in September, after our little stint on the radio! You were babbling into the mike like it was the most natural thing in the world. 'Gastinel and I work like this . . . revise each chapter like that . . . Gastinel writes faster than I do . . . most of the details about the Occupation come from him . . . he lived through it all, you understand . . . he was just a kid, but he remembers . . .' And on and on!"

"Yeah, well, tonight something snapped! What really got me was that elegant little joke of yours . . . about our style . . . 'I hold the score while Dochin blows into the instrument!'"

"Ah! Monsieur is so proud of his 'little music,' like those la-di-das are always calling it! Monsieur's starting to take himself for Céline!"

The mastodon lit a cigarillo.

"Look, if it meant that much to you, you should have said so, smart guy. Go ahead! Don't hold back! I can't write, not a single idea in my head, too thick to have an imagination of my own, one of those losers who have to scrabble around for subjects in everyday life, in the newspapers . . . in their own pathetic little existence, if need be . . . but who shamelessly claim to be creators all the same . . . And even then, even like that, I'll never write squat! Fine, I'm hopeless as a writer, I'm just an ex-butcher, handy enough with a cleaver or a boning knife or a hamburger grinder, of course, and not too shabby at getting a laugh out of the kids with my puppets, but give me a pen and there's nobody home. You're right, you're right. Only you're forgetting one thing, buddy boy: we committed a crime."

"My turn to tell you: put a cork in that blowhole of yours, will you? See all those windows? Behind every one there's some asshole asleep in his bed."

"What, do you want to live out the rest of your life in the pen? Rotting away in the slammer? In the company of gentlemen far less distinguished than writers? Remember, I told you how it works: automatic fixed sentence, then when you get out you've got the shrinks on your ass, and they can be worse than the screws! You'll come out a doddering old fart, with one foot in the grave. Is that what you want, bright boy? Some way for a literary genius to end his career!"

Lowering his voice, the ex-tripemonger went on:

"And what a filthy crime it was, too. Despicable. A fourteen-year-old girl, with her whole life ahead of her . . . And the way we went about it! You, who take yourself for Céline! . . . Sure, he had a bad habit of shooting his mouth off, and some of his books can be pretty hard to swallow . . . but as far as I know he never killed anybody."

"What, don't you think books can kill?"

"Oh, you're a riot! No, old Céline never killed anyone . . . but you, on the other hand . . ."

"What do you mean, 'me'?" Dochin mumbled, suddenly paling.

"Poor sap! The thing is, pal, when you're an up-and-coming writer, you're supposed to steer clear of murder. Or, you know, if you absolutely can't help yourself, you make your sick little crime a solo act. Not a duet with a guy like Charlot Gastinel."

"God, the drivel you come out with! . . . As if I was expecting to become a big, successful writer! Successful! As if I wasn't convinced what I write's not worth shit!"

"Listen to him whine! Such a modest young man! But it's true, success kind of took you by surprise, didn't it? You couldn't believe it, you worm, I'll give you that! Shook you up good! Monsieur was so afraid . . . racked by doubt . . . Like every great artist! Monsieur had no faith in his genius!"

"Shut your face!"

"And so, with his yellow stripe glowing in the dark at the thought of approaching Gallim's or one of the other big publishers, Monsieur decided to send his magnum opus off to some little nobody press! Can't you just see their faces on the Rue Sébastien-Bottin? *Why didn't he*—I mean *they*—*come to us? What were they thinking?*"

"Son of a bitch!"

"I repeat: when you're aiming to top old man Destouches, you're not supposed to go around killing people. And you don't pick a Charlot Gastinel for your accomplice! Ah! my feckless friend! You were only too happy to play along with me when you had blood on your hands! Well, this is the same deal, but now it's ink on our mitts instead! Got it? You don't commit murder alongside a guy who's always wanted to be a writer but unfortunately—oh! and I know it all too well!—hasn't got what it takes. Am I getting on your nerves here?"

He chuckled.

"Well then, why not just kill me? Ha ha!"

They were nearing the car. The mammoth pressed the button on his keyring to unlock the doors and they climbed inside, Gastinel's fat stomach compressed by the steering wheel. They turned onto the Boulevard Saint-Michel, passing a handful of straggling night owls, then headed toward Montparnasse, the Porte d'Orléans, and the autoroute beyond.

"Without me . . ." Gastinel went on. "Yes, if it weren't for me, then what? You'd be making twice the dough, that's true. But I'd still be mired in poverty, hawking *Le Réverbère* to the heartless mob or blubbering to my friendly neighborhood socialist deputy to find me a little place to call my own somewhere in this stinking-rich town. Whereas with you beside me, my fine blond friend . . . I'm in with the in-crowd . . . Sure, some of the big shots can't help feeling a little jealous . . . the guys with a Goncourt or an Académie Française prize under their belts . . . they envy me, try to make me look small . . . Just forty days our book's been in the shops, and already their aspersions are raining down! But at least that shows people are reading our work! 'A certain stylistic slackness, *little music* or no . . . a cacophony, truth be told . . . Populist in tone . . . Coarse language, vulgar, scato-logical . . . Gossip dredged up from the gutter . . .' Forgive me, Jean-Rémi . . . I'm only quoting . . . And then, like it says on the back of the book: 'Spent his childhood and youth in a tripe-shop'! Obvi-ously, that makes a change . . . Some authors are so scared of looking like clods they list all their degrees on the back of their book! Like somebody'd asked to see their credentials!"

"You're just as jealous as they are! You wish that populist tone could have been yours . . . and those vulgarities . . . and the gossip, as you say . . . Not that there's much of that, really . . . Admit it: you'd be in heaven if you could've come up with all that!"

"Well, as it happens, everyone's convinced that I did. Or at least . . . that we did. Half the glory is mine, pal! That's how it is. Just you try and tell them I didn't write one single comma in *Dancing the Brown Java*! Oh, I know, I'm exaggerating a little—I did take the liberty of touching up two or three sentences on the galleys. And wasn't my signature right there next to yours on the contract? That's what it means to be a celebrity, pal. Nobody busting your balls anymore! People treat you nice. Just an occasional green-eyed loser looking down his big fat nose at you, and all he can do is make you laugh!"

"And I suppose abandoning a wife and four kids is just another of your quaint little quirks?"

"That's my private life. Strictly off-limits. Reserved for our bi-ographers, fifty or sixty years from now, if they can tell true from false about two oddballs like Dochin and Gastinel. Good luck to them! I'm somebody now, thanks to you. Did you see those other guys on the show? Couldn't take their eyes off us! You get a load of that one type, the four-eyes with the contract at Charpentier, the regular at the Café de Flore, with his book so thin he could use it as a shoehorn, and that hoity-toity way of talking, that little tiny trace of a sneer? Oh, the loathing in his eyes when he heard me talking about our style! He just couldn't handle it! Seeing a guy who grew up in the meat business compared—along with his old pal Dochin, of course . . ."

"Oh, thanks."

". . . compared to a Céline or a . . . what was his name? The one who did time, liked to steal books . . ."

"Genet."

"Yeah, him. Boy, did that ever throw that guy for a loop!"

"He seemed pretty sharp to me . . . And don't you think . . . if they took the trouble to look into this thing . . . all those critics, those columnists, those jealous mediocre novelists . . . even the publishers, the editors . . . If they started delving into our lives a little, don't you think they'd find it sort of odd that I ended up writing with a meathead like you?"

"A meatheaded butcher! Say, that's a good one! Oh, sure! They're going to find the skeleton in the armoire! Listen, take that Chatrian guy, probably not worth shit as a writer, since it was Erckmann who did most of the work: how do you know he didn't off somebody just for the pleasure of signing his buddy's books without contributing so much as a comma? Unless it was the other way around. And what about old Boileau and Narcejac? After all, did anyone ever actually see them writing? Narcejac . . . You ever notice that look in his eyes? Kind of mysterious . . . even a little disturbing? Believe me, the man has yet to be born who'll figure out the truth about us. But after all . . . why shouldn't Dochin be the hopeless hack?"

"That's right! I can just see it, you bastard. After two or three volumes of *Brown Java* you'll be wanting your name on the cover all by itself."

"Bite your tongue, Jean-Rémi. Suppose you were to kick the bucket unexpectedly. In six months, a year . . . Who'd look like a dumbfuck then? The guy in the coffin or the one still on his feet? Hm? Suppose you disappeared? Just like that! Plop! All of a sudden! Happens to the best of us, and don't forget, we're all in the hands of our Heavenly Father above. Who'd be left sitting there like a twat, incapable of writing a single blessed line? You've never given that a moment's thought, have you, my dear son of a bitch?"

"Look, enough already, okay? . . . You're going to kill my inspiration. Because I just had a great idea for volume two . . . Philippe Henriot's last night on earth . . . just before he got whacked . . . You know who was in his bedroom?"

"More of your smear jobs! You want to drag them all through the mud—as if they didn't have enough shit on them already! You going out of your way to make life hard for our beloved publisher?"

"Well, if that's how you're going to be, then fuck it, I won't tell you. You'll just have to wait and read it in my manuscript."

"Speaking of which, perhaps you'd be so kind as to pick up the pace a little on volume two?"

"Come on, I'm beat! You're forgetting, I just got out of the clinic. What I need right now is a nice, cushy retirement, somewhere in the sun. The Riviera!"

"On the shores of the Riviera . . . ni na ni ni na ni . . . ni na ner . . . in the balmy breeze . . ." the giant warbled through his teeth, a bit like Boudu but without Michel Simon's accent.

The car cruised down the street. They drove through Montparnasse, the lights of Paris gushing and the sidewalks still packed, especially at the Vavin intersection, where huge crowds were emerging from a movie theater showing *The Horseman on the Roof*.

"It's time you learned: a writer worthy of the name never retires," said the hulk at the wheel. "First of all, sleep's for when you're dead. Victor Hugo had seventy-two summers behind him when he squeezed out *Ninety-Three*! And what about that Julien Green? Ninety-four candles on his cake, and still hard at it! There's an example for you! Does a painter stop painting just because his mug gets all wrinkly? Why should a writer be any more of a jerk-off than a painter?"

"Will you keep quiet? You're going to make me sorry I ever put *Brown Java* down on paper. My so-called masterpiece! More like my own little nightmare . . ."

The Mercedes turned down the Boulevard Raspail, heading toward Denfert. The streets were deserted. Gastinel sped up to fifty-five miles an hour.

"I repeat," he said. "The man has yet to be born who'll discover the truth of our little alliance. Everyone thinks I wrote half the book, when in fact . . . What a joke! Bunch of morons! So eager to believe you can spend half your youth surrounded by veal sweetbreads and pork kidneys, and still become . . ."

Here Gastinel's sentence dissolved into a cynical cackle.

Now the mighty vehicle had merged onto the autoroute, traffic-free at this late hour. They sped through the night in the left-hand lane, toward Orléans, Tours, and so on. The victim of adiposity was driving Dochin back to the Limousin, where he lived, not far from Brive.

"Suppose you decided to talk . . ." the obese one resumed. "Suppose you were to tell everyone I can't handle a pen. Let's imagine. What happens? I head right off to the police and hand over the evidence of our dirty little crime. And then so much for your glory . . . our glory . . ."

Ashen, shrinking back into his seat, Dochin clenched his teeth.

"And what a waste that would be!" belched the mountain of flesh. "Wouldn't you say, kid? Hey, what's this asshole think he's doing? Look at him poking along, and in the left lane yet! Got to be a Brit."

Having flashed his lights without effect, he passed the English-man on the right, accelerating furiously, leaving the laggard far behind, swallowed up by the darkness.

"What can it possibly matter to you that my name's next to yours on our books? You think things would be any better for you if you were the only one? Sure, you'd be raking in twice the royalties. Sweet, huh? But half a fortune's better than no fortune at all. Am I right, brother? Oh, if you could see the look on your face. What's the matter, the *tête de veau* not agreeing with you?"

"You piece of filth! You turd! Oh, you make me want to puke!"

"Hey now, that's no way to talk if you want to make the Aca-démie Française."

"You're nothing but a bastard . . . Blackmail! How spineless! How slimy! Revolting beyond belief!"

"Writers aren't always saints, you know. Especially humorists, I've heard they're the worst."

"Get a load of this louse! He didn't write one single line of *Brown Java* and he calls himself a writer!"

Gastinel merely snickered into his double chin. Then silence. The giant drove for some time without opening his mouth. The il-luminated highway signs heralded Artenay, Orléans, and the turn-off to Blois. The radio was quietly emitting South American tunes. Fists clenched, lamenting his own impotence, Dochin glanced toward the Goeringesque profile of his tormentor, his conqueror, then stared out at the endless ribbon of highway ahead of them.

In counterpoint, a conveyor belt of images from his past rolled by in his mind, images somewhat at odds with the *curriculum vitae* concocted for the general public: their auspicious encounter under the Mirabeau bridge . . . the Belleville squat where *Dancing the Brown Java* was born . . . the stolen typewriter . . . their heated disputes as they feverishly constructed their masterpiece . . . the whole elaborate spiel, spun out to take in the marks . . . the usual back-cover stuff, the "about the author" bit, sure, but in their case they'd laid it on pretty thick . . . in the papers, on the radio, on TV, the works . . . The reality was quite different, but that was none of the public's business.

3   A Not-So-Simple Past

1990. Five years before. Jean-Rémi Dochin, aged forty, is at something of a loose end. Behind him lies an endless string of dead-end jobs, most recently four years in the shipping department of a now-defunct surgical-goods company; before him lies a long career in the ranks of the terminally unemployed. He finds himself adrift in a Paris where he knows no one worth knowing. He's spent fifteen years in the capital, but—timid, unsure of himself, not much of a go-getter, lacking the kind of personal charm that's so useful in Paris—he's never made one useful contact. He bums around. His life is going nowhere. Everything's falling apart. Dochin is just one more of society's castoffs, another member of the vast herd that interests no one and can just crawl off and die for all anyone cares. Paul Gauguin's famous little sentence echoes in his head: "Paris is a desert for a poor man." The Paris of the people, the real Paris—that Paris is dead. It's a plutocrat's playground now. A dazzling window display for the rest of the world, but the empty-wallet crowd who once so enlivened the capital have now all been shooed off into the sordid depths of the outlying suburbs. Paris, for Dochin: a desert indeed, a monstrous parade of locked doors with secret security codes, a city where the hard-up have to search high and low for a helping hand. Sure, they've got the food banks, the "Restaurants du Coeur," so the fat cats won't feel too cold-blooded, but only from December to March, after that it's *get lost*, don't show your face around here. He spins his wheels, doesn't know where to go, what to do. In hole-riddled pants and worn-out shoes that go flop-flop when it's wet, he trudges the sidewalks hawking *Le Lampadaire* to an indifferent crowd. People pass him by without so much as a glance. He makes the rounds of the homeless shelters, dreaming of giving it all up for good. He's even thought of going back to the Mayenne, the Mayenne of his childhood, at least people are friendlier there, more welcoming, and most of all more human. But to do what? Oh, for some way out of all this! All his life he's dreamed of becoming a writer. Pages and pages covered with ink. Poems just barely fit for the trash can. Unfinished short stories. From adolescence on. A fixation! In that business, it's a miracle if one in a thousand actually makes it. He's even written—not so much to indulge his own tastes as because it was the fashion—two sort-of crime novels, carefully keeping them "current" so they'd have some chance of being published, loading on all the socio-populist bells and whistles: the inevitable suburban setting, with its hopeless daily life, its dumbfucks, its drug addicts, and its poor slobs who'll never make good—an updated rehash of those *apaches* stories so popular in the late nineteenth century, so hair-raising for the genteel bourgeoisie—and of course lots of dope, governmental corruption, drug dealers, unemployment, con games, youth gone bad, all the standard-issue tropes of a kind of writing that hides behind the label "thriller," but in which Clouzot and Hitchock, if they found their way back to us—hopefully not too decomposed—would never recognize their offspring; not to forget all the inevitable little dramas of the housing projects: Totor the welfare-king stole Riton's motorbike, Ali ben Whatever got called a haji by the redneck concierge and it ended pretty badly, since Ali had a pump rifle at home, like everyone else in the suburbs, a rifle and a satellite dish . . . Oh, he didn't skimp on any of it; he loaded it all into two very dark, very gory books, crammed it all in any which way he could.

There were swarms of novels just like that . . . Most of them, as it happens, written by people who'd never lived in the suburbs. So why not him? Two little novels, which he'd signed Jean Rem. The people at Série Noire slammed the door in his face; François Guérif, at Rivages Noir, turned him away more politely. Narrow-brained assholes, he branded these naysayers. Classic. People can get a bit foul-mouthed when their manuscripts are turned down. So then he tried some slightly less upscale publishers. Same result. The standard mimeographed letter: "Madame, Monsieur, while we found many remarkable things in your work . . ." etc. In the end, he managed to sell one of them, *Mayhem in Les Minguettes*, to a desperate, half-broke little publisher with offices at the end of a cul-de-sac, one foot hovering over the world of the fanzine, as part of a new collection christened *Suburban Jungle*, which gave up the ghost after only eleven volumes.

This was as far as Dochin got. His book went unnoticed like so many thousands of others, no one having had the kindness to compare him to Jean-Patrick Manchette or James Hadley Chase. So much for crime novels. "Not really literature anyway," he told himself in the end, embittered. "Serves me right."

Then came a more serious endeavor—then came the misstep into the cesspool that would soon suck him in, body and soul, with a sickening, ignoble gurgle.

Almost three hundred pages packed with teeny-tiny writing, scrawled out in a malarial fever. A sort of saga, mostly set in Occupation-era Paris, with two heroes serving as guides, a couple of kids fallen prey to the tragic events of the time, word jammed against word as if he feared his sentence might make a run for it, a torrent of images he lined up end to end at a blistering speed, haunted by a terror of disturbing his tale's progression and never finding his way again, a rat's nest of cross-outs and insertions, a virtually indecipherable rough draft. He'd got the idea from a handful of films seen almost back-to-back in various revival houses—he had enough cash for a ticket now and then—or on homeless-shelter TVs: *Four Bags Full, The Last Metro, Army of Shadows, Mr. Klein, The Sorrow and the Pity*, and there were others too . . . Plus the reading or rereading of Céline's book on Sigmaringen, short stories by Marcel Aymé, the works of Jacques Delarue, Dutourd's *The Best Butter* . . .

An undertaking that left him gasping for breath. The blank page. The terror it inspires. Don't make me laugh! What a load of crap! For the highbrow crowd, maybe. But in this case, he who had struggled every step of the way to squeeze out his two crime novels now blackened his pages like a bat out of hell. The blank page, so unnerving to others, so cold-sweat inducing . . . nothing but nerves, like an actor before he goes out on stage . . . no, that blank page didn't scare him a bit: he threw himself at it, peppered it with letters, like a hailstorm where the hailstones were tiny droplets of ink—and the lines racing along like lightning, or like streaks on a broken computer screen. Was that what they call inspiration? Absolutely no telling where it came from. It was mysterious, it just took hold of you all of a sudden, and then it never let go.

But no matter how frantically his pen danced over the paper— words, sentences, situations coming effortlessly, jostling for space, cramming themselves in—he knew full well that no publisher would ever accept such a mess. And if someone, miraculously, did deign to see something in it, they'd ask him to cut it by a good third, maybe more.

He himself had a hell of a time rereading what he'd written—or rather what he'd shot out, what he'd thrown onto the paper like you throw grain out for chickens. He'd have to type it all up, to begin with, come up with a presentable manuscript. And then, above all, he had to finish the book. Because his novel wasn't in any way finished yet—far from it. And he'd also have to find a title.

"What's that you're reading? My heavens, would you look at that pile of papers! It's like the railway timetable, back in the old days . . ."

He raised his eyes from his page, teeming with tiny black letters, smudged like spatters of bug shit, like a sheet of standing-room-only flypaper, an impressive stack packed into a torn red file folder. His great work! Thirteen months of labor bordering on insanity. And he looked at her.

A woman. An old lady, rather. Céline Ferdinaud. But he won't learn her name for a while yet. For the moment she has none. Just like his book. He's still got a ways to go. Some three hundred pages behind him, and he's guessing it's going to end up grazing five hundred, maybe even more. A manuscript as fat as Céline's *Journey*, that's what he wants! An obsession!

As a working title, he's scrawled *Max and Mimile* at the top of the first page, but that won't last, he'll have to find something else, a real grabber if possible.

He looks at her. She doesn't have a name yet, but Lord, what a sight! Getting on a bit. Oh, she's held up well enough. How old? He studies her. Probably not far from seven decades.

The turkey neck never lies. Looks a little younger, presumably thanks to her makeup. Though in its extravagance it seems more like a Rouault canvas than mere makeup. Bright green battles vermillion, bullfighter's-cape pink snuggles up to blazing violet, an alliance of raw sienna and bronze trades blows with various shades of orange, yellow lets out a great triumphant laugh in the face of dull white, this latter whimpering for help, and don't even ask about the blue—sky, ultramarine, or Prussian. It's everywhere, she's even got some on her chin.

A slightly exaggerated description, of course, but the point is, this lady has one hell of a mask—base, blush, rouge, powder, and all the rest—on her kisser.

Her lips are thick and fleshy, plastered with enough lipstick to patch an ineptly stuccoed wall; the mauve around her eyes endows them with a force and a fixedness to rival any hypnotist's. As for the nose, you could almost drape neckties or scarves over it, and no doubt it's suffered more than its share of collisions with oncoming soupspoons.

That said, don't go assuming she's ugly. She's just a little too made-up, that's all. No crime in that.

"What's that you're reading?" she repeats. "Articles? Are you a journalist?"

"No, I . . ."

"Do you mind?"

She lights a cigarette, then lays a wrinkled hand on the masterpiece-in-the-works, the fat pile of papers sitting in Dochin's lap.

The woman's apparel is of a simplicity verging on extravagance. She's nothing like a bag lady, of course—she's not wearing one of those sacks they use for potatoes, although the color's about right. No, she's more like a kindly old biddy of a concierge heading off to do her shopping. For that matter, Dochin can just about picture her with a shopping basket on her arm, a tote bag overflowing with carrots, cabbages, and leeks, and suddenly he thinks of Paul Léautaud. Or rather, he sees him. He has before him a sort of Léautaud in skirts, or shall we say a creature born of the coupling of Léautaud and the Madwoman of Chaillot. Her dingy, soot-colored dress must have come from some flea market, snatched up once the vendor had gone on his way, abandoning the four hopeless rags that had been hanging unsold from a nail for the past few seasons to the mites and passing bums. So maybe she *is* a bag lady? Probably not. Still some remainder of dignity about her, thanks to that painterly makeup, that phalanx of jewels jiggling on her wrists, throwing tiny glints over her long, enveloping hands and salmon-pink manicured nails, that mauve bun, coquettishly coiled, agreeably and even elegantly highlighting her shapely nape. But surely not a bourgeois either, not even of the "artistic" variety.

"Mind if I have a look?"

He abandoned the sheet to the hand of the walking Rouault.

4   The Unwelcome Guest

What was he doing here, with this woman beside him? It's very simple. Less negligent in his dress, he would surely have wound up someplace else. And then he would never have met her. In short, it's all thanks to his decrepit, spattered ankle boots, his soiled, patched jeans, his shiny black jacket—which by all appearances might have been used to wipe down a good thirty tables in some sordid café after meals full of tomato sauce, fried fish, raspberry creams, and black sausage—not to mention his faux-rag-mop scarf: yes, it's thanks to all this that he met Titine. Titine is the old lady now standing beside him, politely asking to read his work, or a few lines of it, anyway, because she's rather busy, and has other things to do at the moment, does this Titine, this Céline, this Céline Ferdinaud.

It's very simple. As a dumb-ass's adventures generally are. You don't need a degree from the École Polytechnique—or from the École Normale Administrative, let's not leave anyone out—to find yourself in such seemingly exceptional circumstances. After traveling to the vineyards around Béziers to earn a few sous working the harvest—this was in September 1991—he'd set out to hitchhike his way back to Paris. Hard enough for a young person. Now imagine a guy in his forties inviting you to stop your car, especially when the individual in question seems precisely the type you wouldn't want to pick up on a highway. Even from afar, Dochin resembled neither Alain Delon nor Christophe Lambert, and not even a Robert

Hossein or a Bernard Tapie after a good seeing-to by a skilled plastic surgeon. Wiggling his thumb, shouldering a backpack stuffed with a few pairs of spare socks, a handful of underwear, two or three favorite books, his toothbrush, and three hundred ink-covered pages in a file folder. A handful of good-hearted truck drivers consented to pick him up, and even one normal motorist, a doctor on his way north to Bourges with his middle-aged wife. But Madame wouldn't stop wrinkling her nose. Oh, the sinister glare she gave him—a one-eyed barn owl would have gone green with envy—when, with his filthy clothes, his shoes polished by a chimney-sweep's brush, stinking to high heaven, he sank onto the backseat of their Renault Espace minivan! Just like he owned the place! Oh, that grimace, so eloquently suggestive of a violently heaving stomach! At Brive, weary of seeing his wife on the verge of regurgitation, the good doctor stopped his heap:

"We'll drop you off here, my dear fellow . . ."

At least he had the delicacy not to stop by a public dump. There were houses around, it was the middle of town.

"It just so happens we were planning to visit some friends around here, and . . ."

Yeah, right!

"Should you have any difficulty finding another helpful motorist, there's an excellent hotel just across the way, on the square . . ."

It was then about three in the afternoon. At six he was still going nowhere, so he made for Le Hôme Fleuri, a cozy-looking hotel. With the modest nest egg he'd earned giving himself lumbago in the vineyards, he figured he could indulge in a room with a shower, a meal, maybe even breakfast. Hitchhiking's a mug's game at night. Besides, it was hot enough to roast a lizard. Might as well call it a day.

"I'd like a room . . ."

"Do you have any luggage?"

With one glance, the woman at the counter took his measure: unpolished shoes that could probably walk on their own, a pair of jeans frantically sending out fruitless SOSs to all available launderers . . . Next to the scowling hostility of the Hôme Fleuri's owner, the wife of the doctor from Bourges would have seemed as amiable as one of those chipper little minxes who do the weather on television . . .

"Uh . . . I have my backpack . . ."

"I'm afraid we have no free rooms, Monsieur. We're full."

Said with a certain coolness, that. It was a lie, of course, confirmed on his way out, when, not ten yards from the front door, he turned around to see four Dutch tourists climb out their car, along with two young women newly arrived in a Volkswagen Golf, and follow the chambermaid upstairs to the rooms, suitcases in hand. Perhaps out of masochism, he stood there staring up at the second floor until the shutters opened and the Dutch folk leaned out, eyeballing the view. Some hospitality.

He now had the good fortune to be invited aboard a little Citroën van, driven by a zigzagging lush, an avid collector, as he confided, of Breathalyzer balloons. He bought them in batches of twelve or fifteen and served them to his mother-in-law at dinner, hidden in the pureed peas or beneath the crusted cheese atop her onion soup.

"Rolled up into little balls, you understand. They open up in the bowels, see? Some air gets in there, and you've got a nice little intestinal blockage. She's been bugging the shit out of me ever since I got married. As you see, I'm doing just the opposite to her."

Having successfully dodged all oncoming roadside plane trees, this architect of the perfect crime dropped his passenger off in Tulle, a few kilometers along, where Dochin found himself beckoned by another hotel, the Sanglier Royal. There too, the owner—a man this time, brutish face, shaved nape, the inevitable jug ears, with a wolfhound half asleep at his feet (who says we'd never find qualified personnel if, God forbid, we one day decided to open our own concentration camps in France?)—there too the owner ogled Dochin's shoes and the none-too-fresh clothes on his back.

"I'm very sorry, Monsieur. The only rooms left have two beds."

To the drifter's right, doors open, lay a TV salon and a dining room. Probably bored out of their skulls, a handful of guests were digging in to an early dinner. Dochin saw several eyes come unglued from the china plates and turn toward him, round as nail heads, riveted to his person: "Who the hell is this guy? How did he get in here? Under personal escort from Mother Teresa, maybe? With Bernard Kouchner carrying his bags?"

"That's all right," Dochin answered. "Two beds is fine. I'll pay for both. Don't worry, I'll only use one."

"Yes, but . . . the double—there's only one left—is reserved for a couple from Madrid I'm expecting this evening. Married, but they've been sleeping apart since 1939. She was a Republican, and he was more of a Francoist."

"Anything you've got would be okay with me . . . Just a little cubby hole would do . . . it doesn't matter . . . a closet . . . a maid's room . . . in the attic . . . You understand? I just want somewhere to sleep."

"We can't accommodate you, Monsieur. Our guests sleep in bedrooms."

Dochin did his best not to take no for an answer. The owner hadn't bothered to offer him a spot in the cellar or the doghouse. He didn't even threaten to throw him out. He simply opened a drawer and took out a blackjack, calmly placing it on the counter without a hint of hostility in his manner. Then he took his leave of Dochin.

"Excuse me . . . I've got guests waiting in the dining room. We're a little busy."

Dochin hung around for a while all the same. He drifted into the bar and ordered a Ricard. Handing over the carafe of cold water, the chambermaid eyed him sympathetically.

"You've been looking for a room for a while now, haven't you?"

"This is the second hotel I've . . ."

"There's the Coq d'Or a little ways down the street, they've got forty rooms. But I wouldn't advise you to try them. If you like, I can give you the name of a nice place where they'll take you in with no fuss. It's a sort of motel, just outside Térignac on the Plateau de Millevaches road. Kind of a deserted around there, but a lot of people like the peace and quiet. Very restful, apparently. You'll see, it's about a half-mile past the village. There'll be a row of willows on the left, the motel's by the water. Just look for the sign, you can't miss it. There's a garden out front . . . kind of a park, if you like . . ."

"Is it far from here?"

"Maybe 15 miles . . . Oh, I see, you're on foot. Try walking with a limp. Someone will give you a lift. We've got lots of nice farmers around here."

"I hope this motel of yours isn't some kind of dump. I'm not saying it's a fleabag or anything, but still . . . I've got some money, you know."

"Don't worry. It's quite well kept up. The owner's a very friendly woman, you'll see."

He walked out of Tulle on the Limoges road, limping a little. As promised, a local farmer invited him into his cauliflower-laden pickup and took him straight to the motel, which did indeed stand all on its own, beside a dusty, unkempt little road that climbed toward the Plateau de Millevaches and the town of Aubusson.

The Halte du Bon Accueil, it was called, as indicated by a little dormouse-shaped sign on the rickety wrought-iron grill that served as an entryway. And then, below the name, in small letters, *Rooms. Meals. Outside food allowed.* It was sort of like a manor-farm, but on a smaller scale, and not particularly well looked-after. Judging by the windows—their wooden shutters slightly dilapidated, in need of a fresh coat of paint, some graced with more than the usual four holes in a cloverleaf design—there must have been some fifteen rooms. Maybe a few more in the attic. The façade seemed to have been lovingly treated with heavy machine-gun fire, and the right half displayed long, black streaks, bespeaking some recent blaze, evidently extinguished just in time. A little manor farm sprinkled with the dust of five shattered cliff faces. On either side, under spiny locust trees, in a tangle of brambles and bushes, the grounds were scattered with kiosks, gazebos, rabbit hutches, and chicken coops. In the distance, half hidden by the greenery, stood a little grayish house, charmless, almost sinister, of the sort you still see in the drab outskirts of big cities. The highlight of the grounds was a huge garden, park-like in places, stretching out in front of the main building. Not too badly maintained. A profusion of flowers, but vegetables too, even a few fruit trees, mostly cherry and pear. Tables and garden chairs were strewn here and there, and parasols unfurled their cheery colors against the light green of the lawn. Three or four cats strolled lazily this way and that, sniffing at the grass.

PART II   Céline

5   The Halte du Bon Accueil

The gate was open. Probably stayed that way all night, he thought. He walked through the garden toward the main building. On his right, three or four cars of various nationalities—he even saw one with a GBZ sticker, from Gibraltar—were angle-parked in a sort of carport.

The building was silent. He stepped into a little room that must have served as a front office, more redolent of coffee than of wood polish.

"Excuse me? Anyone around?" he called out after three or four minutes.

A door stood open at the far end of the room, and he glimpsed a long, bookshelf-lined hallway, the volumes not set out in neat rows but jammed in every which way, an endless parade of titles, covers, brightly colored dust jackets, almost up to the ceiling.

"Anybody home?"

No point hanging around, clearly. He headed back to the garden, pulled up an iron chair, and sat down under a parasol, since even at this hour the September sun was beating down with some force. After a moment, no human being having appeared, he opened his backpack and pulled out his manuscript. He plunged into it whenever he had a spare moment, endlessly rereading his work, plagued by anxiety, overcome with self-doubt as he counted the superfluous words, the repetitions, the pointless descriptions hobbling the flow of the action, the heavy-handed phrasing of sentences that had nevertheless pleased him when they first spewed from his brain, the graceless or stilted dialogue, the absence of humor just where it was needed most, the dumptruck-loads of clichés . . . He crossed them out with a furious swipe of the pen. But the cross-outs were starting to pile up; at this rate, his manuscript would be nothing more than an oversize scratch-pad before long. So many cross-outs . . . if you could lay them end to end, he thought, they'd probably stretch all the way around the Place de la Concorde. But it wasn't enough to X out whole lines at a time, he'd have to replace them with something, or his manuscript was going to end up no longer than a slim little volume of poetry. He reread, reread until his eyes glazed over, and after three or four minutes he reached into his pocket for a pen or pencil stub, and then slash went the scalpel, pruning without pity. What would be left of his work, if he kept this up? And then tomorrow he'd start all over again, laying down new sentences, somehow spurring his saga on, so difficult to guide, so headstrong, like a stubborn old mule! A mule that would carry him God knows where, him the author, perhaps only to that frosty little letter that says "in spite of the originality and brilliant writing of your manuscript, we regret to say that we cannot accept it for publication. Rest assured that . . ." etc., after which the text would go into a drawer, or else he'd face facts and pass it along to some sad little vanity press, and that would be that.

But now he was roused from his labors by the sound of footsteps on the gravel path. He looked up. A most curious couple were passing by. The man was short and hunchbacked, the woman tall and broad-shouldered, florid of face, sporting a goiter the size of a head of broccoli under her chin. He was dressed in a checked suit with knickerbockers, a jogger's cap on his head, she in a very low-cut floral dress. They gave him a friendly smile as they passed by, threw out a cordial "Hello!," and wished him good day in an English accent. They were holding butterfly nets, and from the woman's shoulder hung a little bag that seemed empty but probably contained the few anglewings and Clifden Nonpareils they'd managed to capture, no doubt destined to be glued into an album and displayed to their neighbors in Sussex on long winter nights before steaming cups of tea. At first taken aback, Dochin soon responded amiably to their greeting, then plunged once more into his manuscript. But not for long, because now, out of nowhere, came a man of about fifty, absolutely average in appearance, the standard middle-management type, short hair, sporty clothes—navy-blue jogging suit, tennis shoes. The one jarring note was the leash he was holding, at the other end of which stood a good-size orangutan, emitting a strong wild-animal odor.

Seeing Dochin start and nearly drop his manuscript on catching sight of the beast, he said with a smile, "Don't be afraid. Jojo's very well behaved. Shake hands with the nice man, Jojo."

The orangutan reached out and grazed the writer's trembling paw with its own.

"Was he born here in France?" Dochin asked.

"No, he's from Borneo."

"I don't mean yours specifically, but I've heard monkeys carry all sorts of diseases. Serious ones, I mean, contagious and everything. Maybe even AIDS."

"Oh! We know almost nothing about AIDS. Even today, it's an illness we only partially understand, we have so far to go. Now they're starting to talk about saliva . . . when that used to be nothing to worry about. But rest assured, Jojo's in fine health. He's got a very good veterinarian looking after him."

Amused, Dochin kept his eyes fixed on the animal:

"Does he understand much?"

"I managed to train him . . . With patience you can do a great deal with these beasts, you know. There's no doubt: the orangutan is considerably more observant and above all more thoughtful than the gorilla or the chimpanzee. But the champion of the monkeys, their Einstein as it were, is the capuchin, a South-American species, gifted with remarkable manual dexterity. Give him the parts, and a capuchin could build you a working plumbing system! It's astounding. You know, men are supposedly descended from monkeys, but the monkey himself is descended, I strongly believe, from a sort of . . . let's say a pre-monkey or sub-monkey, vanished today, next to which our marmosets and mandrills are great minds. Same difference, probably, as between a monkey and you or me. For centuries and centuries sub-monkeys and monkeys cohabited on our earth. Then came the superior monkey, man. But only after the sub-monkey had disappeared. Only two sorts at a time. The chain will go on, it's a law of biology. Always moving forward. The simian species are already well on their way to extinction, it's been proven. Reach your own conclusions, Monsieur. To return to the capuchin, I've been trying to adopt one, but they're very difficult to find. You know, these poor beasts are better off either in their own habitat or else with a master—for you must understand that they die of boredom in zoos, even with great floods of idiots hanging around to watch them run and jump and masturbate. I suppose you're waiting for the owner?"

"Yes. I just got here. But since there was no one around . . ."

"She won't be long. She's busy out back with the maid. The ladies are out slaying bunnies. They've got rabbit cooked in beer and morels on tomorrow's menu. Oh! I know everything that goes on around here. I've been here ten days already, and I'm so happy I can't tear myself away and head back to Villefranche-sur-Saône. Jojo likes it here too, and says 'fuck you' to all those asshole hotel owners who don't want him around. As if he was going to break their china just by going and giving a friendly handshake to all the guests stuffing their faces in the restaurant! You see, dear Monsieur, the sorrow of animals is that they're unlucky enough to have us humans as their neighbors on this planet. Tell me, was it animals that invented war and torture and racism? Good evening, dear Monsieur. Come on, Jojo, let's go for a dip in the water. Warm day, isn't it?"

The man and his orangutan wandered off into the garden, heading for the row of willows that stood by the murmuring river.

6 I Say *Tu* to Everyone I Like

Dochin went back to his manuscript, only to receive a body blow to the pit of his stomach on discovering three redundancies in two lines, then a great string of repetitions, as if his pen had developed a stutter. Well, there's plenty of that in Stendhal, he thought to himself. On the other hand, he wasn't Stendhal. Just Dochin, a guy who had the devil's own time putting three sentences together, and who didn't know where his book was going anymore.

"I'm so sorry to keep you waiting, Monsieur. What's that you're reading? My goodness, would you look at that pile of papers! It's like the railway timetable, back in the old days . . . Have you been here long?"

"No, just a few minutes."

"You have a car?"

Here too the newly arrived guest's shoes were treated to a quick inspection. But this time the gaze was indulgent, even friendly, and a touch amused.

She wiped her blood-spattered hands on her apron:

"I'll bet you're on foot . . ."

"As a matter of fact, yes."

"Your shoes sort of speak for you . . ."

"I heard you have rooms for rent . . ."

"I have a few left, yes. Let me guess: you got our address from a chambermaid in one of the local hotels?"

"That's right."

"I'll give you number 4. In back, overlooking the water. Lovely view, you'll see. You'd think it was put there by an Impressionist. You'll have the Slovaks as neighbors. Nothing special about her—she's a very beautiful woman, in fact, a dancer in Bratislava—but he's got a touch of epilepsy. They're very polite. The poor man had a fit just as they were asking for a room at L'Aigle Moderne, in Limoges. The hotel wouldn't touch them, of course. Is that your only luggage?"

"Well, yes. When you're alone, you know . . ."

She gave him a conspiratorial smile:

"Backpacker?"

"If you like . . ."

"We must see fifteen like you every day, in the summertime. They're always headed up to the Plateau de Millevaches. But generally they don't stop. Young people, mostly. They sleep under the stars."

"Unfortunately, I'm not equipped to sleep outside. And I'm not eighteen anymore."

"Good evening, Monsieur Jouffroy. Your wife's already back. She was helping us pick plums."

A customer had passed by, a potbellied little gentleman with a naïve look in his eye, like tens of thousands of others who sit watching their TVs at night, or who show up every four or five years in the front hall of a school to slip their ballot into an urn. He was dressed in a white summer suit, with a baseball cap on his head and a tennis racket under his arm. He had a muzzled pit bull on a leash. A moment later they'd trotted off.

"That's Monsieur Jouffroy, one of our guests. Runs a candy store in Charleville. His pit bull isn't mean. It just doesn't like to be bothered, that's all. Two years ago it tore off a little girl's cheek, but the kid was teasing it. Monsieur Jouffroy didn't have any trouble, thanks to the mayor. But oh, how that beast can eat! An appetite like a tiger. I'd simply advise you not to pet it. Especially because Monsieur Jouffroy doesn't always put the muzzle on—the creature can't stand it. As you can imagine, no hotel would agree to put up with that cur, not even the ones that claim to take dogs. Here we're not so fussy, it's just come as you are. Besides, Monsieur Jouffroy's pit bull and Monsieur Leblond's orangutan are great friends. What's that you're reading?" (She was looking at the paper-stuffed folder on Dochin's knees.) "Articles? Are you a journalist?"

"Not exactly . . ."

"Do you mind?"

She lit a cigarette and extended a wrinkled paw.

"Mind if I have a look?"

He abandoned the sheet to the hand of the walking Rouault.

She deciphered a few lines, her gaze suddenly growing attentive. Her eye raced over the page. From the shifting expressions taking shape on her face, Dochin sensed that his text did not leave her indifferent. He felt a gentle glow bathing his heart, and his mood became a notch brighter. After all, even if it was only a few lines, this no-longer-young woman with the paint-daubed face was his book's very first reader. Without asking, she reached over and pulled a handful of sheets from the folder on his knees.

"Gestapo . . . Gestapo . . . Gestapo again . . . They come up a lot, don't they?" she said, still reading. "Bonny's gang . . . Oh, look at that, Masuy's bathtub . . . Gestapo again. The Marignan Theater turned into a German movie house . . . Gestapo again, that makes . . . What is that, the sixth time? Seventh? Juju, of the Manouchian Group. Whoops! Gestapo again, I haven't missed one. 'Descending into the Combat métro station, the tracks gleaming under the yellow-tinged lights, he . . .' He what? Ah! the old Combat station! I had an uncle who lived right nearby, on the Rue Louis-Blanc. Ran a novelty shop."

She stopped reading and handed the pages back.

"It's a novel?"

"Yes. It's trying to be, anyway . . ."

"Oh, and he's modest, too! Looks like it's set during the war? Under the Occupation?"

"You've got it."

Soon she was calling him *tu*. Evidently she'd taken a liking to him. She tossed out that first *tu* more or less like you'd throw open a door when you have no idea what's waiting on the other side. Heads or tails!

Breezily, then, she attempted a *tu*:

"But really, my boy . . . '40–'44! That's not yesterday! You weren't even born yet . . ."

Dochin was a bit disconcerted:

"But I . . ."

She smiled. He hadn't flinched. So no problem with *tu*, she'd pulled it off!

"You don't mind my calling you *tu*?"

"But . . ."

"Like Prévert said, more or less: I say *tu* to everyone I like. If that rubs you the wrong way, just come right out and say it, we're not Jesuits here, we say what we think. A backpacker, eh? Well, you're no bourgeois, that's for sure. To hell with those small-minded jerks! Let them go their own way, nobody's holding them back. Calling their friends *vous*, carefully knotting their ties, never slurping their soup . . . very nice, I'm sure! Well, they can keep that crap for themselves, don't you think?"

"We hardly know each other . . ."

Suddenly growing somber, her brow furrowed by an ancient memory now painfully rekindled, she said, "It's weird, how you remind me of a brother of mine. My poor brother Hubert."

She let the smoke from her dwindling cigarette veil her face. Dochin looked at the enormous bracelet on her wrist.

"He was just about your age when he died. He really was the best thing I had in my life. Almost everything about you reminds me of him . . . The way you talk . . . the way you pause . . . Your physique too. I can't believe how much you look like him. It's almost like he was standing right here in front of me . . . like he's come back to me, right here in my motel . . . back from a long, long trip . . . Listen, you sure it's okay if I call you *tu*?"

"Oh, it won't kill me. Besides, I understand. If I remind you that much of your late brother . . ."

"You're still calling me *vous*, you dope!"

"I'm sorry, but it's sort of hard for me. I'm not in the habit . . . not right off the bat like that . . ."

She took his backpack and they set off for the main building, him still clutching his manuscript. They climbed the stairs to his room, number 4, nice and clean, very simple, almost monastic, whitewashed walls ornamented only by a cheap reproduction of Van Gogh's *Olive Grove*, looking very lonely against that vast white expanse. The window overlooked the Vézère.

He summoned up the nerve to make a little conversation:

"And what did your brother do?"

"Oh . . . this and that. He wanted to be an architect, but he ended up in business. He bought and sold country houses, mills, things like that . . . Sometimes abandoned shops. All on the up and up, don't get any ideas. I say that because of the things that go on nowadays, now that our whole sense of morality's gone to pot. Upright to his fingertips, was Hubert. Neck-deep in integrity. And we all know how far that gets you! It's certainly no way to make money. Things didn't work out for him. The poor boy never did have any luck. Not with money, not with women. He died in '45. Thirty-five years old."

She nodded toward the manuscript, now lying on a table. "But really, my little pup . . . The war . . . The Occupation . . . The Krauts . . . You weren't even born yet! Or else you were still in diapers."

"Still a long way from diapers. I was born in 1950."

"Forty-one years old . . ."

"Not quite. Next month. I was an October baby."

"Five years older than Hubert was when he left us. But . . . the Gestapo . . . the secret police on the Avenue Foch . . . Masuy and his nice warm bath . . . quite the tongue-loosener, that thing was! . . . Your book's not exactly drawn from experience, now is it?"

"Of course not. But you can find out a lot if you know where to look. Plenty of good writers have written about the war without living through it."

"You might want to doctor the names up a little, you know."

"They're part of history."

"True, but it wasn't that long ago . . . There are the children and grandchildren to think about . . . What I suggest is . . . for example, instead of Bonny, you put Buny or Bany . . . Masuy you replace with Mozuy or Mizuy, something like that . . . See what I mean? That way you don't have to worry about running into trouble. People can be so touchy!"

"I'll think about that . . . The names aren't really that big a deal."

"And of course fake names are loads of fun for the reader. They love trying to figure out who's behind them. A *roman à clef*, if you like. But that's your business. I've got tons of books about war, if you want to bone up. Especially the two best ones, '14–'18 and '39–'45, which so livened up our dull little century . . . I've got books all over the place here. I don't even know where to put them anymore."

"You like reading too?"

"My husband ran a bookstore . . . I used to help out . . . That was a long time ago. I was still quite young when we divorced. We had a big shop in Paris, on the Quai des Grands-Augustins, 'Le Monde à la Page' it was called. And the customers we had! Cocteau . . . Montherlant . . . Salacrou . . . Arthur Adamov . . . All long gone now. Before that I was in the movie business. Script girl. Oh, not for long! I worked with Duvivier, Grémillon . . . Pierre Chenal, too . . . Jules Berry used to make passes at me! What class that guy had! Try finding his equal nowadays! Bunch of slobs, climbing all over each other for a chance to get on TV!"

"And you ended up here, in the Limousin."

"I did indeed. Here you've got all the peace and quiet you could ask for. You can breathe. You can live your whole life in slippers, if you like, without even washing your backside, and no one's going to say a word about it. Almost forty-one years I've been here! This place used to be a post house way back when, before it became a motel. I took it over from a friend, and I never looked back. If I've set foot in Paris ten times since then, I'd be surprised. At any rate, about your book . . . my hat's off to you! I don't suppose it's finished yet?"

"Oh, good Lord, no . . . I'm still a long way from the end . . ."

"All the better. There's nothing I like more than a novel with some heft to it. *Death on the Installment Plan . . . For Whom the Bell Tolls . . . The Brothers Karamazov* . . . Not like those little pieces of Kleenex Françoise Sagan keeps giving us. Those guys had lead in their pencils, and plenty of brawn to get the job done. They had what it takes to go the distance. I'm sure a lad like you is in just the same class."

"Oh, it's hard for me . . . The words don't always come so easily . . ."

"So you're struggling a little? Well, for the few lines I read, bravo!"

"You're too kind . . ."

"Not at all. I'm just an informed reader, if that doesn't sound too pompous. I was reading Montaigne and Proust when I was eleven. You know, your thing isn't a thousand miles from Sartre's *Roads to Freedom* . . . Something in the tone . . ."

"You've got to be kidding!"

"Not at all. It's strange, you don't look much like a writer."

"They have a special physique?"

"Some of them are quite a sight . . . You could at least tell me your name."

"Jean-Rémi Dochin."

"Is that c-h-a-i-n or c-h-i-n, like Benoist-Méchin?"

"See aitch eye enn, like *crachin*. It's a northern name."

"Is that where you're from, then?"

"No, I was born in the Anjou. But the name comes from the Artois. Like Meurchin . . . Gauchin . . . Esquerchin . . . there are a bunch of little burgs with names like that around Lens and Béthune."

"I'm from the Berri, myself. Or at least my parents were. Not far from the Bois de Meillant. Oh, strolling through the Bois de Meillant . . . taking your time . . . early on a summer morning, when the sun's going full blast . . . I don't know anything more glorious in this world. When I think of all those dolts jetting off to Indonesia . . . My niece lives in Bordeaux. I'm Céline. Céline Ferdinaud. Turn it around and you've almost got the author of *Death on the Installment Plan*.

Pretty wild, huh? Relax, we're not cousins or anything. But if I'd had a knack for writing and wanted to be published, I probably would have had to come up with a pseudonym. Don't worry, I'm not much good at prose. Or poetry, for that matter."

"Why would that worry me?"

"They say two writers don't always see eye to eye. Let's come right out and say it . . . often they can't stand the sight of each other! And if one of them happens to be more talented than the other, then someone's got ulcers and insomnia coming his way."

"I wouldn't know. Never spent any time in literary circles."

"I'm not surprised to hear it. You're new to all this. Jean-Rémi Dochin? Never heard of him. Bernard Pivot's never dandled you in his lap on that *Apostrophes* show, that's for sure!"

"That'll come in time," Dochin murmured, seething. "It'll come. Just takes some patience. There's no reason why not! All those no-talent jerks he has on . . ."

"Ooh, he's got the hunger, this one! And thinks all his fellow-writers are boobs. A real author, in short!" Céline chuckled. "But you know, it just kills me, seeing a kid like you writing about the Occupation . . . the black market . . . the double crosses . . . the sheer stupidity . . ."

She'd handed him a can of beer from a little refrigerator. He sat down and took a few sips.

"Like I told you, you just have to dig up some info . . . go through the newspapers from the time . . . or . . ."

"Don't give me a list!" she interrupted. "Research! What a joke. If you want to say anything serious about those days, you have to have been there."

"It's fictionalized. The Occupation's just a backdrop . . ."

"Some backdrop. All full of holes, I'll wager!"

"My book's about two kids, two friends who . . ."

"You ever publish anything before?"

"Oh . . . nothing worth mentioning . . . Just a crappy little crime novel that no one ever even noticed."

"What gets me about crime novels is all the high-class types you see trying to write them. I'm talking about respectable writers, the kind who write books with no picture on the cover . . . The literary white-collar crowd, if you like. When they talk about crime . . . about violence . . . or should I say when they try . . . it's just hilarious. Like slumming aristocrats . . . like yuppies putting on their rattiest old clothes to go tour an underprivileged suburb. I've got bucketfuls of crime novels around here. Especially from before the war, in the 'Not for Nighttime Reading' and 'Black Mask' collections . . . you know, with the big thick covers . . . I've even got some Ferenczis. Like *No Holiday for the Undertaker.* That's the top! My brother read that, he loved it. *The Curse of the Willetts . . . The Resurrection of Monsieur Corme* . . . No one's ever done better."

Suddenly the pit bull barked furiously. Footsteps were approaching in the hallway. The door was half-open, and Dochin and Céline saw the strange couple go by, the hunchback and the woman with the goiter.

"Out for a little stroll," said the hunchback, twisting his neck slightly to one side. "See you at dinner!"

"Have a nice walk," said Céline. "Don't go too far, it'll be getting chilly soon. The altitude, you know. It can be damp by the water at this hour, too. I think Monsieur Leblond's out there somewhere with his orangutan."

"See you in a while!" the begoitered Englishwoman chirped with a charming smile. "We're headed to the mill."

Out front a car horn honked imperiously two or three times.

"You get unpacked, my fine blond friend," said the Ferdinaud woman. "That must be more customers. I've got to go. Make yourself at home. It's a very good bed, you'll see. Help yourself to another cold one from the fridge if you like."

Dochin picked up his backpack and tossed his few belongings into a cabinet, then lay down on his back to try out the bed. He went to the window and watched the Vézère flowing by. Perhaps because evening was coming, the river seemed to hesitate for a moment at the foot of the willows, as if to tarry and chat for a while with old friends. Or so Dochin told himself, endowing the trees with the power of speech. Little eddies could be seen at the foot of the willows, and then the water set off on its way again. The guy from Villefranche-sur-Saône was out strolling on the banks with his orangutan. He was talking to the animal as you might talk to a child, pointing out the fish as they jumped from the water, and the creature leapt with joy.

On his way down the hall to the bathroom, a towel under his arm, Dochin glanced out a window that gave onto the garden. Céline Ferdinaud was standing beside a dusty Buick, chatting with two newly arrived guests: American tourists, their voices as loud and piercing as deaf peoples', their bodies enormous, more than obese (the film director Ivan Noë would surely have turned them down for leading roles in his masterful *Le Château des Quatre Obèses* on the grounds that they were simply too fat), wider than they were tall, the man in a Stetson, they must have spent years gorging on gut-popping quantities of sweets or frozen junk food, unless, Dochin thought, it was simply some glandular thing. They must not have dared try their luck in a normal hotel, or perhaps they were politely shown the door lest they inconvenience the more presentable guests in the dining room.

Now La Halte's aged chambermaid made her appearance. She looked a bit like that extraordinary actress Gabrielle Fontan, so unforgettable in Duvivier's *Deadlier Than the Male*. She took the elephantine couple's bags and led them toward the main building, unhurried, her legs heavy. The two roly-polies seemed delighted not to be—yet again, who knows?—spending the night outdoors or in their car.

"When you're made like that, the best thing you can to do is stay home," said Céline, back upstairs, Dochin having just torn himself away from the window. "Or else buy yourself a camper. With industrial-strength shock absorbers, of course. There are plenty of bed-and-breakfasts along the road—more all the time, in fact—but I'll bet our fat friends couldn't work up the nerve even to try one of those."

Dochin entered the bathroom, and Céline turned on the taps in the tub.

"I'd rather take a shower," he said.

"Oh, go on and take a bath, idiot. It'll relax you. You've been out pounding the pavement like a fool in this heat, a bath'll do you good."

"Oh, all right, a bath it is."

"I'll make it nice and warm."

Testing the water with her fingertips, she went on:

"To return to our two Yanks, you can't stop people traveling just because their butts are too big, after all. Those hotel owners shouldn't be so particular. In the wintertime, when no one's around, they might turn a blind eye when a freak or a drifter like you stumbles in . . . But when summer comes it's a different story altogether."

The bathtub was three-quarters full. A cigarette stuck between the scarlet slugs that were her full lips, one eye closed against the smoke, Céline looked on unblushing as Dochin slowly undressed.

"You know what you make me think of, standing there by that tub?"

"No."

"All those guys Masuy interrogated in the Gestapo offices. It must be your book. The old fake drowning trick! The bathtub . . . That was his invention. A nobody, he was. Before the war he was a traveling toy wholesaler. A Belgian, to boot! Belgians are a lot more fun nowadays."

"I talk about him a little in my book, as it happens . . . Did you read that part?"

"Just a couple of sentences . . . But back to hotel owners. You know, the clientele can be awfully demanding, and they don't want to eat dinner with a roomful of fatsoes and dwarves. The foreigners are the worst. Particularly the northern Europeans. Your Frenchman isn't so prissy, everything cracks him up. I had a religious education—I don't believe in anything anymore, but a few of their little teachings have marked me for life—and that sort of attitude seems scarcely charitable to me, but it's human nature, after all. This planet's full of assholes and bastards, you've got to get used to it, there's no other place for us to go on our little journey."

Dochin stood waiting, not daring to take off his jeans, one hand vaguely hovering about the fly.

"I've seen a man's backside before, baby doll. I may be a bit over the hill, but you've got to understand, I used to be a beautiful woman, and I've had my share of lovers. Go ahead and take your bath, I'm not going to bite your balls."

He consented to bare all and sank one tentative foot into the bathwater.

"That's life!" sighed Céline, a fresh cigarette between her lips. "Just this morning I had a couple of dwarves wanting a room. Two gentlemen straight out of a Tod Browning movie. They got out of their car and stood there gawking, the idiots, they didn't even have the guts to come in, at first."

Dochin relaxed blissfully in the warm, perfumed water.

"Two brothers from Luxembourg, with a lemur. They had a teeny little car, one of those ridiculous buggies you can drive without a license, poking along at ten miles an hour and pissing everyone off. I put them in room 8. Quiet as ants. If you could see how happy they were, just for the chance to sleep at long last! As if the world wasn't ugly enough, without those two poor bastards! In their case, they've got *two* strikes against them: one, standing knee-high to a house cat, and two, carting a strange animal around."

"I haven't met many of your guests, but I'm thinking you like to take in people who are . . . shall we say . . . a little unusual."

"That's right. We don't care about nationality around here, we just have a soft spot for cripples and freaks. Folks who have trouble getting into a hotel, where nobody wants to eat dinner next to someone a little bit different. You don't have to be funny-looking, though. I also take ordinary people, but usually ones who travel with animals that some might find a tad . . . problematic."

"Like the guy with the orangutan."

"Right. This isn't the Rue Morgue. That animal's no bother at all, it sleeps in a nice, airy shed by the cellar door. Our ever-vigilant police came by to check up on it, but they couldn't find a thing to complain about. Just like the name says, this place is the home of the friendly welcome, and it's cheaper, too. The hotel maids send me most of my customers. Such sweet girls! I always give them a nice tip when I see them, it's well worth it. This place has always welcomed outsiders, people who are a little lost, wanderers with no car, like you . . . The guy who was here before me used to put up that actor who worked with Jean Renoir . . . you know, Max Dalban . . . The poor man suffered from some sort of elephantiasis, in the end he could only get roles as a mover, that kind of thing, and since the hotels didn't much care for his looks, he came here for his vacations sometimes . . . He fished in the river . . . he loved it here. We had a couple of double amputees once, two cousins from Colmar, oh they were a riot, they could even play ping-pong . . . Of course, we had to take the legs off the table . . . Oh, how those rogues made me laugh! I peed my pants! They got run over by a truck late one night in Cherbourg . . . in '77, I think it was. Their little carts didn't have running lights. Life sort of stinks sometimes, doesn't it? They used to hide Resistance members here, back before my time . . . even a few British paratroopers . . . between '40 and '44 . . . Then later it was Collaborationists on the run . . . Sort of like the padres used to do, in the monasteries and abbeys . . . giving succor to human misery, that was their only concern . . ."

"Next you'll be telling me Paul Touvier hid out here."

"You talk about Touvier in your book?"

"Not much."

"Not Touvier, no. But lots more just like him, apparently, on their way to the Spanish border. No politicos in our beds nowadays, though. Just poor souls who got screwed over by old Mother Nature. The bitch! Really, instead of shrinking them down to almost nothing or pumping them up into blimps, she would have done better to plant a feather in their ass. That way the hotels might have taken them in, because the normal tourists love a good laugh, especially at vacation time. You like your room? Made yourself at home, I hope?"

"It's very nice, yes. And the view of the river's a real pleasure. You're right, it's like something out of Pissarro . . . or maybe Sisley . . ."

"And there are some lovely fish swimming around in there! Completely unpolluted, too. No factories in this neck of the woods. Let's hope that lasts! Oh, the fish we've got! You'll see, Odette will whip you up a trout meunière with grapes that'll knock you out."

"Odette's the chambermaid?"

"That's right. Thirty-one years she's been here. A real pearl. I love her like a sister. Devoted like you can't imagine."

"Are there other servants?"

"There's Félibut . . . He lives in town, comes out now and then when there's heavy work to be done. But just look at you, Mister! Those arms! Suppose I took you on to help out? We've got plenty of work for a handyman."

Dochin let out a laugh, rocking from side to side in the tub:

"I'm just passing through."

"That's what they all say!" Céline chuckled. "Incidentally, I haven't even asked if you're hungry, my lad."

"Pretty much famished."

"I'll ask Odette to make you something . . . You can eat before the rest of them, you must be half-dead."

"Everyone eats together here?"

"However you like. We have a dining room, but Odette can also bring your meals up to your room. Or if you prefer, you can skip them. Around here everybody does as he damn well pleases. Anyway, I've got to get going, sweetcheeks, take your time."

And out she went. Passing the room she'd given Dochin, she stopped, pushed open the door, and took a quick look around. The bedclothes had been pulled down. On the table, she spied the manuscript in its red folder. She stepped in, picked it up, and flipped through it a little. She read a passage, smiled, skipped to another page . . . then another . . . Finally she put the thing back on the table. Suddenly a thoughtful look crossed her face. She picked up the manuscript again and opened it at random. Quickly scanned the page before her. Finally she left the room and called out:

"Odette, are you around?"

Clean and fresh after his bath, Dochin went down to the dining room. Rustically furnished, the lighting a bit dim. His place had been set at the long table. The two Luxemburgish dwarves were already sitting at the far end of the table, their lemur beside them. Dochin said hello. The dwarves answered congenially, their mouths full, and the writer tucked into his rosette sausage and goose rillettes with rough country-style bread, slightly burned and crusty. A moment later, Odette brought in a sizzling, perfectly runny omelet with porcinis.

"Take your time, Monsieur Jean-Rémi. Eating too fast gives you a stomachache."

"Thanks, Madame Odette. That omelet looks delectable."

"Call me just plain Odette."

All the while serving him from the frying pan with a long wooden spoon, she leaned over his shoulder and whispered slyly into his ear:

"I don't think I'm wrong to tell you this: the boss has taken quite a shine to you, and believe me, she's plenty choosy where men are concerned."

Then she headed over to the dwarves, who were digging into a terrine of foie gras, and amiably asked if there was anything else they might need. One of them requested a carafe of Cahors.

7 An Admirer

Back in my room, my belly full at last, I saw that my manuscript was gone from the table. I searched around and finally spotted it: God knows how, it had ended up in the cabinet, on top of my almost empty backpack. There were pages sticking out of the folder, like someone had been rummaging through it. I picked it up and tapped it on the table to make a nice tidy stack, more or less squared off. Like any writer, I'm always on guard against copycats, so I was wondering if some ill-mannered soul—a stranger, maybe a guest in this place—might have been nosing around in my work. I shrugged. Now I heard voices in the hallway, so I bent an ear. It was Céline chatting with the orangutan guy. Hearing him go on his way, I opened the door. Céline was just walking off:

"Excuse me!"

She turned around. "What is it, my fine friend? Enjoy your dinner?"

"Yes, very good, thanks. I wanted to ask you . . ."

"I'm listening, son."

First she almost mistook me for her late brother, now here she was posing as my mother. I was like one of the family, that's for sure.

"Well, my friend? Speak up."

"Was that you who was fiddling with my manuscript while I was at dinner? I only ask because . . ."

She let out a full-throated, mocking laugh:

"Oh! someone's been messing with Monsieur Flaubert's lovely manuscript! . . . Ah! he spotted it right away! Forgive me, dearie, but, you'll see, I didn't stain it, I didn't dog-ear it, I didn't even lick my finger to turn the pages. I was in your room spraying mosquito repellent—they can get pretty thick around here with the river so close by and this warm weather—and I couldn't help reading a few pages of your opus. Wasn't easy, because frankly you're no calligrapher. Do you mind?"

"Not at all," I said, relieved. "As long as it's you . . . I was afraid it might have been . . . I don't know, one of your guests . . . You're different."

"Well, thank you. But you know, we don't have any cat burglars around here. Anyway, congratulations. Sincerely. You've got something there. And the writing! You're loaded with talent, kid. I can tell. Now, take my advice, don't you go frittering away your gift. You've got to finish that book. Such a change from the tripe that usually gets published nowadays!"

"Oh, you're just trying to be nice."

"Why should I do that? I always say what I think. If it was crap, I'd give it to you straight, right to your face."

"What part did you read?"

"When the two kids—strikingly lifelike, those two—when the two kids are standing on the platform in the Combat métro station, and the guy in the black raincoat asks them if they like . . . chewing gum, I think it was, I can't quite remember . . . Oh! the dialogue! It's like Anouilh! Pagnol! It's all yours, your own style, but I mean in terms of quality. You could eat that dialogue up! You can almost taste it! And then . . . In any case, the writing is masterly, no two ways about it. The story seems captivating enough, but it's the style that matters most. What a gift!"

"You're really being far too kind . . ."

"Don't start up again with your silly doubts! You think old man Céline wasted his time tormenting his noodle when he was laying down his *Journey*? He knew it was terrific, he knew he was the greatest, the most brilliant, and everyone else was a pinhead! Do me a favor and have a little faith in yourself. When you write as well as that, you don't have to be afraid of anyone."

Still hoping to keep me around, she went on:

"Tell me . . . Do you think it would really be so terrible to settle here at my motel? Lots of peace and quiet, fresh air . . . You could help out around the place . . . I can see you're out of work. The grape harvest! That's what you told Odette, isn't it?"

"Well yes, what of it?"

"A forty-year-old man picking grapes! If you were a teenager, then sure, why not? But a guy your age!"

"There's no shame in it."

"No, but it proves you're out work. And homeless too, I bet?"

No point trying to hide it. She'd seen it all. She was like a bloodhound. One glance and she could tell I was a bum, no analysis of my footwear required.

"Well, that's not going to last long, believe me. Not with this novel. It's a sure-fire bestseller. You're going to make headlines in all the literary columns. I'm telling you, it's a cinch."

"You're joking."

I eyed her warily, doubt still squeezing me in its claws. Why this avalanche of praise? My book was just one step above trash, I knew that for a fact. I had to labor like a coolie climbing the Himalayas just to come up with one halfway decent sentence. I didn't even know where to stick my commas! No, those sentences I was spewing out—on pages that would never end up on a classy auction block—were about as fresh and airy as an overgrown wasteland that no one's set foot in for a hundred years. Good luck finding your way through! A wilderness of bumbling, brain-dead words. But the way she was carrying on . . . Still, I had to admit, she probably did know a thing or two about books. She had thousands of them, by almost all the best writers, from what I'd seen in the main hallway. There were even more in the room they used as a library, which I'd stopped by on my way upstairs, once I'd wolfed down my omelet and fruit. What's more, she used to run a bookstore in Paris, right in the Latin Quarter, and she'd been married to a guy who didn't exactly sell lollipops, no, he sold books, real books, and he used to discuss literature—and so did she, for that matter—with all sorts of big writers who came by his place.

"Really, you liked it?"

"We'll talk more about that later. For now, I've only got one thing to tell you: you have to finish it . . ."

"It's not going so great at the moment . . . I've been pretty much stalled for two weeks . . . kind of lost . . . can't seem to get anywhere . . ."

"That won't last. You've got to go back to it, just to make me happy. First, I'll give everything you've written a good, careful read-through. . ."

"You can start now, if you like."

We went into my room and I handed her the manuscript. She pressed it to her bosom:

"I'll read it tonight. Or I'll try, anyway . . . because with your chicken-scratch handwriting . . . Who knows how many pairs of glasses I'm going to wear out deciphering all this! In any case, think about sticking around here a while. There's plenty of work to do, I told you that already. Félibut's getting on. We need a young pair of arms. There's wood to be chopped for the winter, to begin with. We're running low."

"I don't know . . . out in the middle of nowhere . . ."

"Don't tell me you're lazy! I'd be most disappointed. Shirkers aren't really my cup of tea. I know, you're more brains than brawn, but . . . Not big on sports, I'll wager, are you?"

"As a matter of fact no . . . or on . . . long hikes."

"That's right. Long hikes through the streets of Paris, looking for work! Because you're sure not earning your daily bread with your pen!"

After a pause, she added:

"For the moment."

And then she went on:

"A little honest work now and then won't hurt you, and it'll aerate your gray matter. There are enough writers with fat asses and potbellies as it is, don't you think?"

She named a few names . . . People you sometimes see on television . . . healthy eaters . . . august faces with lovely plump cheeks . . . dimpled hands . . .

"I'm skinny enough, aren't I?"

"It's true, you don't cast much of a shadow, but with the princely fare you'll get here, you'd better watch out for the spare tire, the double chin, and the sagging backside, little piggy! Have to expect it. You could look after the garden, too. No harm in a little hoeing or raking . . . you can't die of blisters! And there are wine casks to be stored away . . . And errands to run! Plus we've got three rooms that need painting. Odette's getting on in years, you know."

8   The Latest Julien Gracq

Obviously, the next day I said yes.

She'd only got through the first quarter of the manuscript, what with my cramped handwriting and my cross-outs and rewrites and little glued-on additions all over the place, but when she came to see me she was half-speechless, like she was still stunned by what she'd read. She told me she hadn't seen anything so wonderful since Céline, Cendrars, or Mac Orlan, and that my book was going to be a smash hit for sure. I asked her to stop playing me for a fool. She shrugged her shoulders.

"My poor Jean-Rémi . . . what a dimwit you can be sometimes! Keep doubting your talent, shove it away once too often, and it'll end up ditching you for good. Talent's like a beautiful mistress, it needs some maintenance . . . or like a pot of stew on the fire, you've got to give it a stir now and then, see how the sauce is coming along . . . Otherwise your talent might tell you thanks and so long, and never come back. And to think: of all the hotels in the world, this great writer ends up in mine! My lucky day . . . A good writer's such a rare thing, especially nowadays. All the great ones have bid us farewell . . . never to return! 'I leave you my books, enjoy yourselves.' Céline . . . Aragon . . . Giono . . . Beckett . . . Henry Miller . . . and of course Marcel[1] . . . When you see all these posers cobbling together that dreck on their computers, it makes you want

---

1   Presumably Aymé. (Author's note.)

to give literature the finger once and for all. But there's one thing I wanted to tell you: you cross out too much. You've got rid of some great stuff! When I think of all the sentences you've scratched out! Drowning them in ink till you can't even read them anymore! But when, by some miracle, one of them still shows through, it's a stunner. Such gems you've wiped out! Makes me wonder what the hell you were thinking."

It was a skeptical smile, I imagine, that now took shape on my lips:

"Just one little question: was that really my manuscript you were reading?"

She gave me another irritated little shrug:

"No, it was the latest Julien Gracq!"

9 A Lingering Doubt

I didn't stay a hired hand for long. You've guessed it by now: Céline Ferdinaud became my mistress. She wasn't bad for a seventy-two-year-old woman—well preserved. I probably would have preferred someone younger, of course, but what can you do, she sang me the old siren song, and we wound up in the sack quicker than you can stir a pot. And speaking of pots, don't remind me of that old saw "Old pots make the best . . ."—that would be vulgar. She led, and I followed. For one thing, I was unattached. No relationships. Women don't exactly go throwing themselves at you when you live in the street. And who can blame them? Hard to get turned on by a guy in saggy old trousers with holes in the ass, and shoes that look like they've been all the way from Paris to Dakar, only not in some candy-ass racecar. However dewy-eyed you may be, love stories get to sound a little uninspiring when you're facing down a can of cassoulet and a hunk of moldy bread. But Céline didn't give a holy hoot about all that, she'd never been the lace-and-lavender type. The fact that I was a bum and a drifter just amused her. She said I had a certain hobo charm about me, like some American writer before he got famous, the beautiful loser type, one of those guys who's dragged his broken-down clodhoppers all over creation, who knows what it's like to be down and out, who's used to sleeping rough, who takes it into his head to write like it's a sort of revenge, and who writes pretty damn well at that, because he knows all about life and has a head full of images, and of course success is waiting for him at the end of the line, come on, everybody knows that! It's true I'm not much to look at. I've already thought it worth mentioning that I resemble neither Alain Delon nor Christophe Lambert, not even a Robert Hossein or a Bernard Tapie after visiting a good plastic surgeon. But what Céline liked, what really attracted her, was the writer in me. (The scribbler, I should say.) She wouldn't leave that alone; more than once she gave me a good, long talking-to about my talents. Of which I had plenty, according to her. Myself, I was still full of doubts. But why should Céline shower me with praise if she wasn't genuinely thrilled by my work? She'd read practically all the great classics and all the good contemporary writers, she'd run a bookstore for ten years, and not just any bookstore, but one frequented by the cream of the literary crowd, so for what weird reason would she have looked at a piece of writing as flat and lifeless as a dead slug and seen something interesting and even brilliant in it? But, regardless, I was perfectly aware of one thing (in truth, I was as blind as a bat): what I wrote was absolutely not going to revolutionize the art of the novel, and you didn't need a magnifying glass to see that my text reeked of pointless, plodding labor. To tell the truth, I couldn't even understand why I went on covering all those pages with ink, or how I could have managed to fill up three hundred pages already. I half wondered if some strange being was vibrating my meninges with some diabolical remote control, my brain having become its plaything, sort of like a remake of that Siodmak book; and, though it crossed my mind, it really would have been the height of presumption to apply Stefan Zweig's portrayal of the pre-*Human Comedy* Balzac (back when he was writing serial novels under various pseudonyms, like Lord R'hoone) to my present circumstances: "In vain does he write and write and write, day and night, eager as a starving rat bent on gnawing into the pantry whose enticing aromas set his soul and entrails aflame. His superhuman efforts bring him not one step closer to success." How could I react, hearing Céline use the words "masterpiece in gestation" for the work of a guy who had nothing to show for the last five years except two crime novels—"not to be read at night," and not in the daytime either!—the published one making about as much of a splash as the one that stayed in my drawer (if you want to know the truth, it was dumped into a sewer)!

"You'll outdo them all, my son. You'll see!"

I said she became my mistress. Let's get it right: mistress and mother. Good Lord, she was born in 1918! And me in 1950, during the reign of Vincent Auriol. Find a pencil and figure out the difference.

"Remember what I'm telling you! Right here and now, cross my heart and hope to die, I swear that this novel you're making through all your toil and torment is a truly great book! Except, my little lamb, you're going to have to get back to work. I can see it now, you're not made for chopping wood and cutting down trees and weeding a vegetable garden. You're not the laboring type. Your place is in front of a sheet of paper, by gum! You're not going to get anywhere fussing around with yard work, I can tell you that much for sure!"

In any case, for a homeless guy, this wasn't a bad setup: dry feet, a guaranteed bed for the night . . . We'd even gone to a department store in Brive, where she dressed me up nice from my head to my toes, no more pants with holes in the ass or shredded shit-kickers on my feet, I was finally presentable. I even got some more or less "sporty" clothes, suitable for the countryside. Nice spread at mealtimes, lots of little dishes concocted just for me, the fresh air of the woods and pastures filling my lungs, and the continual, almost maternal kindness—occasionally mingled with a few grumbling reproaches, but it was all for my own good—of Céline and Odette, my adoptresses, both of them sort of homey, always trying to find new ways to please me. I would have had to be a real brute to complain. Next to what I'd endured in Paris the past few years—the loser community centers, the homeless shelters, the dubious company of the Salvation Army dormitories, the stinking squats, the emergency aid offices—next to all that the Halte du Bon Accueil was a real four-star hotel, a new lease on life for a broken-down bum like myself.

But I didn't know yet exactly where I'd ended up.

Now that I do, I tell myself I probably should have gone off and slept in the woods when that chambermaid pointed me toward this quaint little inn! Because if you knew where that novel of mine's taken me, if you knew everything it got me into! . . . The lake of eternal fire sounds pretty comfy next to all that!

At Céline's, someone had finally reached out a helping hand.

If I'd said no . . . The money I'd made from the grape harvest wouldn't have got me far. Back to the streets, back to the grinder, in Paris or elsewhere, no thanks, not for me.

Céline moved me into the little house behind the main building. I settled in, right at home.

"This is where my niece used to live before she left for Bordeaux."

"What does this niece of yours do in Bordeaux?"

"She teaches high school. She's an old maid, never married. But a pretty nice-looking old maid."

"Your late brother's daughter?"

"You got it, baby doll. She was born just about when Hubert went. I looked after her."

"What about her mother?"

"Vanished . . . Into thin air . . . A real airhead. A little actress. I don't know what became of her. No matter. You know, my niece may live alone, but she still has her share of lovers. She knows how to have a good time. She's no wallflower."

"And you . . . Since you divorced your bookseller . . . Ferdinaud's your maiden name?"

"Of course. I used to be Mme Courville. We separated in '46. He sold the bookstore. It got turned into a nightclub . . . a sort of bistro, existentialist-style. I never set foot in the joint. Oh, you're going to get lots of work done in this little house. Just look at those trees, right in front of your window! Don't tell me your inspiration's not going to come back! You're going to have to buckle down to work on that book, and double-time too! I'm going to lock you in and keep you under surveillance, my boy. I'm going to make you write! Just like Madame de Caillavet did for Anatole France."

Yes, there was no choice but to end up in the sack with her. It strengthens the ties that bind, she told me. She even asked—I'm talking about the first time—if I knew what they say about women with big noses like her . . . You can probably guess the rest, the kind of risqué little pleasantry we've all heard more than once. Dirty talk wasn't really her style—her, a former bookseller! who used to talk literature with Henry Miller and Léon-Paul Fargue, who sold books to great writers, famous critics!—but she unloaded that little quip on me all the same.

I really was stuck there in the Halte du Bon Accueil, balled and chained, and besides, like I said, the ladies had taken me under their wings, almost the perfect little nest, and I didn't stay a hired hand for long. My chores—cutting wood, running errands, hauling magnums of mineral water and sacks of fruit or spuds at the wheel of the old *deux chevaux*, all that came to an end after just a few weeks.

"Maybe it's time you went back to your book, my friend," Céline told me toward mid-October, after I'd spent a month taking it easy in this quiet, slightly wild spot on the edge of the Plateau de Millevaches, farting around, picking mushrooms, maybe trying to tease the odd carp or pike out of the Vézère. "You're not going to let a book like that just lie around gathering dust, are you? What's the matter, my little sparrow, your inspiration run out on you?"

10   The Poor Man's Laure de Berny

The flood of refuseniks from the hotels slowed to a trickle a little before All Saints' Day. After October 21st, Sainte-Céline's day, we only had one or two wandering losers, unshaven, dressed like rag-and-bone men, and an oldish lady with a nice case of dropsy. No hotel in the region would have anything to do with them, of course, and they were all full up anyway, owing to an oenologists' convention (or so they said).

After that, things really slowed down, absolutely nothing going on, beautiful Novembers they have around there! The colors! Around November 11th we had two tiny, bowlegged Asians who stayed one night—them and their boa constrictor—and then it was just the three of us in that charming, peaceful abode. Félibut, the handyman—a very sympathetic drunk, with a nose you could probably squeeze a full glass of wine from—only came by every five or six days now, when there was some major chore to be done. I'd started writing again. It wasn't coming easy. I spent my time crossing out lines and tossing away crumpled pages (when evening came I burned the contents of my wastebasket out in one corner of the garden, because I never liked to leave paper bearing my handiwork lying around ... which is probably dumb, especially when you consider that what I write isn't worth beans—as I keep telling you, maybe in hopes it'll end up really sinking in, so when the time comes your jaw will drop right open with astonishment ...).

So she shut me away in the little house at the far end of the garden and made me fill up my pages, sort of like a schoolboy in detention. I don't know how hard Madame de Caillavet had to bear down on Anatole France to get him to come up with a book, but in my case I can say I got the full treatment! Almost twenty-four hours a day I was exiled to the little house in the brambles, behind the old post house, right next door to the river, the Vézère just ten feet away, let the water rise a little and here comes the muck. She left me to my own devices, but only under lock and key. And like a pussy I didn't put up a fight. Incidentally, I should tell you, those first three or four rolls in the hay weren't the end of it. This was a real relationship. Not only did I have to lay down shitloads of sentences on paper, I also had to lie down on Madame's belly on a regular basis. She was a fan of the no doubt very restful but not particularly original missionary position. Wears thin pretty quick, if you want my opinion. But I never crapped out on her. Too scared of being tossed back into the big wide world. So no choice but to keep on keeping it up. Apart from that, Céline wasn't disagreeable at all, I liked her common-folk ways, and all in all she was a pretty nice girl, a good grandma, a decent mother. It's just that I was expected to screw her every now and again. What was I supposed to do? She kept cooing about how much I reminded her of her late brother. I'd seen a framed portrait in her room of the dear departed in question, with a strip of black crepe across one corner, and a little bouquet of dried flowers. I saw no—and I mean absolutely zero—resemblance. What I saw was a guy with short, dark hair (mine is blond, shoulder-length, with an eternal cowlick), a square face (mine's sort of long), a strong, decisive jaw (the shape of my lips denotes cowardice, lack of will, physical weakness, and more besides, none of it very attractive), and an overall air of vitality, determination, and practicality (you might already have noticed my regrettable lack of maturity, my infuriating penchant for indecision . . .).

The fact is, it wasn't just because of her long-lost brother that Céline took an interest in me the moment I showed up at La Halte. No, it was those four or five sentences she'd read when she first cast an eye over my prose. Something clicked at that moment, I imagine, and her heart must have started beating a little faster. Deep down—yes, that must have been it—she probably had a touch of the Zulma Carraud or Laure de Berny or Éveline Hanska in her. Women who would undoubtedly have wound up somewhere in the dim background of history if it weren't for the great writer they loved. But, unfortunately for her, my writing wasn't worth one quarter of the first comma Balzac ever committed to paper. I was just a lumbering malingerer, and that's all I'd ever be. Poor woman, she could have done so much better. She'd taken it into her head that my book was going to be a tremendous success and make me a household name, when in fact six dozen hack novels get published every month in Paris that are exactly like the one I'd been killing myself to write for the past year—and most end up getting pulped. What made her quiver with excitement was the idea of having and holding, all to herself, a sort—these are her words—of new Céline (for such was the nickname—a bit intimidating and burdensome—that she'd two or three times poured into my ear canals). Understandable, for someone as well-read as her, someone who'd once been a high-class bookseller and then got stuck in the middle of nowhere for forty years. And if she talked to me so much about her dead brother—never at any real length, just two words here and there—I imagine it was essentially a way of appealing to my emotions, a way of tugging at my heartstrings, touching a sensitive chord. Well, that's okay by me, I told myself, let's play along.

11   Anatole France and Madame de Caillavet

But the bedroom stuff wasn't that big a thing, really, just a now and then deal, sort of the icing on the cake. Once fall came and the clientele turned invisible, so to speak, La Halte practically shut down. This was when things really got going for me. Locked away in my little house—I'm exaggerating a bit, I did have the right to go out for a walk in the garden now and then—I found myself living the life of an actual writer, by which I mean sitting alone at a desk with a blank page in front of me and fistfuls of pencils and pens all around, plus five or six dictionaries keeping me company. And, in place of the smog-choked skies and fucked-up ozone layer of Paris, cool breezes from the Plateau de Millevaches, and all the fresh air I could ask for. Things were a damn sight better here, I have to say. Better than wearing away your artistic temperament scribbling in a drafty park or on a subway bench or a cot in a homeless shelter with your neighbors all groaning and farting and belching, better than trying to write at a grimy old table in some sad wino bar. I've already mentioned the grub they laid on at La Halte. Wholesome and abundant, that's what it was. Regional dishes, daubes, river fish lovingly prepared by a veritable wizard of pots and pans, hearty peasant pots-au-feu. What does the man in the street want most of all? A nice, full belly. Well, it's the same thing for a writer—isn't there an expression "hungry as a novelist"? He can't churn out his pages when his stomach is rumbling, and if it weren't for the sweat trickling over my temples as I sat there working my fingers to the bone, I think I could easily have gained a good twenty pounds from Odette's wondrous creations.

Now and then Céline stopped by for a surprise visit. She leaned over my shoulder and read what I'd just put down. Sometimes, when I felt like going for a stroll to wake up my sleeping feet, she bitched:

"I'm keeping you under lock and key, Mister! Like that Caillavet woman did with the author of *The Red Lily*. Please be so kind as to finish this chapter."

Looking over my sentences, my snatches of dialogue, my descriptions, my short bursts of would-be poetry, she exclaimed in delight, on the verge of clapping her hands, it seemed like, even comparing me—"within reason, of course," she was always careful to add—to Céline . . . Chekhov . . . Simenon . . . Aragon . . . Hardly a day went by that I didn't find myself graced with a new name from the literary pantheon. One morning I even got a Gogol, thrown out just like that, without a trace of a smile!

What if I'd rather be just plain Dochin?

Maybe my writing wasn't so bad after all, I thought. And inside me, sweeping away the insecurities that had been gnawing at me ever since I first got my book underway, a sort of self-satisfaction started rearing its head. It didn't last, of course. The smothering black clouds of doubt drifted back soon enough.

For Céline, trumpeting all these glorious names at me as she watched my sentences march by, I was no longer just some poor drudge sweating over his page, but a whole shelf in the Bibliothèque Nationale.

"You've got almost all of them inside you . . . There's even some Réstif de la Bretonne, here and there . . ."

It had been smoldering inside me for some time, and finally it flared up:

"You're sure you don't mean Ponson du Terrail?"

Poor old Ponson! Literature's whipping boy. How lucky we are to have him around!

Meantime, I was running seriously short on élan. I filled up my pages like an automaton, completely devoid of enthusiasm. But I must have been missing something, the way Céline kept cheering me on, genuinely overjoyed with my work . . . Doubts or no doubts, this book really was—apparently—going to land me a spot on Eyebrows's show, and a place of honor in all the booksellers' windows.

So, one way or another, the manuscript was coming along. Toward mid-November I hit page 325.

I probably wouldn't have been in such a hurry if I'd known the sordid cesspool this goddamn novel was going to drag me into. Less of a hurry? Unless I was completely out of my mind, I would have thrown away my pen, yes indeed! Like a flash, like it was red-hot, singeing my fingers!

The days went by.

No, I never heard her coming when she stopped by to make sure I was still hard at work and not jerking off or snoozing on the couch or chasing flies. Quiet as a mouse. Suddenly her voice would tickle my ear, and I'd lift my nose from my paper. I had pounds of the stuff, seven or eight reams to spare. Céline had headed off in her old 2CV to buy more several times already. Once I saw her come back with a whole trunk full, enough paper to write ten *Gone with the Wind*s. I'll bet the stationer came this close to asking if she hadn't made some mistake, if it wasn't toilet paper she was wanting, in which case she'd have done better to shop at the mini-supermarket next door.

"Whatever are you going to do with all that paper, Mâme Ferdinaud?"

"Can you believe it? Along with the hunchbacks and goiter victims and amputees, that hotel maid in Tulle sent me a writer . . . That's all I need!"

"It's true, when it comes to strange-looking characters, you can't do better than writers . . . I'm thinking of that one they showed on TV . . . walking along with his shopping bag full of carrots and cabbage, fifteen cats milling around his feet . . ."

"Paul Léautaud."

"And there was that other one, dressed like a bum, wearing five or six sweaters at once, with safety pins holding them together . . ."

"Louis-Ferdinand Céline. There was also the one who ate five or six meals a day, Raymond Roussel. But generally, the weirder they are, the more talent they've got. A real writer has to be a little nuts. Mine has smelly feet. Maybe that's why the hotels wouldn't take him."

But let's get back to my paper and my writing desk. Hearing her whisper something in my ear, I looked up from my half-covered page:

"You say something? I didn't hear you come in . . ."

She was looking at my ink-stained hands, sympathetically shaking her head. My back was aching from too much work. I'd been at it since nine in the morning, and here it was almost two. Once again I'd skipped lunch, for fear of losing an idea.

"You really should have come, Jean-Rémi. Odette made us a lovely little veal Marengo. We saved you some for tonight, but it's never as good reheated, even in a bain-marie."

"Thanks all the same."

"If you get too hungry, you can eat a little something at four."

The old four o'clock snack! Just like a schoolboy!

"Félibut brought some rosette."

"How's everything going in the motel?"

Locked up in my little house, absorbed in the creation of my life's work, I felt like the Halte du Bon Accueil was miles away. I hardly ever went into the main building anymore, just a shadow, barely a ghost. I was in my novel.

"This morning we had a guy with a big port-wine stain on his face, and a hare lip to top it all off. Couldn't find anywhere to stay. He tried three hotels in Figeac and the Cerf Royal in Brive. They told him to come back after the holidays. Some people just don't have the luck. He's in number twelve. Doesn't make much noise. I think he collects stamps. He borrowed a magnifying glass from Odette so he can look through his albums at night. Apart from that there's not much to tell you. It's all very quiet. Nothing to report. You know, very little goes on at La Halte. Maybe that's part of its charm. But I'm not telling you anything you don't already know, you've been here almost four months now."

Hands on hips, she bent over my page to decipher my minuscule writing. "Boy, you really do like wasting your time, don't you?"

"What are you talking about? Jesus, I never stop working!"

"There's one thing I noticed right off the bat. You rewrite every sentence thirty-six times. You give every one a new turn, but it always means the same thing. You spend all your time crossing out words and adding other words. It never ends! And those little scraps you glue on all over the place! Your manuscript's got more add-ons than Paris has assholes. You really don't know how to write."

"You're always swooning over my great talent."

"And I repeat, great talent's just what you've got. But technique-wise, you're shooting yourself in the foot. All those additions . . . those revisions . . ."

"Well, what about Flaubert? What did he do? Needlework?"

"Flaubert's Flaubert. Jean Anouilh got it exactly right on the radio once: you should almost never revise what you've written. The best thing—or the least bad—is always the spontaneous thing. The first thing you write. Rework it and you almost always mess it up."

"What about Flaubert, then?" I repeated.

She stuck a Marlboro between her lips. "To hell with Flaubert. Paul Léautaud compared old Flaubuche's books to fine woodwork. It all fits together beautifully, it's impeccable, it gleams . . . Result: boredom."

"Léautaud's an asshole."

"Spontaneity! Immediacy! Even if it's a little sloppy . . . a little rough around the edges . . . too bad. It's like andouilette. Herriot was right. It needs a little shit to be good."

"Herriot is the king of the assholes."

12   My Typist Céline, and Céline's Typist

About mid-March 1992, I was in the mood for a breather. My head was stuffed full of that book. A little trip to Paris or Bordeaux or the seaside or somewhere would make a nice change, take the pressure off. Dream on. I'd been planning a break around page 400, but Madame insisted I keep at it, she wanted pages by the pound. I couldn't think of anything else to write. Furthermore, it wasn't clear what had become of the two kids, my two heroes, Max and Mimile, who'd mysteriously disappeared after spending half the night in the lantern-house of the Chatou station, outside Paris. I couldn't quit now, especially not there. She read every page as it dropped off the end of my pen, often putting on her glasses because her eyesight was going, taking the pages I'd finished that day or the day before, devouring it all and again pronouncing me a genius. For a while I thought she was very gently pulling my leg, laughing up her sleeve at my feeblemindedness. Or else, if she really did like it, it was only because she had a thing for me. She was crazy about me, really hot for me—you can be just as much in love at seventy-two as at twenty. End result: everything I did was good. No way this strange castaway she'd adopted could be an eighth-rate writer; I had to be another Cendrars or Dos Passos. And she expressed her enthusiasm not so much in the admiring cries of "Hurrah! You've got them all beat!" I've already reported, as in thoughtful observations worthy of an enlightened reader (I'd come a long way from my two-bit crime novel!), book-critic-style analyses, in-depth discussions—slightly dull, might as well admit it—a mound of keen exegeses that would have been right at home in a high-class literary revue. If she were some serving girl with a subscription to a photo-novel club or a concierge addicted to the 8:30 TV movie, then I would have kept up my guard . . . but the troubling thing—troubling? yes, let's keep that word—the troubling thing was that Céline was a sophisticated woman where books were concerned, someone who could just as easily spend a quarter of an hour telling you about Tolstoy as about Samuel Beckett or Marguerite Yourcenar without giving you a single emptyheaded commonplace, and without putting you to sleep either—and after all, what she'd sold for ten years in her bookstore bore only the most distant resemblance to electric drills or videogames . . .

Anyway, at the beginning of April, with the pages piling up—I now had a respectable stack of sheets covered with my cramped writing, something like four hundred and twenty—she raised the question of putting together a proper manuscript, presentable, the way they're supposed to be. Somehow, it was all going to have to be typed up.

"I hope you're not thinking any publisher's likely to waste his time trying to wade through this . . . this virgin forest of words? He wouldn't need reading glasses, he'd need a scythe! A machete!"

"Who could possibly type this thing up?" I asked in dismay. "You know anyone?"

With my crime novel—just a hair over 140 pages—it was all so much easier: an old lady at the Salvation Army helped me out with her little portable Japy. Here, on the other hand, we were dealing with a genuine doorstop, and—so it seemed, at least—a real piece of writing too.

She thought it over, gnawing her thumb.

"You know anyone?" I repeated.

"I know two or three ladies in Brive who do that . . . but you can't be too careful. We need someone we can trust. When Céline was ready to have his *Journey* typed up, he called on Aimée Paymal, a secretary in the suburban clinic where he practiced, very trust-worthy and discreet. For most of his other books he had help from Marie Canavaggia, a translator, an extremely competent woman. She watched the manuscript like a hawk, supervised the whole thing. She even let him know when she found some tiny goof that needed fixing, just little things here and there, nothing much . . . For *Death on the Installment Plan*, he found Madame Dugué, also a very trustworthy person."

"In other words, if I'm understanding you right, I need someone to put my commas where they belong, drain off some of my ad-verbs, maybe beat some sense into my whacked-out verb tenses?"

"Now, now, don't get all snippy about it . . . Every writer, good or bad, has to take that kind of treatment—except the ones who end up in the Académie, of course. The big publishers pay people to do just that. Don't worry, they're not going to 'tamper with the text.' That would be idiotic with writing as powerful and personal and vibrant as yours. They'd only be ruining it."

"So do you know a good typist or don't you?"

"Like I told you, we need someone we can trust. You can't be too careful . . ."

I let out a belly laugh. "You're afraid someone's going to swipe my ideas?"

"You're the one who's afraid, you dope! Burning all your rough drafts in the garden at night!"

"So do you know someone?"

"Well, how about me? I can't think of anyone else. Better than someone we don't know. Because no matter what, you can't be too careful. Such a lovely text . . . This isn't just any old novel, after all. And that way it'd never have to leave the house."

She sighed, lifting up one corner of the stack and letting the pages fall almost one by one:

"Oh, lord! This thing's going to do me in."

"What about Odette?"

"She types with one finger. Besides, she's got a lot on her plate as it is, poor old thing. Can you see her tending the stove and washing the sheets and dealing with the chickens and cleaning the rooms and then shouldering Monsieur's output on top of all that?"

"You think you can manage?"

"I have an old 1930 Underwood, a real tank. I got it from my mother. She worked in insurance."

"You can do it?"

"Well, my dear son of a bitch, with that writing of yours . . . It's not going to be a picnic! My eyes are aching already. And to make matters worse I'm starting to get rheumatism in my fingers, just like old man Renoir. But I'll have to manage. As long as we're not in too big a rush, it ought to work out. And don't let that keep you from writing, because it's a long way from done, this novel of yours, to judge by the story."

"Put in a sheet of carbon paper and make a couple of copies."

"No, carbon paper smudges. I'll just make the one copy. If we want more we can deal with that later. We can always photocopy the original."

My little nobody's heart—that's how I thought of myself, any-way—was beating hard:

"So then it'll be done . . . The book will be there . . ."

"And then you really get to work, kitten."

"What do you think I've been doing for the past two years?"

"I mean get to work on the publishers. Make your move. The moment of truth."

"But you keep telling me I . . ."

"I'm not in the business. I have my tastes, they have theirs. If they match up, congratulations."

I shrugged, as if I were trying to shake off a fly:

"What a lot of crap we're talking! I think we might as well just shove the whole thing into a drawer right now and be done with it."

"Bite your tongue, you idiot. You'll be on Eyebrows's show within two or three years. And in the seat of honor! Every camera trained on your little puss. Remember what I'm telling you."

13 Q w e r t y u i o p

I laid down another twenty pages or so, and soon came the first days of May. She'd started in on the typing. She picked up the stack, headed into her bedroom, and set it down on the big round table she used as a desk.

"We ought to have a presentable manuscript within a year," she told me after she'd knocked out the first few pages. "The slow part's deciphering that sparrow-scratch writing of yours. And don't even think of looking up from your page and daydreaming just because I'm not there hovering over you . . . Anatole France."

Some days—many days, actually—she typed from morning to night. Once I even heard her working at dawn. Tap tap tappity-tap, *q w e r t y u i o p*, I could hear her plugging away whenever I opened the window or strolled in the garden outside her room. She was going at it for all she was worth, full speed ahead on that old rattletrap typewriter, battered but still ready to serve. It wasn't unusual to see her lamp lit till late at night. Typing was just about all she did anymore, and I can tell you, she believed in my book all the way, much more than I did, I who still doubted the thing would ever be published, almost positive I'd soon be reading another of those insulting little letters that tell you "In spite of the unmistak-able skill and even the brilliant writing of your . . . we regret to inform you that . . . and, thanking you for your kind submission, we assure you of," etc. There she stayed, hunched over her machine, and from summer 1992 to the end of the year she only made three trips to Bordeaux to say hello to her niece—which also gave her a nice little day off.

I looked over the start of the typescript and reread a few passages, more or less at random. Nothing had changed, apart from a few little slips that—with my permission, of course—Céline had touched up. I reacquainted myself with my prose, much easier to read now that it was so tidily typed, with the obligatory double spacing and elegant margins to give it a nice, uncluttered look. First-rate work.

Céline always handed back my handwritten sheets along with the typed pages. Rereading the book up to page eighty, with the manuscript beside it to compare, I realized just what she'd gone through, deciphering my impossible, tiny, irregular, shaky handwriting. Yeoman service, that's what that's called!

I put the first draft into a folder, then carefully slipped that manuscript-to-be—the "fair copy," as they say—into a thick red cardboard file, with an elastic strap to keep it shut. One day this book was going to land me a spot on Eyebrows's show, but—respecting as I do the delicate sensibilities of the tenderhearted among you—I won't say what happened next.

Céline had typed up a little more than a hundred pages. Still plenty of work ahead of her.

Yes, very presentable. But my doubts hadn't faded one bit. Nothing had changed, I still found what I'd written as god-awful as ever. Easy to read, sure, but so nauseatingly flat! Oh, how I longed to hear what the critics would say, and how I hoped they'd confirm everything my ecstatic protectress was telling me!

14 To Hell with the Goncourt!

Spring 1994 rolled around. Thirty months now since I first showed up at La Halte. I'd all but forgotten the many miseries of my former existence, my pathetic life as a drifter. I was still hard at work on my book, still nowhere near done. Céline was still scurrying off to type up my pages as soon as I finished them. The typescript was getting fatter by the day. This was going to be some kind of book—in terms of volume, weight, and thickness if nothing else. A doorstop. Heavy as a cobblestone. And suppose that cobblestone were to fall on my head one fine day? I didn't quite know what it was, but something was telling me to be very, very careful.

It still didn't have a definitive title. For the moment I was call-ing it *Max and Mimile*, but I'd have to find something else before long. Céline was already talking about submitting it to Gallim's or Furne or Charpentier, the biggest publishers in Paris. I felt like I was caught up in some weird dream.

"Sure you don't want them to give me the Goncourt Prize, while they're at it?" I said.

"To hell with the Goncourt! It's gotten so common! And it's all about money anyway. You've got to aim higher. Sales through the roof! You'll see! I can feel it! Translations by the truckload! The subject is pure gold . . . And that style! Completely new! Like noth-ing on earth! They'll still be talking about it in fifty years—and trust me, I know a thing or two about books!"

"Come on, Céline, I'm not that dumb. Quit messing with me, will you?"

"You can't see it . . . You don't understand . . . Oh, you talented young authors, you're all the same! You don't get it! They say Proust was like that when he started out . . . Chekhov too . . . and Zola . . . never suspected just how brilliant they were . . ."

"Stupid literary café chatter."

"Now Céline, on the other hand, he knew from the start he was going to knock them dead. Your problem is, you're too timid, too anxious. If only you had his balls—Céline's, I mean—you'd understand: what you've been writing all these months is going to land on the world of books like a big, juicy bombshell! They'll be wondering what the hell hit them!"

"Come on, quit babbling . . . Odd, you really don't seem like much of a drinker . . ."

Doubt still held me in its clutches, stubborn as an octopus. The closer I got to the end, the more I dreaded handing it over to a publisher, to the point where I eased up the pace when I hit page 525, like someone who suspects there's a big black hole waiting for him at the end of the line, a deep, gaping hole eager to swallow him up. But that's chickenshit, next to the way it actually turned out!

"Listen, Jean-Rémi . . . You can't possibly be so dense that you won't at least give it a shot. If the publishers don't like it, they won't hesitate to tell you. Nothing to fear, they're not going to tear you a new asshole. Those gentlemen will turn down your great work, and that will be that. But I'm telling you, you'll be getting a call after five days at most! Just like Destouches got from Denoël!"

"All these wondrous predictions . . . are you trying to cast a spell on me?"

"Why should I lie? I've got nothing to sell you, kiddo. If I thought your book was worthless, I wouldn't go telling you to send it to Furne or Gallim's, now would I? I'm not out of my mind, you know. Who'd be the one looking like a fool when they sent the thing back with their dreaded little letter? Oh no, I have every certainty it'll be published."

"Yeah, at author's expense . . ."

"Oh, be quiet."

"Every certainty, eh? . . . An endless string of inkblots from the pen of a slow-witted schoolboy . . . Quick, put a cork in my inkwell! Jesus, the bullshit you hand me! What a laugh. Gallim's! Furne! Charpentier! The stars will rain down! Baloney!"

"Just you wait two or three years and see what you have to say then. By that time you'll be someone, a real man of letters. And you'll have long since forgotten your old Céline. When I think that just last summer Monsieur was planning to abandon his novel and throw out everything he'd written! Good thing I was here to rescue it! But don't worry, I don't want a reward. I just like good books and real writers, it's as simple as that."

15   Céline Loses Patience

Nothing much changed from April to October. Still the same parade of outcasts from the high-class hotels. Céline was getting more and more worn down by her labors as a typist and decipherer of the chicken-scratchesque handwriting of the one trying to tell you this story—which is going to end very badly, it doesn't take a fakir to see that.

Poor Céline, she really threw herself into her work. I myself was in no hurry to get the thing finished and sent off. But her! She was bursting from impatience—hour after hour at her old Underwood, almost putting her health at risk, even going without sleep. And all the while I was shaking like a leaf at the mere thought of approaching a publisher: every chance of getting a good, bone-crunching smack to the face, I sensed . . . and humiliation virtually a dead certainty.

With Céline almost always yoked to her typewriter, the ladies of La Halte du Bon Accueil had hired a housemaid, Camille Bihoreau, just a kid, barely fourteen, the daughter of a wine merchant in Les Chartrons. She was looking for a way out of school, where she was bored and not learning anything, but she wasn't dumb at all, no, kind and thoughtful, and discreet too, no chance she might sneak a peek at what Céline was typing or what I was writing so breathlessly with my face glued to the paper, a girl with a perpetual smile on her face, lively and hardworking, and an immediate hit with our amputees, mange cases, drifters, and hunchbacks. Céline's niece Colette Ferdinaud brought her up in her Golf, then spent the rest of the day at La Halte, which gave me a chance to meet her at last. The high-school teacher turned out to be a pretty brunette, about forty, athletic, self-confident, wearing a denim suit. Strong family resemblance with the man in the portrait. She greeted me pleasantly enough, looking me over for five or six seconds. Obviously her auntie had told her all about me. "Yes, the literary genius, that's me. Don't tell me I don't look just like anyone else. I'm sure your aunt told you all sorts of wild stuff about me, but I'm really just your average, insignificant Joe," I wanted to say. But she didn't say three words to me. She stayed with Céline the whole time. Then she kissed her aunt and the new maid and went on her way.

I never saw her again.

Usually it was Céline who made the trip to Bordeaux for these family reunions. One or two days in the City of Wine made a nice change, my protectress told me, and I could certainly understand that. "Stay three days if you like," I'd told her. "Even a week . . . The manuscript can wait, no point complicating your life just for a book."

When summer came, I sometimes went for long strolls through the garden and the orchard, just as night was falling. I inhaled the warm air and the scent of the flowers. I felt the coolness of the Vézère, so close I could hear it lapping away. Everything was calm and harmonious. Nature really comes into its own after dark. I walked as quietly as I could, like a stranger out for a stroll trying not to bother the guests. I tried to empty my mind of everything I'd written in the course of the day. Often, like I said, the lamp in Céline's room was still burning, a tiny distant sun in the window. The tippity-tap of her typewriter drifted out, a monotonous little tune, a machine gun shooting out letters rather than bullets. My turn to surprise her. Limboing under the pear and apple trees, I climbed the old staircase. The upper steps let out a sad little creak as I passed, sort of like a mewing cat, probably halfway gnawed through by mice. I crept down the dark hallway and gently pushed open the door to her room, full of smoke even with the window wide open—she really sucked down the cigarettes when she was working. I tiptoed toward her broad, bony back, bent down and deciphered my sentences, my prose, things I'd written two or three days before. On her left sat my handwritten pages, and a ream of fresh paper in front of her, next to the big jam-packed Martini ashtray. I peered over her shoulder and rediscovered my dialogue, my descriptions, all neat and tidy now, not a comma out of place. Céline was a very careful copyist. When she thought some adjective or a punctuation mark could do with a change, or maybe some sentence's phrasing was too convoluted or bore only a distant resemblance to respectable French, she always set the page in question aside and asked me about it—just like Mme Canavaggio did with Destouches, she reminded me—whereupon I picked up a pencil and redid a word there or an adjective here or an overly audacious neologism over yonder, threw away a repetition or a pair of homophones strung too close together, or reconstructed a sentence completely. Occasionally—but always with my permission—Céline would correct certain points herself, insignificant little things, punctuation stuff, paragraph breaks, spaces between scenes, junk like that, maybe a sentence that had come out a little wordy or obscure and flaunted its irritating penchant for refusing to be French.

Once my little surprise visit was over, I went back to my vesperal or nocturnal promenade, strolling aimlessly around the old post house, crossing through the orchard, sometimes pulling a plum or a handful of cherries from a low branch, heading on to the Vézère, where the cool air was like a damp cloth against my face.

One time when I came sneaking into her bedroom like that, I realized I'd caught her off guard. She must not have been expecting to see me, because at dinner I'd told her I was tired, and was planning to knock myself out for the night with a sleeping pill. But I was feeling a little more chipper by the time I got up from the table, so the gelcap had stayed in its bottle. She jumped halfway out of her chair when I came in, making a funny movement with her shoulders, like an uncontrollable shudder. The sheet in the typewriter was almost completely covered with words—she must have been on the last or next-to-last line—but all of a sudden she ripped it out of the roller, crumpled it, and tossed it into the wastebasket. Then she slipped a blank page into the Underwood, leapt up, and rushed over to close the window, roughly—even violently—shoving me aside on the way. I'd never seen her looking so pissed. She whirled around and hurried back to her table, her shoulder and hip slamming into a full bookshelf halfway there. The shelf toppled forward and dozens of books went flying, all over the floor, the table, and the papers. She spat out a resounding "shit!" and asked me to leave.

"Don't go getting underfoot like that!" she shrieked. "If I'm not going fast enough, at least have the decency to come out and say it!"

For ten seconds I nearly didn't recognize her, her face all clenched up, almost ugly—and that overblown makeup of hers certainly wasn't helping any. She started clearing away the books that had tumbled onto the table.

"What's the matter, Céline? I'm not trying to spy on you . . . I was just stopping by to say hello, that's all. You know, a friendly good day. Or good evening, rather."

"You ought to be working on your book! We're wasting a lot of time . . ."

"But *Dancing the Brown Java*'s almost done now, Céline . . . Just a few more weeks, I think . . . I gave you pages 545 to 560 the day before yesterday, right?"

"You get on my nerves, looking so lost all the time! Try just a little to be an adult, will you? You're a writer, Jean-Rémi. Sometimes I feel like I'm talking to the village idiot."

"Gee, thanks . . ."

She was waiting for me to clear out of there, that much was obvious. She still had the books in her hands, but she didn't make a move. Always wary by nature—it had become almost pathological with me—I looked around the room. It was sort of dim in there, just the one lamp shining, and even that one was aimed mostly at the paper-strewn table. I wondered if somebody might be hiding in the closet or something.

"What are you looking for?"

"Nothing . . ."

I couldn't very well peek under the bed, could I? This might have been the start of a dark comedy, but not a play by Feydeau or Labiche. All I did was open a big cabinet. There, behind the clothes on their hangers, I saw reams of blank paper, enough for all the volumes to come, because Céline had insisted I write a sequel, and even several, so great was the success she foresaw for *Brown Java*. *Dancing the Brown Java* was the title, by the way, discovered at last. I liked it well enough. It was Céline's idea, and I got the feeling it'd be best if I agreed to it without a fuss.

"Volume one will be done soon, Céline. So why get so upset?"

"Don't you go thinking it's vacation time just because the book's almost done. You're going to launch right into volume two. That was our agreement, right?"

"Of course," I mumbled, every inch the pushover, exhausted in advance and half ready to give up for good, because it was getting harder and harder to believe in the success Céline claimed she could already taste.

She went on clearing the books off her table. "Put that thing back where it belongs, that'll give you something to do."

I stood the shelf up on its feet and left the room, telling myself she could be a real cow sometimes. Was that how it was between Anatole France and Madame de Caillavet? I even went so far as to remember that he'd ended up tossing his muse into the street—she'd withered away and died because of it, in fact—to take another mistress, who he married just prior to kicking the bucket.

With the first snows of January—this would have been in 1995—I let out a great sigh of relief. The words "End of Volume One" were finally about to be placed below the last line of the manuscript. Volume one of *Dancing the Brown Java* was going to be done at last. Begun in August 1990, the novel would in all likelihood be finished sometime in March or April. Fifty-four months of work, thirteen as a drifter, a homeless person, a demi-tramp, forty-one or forty-two at Céline's, snug and cozy. An epic!

Thinking I'd stop at the end of the summer, I'd then decided that volume one would include a long episode I'd been saving for the sequel, the first scene with Galette, an important figure in Pétain's Service d'Ordre Légionnaire, and Le Mammouth, an old friend of Lafont, where we see two former typesetters from *Je Suis Partout* planning to kidnap the collaborationist Laubruche and burn the soles of his feet, this latter having been responsible for their eviction from the newspaper after they'd imprudently praised De Gaulle and condemned as Judases everyone who wore the Francisque medal awarded by Pétain for services rendered. That cost me another four months of work. But now it really was done. Nothing left but some last little niggles, tiny changes, an occasional transition to clean up, which would take me into the Easter festivities. In four and a half months I'd laid down nearly six hundred pages, not counting the ones I'd had to redo because there were too many cross-outs and additions to be readable. The first drafts ended up on the fire, as always. Maybe forty more pages and I'd have volume one in definitive form. Céline had already typed a little more than five hundred pages; she too was finally going to get a breather after her arduous, almost mind-numbing labors.

I went on putting those precious "fair copy" pages into the thick red cardboard folder as she handed them over. Wary as a cat, I kept my manuscript under lock and key. I'd decided to make only one photocopy, just before I got in touch with a publisher. I'd need that, because the contracts always say that the author's supposed to keep a second copy in his possession.

The manuscript—not yet finished, but getting close—lay in a suitcase I'd bought in Térignac, under some personal belongings, pairs of underwear . . . A suitcase locked twenty-four hours a day, whose key never left my person. I had good reason to be careful, because we got some odd types staying at La Halte. The sort who don't exactly inspire confidence. But I was probably imagining things.

In any case, the first person to hold the whole manuscript in his hands—I made dead sure of this—would be the publisher.

16   The Trip to Paris

The more Céline assured me I was about to hit the jackpot—"Don't let me down, don't be a dumbshit!" she exhorted me, foul-mouthed as always, but good-humored about it—the more my anxieties grew. It couldn't be true . . . An exceptional novel—this thing of mine? The quasi-pathological hobbyhorse of a sad loser who didn't know fuck about anything else . . . that's what it was. Line up words on a page so you don't die of boredom. That was the explanation. Delirious scriptomania.

"The more I type your whatsis, the more I'm convinced you've really got something here. I'm telling you, Jean-Rémi. Don't make that face when people say you're one of the greats. Don't worry . . . there are plenty of hacks out there, plenty of specialists in the been-there and the done-that who never hesitate for a second to bask in the limelight . . . especially when their connections get them invited on TV. Whereas you, you're actually someone, literature-wise, and you'd rather stick to the shadows? Rather crawl back under your rock? Wake up, old man! Snap out of it!"

And then, one morning, it got hold of me. I decided to go for it. Dive in. What the hell? We'd see how it went. Fuck it. Since, apparently, what I wrote had some value . . .

Downing my morning café au lait in the kitchen, my eye landed on a special feature in the *Figaro Littéraire*. An interview with Galice on the occasion of his eighty-fifth birthday. Everybody knows who Galice is, even people who don't read, the TV-movie watchers and the rest. Our greatest living writer. There's nothing more to say about Galice. A monument unto himself. No Goncourt Academy for him, no Académie Française. Nothing. Just his books. Nothing but his books.

All the greats were gone, but our Galice was still standing, proud and strong, his mind clear, still writing, almost a young man with his round, pink, barely wrinkled face and his mane of white hair. Homosexual. Not that I cared about that. I wasn't planning to come on to him.

"Do I dare?" I asked myself. Another voice inside me shot back, "Dare, you pussy! What have you got to lose?"

When Marcel Proust was starting out with *Pleasures and Days*, he sought out the opinion of Anatole France, the Galice of his time, back at the end of the last century . . .

"It's settled, I'm going to give it a try," I told myself. "Time to find out. They say Galice is very approachable, kindness itself, deeply human, and there's no counting the prefaces he's agreed to write for very young novelists. A great guy. A great mind. I'm going to lay *Dancing the Brown Java* on him, and we'll just see what comes of it."

I was determined not to breathe a word of this to Céline. I was sure she would have warned me off. "What, my opinion isn't good enough for you?" she would have shot back, probably furious. I didn't want to piss her off. Maybe even hurt her.

I'd been given to understand that lots of young novelists did just what I was doing, submitting their first book to a great writer to humbly and respectfully ask for their blessing. For one thing—maybe I'm being uncharitable—it flatters them. I'd read two or three of Galice's books in paperback, *The Shrew-Mouse* among them, but he's not my favorite writer. A little precious, stylistically, for one thing, but above all an out-and-out moralist. The one I place above all the rest is good old Ferdine. Ferdine the bigmouthed brawler. But if I'd knocked on the door of the semi-bum of Meudon with a manuscript under my arm, he certainly would have swatted me away like a pesky little gnat, without bothering to put on his kid gloves first . . .

So, Galice.

Where was I supposed to find him? How to get in touch with him? I'd heard he lived in a beautiful house with a big garden at the edge of the Forest of Rambouillet. Should I write him a letter? Call him up? I wasn't eager to send my monster through the mail and have it wind up God knows where. I'd have to get my stack of pages straight into Galice's two hands.

"Céline, I need a break. I'm wiped out, literally. Besides, it's almost done . . ."

"I don't understand what you're telling me. You need to break what? Wind?"

Amazing, she was cracking jokes. I'd noticed the titanic task of typing my book had, well . . . not really addled her brain, no, but certainly stamped a permanent expression of deep weariness on her mug. She'd also been biting her tongue a lot when she ate. The work was getting to her. She was within sight of her seventy-seventh birthday cake, after all. Still, there was absolutely nothing of the kindly old grandma about her. The *mammy*, like those jerks who try to talk what they think is American would say. Nothing of what people who think age is an insult euphemistically call "the senior citizen" either. She was holding up very nicely, better-looking than a lot of young women, as a matter of fact. No sign of anything going to seed in her figure. A certain grace about her, even. And most of all, positively bursting with energy. Still, seventy-six isn't thirty-five. And think of all the backbreaking work my book had put her through! Thousands and thousands of words all crammed together, every line practically touching the ones above and below. Next to my writing, a Tokyo subway car at rush hour would have seemed like the wide-open spaces . . .

"You know, just a break . . . So can I . . . uh . . . ?"

"So can you what?"

Where were we at that moment, come to think of it? Doesn't matter. Standing face to face. Very important, for a proper dialogue. There's always the telephone, of course, whether portable or sitting on the nightstand, just above the chamberpot, wherever, but . . . No. Face to face. Your services are not required, France Télécom. Let's put us in the kitchen. I've just slurped down my café au lait and she's standing in front of me, supervising Odette and Camille as they peel the turnips and carrots—or pare, not peel, in the case of the turnips, I guess—for the noontime lamb stew, the hunk of meat sitting on the table, wrapped up in special butcher's paper.

"What do you want to do?" she asks again.

"Oh, nothing much . . . You know, a little trip . . ."

A six-year-old kid asking the headmaster of his boarding school for permission to take the train all alone and go see his parents for two days, that was pretty much my position.

"A trip? Well, what's the big deal? I've seen you go off on plenty of little jaunts."

"Oh no, not around here. A trip. A real trip."

"A real trip? Well, now . . ."

"That's right. A chance to relax, a change of scenery. The air around here's plenty fresh, but . . ."

"What's going on in that little brain of yours?"

She was eyeing me closely, probably searching for the crack, the weak spot. Something wasn't right, she could tell. She'd glanced at the *Fig'Litt'* lying open on the table, with Galice's picture in it, but she didn't pay it much mind.

"You want to go on a trip? To Egypt? Greece? Thailand? With all those tour-group rubes who can't survive without a guide, all lined up like pathologically gregarious lemmings?"

"Oh no, nothing like that. No, maybe a vacation in the Bois de Boulogne. It's true, the Bois de Boulogne, that's somewhere nobody goes anymore."

"Be patient. You'll see the big tourist buses there soon enough . . . They're even talking about organized tours of the forests nowadays. With guides to explain it all. It's going to drive the trees barking mad."

"You see, Céline, the thing is . . . I guess it never occurred to you I might be wondering how my parents are doing?"

"You have parents?"

"Of course."

"Strange, you seem more like the orphan type to me."

"My mother and father. In the Mayenne. Almost five years since I last saw them. No letters, nothing. You don't think I'd like to catch up with them a little bit? So I was thinking, with the book practically done . . ."

"Go ahead . . . Take off. It's only natural. Besides, you're a free man, pal. I've never tried to tie you down."

"That's a great relief. Thanks."

"You're all grown up."

"I'll be gone . . . what? three days? Or maybe closer to a week . . . The book's not going to die of loneliness."

"What page are you up to now?"

"Six hundred and ten. On my draft, I mean. Up to where Mayol de Loupé comes to bless the Militiamen in the old château on the banks of the Loir. The fair copy's hit six hundred and forty."

"You'll be taking it with you, I bet?"

I noticed her anxious air.

"Well, I . . ."

"What are you going to do with it?"

"Uh . . . well, you know, look it over. Read a little bit here and there . . . You can't do too much rereading. In the TGV, for instance, what else do you expect me to do?"

"What do you mean, the TGV? To go see your parents in the Mayenne you take the TGV? Why not the Trans-Siberian Express?"

Shit! I'd given myself away.

"Oh . . . I mean the train. The regular train. Um . . . unless I change trains in Paris."

"That's right. You could even make a little detour to Dunkirk. Why not? In any case, don't you go losing that manuscript! I hope you're not thinking I'd start the whole thing over from scratch, if I had to? Head in the clouds, as always! Why didn't you have it photocopied?"

"Let's wait till it's really done. Don't worry, I'll deal with that. I'll do it once I've made up my mind."

"Made up your mind about what?"

"Will this be enough, Madame Céline?" asked the girl, half lifting a big porcelain dish full of peeled carrots. (Odette had wandered off toward the toilets.)

"Five or six more, Camille. Looks like we're going to be two more for lunch. A Hungarian giant, almost eight feet tall, and his one-legged girlfriend. Retired circus artists—now they spend their days traveling around in a 4 by 4. Turned away at the Hôtel de la Liberté in Argentat, the Progrès in Aurillac, and the Bouche d'Or as well. The maid from the Bouche just called me."

Abandoning the subject of the carrots, she turned back to me:

"Made up your mind about what, big boy?"

"Well, you know, the whole deal . . . the publisher . . ."

"Charpentier or Gallim's, I told you. Or Furne."

"Oh please, don't start that up again. You're turning into a broken record."

"I promise they won't bite you at Gallim's. Why are you so scared of them?"

"No . . . They're too big. I'd end up looking like a fool . . . Proust . . . Céline . . . Aragon . . . and then all of a sudden, splat! who's this? Dochin. No, no!"

"You shouldn't get so worked up about this. They're used to these things, you know. They must get three hundred shitty manuscripts a month. They'll write up a little rejection letter, very polite, and that'll be that. It won't kill you."

"No, I have to think about this. Hey, that's what I'll do while I'm gone. I'll choose a publisher. A good one. One I can go to without looking like an idiot, I mean."

"Listen to him! This from the guy who wrote *Dancing the Brown Java*! It's enough to make you think the poor bastard's losing his wits!"

Galice could tell me if my book was worth anything . . . It wasn't quite finished yet . . . but . . . What was left to write? Twenty pages at most. If necessary, I'd tell Galice what happens after the scene with Mayol de Loupé and the Militiamen. Surely he'd understand: I just couldn't stand to put off hearing his opinion, even without the last twenty-five or thirty pages. Which I might just write in the TGV, come to think of it. Why not? We'd see. Should inspiration strike, of course . . . But whenever it comes, you've got to take advantage of it. Even in the middle of the night. And who cares where you happen to be at the moment. Grab it, whenever it comes along. That's what a real writer does. Yes indeed.

Above all, see Galice. And if I had time, I'd hurry down to the Mayenne to hug my parents, who'd so vehemently deplored the bumification of their adult son! But no point holding a grudge. Anyway, we'd see about the family reunion when the time came. First of all, the manuscript. Galice.

Naturally, no Galice in the phone book. That was when I remembered Urbain Langillier, a journalist, very decent guy, a real mensch. I'd met him back when I was moldering away in a homeless shelter run by the Sisters of Charity near the Place d'Italie. He was writing a big newspaper story on the plight of the homeless, and he'd come by to ask questions. We hit it off right away, he even took me to lunch in a little restaurant, nothing snooty, the kind of place where you can eat with your elbows on the table. As I remembered, Langillier had been in the book game for a while. I got the feeling he knew lots of people in the business. He'd put out some remarkable poems around 1960, and then he signed on as literary advisor for a big publishing house. I can't remember which one, Furne or De Broise, I think, but it doesn't matter. Ten years at that job! Obviously, he'd read a buttload of manuscripts. He was an expert, no doubt about it. I think he'd also translated some American writers. Surely he'd know Galice's number. I still had Langillier's address in my tattered little notebook, I'd never thrown it away, still packed with names . . . names of charities, mostly . . .

"Langillier, Urbain . . . it's a Paris number . . ."

I got him right away.

This was all done on the sly, of course, because I didn't want Cé-line catching on. Fortunately she was up in her room, typing.

Langillier lived near the Sainte-Anne Hospital. I tried to help him summon me up from his memory.

"Jean-Rémi Dochin! Well, what do you know? Of course I remember you, my friend. What have you been up to? Still tramping all over creation looking for work? No? Things going a bit more smoothly these days?"

I told him flat out that I'd written a book, a big fat book, and . . .

"Get Galice to read it? Why, of course . . . Why not? But you know, he's a very busy man. Yes, of course I have his number . . . But . . . it's a crime novel, this book of yours?"

"Oh, no, not at all!"

Those last words came out in a horrified yelp. No, I'd moved up the ladder a few rungs, joined the high-class crowd. Steeped in literature as she was, Céline would never have sung my praises for a crime novel.

"You were writing one back then, I think . . . Or maybe you'd published one . . . I don't quite recall . . . You told me a little about it . . ."

"Yes, I remember . . ."

"So? How did it work out? Did it sell?"

"Oh . . . that doesn't really matter . . . No, I'm calling about this book, my other book, the one I've just finished. A serious book . . . the kind they publish with plain covers, if you like . . ."

"All right then, but if Galice finds out you've published a crime novel . . . He absolutely loathes them . . . Our friend Galice is no Gide, no Giono, no Cocteau. He doesn't like that kind of book one little bit, says he's incapable of reading them. In fact, you'll have to come clean and tell him you've written one, because if you try to keep it a secret and he finds out some other way, he might hold it against you, and that could spell disaster for your manuscript. You know, Galice is sure to ask what else you've done . . . if you've ever published before . . ."

"Okay, I get it. Never mind. So much for Galice. Too bad. But really, there's no shame in having published a crime novel. Why couldn't he just judge my work from whatever I give him?"

"Of course . . . But you know, they can get a bit persnickety at that age . . . Listen, I've just thought of something . . . If you don't mind . . ."

Long story short, Langillier kindly offered to read the thing himself.

"I'll give you my frank opinion, my friend . . . You can be sure of that . . . If I think it's . . . uh . . . not particularly good, well then . . ."

I accepted right off the bat. After all, Langillier's opinion was just as good as Galice's. And no worries about having my ideas stolen. Langillier was a real stand-up guy, perfectly honest, every bit the equal of Galice in the morals department.

"Where are you now, Dochin?"

"In the Limousin."

"But you do come up to Paris sometimes? You were hoping to meet with Galice . . ."

"As a matter of fact yes . . . I can drop off the manuscript . . ."

"Come by my place. Just give me a quick call beforehand. It'll be real pleasure to see you again. Listen, I've got to get going, Dochin. I'm in a bit of a hurry, they're expecting me at the *Info-Matin* offices. See you soon, my friend. Have a good day."

Well, that was just ducky. Suited me fine. I liked Langillier, I had very fond memories of him. Publishing was no mystery to that guy.

His opinion would mean a lot. And there was no reason why it shouldn't match up with Céline's. First Ferdinaud, then Langillier . . . Two thumbs up. That would give my morale a nice shot in the arm, because I was still thinking *Brown Java* wasn't worth a cup of cold soup. Sure, I would have liked to know what Galice thought, but . . . Oh, well. I wasn't going to let it get to me. Galice didn't care for the kind of things crime novelists write about . . . Oh God, let's hope that almost-forgotten thriller doesn't end up queering the deal! What, was I going to have to drag that old thing around for the rest of my life, like a crutch? I'd signed it Jean Rem. Still, if *Brown Java* did end up getting published, I'd have a hard time hiding my crime-novelist past—a black eye, a big blop of shit on my escutcheon in the eyes of certain highfalutin know-it-alls: the literary yellow star. I'd deal with that when the time came.

I got the ancient Citroën sedan out of the garage. It's falling to pieces, but it still runs. Félibut uses it for carting around wine barrels and for mushroom hunting and walnut picking and collecting dead branches. Sometimes I took it to run errands in Tulle or Uzerche, and occasionally for a quick little spin around the area to air out my brain, out to the Plateau de Millevaches or the Lac de Vassivière or the Château de Ventadour. I got on the road to Limoges, and I left the old jalopy in the train-station parking lot.

Needless to say, I didn't write a blessed line on the TGV. I hardly even glanced through *Brown Java*, my stomach churning all the while. I was too anxious to think, too tense, so I just sat there with my fat manuscript in my lap.

The train stopped at the Gare d'Austerlitz, and I looked around for a hotel. Thoughtful as ever, Céline had slipped me some cash. "Be careful crossing the streets when you're changing stations in

Paris, you've forgotten what it's like in the big city," she'd warned me. "And watch out who you talk to in the subway."

I took the métro to Denfert-Rochereau. Langillier was just on his way out. Places to go, things to do. Tall guy, about sixty-five, relaxed, affable, sporty, kind of like the journalist Jean Lacouture.

"Do forgive me, I'm in such a hurry . . . I've got to be going . . ."

He took the time to open the folder and read my title:

"*Dancing the Brown Java* . . . Hey, what about you? You didn't put your name on it!"

It's true, all it said on the first page was *Dancing the Brown Java*, in black magic marker. No author's name, because I hadn't quite made up my mind about that. Should I call myself Jean-Rémi Dochin, or Jean Rem like for my crime novel, or should I come up with some other alias? At one point, back at La Halte, I'd thought of calling myself Jean-Rémi Céline, in honor of my protectress, but I shrugged that one off right away. It was a ridiculous idea, not to mention all the morons who'd think I was trying to pass myself off as a descendent of the recluse of Meudon, there's just no limit to some people's stupidity.

Langillier tossed the pile of pages onto his desk. "You've written your address on it, at least? You never know . . . Suppose I had to get in touch with you urgently . . ."

"I put down my phone number . . . Dial 16 first. It's in the Corrèze."

He gave me a little nudge from behind and we hurried toward the door.

"I've got to stop by *Paris-Match* as well . . . before noon . . ."

Now we were barreling down the staircase of his swanky apartment building on the Avenue René Coty.

"Can I drop you off somewhere?"

His Mitsubishi Space Wagon was waiting out front, a parking ticket under the wiper.

"No, I . . . I'd rather walk around a little . . ."

I must have seemed like a real moron, the classic hick visiting the big city. Still, his laugh was good-hearted. He stood by his car for a moment, flashed a big toothy grin, and clapped me on the shoulder.

"I can't believe it's you! What a pleasure to see you again. Looking so healthy, so rosy-cheeked . . . so decently dressed . . . What a change! You remember the state you were in back on the Rue Croulebarbe? Out on the street, weren't you? You hated everyone . . . Even the kids . . . Even the little dogs trotting by . . ."

"I'm doing my best to forget all that."

"Seeing you again like this . . . with that enormous manuscript . . . Bravo to you, that's all I can say!"

He hopped into his car:

"Call me in ten days or so! I'm hoping to read it right away. And I hope we'll find a moment for lunch and a peaceful little chat, too. See you soon, friend."

The car sped away. A moment later it was probably passing by the Lion of Belfort. Suddenly I felt all alone, and a sort of shiver ran through me. Which proves just how warm the journalist's friendly welcome had been.

17   A Boneheaded Blunder

I decided to spend a couple more days in Paris before heading back to La Halte. I was sure Langillier would give the manuscript a serious reading. His opinion would mean something. But impatience was eating me up inside, and I paced back and forth in my room like a bear in a cage. Now and then, to get some fresh air and keep from losing my mind, I went out for a stroll on the boulevard.

I walked up to the Place d'Italie. Or maybe the other way. Across the Seine, the Avenue Ledru-Rollin, the Saint-Antoine neighborhood with its furniture stores, the Place de la Bastille. It had been years since I last strolled the streets of Paris in normal clothes, in the kind of respectable getup that doesn't earn you disapproving stares from everyone you meet. I'd dressed up for my little solo journey, courtesy of the duds Céline bought me at L'Homme Élégant, the big men's shop in Brive. First time in a good while I'd been a Parisian without all the telltale signs of bumdom. But I couldn't figure out what to do with myself. I was kind of bored. I treated myself to a movie, where I dozed for a while. I dined in a not overly hygienic little restaurant near the Saint-Paul métro stop. I wasn't going to go find a hooker. Like a lot of people, I'm scared of AIDS, and using a condom seems to me a bit like putting on boxing gloves to play a Chopin nocturne—and besides, there's a lot we don't know about that disease, those rubber dealies only lower the risk, they don't get rid of it completely. Anyway, I wasn't really in the mood for love. I realized that Paris bored me to tears. It just wasn't the same anymore. Almost everyone in the street had a scowl on their face. I missed the Limousin, and I hoped the provinces would stay just like they are, friendly and beautiful. Most of all, of course, I just couldn't get that goddamn manuscript out of my mind . . .

On the third day, all the waiting around became unbearable. I couldn't take it anymore, I had to get out of there. I was going to lose my mind if I spent one more day in Paris, dicking around and biting my nails.

I had enough cash left for a little excursion. I got the Angers train at the Gare du Maine, then a bus to Rechangé, where my parents lived. They were doing fine. My father, who now had a big red nose—Bourgueil can be a merciless red paintbrush, if you overdo it—had sold off his little housewares shop a year before. My mother seemed sort of tired, she had some kind of kidney problem. The Dochins hadn't changed: still highly regarded in the area, still that same "French heartland" air about them . . . the su-permarket . . . the TV . . . caught up in the mug's game of the eight o'clock news, believing everything they were told . . . all that crap . . . game shows . . . *Missing Persons* . . . (I guess they'd never bothered to set the TV bloodhounds on my trail!) . . . Good people . . . They made a more or less acceptable couple. Certainly not the type to be sent packing when they asked for a room in a hotel. Within the norms. They were overjoyed to hear I wasn't homeless anymore, no longer the shame of the village. ("Can you imagine, the Dochin boy sleeps on the subway gratings in Paris, with a bunch of guitar-strumming hoodlums . . .")

"What are you doing with yourself these days? Keeping busy? I know hard work's sort of gone out of fashion lately, but still . . ."

"I . . . I'm writing . . . I'm trying . . . hoping I might find work in the publishing business . . ." (Right.)

My father furrowed his little red eyebrows:

"That's no trade for a man . . . What, are you hoping to get on that guy's TV show or something? You know, what's-his-name, the guy with the eyebrows?"

It wasn't long before they started getting seriously on my nerves. I didn't stick around long. No trace of the family spirit in me. Once lunch was over with, I gave them a hug all the same and said, "So long, take care of yourselves." Maybe they'd see me on TV, if the book ever got published and sold well enough. Quite a shock for the village!

I called Céline from the Angers station:

"I'm on my way. I'll be back sometime this evening."

On the train, I got to thinking about that goddamn manuscript again. We were speeding through a little station just past Poitiers when I suddenly jumped in my seat, like I'd got a big electric shock, and the mint I was about to put in my mouth flew out of my fingers. I'd just had a thought that hit me right in the gut. A dumbass little detail. A screw-up like only a really top-of-the-line idiot ever manages. What you might call a boneheaded blunder, even. Very simply, I'd forgotten to warn Langillier that the manuscript wasn't finished. The end was missing, hadn't even been written yet, plus the few pages before it, which Céline still hadn't typed up when I left. It broke off at page 642. What a moron! What would Langillier think, assuming he read it all the way through? He was so helpful, so honest, so intelligent and fastidious . . . Seeing the story come screeching to a sudden, completely senseless halt, like a movie cut short by a power failure, wouldn't he assume—oh, what a hamwit I was!—wouldn't he assume he'd somehow misplaced the missing pages, and waste his time searching for them God knows where, just to be sure, under his desk, in the wastebasket, under his bed, maybe in the bathroom if he'd taken it in there to read while he was washing his feet?

The moment I got to Limoges I called Langiller to confess my mistake. But all I got was the answering machine. Langillier was away for a few days, on assignment in Phnom Penh. Maybe he'd stuffed *Brown Java* into one of his suitcases? Trundling my manuscript into the depths of Asia . . . Unstable regions . . . Careful now, that's precious cargo you're carrying, wouldn't want to go losing it . . . The typescript still hadn't been photocopied, and I could hardly see Céline going back to the original and killing herself redoing the damn thing.

She came running the moment I reached La Halte:

"How're your parents doing?"

"Just fine. A little older, not quite what they were, but everything's going okay."

"Great. So now you can get back to work."

"Of course, Céline . . ."

"First you're going to finish volume one, and then that little volume two is waiting patiently. I kept it company while you were away."

I went right off and plunked my ass down at my desk. The inkwells were all open, black ink for writing, violet for added words, red for changes in the margins, everything was in order.

She started putting my things away—my suitcase, my briefcase, my three shirts—poking through them a little as she did, of course, the way women do.

"What did you do with your manuscript?"

From her tone, you would have thought I'd come back with one arm. And this despite the complete absence of terrorist attacks during my stay in the great city of Paris.

I stood there like an idiot with my mouth hanging open, gnawing on one thumb.

"You didn't leave it with a publisher, did you?"

She was giving me a good cold stare.

"A child, that's what you are! What—did you forget your novel isn't quite done yet?"

"I . . . Well, the thing is . . . I have to go back to Rechangé . . . My father wanted to read it . . ."

Here she turned openly suspicious:

"Oh, so he's a big reader, is he? What does he do, anyway? You've never told me about your parents."

I nodded toward the desk, where a stack of white sheets lay awaiting the caress of my pen.

"You really think we have time to . . ."

"What does your daddy do for a living?"

"He's retired. My parents ran a little shop."

"Not a bookstore, I don't suppose?"

She let out a little snicker, just this side of insulting, with a teasing look in her eye, like she'd cracked a good joke.

"And what makes you think my parents wouldn't have been capable of running a bookstore?" I asked, offended.

"All right, kid, don't get mad. I didn't mean any harm. What did they sell?"

"Notions and sundries, cleaning supplies, beauty aids."

"Well, that's perfect. I might almost say they've put the blush back on my cheek."

"Say, why *do* you wear all that makeup, anyway? You really plaster it on, you know that?"

"It's my greasepaint. I want to look like a clown, just like you. They always come in pairs, you know: Pierrot and Auguste."

"Enough already. Give me some time to myself, okay? . . . I've got to think about my ending . . . And it's looking a little tricky."

"In any case, you're not going to leave the manuscript at your parents'. You could have told your father to wait till it's done, and . . ."

Here I started to yell:

"Listen, quit watching over the manuscript like it was your first-born, will you? Jesus! It's *my* novel, isn't it?"

"And who typed it, you wicked child? Don't be an idiot, Jean-Rémi. I repeat: this close to the end, losing the thing would be the fuck-up of the century—where literature's concerned, anyway. Next to that, Gallim's turning down *Journey* would be as trivial as an unbuttoned fly."

I calmed down. She was wearing me out:

"I'll be going back to the Mayenne in a few days . . . I won't stick around long . . . A week . . . Two at most . . . One of my cousins is going to be visiting. She lives in Canada, and my mother wouldn't take it well if I didn't stop by . . . Twelve years since we last saw her . . . And then, as for my father, don't you think it might be interesting to know what an ordinary reader thinks of the thing? Don't worry, you'll see your precious typescript again."

"I hope he's not going to go dragging it all over creation and leave it lying around who knows where! Can you see me going back to that thing and starting again? Over six hundred pages!"

"Don't worry, Céline. My father's very careful. And it won't leave the house. It'll be just like I still had it around my wrist, like a watch."

"It's for your sake, Jean-Rémi. Nothing to do with me . . ."

All very well and good, but Langillier still had a book with no ending on his hands. "I hope that's not going to shock him too much," I said to myself. Then, to get her the hell out of my room—there were times when I just couldn't bear to be around her—I put a white sheet down in front of me and picked up a pen. Black ink. Once more into the breach.

"Still, let me know what your father thinks of *Brown Java*," she said as she left the failure's—I'm sorry, I mean the genius's—study.

18 Chiboust-Lormeuil

Returning with his wife from a symposium in Gijón, Spain, in mid-March, 1995, Emmanuel Chiboust-Lormeuil, professor at the Collège de France, appeared for the second time at the front desk of the Hôtel Mon Repos-Palace in Eymoutiers, only to find himself politely shown the door. Having first come to the desk alone—his wife still in the car—he had been assigned room 31, two beds, private bath, view of the Vienne River. But now his wife stood at his side.

"It's so stupid of me, and I couldn't be sorrier, but I've just realized number 31 isn't free after all," the innkeeper told him, his nose buried in the register. "In fact, I see we're completely full," he added, eyeing Madame Chiboust-Lormeuil, a woman of some sixty years, her figure deformed by an enormous stomach, an abnormally voluminous derrière, and above all those two horrifically swollen legs, those ankles puffed up like wineskins, swathed in grayish stockings not unlike the leggings our brave boys wore in World War I. A victim of Hodgkin's disease, the poor woman dragged herself along with great difficulty, leaning on a cane, her entire body bloated with serous fluid, a walking martyr. She'd insisted on traveling to the symposium alongside her husband, whom she greatly admired.

"Spring came early this year," the hotel man explained. "We're getting lots of business. I'm so sorry. Only 7:30 in the evening, and already the dining room's full, as you see."

The Chiboust-Lormeuils returned to their car and tried again at the Coq d'Or, a little further on.

"Madame might perhaps prefer . . . uh . . . to dine in her room?" the woman at the desk purred in honeyed tones.

"Why no, not at all," the intellectual luminary responded. "We'll take our meal in the dining room like everyone else. Why on earth not?" Chiboust inquired, somewhat taken aback.

The owner never took her eyes off the poor woman's monstrous legs, her backside like a great thick eiderdown, her slug-like demeanor, her labored gait, her moribund movements . . .

"We have a great many English and Swedish tourists at the moment . . . a whole busload of Dutch people too . . ."

"And what has that to do with us?" asked Chiboust.

"Well, I've just realized we don't have a single room left. I'm so very sorry, Monsieur, Madame . . ."

The Chiboust-Lormeuils headed back to their car, him supporting his gout-ridden wife, their gait painfully slow. The chambermaid caught up with them on the front step to give them the address of the Halte du Bon Accueil.

Needing some rest, the couple spent three happy days at Ferdinaud's place, delighting in the locale and the friendly reception. Meanwhile, no sign of Dochin. Closeted away in his little house, feverishly covering his pages with ink, he never once saw the new guests. He himself remained invisible, with his novel advancing—slowly and painfully, but advancing all the same. Nearing its end, as a matter of fact, since on the very morning of the Chibousts' arrival he'd attacked page 638 of his manuscript.

Madame Chiboust spent many long hours in an armchair near the basin, reveling in the balmy sunshine of this unusually spring-like March, waited on hand and foot by the motel's three women,

Céline, Odette, and Camille. An inveterate walker, the genius from the Collège de France strolled the grounds of the former post house, along the banks of the Vézère, but also in the orchard and behind the motel, along paths that sliced through the tangled undergrowth, sometimes engaging his amiable hostess in conversation, her face having reminded him of something or other, a vague sense of déjà-vu whose origin he couldn't quite place, and then there was that rather overdone makeup . . . those reds . . . that turquoise . . . those violets . . . A delightful woman, rather cultivated too, her language a bit crude, perhaps, a bit freewheeling, but after all . . .

"My wife has terrible circulation troubles . . . dreadful pain in her legs and feet . . . It's been this way for five years . . . Nothing can be done. Our travels are a real torment for her. It can cause problems in hotels. All eyes turn toward us the moment we come into the dining room, everyone staring at my wife's legs, they don't even look at their plates . . . It's very distressing, you know. Even after we've sat down and my wife's legs are out of sight, the others are always turning our way . . . And it's strange, all those lively conversations underway when we came in . . . they all go quiet . . . We finish our meals as quick as we can—sometimes we even skip the cheese and dessert to get out sooner! And then, once we've left the dining room—which takes a good five minutes, my poor wife shuffling along, clutching my arm—the conversations start up again, as animated as before. As if we'd forbidden them all from talking!"

All the while, Dochin sat in his room writing, scarcely so much as glancing up from his page. Like a homeward-bound horse smelling his stable! He spurred himself on, knowing that the end of volume one was now near at hand. His desk was littered with pages he'd left out to dry. The ink itself congealed quickly enough—apart from the blots, now too numerous to count—but now and then he pasted on a little addendum, and as his glue wasn't exactly of the finest quality, it took some time to set. Running out of room, he'd laid a few pages on the windowsill. One day the weather was fine, and the window stood wide open. Emmanuel Chiboust-Lormeuil came strolling by. Through the tangle of bushes, the intellectual powerhouse couldn't see the writer bent over his desk, his nose against the page, his cervical vertebrae aching. A sudden gust of wind sent one of the sheets flying. It fluttered merrily through the air a few times, then landed at the feet of the great thinker from the Collège de France. This latter, endowed with an intelligence so vast as to make the best minds of Paris seem pitifully stunted, bent down, picked up the page, and ran his eye over the words thereupon, suddenly amused, gently affectionate . . . He chuckled quietly, shrugged, smiled, and carelessly stuffed the sheet into his jacket pocket, then thought better of it, for he'd just spied the open window. Exceptionally lucid creature that he was, he immediately deduced that this was the starting-point of the paper's brief flight. He went and discreetly laid the sheet on the windowsill, but, as befits a man of infinite tact and superior breeding, he refrained from looking into the room. And so he went on his way, without having caught sight of the writer.

Three or four hours later, in the early afternoon, another gust of wind came along, and another page of Dochin's manuscript went flying . . . Once again, the intellectual titan was passing by. Chiboust was fond of this wild spot, with the river so close . . . The paper fell onto a bramble bush. The cerebral heavyweight—of a sort virtually no longer seen, alas, in the vast city that is Paris—picked up the page and perused it as he strolled on, moved and amused in the most benevolent way, indulgently shaking his head. Chiboust turned back to return the sheet to the sill, but now found the window closed. Seeing his page fly away before his impotent eyes, an exasperated Dochin had slammed down the sash, cursing the wind and vowing to venture out later on and liberate it from the barbed-wire-like brambles surrounding the house. Finding the window closed, Chiboust folded the sheet in four and thrust it into his pocket. A little later, returning to the main garden to join his wife, who was still resting in a wicker armchair, he—or rather they—had the pleasure of visiting with Céline, who'd come out for a little chat with her guests. Her endless typing left her with an aching back and sore wrists, and she sometimes stepped outside for a break. Those long hours at the machine were taking their toll. A major undertaking, the typing of this novel, which some days absorbed her from dawn to dusk. At times she even rose from her bed in the middle of the night, when sleep eluded her, to attack the masterly manuscript once again . . .

"So," asked she whose immense physical courage is no longer in doubt, "you'll be leaving us tomorrow morning, Monsieur, Madame? You've had a nice, restful stay, I hope?"

"Wonderfully restful, dear Madame Céline," answered Madame Chiboust. "Such a lovely spot this is! And so much less polluted than our Boulevard Beaumarchais! I do believe we'll be coming back."

"We would have been so happy to meet the young lad, however," said the luminous representative of the French Intellect, his kindly smile shot through with friendly curiosity.

"The lad? What lad?"

"The one who likes to scrawl out these stories," said Chiboust, pulling the folded page from his pocket.

He showed it to the hotelier:

"I found this outside . . . It blew out of a window in back . . . I was walking not far away . . ."

"What's that?" asked Céline, stunned and quivering, one hesitant hand reaching out for the paper.

"At least I assume it was a child, trying his hand at writing," replied that high priest of Knowledge, still smiling with gentle amusement. "Doesn't he ever come out to play? I guess he'd rather stay in his room and scribble away? Such touching naïveté in these words, such a sweet gaucherie . . . How old is he? Oh, kids! When I was his age, I copied out Perrault's fairy tales, and so badly! *Puss-in-Boots*, *Cinderella*, that sort of thing . . . La Fontaine's fables too . . . I left out half the nouns, and it was even messier than what this boy has scratched out. But in his case, one has the impression he's making it all up . . . and such whimsical silliness in that cute little head! . . . I'm very fond of children's drawings, as well . . . Incidentally, I keep calling him the lad, but perhaps it's a little girl?"

Pale, speechless, her jaw trembling a little, Céline unfolded the sheet and discovered her protegé's fevered handwriting. She held in her hand page 643 of Jean-Rémi's manuscript, recounting Bonny's discussion with one of his informers, a bus conductor, in the back room of a café by the Porte Champerret—a page as yet untyped, overladen with rewrites, an addendum pasted to one side.

"You read this?" she asked the Great Mind, alarmed.

"Oh . . . just five or six words . . . two or three lines," said Chiboust-Lormeuil, a tender smile illuminating his wizened face. "My wife and I love children. Unfortunately, we weren't able to have any of our own . . . It's a boy, I suppose?"

"Who?"

"Why, the author of this page . . . Your grandson, perhaps?"

Speechless, as if a fishbone had lodged in her throat, Céline slipped the folded sheet into a pocket of her dress.

"It's just as good as playing cops and robbers or knocking birds' nests from the trees," said this awesome storehouse of Gallic gray matter, with a burst of warm-hearted laughter. "My wife and I had a great-nephew who . . ."

Céline didn't hear the rest. She turned on her heel and made for the little house, entering silently so as not to disturb the Master. She crept up discreetly behind Dochin, who sat lost in his prose, his tongue sticking out of his mouth, his pen racing over the paper like some monstrous insect afflicted with Saint Vitus's dance, and delicately placed the page next to three or four others drying on the sill. Dochin saw none of this. She bent over her protégé's bony shoulder. Finally realizing she was there, he lifted his head and his pen from the paper.

"Coming along nicely now," he said.

"Keep it up, my treasure . . . Keep it up, my Flaubert," she said softly—a profound gentleness in her voice, as you might speak to someone whose feelings you're anxious to spare. "Who's going to write us a masterpiece?"

Dochin was in a relatively sunny mood. He smiled, and with one voice they shouted out the answer: "Jean-Rémi Dochin!"

She lay a hand on his forehead—a caring, nurturing hand—and gently caressed his nape, massaged his shoulders for a moment . . .

"Keep it up, my boy. And believe me, we're going to beat them all. Beat them into the ground! We'll show them who's who! Yes we will!"

Then she added, her eyes suddenly hard and commanding, as if she had some idea in mind—but not just any idea, the sort of idea one has only two or three times in one's life, the kind that throws a little splash of light onto the long, gray ribbon that is a human existence . . .

"They'll love it. They damn well better. They'll be singing your praises from every rooftop!"

Then she stepped back from the Master's armchair:

"I'll leave you in peace, hen . . . Keep going . . . You'll be wanting dinner soon?"

"I don't think so . . . I don't want my ideas to get away from me."

"Yes, hold on to those ideas, Jean-Rémi. Hold on tight. For all you're worth. Don't let go! I'm sure they're very beautiful, my love."

"How's the typing going?" he asked.

"I never stop, lamb. I've got cramps in my fingers. Don't worry. Besides, there's almost nothing left to type. We'll be all done in May, June at the latest."

She let him go back to his work. Once again the pen scurried over the paper, hurried, unrelenting, almost frenzied.

19   The Thirteenth Day

Twelve days went by. The tension was building up inside me, it was almost more than I could bear. Had Langillier read it? The waiting was killing me. I worked on the book a little, wrote a few pages, but it was a real struggle. It just wasn't coming at all lately, or it was coming out all wrong. Sick of the whole thing, I came close to ripping up everything I'd done.

Still plugging away, weary as an old workhorse yoked to a creaky, rundown cart, collapsing under the weight of its load, Céline hurried to type up the last pages. She'd spent three days with her niece Colette in Bordeaux, and that put her a little behind. "I'm doing the same as you," she'd told me in a spiteful little voice, "I'm going to see my family. It'll relax me—as you put it so eloquently with respect to your own sweet self." She'd come home the day before in her old *deux chevaux*, and Camille helped her unload the usual trunkload of packages: fine candies given to her by her niece, for example, but mostly cans of top-grade foie gras or duck pâté from the Landes, as well as some genuine artisanal cassoulet, because Colette Ferdinaud's boyfriend ran a big duck confit operation in Mont-de-Marsan, with a real high-class clientele, including several embassies.

"I hope you got some good work done," were her first words, before she'd even said hello.

On the thirteenth day I started to wonder. Should I call Langillier? I couldn't keep still.

"What's with you, coming and going and pacing around the basin all the time? You got a perpetual motion machine up your ass? Don't you have writing to do? If not, at least try and make yourself useful. You could always drain the basin and clean out the crud in there. Félibut doesn't seem too eager to tackle that little job."

Langillier must have come home from Cambodia by now. But no way was I going to call him from La Halte. Ever since I got back from Paris, Céline seemed to be watching my every move. She must have sensed something was up, wondering about all those trips to the Anjou, asking herself why I'd left the manuscript 250 miles away.

I had some errands to run in Térignac anyway, so off I went in the old Citroën. And from there I pressed on to Tulle, where nobody knows us.

My plan was to call Langillier from the post office, but I chickened out at the last second. My nerves got the better of me. Blind panic. A really craven kind of terror. My hands were all clammy. Like some pimple-faced teenager waiting to hear if he passed his *baccalauréat*!

So, bottom line: I couldn't bring myself to call him. What a pussy. Tomorrow I'll head for Paris, I told myself. Besides, it'd be better for Langillier to give me his thoughts in person, I mean with me physically present. He'd probably have a whole lot to say, good or bad, we'd see, maybe a little of both. You can't very well do that on the phone, not with a big fat manuscript like mine. This wasn't some short story by Maupassant, after all. All bullshit, of course. Langillier could have given me his thoughts perfectly well on the phone, it just takes a few words, no big production required. But no, like a true dumbass, I felt the need to wrap my cowardice up in a pretty little package of elaborate excuses.

I had to go to Paris. After all, didn't Langillier say he wanted to get together? Have a chat, eat some lunch, make it a real reunion, without the mad dash? Besides, sending the manuscript back in the mail was obviously out of the question.

That evening, digging into my gratinéed cauliflower in white sauce, I told Céline I was planning to go to see my parents again the next day, because my cousin Ginette had just landed in France (my mother had called, as Céline could verify for herself).

"Don't forget to bring back the manuscript. That's what really matters. As for the rest, frankly . . ."

I took the old sedan to Limoges. Then the TGV again . . . eating my heart out with impatience . . . getting the cold sweats . . . I took a room in the same hotel as before, on the Boulevard de l'Hôpital. In any case, Langillier hadn't called. "In case of urgent necessity . . . you never know . . ." he'd told me. Give me a break! If he'd found himself with another *Journey* or *Molloy* on his hands he would have called right away, even in the middle of the night. I thought about all that as I got settled into my room, putting my things away in the armoire. But then again no, even if he was in love with the thing, he had no reason to call me. Langillier was a journalist, not a publisher. Why should he call? He didn't have a contract to offer me. He'd read my work—or so I hoped, at least—and now he was calmly awaiting my call, it was as simple as that.

Returning from Southeast Asia, Urbain Langillier found his apartment neat and tidy, everything well-looked after by his new maid, a recent immigrant from Ethiopia known to him simply as Titi, her real name being more than he could handle. On his desk, beside his blotter—next to Dochin's manuscript, a stack of newspapers, three or four folded road maps, and several notebooks—a square of white paper lay under a stone paperweight. It was a note. Written, he soon realized, by his young servant:

Monsieu La Gilié (having arrived in France only a short while before, she still had some difficulties with the language), *I went too let you no that . . .*

"I want to let you know that . . ." the journalist interpreted. But the note ended there. She must have been interrupted while she was writing, then never thought to come back and finish it. So it can't have been very important. Some phone call, presumably. He'd just have to wait; if it was that urgent they'd surely call back. Or should he call Titi? Langillier shrugged: it's not like the house was on fire, why worry about it? And in any case, it now occurred to him, there was no way to get hold of her anyway, because she'd told him she was going off God knows where—Cairo, who knows?—to spend a few days with her family. He crumpled the paper and threw it into the wastebasket.

Right. He'd got back twenty-four hours earlier than expected, so he had the whole day to himself. No important meetings until tomorrow. So let's have at it. Dochin's manuscript. He rubbed his hands, pulled it toward him . . . opened the folder . . . Page 1. Chapter 1.

On that fine day in . . .

Well, that settles that, he told himself scarcely three-quarters of an hour later, completely put off, a sour feeling in his stomach. I think I can do what I like with myself today, he thought. Most of it, anyway. This'll give me chance to take care of some errands.

It was on reaching page thirty-three that he'd decided there was no point going on. He hesitated for a moment, lit a cigarette, and took three puffs; then, just to be sure, he jumped back in and read three or four more passages at random, most often just skimming them, shaking his head, horrified, aghast. It was absolutely and completely devoid of interest. Worse: it was garbage. And the writing! He heaved a weary sigh, still reading—or rather glancing over—a page here, a half-page there, a quarter of a page a little further on . . .

"Poor boy . . . I don't know what got into him . . . Pouring so much energy into this tripe . . . He must have been laboring over it for months . . ."

Page after page after page . . . All of the same sad ilk.

With the price of paper today, he caught himself thinking, immediately ashamed of himself, because after all he was very fond of this Dochin . . .

Then in a whisper:

"Who the hell is going to accept this?"

Was Dochin's manuscript meant as some sort of practical joke? Paging through it again, he wondered—but rejected the idea almost at once—if the book might be something other than what it seemed. But what? Some sort of put-on? A prank? If it were only ten or fifteen pages long, then yes, maybe . . . But . . . this great raft of paper!

He wrote nothing in the margins, no observations of the sort he used to note down in his days as a literary advisor, but the words came flooding into his mind all the same: Plot impossibly incoherent . . . Vocabulary highly limited, prosaic . . . No notion of how to tell a story . . . No skill at creating lifelike characters . . . Scene transitions clumsy and arbitrary . . . Not to mention the unrelenting, unending riot of aphaereses and apocopes . . . Only the humor—or more precisely, the absurdity—occasionally compensates for the stuntedness and triviality of the plot, but far too feebly to salvage much. Poor guy! I can't even imagine what Galice would have said if this thing had ended up in his hands . . . Poor boy, caught up in this mess! What makes people take it into their heads to write when they've got nothing to offer? . . . But what I find most depressing are the many passages . . . and mind you I've seen only a tiny fraction of the manuscript! . . . the many passages he's lifted from movies . . . almost cribbed word for word . . . *The Last Métro . . . Black Thursday . . . Four Bags Full . . .* films on the Occupation . . . *Jericho* too . . . And look there, virtually a whole scene from Melville's *Army of Shadows*! I don't get it, Dochin's not the dishonest sort . . . He must not have remembered. . . must have thought he was inventing when he was only recalling films he'd seen years before . . . He's touched them up a little, of course, even if he made a hash of it. Nevertheless . . . But maybe he'll realize it, and take all that out. I can't very well bring it up with him. Touchy subject. And then the names of all these collaborationists . . . all these Gestapo members . . . Tons of them. He's changed a letter here and there, but you can still see who he means. He's trying to give us new dirt on the sad leading players of the Occupation, but there's just nothing there, we've heard all this a thousand times before. And so heavy-handed! It's not *noir*, it's not anything. Obviously, since it's set in Paris, with the Krauts, he thought . . . He must have scoured the newspapers of the time . . . What a mess! A complete waste of time.

Having given up on plowing through to the end, Langillier never realized that the last line of the last page read "and the door to the shop, which he." Which he what? Wait and see, we'll find out on the next page, but no—incomplete manuscript. He was about to put it away, bemused, irritated, and downcast, wondering what he could say to Dochin, when the telephone rang. It was exactly eleven o'clock. Too bad, he thought as he picked up the receiver, this could have been his ticket off the streets.

"Hello, this is Urban Langillier. Ah . . . it's you, my dear friend."

He did his best to sound casual. It was Dochin. An ambush. The eager, terrified "So?" that the author immediately blurted out hit him right in the pit of his stomach, like a billiard ball launched from the table by a furious thrust of the cue.

"Yes, I've read it, I've read it. I . . . Listen. If I tell you I'm drowning in work at the moment, you're going to be cross with me. Am I wrong? Yes, yes, I can tell from your voice you're upset. Listen. Yes, yes, I read it, I did. No, I assure you, it's not uninteresting at all. All those things about the Occupation . . . sometimes sort of historical . . . A bit like Dumas . . . Marshal Pétain . . . Abel Bonnard . . . De Brinon . . . all that . . . Really compelling at times, I assure you . . ."

I've become a coward and a bastard, Langillier thought to himself. I'm getting old. Still, some things you just can't say . . . It's impossible, if you know the person a little . . . if you have some regard for him . . . Lousy thing to do to him, though, it's true. Something more than lousy, in fact.

"There are some very funny bits, now and then . . . It's . . ." (He let go, tossed out this remark, only to regret it at once): "The sort of goofy aspect of it, with the two kids . . . That's really the best thing about the book . . . No, no, that's not what I meant . . . The rest holds together nicely, but . . . Not at all . . . No, it's just that . . . I was a little reluctant to tell you this, but there are many passages that might need some revision . . . Might even need to be rewritten entirely . . ." (He forced out a jaunty burst of laughter.) "Oh, no! Let's not get carried away! Not the whole book . . . that's not what I said, my dear Dochin . . . And above all don't take this the wrong way. Listen, I'm absolutely ashamed to shove you aside, but my plane leaves from Roissy at five past twelve. Oh yes, yes, I read it through to the end. The end works rather better, now that you mention it. There's . . . how to put it? A sort of momentum . . . the story moves along a bit quicker, it's livelier . . . Oh yes, it is, yes . . . Listen, Dochin. Here's what we'll do. I'll get your manuscript right back to you, and then I'm sure that like a big boy you'll launch right back into it and fix everything that needs fixing. You're thinking about it, right? That seems like the best idea to me. And don't be afraid to take your time." (I can't very well advise him to dump the whole manuscript . . . I'd seem like a first-rate bastard, I was the one who asked to see the damn thing, I don't know what got into me, I thought maybe the boy had something . . .) "Excuse me. Again, I'm so sorry. Forgive me. We'll have to get together one of these days . . . Yes, I hope so . . . It'll be with my concierge, yes. In a sealed envelope, don't worry. See you soon. Courage, my friend."

Langillier hung up the phone and sat mopping his brow with his handkerchief. The impaler's spike was still in him, thrust deep into his skull. He spent three minutes recuperating. A messy execution, full of missteps. Wasn't it better to come right out with it, no matter how harsh it might seem, if there was an execution to be done? But all that beating around the bush . . . those *maybe yes, maybe no*s . . . kind of like a slow-motion decapitation, the blade starting to fall, then pausing, climbing again, falling again . . . an abominable tease . . .

I'm an asshole, a coward, a bastard, he told himself. But for God's sake, why write such things? Poor boy. There was nothing else to do. Shouldn't you leave people just a glimmer of hope, though? After all, I've been wrong about manuscripts before . . . often, in fact . . . both for and against. But in this case I think it's safe to say . . . the margin of error is as thin as a sheet of cigarette paper.

He evened the disordered manuscript pages into a nice, tidy stack and slipped it into a large padded envelope, on which he wrote in red felt tip: *Monsieur Dochin*. He'd leave the envelope with his concierge. And what if Dochin called again? Well, since he was supposedly on a plane bound for God knows where, might as well turn on the answering machine for the next two or three days. But he won't call, he told himself. Poor boy! Really, I pity people like that. Good God, there's no justice in this world! All that work . . . If only there'd been, I don't know, some little thing to hold onto . . . we could have tried to rescue his book . . . This could have done him such a lot of good, poor guy! When I picture him in those filthy clothes . . . that tattered parka . . . We can't let him fall back into that again. But, for the love of God, what on earth could anyone do with that manuscript? Can't just do a quick rewrite job on an unholy mess like that! Unimaginable. Poor writers . . . all blind, they never see where they're putting their pens . . . And then there are those few very, very lucky ones—the greats, mostly—who've got the finesse and the sense to tell right away if their work is good or unsalvageable, who can say straight out, with no hesitation, "This one goes in the drawer or the trash or to Furne or Gallim's or Charpentier . . ." Fur-gal-char, as they say in the Goncourt season . . .

20 Page 111

I'd called Langillier from the Gare d'Austerlitz. Once the hammer dropped—so I was right all along, *Brown Java* really is shit, Céline must be touched in the head—I trudged back to my hotel, probably white as a sheet. I can't imagine what I must have looked like, though no one I met on the street seemed to be paying attention. This thing had hit me pretty hard. Like a fool, I'd got my hopes up. What a comedown! And yet . . . Yes, and yet—I had to see things as they were—yes, it's true that Langillier hadn't blasted it outright. Maybe it was so good he got jealous? No, that's not his style. That's for losers. First of all, he was a pro. He just didn't like it, and that's all there is to it. That was clear. But after all, in the end it was kind of a mixed review, wasn't it? And besides, there's such a thing as a matter of taste.

In places, he'd told me . . . I can't remember his exact words . . . in places, it wasn't uninteresting at all, something like that . . . Hmm . . . the kind of thing people say when they're handing out consolation prizes. I sensed a real lack of conviction in his voice, it's true. Many passages need reworking . . . But not all of them. So that means some of it's good. He could have told me which parts, at least. But on the fucking phone like that . . . I wish I could have seen him, talked it all over a little. In any case, there are some passages that don't need revising. That's something, at least. But did he really mention Dumas? Dumas! I must not have heard right . . . Oh, but he's been out of the publishing game for years now. Maybe he's lost his knack for judging manuscripts . . . Does this guy even have time to read novels? Always dashing off, hither and yon. Nobody reads on airplanes anymore. They're all watching the movie nowadays. He mentioned the ending, thought it seemed better than the rest . . .

Just then, still stumbling like a sleepwalker down the boulevard, lost in my thoughts, I felt a sort of sudden shock run through me.

Jesus, wait a minute! He was bullshitting me! The ending! But the ending wasn't in the manuscript! Hasn't even been written yet! So he *didn't* read the thing all the way through! Talking through his ass, in short! They're all the same. No balls. Be polite, don't hurt anyone, don't ruffle any feelings. Pantywaists! He could see that *Brown Java* was a piece of shit all right, but he didn't dare say it to my face.

Kindness and tact, yes, very nice . . . but I had to accept it, he wasn't quite as impeccable a mensch as I'd thought, not quite the direct, forthright man I took him to be . . . "There are some amusing bits" . . . Don't make me laugh! And to think I almost gave it to Galice!

And what about Céline? Is she just nuts? Former bookseller! Comic books and *Girl's Weekly*, that's what she sold, I'll lay you even money! What is she, a lunatic? I'm starting to wonder if all these people aren't deliberately taking me for a ride. And there I was like a dumbass picturing myself in the seat of honor on Eyebrows's show! In any case, not a word of all this to old lady Ferdinaud. We'll see if she goes on pretending this is some great work of literature. Jesus, what a joke! Damn it, I didn't write six hundred pages to see them thrown down the toilet!

I stopped by the Avenue René-Coty and picked up my manuscript from the concierge. Back in my hotel room, I paged through it a little. No grease marks, no wine stains, so Langillier hadn't read it at the dinner table, like some people do. I found all my sentences right where I'd left them. How empty they seemed to me now! About as lively as a stiff . . . Nothing . . . Six hundred pages of nothing . . . Journey to the end of inanity. The great writer Dochin, where's his pen? Up his ass, that's where!

With all the conviction of a maimed hedgehog limping down a long, dusty road, I started rereading a passage I thought was pretty good, in the first quarter of what once mistook itself for a novel, a passage where Max and Mimile . . . Hey, it jumps from page 110 to page 112. No page 111. So Langillier must have got that far, at least, and somehow the page got stuck someplace else in the manuscript. I reread page 110, then 112. Not much happened between them. Nothing special. Max and Mimile in the Normandy countryside, where they try to steal some eggs from a henhouse, yes, that was the spot. The farmer catches them, and instead of chewing them out offers them a drink of cider in the farmhouse kitchen, yes, yes. At the bottom of page 110 they're leaving the pigsty to sneak into the henhouse, and at the top of 112 the farmer's wife shows up, sees her husband drinking with the two kids, and gives him a piece of her mind. Oh well, I'd get that page back, no problem. It had to be at Langillier's. Maybe it was drafty in there, who knows, and since the pages weren't bound together . . . But calling Langillier after he'd swatted me down like that . . . Gently, it's true, but that's what had happened, all right. Given the circumstances, the idea didn't appeal to me much, and I didn't want to be a bother. Unless . . . I found the patience—not that I had anything better to do anyway—to go through the manuscript one page at a time, checking the numbers in the upper right-hand corner. No sign of page 111 anywhere. So it was still at Langillier's. Unless he'd taken the manuscript with him to Cambodia . . . I hadn't asked him about that. Page 111 of the masterpiece lost in Cambodia! The scoop of the year! No, it had to be at his place. On his desk, something like that . . . in his bedroom . . . Still, I really didn't feel like calling him back. But didn't he say he had a plane to catch? That gave me a tiny dollop of courage. He almost certainly wouldn't be there. So . . . There was a phone in the hallway. I went out and dialed his number, my buttocks clenched in terror. To my great relief, Langillier wasn't there. An answering machine. Away for four days. Needless to say, I didn't leave a message. I hung up, heaving a cowardly sigh of relief. Fine. The loss of page 111 wouldn't pose an insurmountable problem, since the original was still back at La Halte. I could easily find the passage again. For that matter, I could always rewrite whatever was missing, if need be. Céline would just have to retype it. No big deal.

I packed my bags, paid my bill, and caught the first TGV to Limoges. A crappy day, the kind I wouldn't wish on any novelist, talented or otherwise.

21   Death's Not in the Cards

Before long it was dinnertime, and from the way I was picking at my fricandeau Céline could tell something was wrong. I was still reeling from the blow. I must have seemed thoroughly down in the dumps, I'd spent the whole train ride wallowing in my sorrows.

"What's the matter with you, Jean-Rémi? Aren't you hungry?"

"Oh yes, of course I am . . ."

Odette and Camille were looking at me too. A most unusual stare. They could tell something was up. Women are intuitive, that's not just an old wives' tale, you really can't keep much from them.

"Well then eat, if you're so hungry. We've got stuffed tomatoes next."

"With tarragon," Odette elaborated.

"If you could see the look on your face, my boy! But your father loved *Brown Java*, isn't that what you were telling me?"

"Yes, yes, of course . . ."

She'd collared me the moment I got back:

"So? What did your father think? Liked it?"

I'd set the manuscript down on the table in my bedroom, my "study." She'd given it a quick, automatic little glance, and I'd told her that ridiculous lie about my father liking it, I didn't know what else to do, I was beat, I was crushed. I couldn't even see why I should keep up the pointless labor of finishing the damn thing.

She was almost done typing the last pages.

"I'll give them to you all at the same time," she told me. "I've got to get through the proofreading, after all. The closer you get to the end, the better it looks."

"Stop fucking around with me, Céline."

"What's up with you? I guess travel doesn't do much for your mood, does it?"

Just a few more pages to write and that would be it. And then what was supposed to happen? I was doing all I could not to think about that.

After dinner, Céline took me aside. My face was as long as your arm. Langillier's reservations (how's that for a euphemism!) were still echoing in my head. And since kicks in the gut never come along unaccompanied—like Siamese twins, those things—there was also the business of the missing page. I hadn't yet mentioned that to my protectress.

"Let's go to your place," she said.

I thought at first she wanted to screw. Back to that again. Generally when a lady asks to go to your place, it's not to admire the carpet. But let's leave the delicate subject of boot-knocking aside and get down to more serious matters. Along the way, Céline ran off to get something from her room. Something like a little box—shit! I hoped it wasn't condoms, they're all so crazy about those things nowadays! I saw it when she was coming out of the main building, a little box she was slipping into a pocket of her dress. We headed for the house in the brambles.

I plunked down at my table. She took a chair and sat facing me, her back to the window.

I was wrong. She just wanted to talk.

"So, big boy, what's bothering you?"

So now I was at confession?

"If you could see yourself! Really, you worry me sometimes. You went on your trip, had a nice break, and I was hoping it might relax you a little. That's what you wanted, right? So did you see your cousin?"

"I . . . Yes, of course . . ."

"And what did this cousin have to say?"

"Would you mind not bugging me about all that?"

"How very pleasant you are tonight. Nobody happened to stick a jagged stick up your ass while you were away, did they? Come on, how about a little smile, big boy? The book's almost done, and here you are all in a funk. Still your old lack of self-confidence, obviously . . . You have doubts . . . Monsieur has doubts . . . doesn't believe in his own talent . . ."

She started in with the compliments again, the soft soap, the censer swaying over my head . . . I'd never asked her for any favors! Why keep telling me my writing was worth something? Almost from the moment I set foot in La Halte. What the hell was she up to? She couldn't have been as hot for me as all that . . . We didn't even screw anymore, not really, that was all over and done with. At this point, Céline was more a mother to me than anything else. Was she trying to sweeten the pill, or what? Why won't she leave me the fuck alone already, for Christ's sake!

And now it all finally came bursting out as we sat there looking at the last pages I'd covered with ink: "Look, if you think it's shit, you can just come right out and say it!"

She looked stunned—and I mean really stunned, her eyes were popping out of her head.

"What? *Brown Java*?"

"Yes, of course *Brown Java* . . . Give me the word, and that's the last you'll hear of it. It's not like I'm going to go hole up in a monastery for the rest of my life."

"What on earth is the matter with you? Who put that into your head? You get bitten by a rabid fly on the train?"

"I'm not going to kill myself, you know. Just tell me: 'It's no good.' Period. That's it. 'It stinks, I only told you I liked it because . . . because I'm fond of you . . . because you're kind of the son I never had . . . because you remind me of my brother Hubert . . .' Just let me down easy, and fine, it's over. But praising me to the heavens like this for no reason, that's where I draw the line! I'm not going to put up with it anymore!"

"You've been like this ever since you got back. You had your little doubts every now and again before those two trips . . . nothing too dramatic . . . But this evening and this afternoon, Jesus!"

She wrinkled up her snout in concern.

"You have somebody read this besides your father?"

"No, Your Honor."

"Well, I'm sure it wasn't him who said *Brown Java* isn't worth shit! Tell me whatever you like, but not that."

"I was thinking . . . on the train . . . that's all . . . That was the first time in ages I had a few hours to myself, all alone . . . So I got to thinking about all this . . . thinking and thinking . . . And I reread, reread . . . No, it's no good. Won't work. Hasn't got it. It's crap, Céline, pure crap."

"I see the trouble, he's sick. Did you eat something a little off, back in the Mayenne? What's wrong? It's your liver acting up . . . you've got bile, maybe . . . your head's full of black humors . . . Textbook case . . . What have your parents been feeding you? Overripe rillettes?"

"Just drop it, okay?"

"You, my dear boy, have let someone besides your father read through the manuscript. That's it, isn't it? Just admit it: you had someone else read *Brown Java*! And that someone turned out to be jealous of your talent. And, being jealous, said all sorts of awful things about your work. That's a classic story, kiddo, nothing new . . . What, you never read that clown Sainte-Beuve's broadsides against Balzac? And his complete silence on Stendhal! Still resounding today! Huh? You ever read those things? It was another writer, I'll bet."

"Stop talking crap."

"A book like this is only to be given to people you can trust, understand?"

There was something sharp in her voice. Then all of a sudden she flew off the handle:

"You fool! Don't tell me you gave it to some literary twat!"

"Hey there, Céline . . . take it easy, will you? Why do you have to yell at me? It's my manuscript, isn't it? Suppose I did want to have somebody read it, it's a free country, right?"

"Oh, you poor fool . . . don't you think you've already fucked up enough for one sad little life? For once you've got a woman with some sense in her head, who knows what a real book is, for once you've got someone like that looking after you, and sometimes giving your ass a little smack to get you back to work—that's nothing to gripe about, right?"

We went at it like that for two or three minutes. Then she quieted down, but she was still determined to wipe that pathetic pout off my lips:

"You've got to get those black thoughts out of there, Jean-Rémi." (She bent forward and tapped my forehead with her index finger.) "You're a little depressed. It's only natural, when you've just churned out six hundred pages. You're a Céline, my fine friend. What am I saying, a Céline? You're a Dochin! That's what you'll be hearing soon enough! It's all about the style. Style, you understand?

They could take your name off the cover, and still your book would never be mistaken for anyone else's. Get it? That's the whole ball of wax. Style, my boy. That's the sign of a real artist, that and inventiveness. Do people mix up a Monet with a Vlaminck, and vice versa? It's all in the touch! Only one Dochin in this world!"

I looked at her for a long time. No doubt about it, something wasn't right in her head. Either she was nuts or she was thinking of a different book. Her very own *Java*, existing only in her own mind, nothing to do with my turkey, nothing to do with the book Langillier had demolished—kindly, diplomatically, and courteously, it's true, but it was still a slapdown, good and proper. I was completely mystified. My only thought now was to figure out what on earth made her think I had talent, why she saw something worthwhile in my pointless manuscript. A sort of mystery. Or else, if she was just taking me for a ride, it still would have been interesting to know why. Now—and this was a completely new thing, a one-eighty—I couldn't wait to show my monster to a publisher. Yes, indeed. Then, when he handed down his verdict, Madame Ferdinaud would have to give in and face facts. Accept the truth, once and for all.

She still wasn't done. And it seemed to me I'd heard her say these words before, like a sort of threat:

"They're going to love your book, my boy, I guarantee it. They'd damn well better."

And she kept on going, the look in her eyes almost scaring me a little:

"And if they don't, they'll be kicking themselves. Black and blue! But don't worry, they're all going to bow down before you, they're going to love it . . . I promise."

Hearing her spit out this prediction, I got the image of a lioness defending her cub. And I was the cub, the hopeless scribbler, the no-talent, down-market hack. She went on: "They're going to find it masterful, very very good—every one of them, you hear me? Anything else would seem to me most unreasonable! That's the polite word for it. Unreasonable for starters . . . Impossible . . ." Her fixed, flashing eyes were starting to scare me. And then, all at once, the lunacy went up to the next level—in three seconds flat, we were transported to a cell in a madhouse. She showed me that little flat package I'd seen her slip into her pocket earlier on. She took out a deck of cards. So that's what she was getting from her room. Tarot cards.

She shoved the papers aside and scattered the cardboard rectangles all over the table, mixing them up every which way, spreading them into a sort of clockwise spiral. Then she gathered them up, shuffled them, and cut the deck twice with her left hand to make three unequal stacks:

"These will tell us what's going to happen."

I almost cried out for help. Security! Madwoman on the loose! She was doing her best to stare me down, her blue and mauve-ringed eyes looking deep into mine.

"When a woman like me—not completely illiterate, let me remind you—says your book has an undeniable something, it just bounces right off you. So now we're going to see what the cards have to say. The tarot never lies, Jean-Rémi. Never. Hasn't let me down once in forty years."

She laid out the cards with a flurry of manual gymnastics that was probably supposed to be mysterious. Looked pretty damn meaningless to me, just a flashy display to dazzle a poor rube like yours truly. She put down five cards, each some distance from the last, more or less in the shape of a Greek cross.

"The question is 'Am I a great writer? Is my book going to be a hit?' Agreed, Jean-Rémi?"

I let out a scarcely audible grunt, accompanied by a shrug that she must have noticed. She raised her eyes heavenward in exasperation.

"Three major arcana . . . Three cards upright . . . That's pretty good . . . Well, look here, my little piggy! The Wheel of Fortune, and not upside down! Jupiter's in the game. Say, you've got a lucky ace up your sleeve, and plenty more to pull out of your ass . . . Nine of coins, head high. Financial success. Six of rods, efforts rewarded, triumph . . . Well, piggy! Ah yes, of course . . . nothing's ever completely perfect, that'd be asking too much."

To my eye all those weird little pictures seemed about as eloquent as hieroglyphs, but just then I spotted one that sent a shiver racing straight down my spine. Upside down, to be sure—its top toward me—but all the same: a human skeleton holding a scythe. Céline noticed the troubled look on my face:

"Don't worry. Death's not in the cards. At least . . . not for you."

Not for me. Well, that's always nice to hear, I told myself. Thanks a lot. But who for, then? Madwoman on the loose! What was this sinister farce supposed to mean?

"Haven't you got anything a little cheerier?"

"Here's the Sun. Right in the middle, the nexus. So Monsieur thinks he has something to complain about? The Sun! Cabalistic correlation: the Hebrew letter *raysh*. The head . . . Thirtieth Path of the Tree of Life: sublime reward. A touch of pride, egoism . . . You'll get over that, you're still just a kid. I'll pass over these trivialities . . . Lord, look at all this, is this good! Forty years I've been reading the tarot, my boy, and it's never been wrong. So do me a favor and stop looking like some halfwit being sentenced to fry in the chair."

And then we were off . . . she started telling me everything she saw in those grimy old cards. It's true, they'd clearly been used before, and more than once.

"Literary glory has already taken you by the little finger, lamb. In a few months it'll be holding you by the hand. And the path you'll walk together—get this all the way through your thick skull—is going to be a long one. At the other end, the Académie Française, or else your complete works published in a nice fat Pléiade edition."

"Why not Sainte-Anne hospital or a padded cell in Lannemezan asylum, while you're at it?" I added (but under my breath, discreetly, because Céline was starting to scare me—fortunately, she didn't hear).

So to hear her tell it, the tarot never lies . . . Okay, let's suppose it's true: but in that case how the hell had Langillier got it so wrong? I just couldn't figure it. How could a major player in the publishing game (that's what he used to be, at least) see no redeeming features in a manuscript that was good enough—Céline's words, not mine—to set me on my way toward the front door of the Académie? Not a word on that from the tarot. On that point, I was all on my own.

22 The Page Recaptured

Two days later Odette came to tell me I had a phone call. It was a little awkward, because Céline was right there in the front office talking with Félibut, who'd come out to install a new water heater in the laundry room.

I jumped when I heard Langillier's voice. She must have noticed, because all at once she stopped gabbing with Félibut, turned my way, and opened her eyes nice and wide, the better to keep me in her sights. This intense surveillance was getting to be a pain in the ass. But she'd been sensing something was wrong ever since she saw me come back from my trip looking so miserable. Did she really know I'd had someone other than my father read my book, someone who maybe tried to discourage me? I didn't quite know what to think.

"Is that you, Dochin?"

"Yes, I . . . I'm here . . ."

"It's Langillier, hello."

"Oh, hello."

Something about Langillier's tone struck me as odd. He sounded serious, grave. Like he had something big on his mind. I immediately realized something abnormal was going on. Maybe worse than abnormal . . .

"I've taken the liberty of calling you . . ."

A brief hesitation . . . an awkward pause . . .

A little less than an hour earlier, searching in vain for some misplaced papers, Urbain Langillier had started clearing the file folders and stacked newspapers off his desktop. A moment later he found himself holding a page from Dochin's manuscript.

"What on earth is this?"

He realized at once—from the type, from the names Max and Mimile—that it came from the manuscript he'd tried to read two or three days earlier. The page must have slipped out of the pile somehow and ended up who knows where, on some corner of the desk . . . And then, purely by chance, he must have put some folders on top of it. But little matter how it happened . . . Had Dochin realized it was missing? He looked at the number. He remembered he hadn't made it past page 33, so thoroughly uninteresting had he found Dochin's work. Nevertheless, after a brief pause, he'd gone back to the manuscript and read a little more, here and there, at random, then a little more, further on . . .

If he notices . . . he said to himself. I'll call him. I'll let him know the page is on its way back, otherwise he might worry.

He hesitated a little longer. Got out his address book, in which he'd very recently jotted the number of the ex-denizen of the homeless shelters. But just then, almost in spite of him, his eye landed once again on the typewritten page.

He read it.

Then read it again.

Three lines . . . Five lines . . . Seven . . . Eight . . .

Little by little, an expression of astonishment took shape on his face. It was incredible. Extraordinary. Mind-blowing. For two seconds he even heard a nervous laugh escaping his lips. In the manner of the actor Pierre Blanchar. It was all just so . . . unimaginable! Still reading, he rose from his chair, eyes riveted to the page, and nearly lost his balance. He caught himself on a corner of the desk.

Deep confoundment draped his face in blanket of purest white. He tried to react, his vision went blurry, a torrent of words raced by his uncomprehending eyes. He dropped back into his armchair and let go of the sheet. Not frightened, no. Dumbfounded. Because now he'd read it through to the end.

And then, in disbelief, he forced himself to read it again.

Langillier thought things over for a few minutes and decided to call Dochin. Oh! no, no question of . . . Not a word about this to him. Not one word. Don't get involved, no matter what. Besides, he had no idea what was going on here . . . Just let him know he'll be getting the page back in the mail. It was his, after all.

"Yes?" Dochin murmured into the phone in a timorous little voice.

He'd almost added "Monsieur Langillier," but caught himself just in time. Céline was still searching his face. Even Félibut looked uncomfortable to see the boss listening in like this, keeping poor Monsieur Jean-Rémi in her eyes' vice-like grip while he talked on the phone, looking so lost, trembling a little . . .

It's got to be about that missing page, Dochin thought.

"I'll have to make this quick," said Langillier. (He seemed in a hurry to get this over with, trying to cut the conversation short, racing along like a radio newsreader, and Dochin had some difficulty keeping up.)

"I'm very sorry to disturb you at home, but I've just found a page of your manuscript in my study. It must have fallen out without my noticing . . . I'm embarrassed not to have seen it, and I do hope you'll forgive me if this page . . . if the absence of this page has caused you any inconvenience."

"I . . ."

Racked with anxiety, not daring to speak, Dochin glanced furtively toward Céline. There'd be hell to pay if she found out he'd given his monster to a journalist.

"I didn't even notice," he said, just to be polite.

"I'll send it to you at once . . ."

"That's very thoughtful of you . . . I . . ."

Céline was still staring at him for all she was worth—two points drilling into his skull, it felt like. He could see her out of the corner of his eye, he knew she was there, she had him in her spell, like a snake hypnotizing its prey.

"I have your phone number, of course, but I've just realized I don't have your address."

Dochin recited it, feeling relieved. So it really was just about the missing page. Nothing serious, in short.

"Okay, got it," said Langillier. "I'll put it right in the mail. You'll have it tomorrow, I imagine. And now I've got to be going. I'm in a terrible hurry. Again, so sorry."

"Thank you very much. And it's . . ."

Dochin stood speechless. Langillier had hung up. Not even so much as a "good-bye," a bit like someone running for dear life. Maybe he was afraid the author might start asking questions about his work. Truly abnormal, that tone of his, Dochin told himself as he hung up the phone. Hey, so he wasn't out of the country after all! I thought he had a plane to catch . . . Weird guy.

"What was it?" asked Céline.

"Nothing . . . Someone at my parents' house . . ."

"And what did they want?"

"How do you mean?"

"Well, I don't know . . . Something wrong, at your parents' place? You should have heard your voice . . . And the look on your face . . . you seemed pretty shook up, if you don't mind my saying."

"Oh, it's nothing."

After all, there was no reason to keep it from her, it wasn't a problem. Might as well come out with it. (And besides, he knew her all too well! She'd worm it out of him anyway, badger him till he . . .)

"My father misplaced a page while he was reading the manuscript. They just found it. It's very simple. It's not like the world's coming to an end."

"All right then . . . Still, from the way you were looking . . ."

"It was my parents' maid . . . I . . . She seemed so upset, and . . . I . . ."

"What about the page? Which one was it?"

Irritated, Dochin headed off to his room. She followed quick on his heels, leaving Félibut to his own devices.

They crossed through the orchard . . .

"I'm talking to you, Jean-Rémi."

"What?"

"What was the missing page? Which one?"

"Oh, nothing . . . Page 111 . . . I noticed it the day before yesterday."

Céline furrowed her brow ever so slightly. She veered back toward the former post house.

"Wait a minute!" she shouted. "Go to your room and look at the manuscript. I'll be right there."

He went on alone. In the little house, he picked up his manuscript. Opened it. Nothing had changed. Page 110, page 112, and nothing in between. He leafed through his work, reread two or three pages in the middle, grimacing in disgust, finding his sentences as emetic as ever. After a moment, Céline appeared at his side.

"So?" she asked.

"It's page 111, all right. Nothing serious."

"I could have retyped it . . ."

She bent over the table, looking for pages 110 and 112.

"There's absolutely nothing happening on that page," said Dochin. "The two kids are trying to steal eggs from a henhouse, and . . ."

"Oh yes, I remember. The farmer gives them some cider, then the lady of the house shows up and chews out her husband because she doesn't want him wasting his time with two guttersnipes."

"That's right."

"Then the farmer goes to check on his old nag, which injured itself two days before trying to jump the metal fence in the field. You're right, it's not exactly the Bovarys' evening at La Vaubyessard, or Bardamu crossing the ocean on the *Amiral Bragueton* . . ."

At that moment, having folded Dochin's page in four, slipped it into an envelope, written *Monsieur Jean-Rémi Dochin, La Halte du Bon Accueil, La Petite Saulée, 19260 Térignac* on said envelope, affixed the proper postage in the upper right-hand corner, and stamped his address on the back—*Urbain Langillier, 30 Avenue René-Coty, 75014 Paris*—the reporter was dropping the letter into the mailbox that stands waiting, ever-faithful, at the corner of the Avenue René-Coty and the Rue de La Tombe Issoire.

The next morning, heading back to my desk after a stroll through the orchard, I spotted the postman's little yellow truck at the front gate. Camille went out to pick up the mail. A little later, after I'd laid down a line of my immortal prose at the top of a fresh sheet of paper, she knocked politely at the door, handed me my mail with a smile, and disappeared just as discreetly. A letter for me. A pale blue envelope. I read the return address on the back: *Urbain Langillier, 30 Avenue . . ."* etc. "Shit!" I muttered through my teeth. "Let's hope Céline didn't see this!" Did she know Langillier's name? He published a lot of articles in *Paris-Match, Le Figaro,* places like that . . . Here at La Halte they mostly read *La Montagne,* the regional paper, and sometimes the *Figaro Littéraire,* and *La Magazine Littéraire* and *Les Nouvelles Littéraires* too . . . Not really Langillier's turf, even if he did use to work in the publishing game. He was mostly an investigative reporter these days. Sometimes Félibut left his old issues of *L'Humanité* lying around the motel, and Odette subscribed to a couple of right-wing weeklies, but that wasn't quite Langillier's cup of tea either, I got the impression he was more of a Gaullist.

I sliced delicately into the envelope with a letter-opener. The rescued page was inside, folded in four. I took it out and opened it up. Sure enough, page 111. I reread it. It's true, not much going on there. Almost nothing, really. A complete absence of events. Max and Mimile on the Norman farm . . . In short, it wouldn't have been the catastrophe of the year if this page had been lost for good. I reinserted the prodigal, still bearing the cross of its fold, between pages 110 and 112, where it belonged.

At lunch—steamed chicken with saffron rice—I tried to figure out what Céline was thinking. Nothing unusual in her expression. Apart from the customary half-pound of makeup, her face looked perfectly normal, perfectly calm. Clearly she'd never had the envelope in her hands, because otherwise she would have questioned me about that name on the back, "Langillier," and that address, so far from the Mayenne that it was, in fact, in Paris. Of course, I could have come up with some story to tell her, because there was no proof it had anything to do with the missing page.

"So you got your page back?" she finally asked, but not till the cheese course (goat cheese from the region, which means no long journeys in the back of a truck where the cheeselets can sometimes get damaged).

"Yes, just this morning . . ."

"So, happy?"

"It wasn't a big deal."

"Still, that was very nice of them to call."

"Would you like some profiteroles, Monsieur Jean-Rémi?" Odette asked.

"Oh, he loves profiteroles, of course he'll have some," said Céline. "Isn't that so, my boy, that you love profiteroles?"

"Yes . . ." (I dared to say it:) ". . . mommy."

"Oh, you ass!"

She stuck a Marlboro between the two plump slugs that were her lips:

"Camille, dear, hurry and make us some coffee. I still have a few pages of the Great Man's work to type up."

PART III   Dancing the Brown Java

23   Gastinel Editions

Early that May I was finally able to write the long-awaited words THE END under the last line, though Céline made me cross them out and put "End of Volume One." Four years and nine months' work.

We bickered a little about choosing a publisher. She was still bent on Gallim's. And then, as a fallback, Charpentier, Furne, or Conard.

"No way I'm giving this to one of the big houses," I said. "First of all, they don't need a little guy like me. And I don't much relish the thought of being humiliated."

She kept at me on that, and then, seeing I wouldn't budge, she gave up the fight. She was going to let me do it my way. Some very minor little house, almost invisible, a non-entity in the publishing world, that's what I wanted, but I didn't know yet which one.

I dithered a while over five or six possibilities, but they were still too important for my tastes, still a little too well known. No, what I wanted was a sort of Good Samaritan for logorrheic hacks, someone who'd let me get this whole demented business behind me as quick as possible. Once the thing was sent back—which it would be, that was as plain as the snot in the nose on my face—Céline would pipe down and give up on the sempiternal, "Really, why don't you just give Gallim's a try? Those little cut-rate publishers are all idiots. As demonstrated by the fact that they never manage to snare a decent manuscript." To which I could then answer, snickering, slapping my fat pile of papers with one hand, "Well, this time they're going to get one."

The last ten or fifteen pages still had to be typed. I left her to toil away in her room and spent most of my time fishing on the banks of the Vézère. Free at last of that endless obligation to write, how light and carefree I felt! Volume two could wait. My idea was to stop and catch my breath before launching back into it, but deep in my heart of hearts I hoped never to have to touch that volume two, no matter how many scoldings—how many beatings!—Céline might dish out. I'd just have to wait for the publisher's verdict. Once *Brown Java* had been turned down by three or four houses, once it became clear that my book really was tripe through and through, then it would be curtains for volume two, and I wouldn't have to write another line.

Fishing's nice enough, for a while. But it can get pretty old, too, especially if you've devoted several days in a row to that restful pastime. I couldn't figure out why Céline was taking so long with that last handful of pages. I asked her what was going on, how she was doing. Madame de Berny was feeling a bit bushed. It dragged on and on, she took almost a month to type up those few pages. She was running out of steam fast, that was clear.

I finally got the rest of the typescript on May 24th. The fucker was 680 pages long! Absolutely insane. The handwritten version—bound for the auction block someday, assuming the mice didn't gobble it down first—came to 655, cross-outs and various graphical gymnastics included. In print, assuming the type wasn't too small, it would probably make a doorstop of six hundred pages.

Proudly, on my protectress's typewriter—though all the while feeling that deep vein of dumbassery throbbing inside me—I concocted the title page, starting over four or five times because I couldn't get the layout right. At the top: *Jean-Rémi Dochin* (I'd finally made my decision, I was going to use my real name), and then, a little below, in capitals: DANCING THE BROWN JAVA, and then *A Novel*. Stick a fork in it, it's done. I went to a big stationery shop in Brive and spent most of the morning photocopying the thing, just one copy to keep in my possession, as every publisher's contract stipulates. Back at La Halte, I stowed it away in my suitcase with the original manuscript and carefully locked the bag, like a miser with his little coffer of gold.

Now that the good weather was back, we had more of a crowd at La Halte, eight or nine rooms taken. The local hotels were still turning away undesirables, the dining rooms still reserved for a respectable, high-class clientele who didn't like having all the misery of the world parading by them as they ate. We had two people with goiters. We had a wheelchair-bound Romanian and his perfectly normal young daughter, along with a magnificent foxhound. We had a Canadian hunchback. We had a little girl with scars all over her face from a dog bite when she was three, who also had to wear orthopedic shoes, poor little thing, traveling with her mother, who was deaf and un-hearing-aided and spoke in a very loud voice, almost a shout, a real nuisance in the dining room of a decent hotel, especially when the person in question is forever asking for bread or salt or mustard or telling the headwaiter the steak has to be cooked medium and the fried potatoes have to be tender. We had two fairly grungy gypsies, one of them always carrying a banjo. The night before, we'd seen a whole family from Sens get out of their car, headed to a funeral in the Lot. There were six or seven of them, all adults, the men in dark suits, with crêpe or an armband, a suitably lugubrious look on their faces, and the four women in full mourning, complete with veils, flounces, black plumes, teary voices, red eyes, sniffles, the whole shooting match. They'd been turned away from three nearby hotels, since people like to dine in a gay, relaxed atmosphere, especially if there are funny things to see on TV before the moronic eight-o'clock news comes on. In short, my mourners, what with their depressing outfits—nobody wants to be reminded of death when they're digging into a nice choucroute or a jugged hare simmered in its own blood—had been pointed toward La Halte by a chambermaid. Céline and I were sort of celebrating the end of the manuscript that night, and we were all merrily stuffing our faces (a bit more reservedly in the case of the folks from the funeral procession), delighting in Odette's veal sweetbreads and morels in cream sauce, a damn sight better than anything you'll find in a snooty hotel restaurant. Céline and I were sitting with the guests, all of us eating side by side, nice and friendly. After the cherry pie was brought out, the hunchback from Ottawa even broke into song, with his Canadian accent:

"Oh what a joy

Is that dear hunchback boy

They don't make 'em like that anymore!"

which led to a warm round of applause, after we'd all chorused that sweet little song's last three lines. Tomorrow morning we'd get back to serious things.

After dinner, Céline got on me to make up my mind, publisher-wise. I sat in her room, unable to reach a decision. Irritated, she pulled a few well-worn volumes from her little bookshelf and spread them out on the table in front of me. I pawed over the books, most of them dime-store novels, one was even porn.

"Here, if you're so scared of Gallim's, why don't you just choose one of these?"

I took them up one by one and dropped them back on the table, like I was picking over some not very fresh-looking cod at the fishmonger's, opening them, leafing through them, this close to smelling them like melons or camemberts, studying the lists of other books put out by the same press, the back covers, the names of other nonentities moved to write books to be read by people with absolutely nothing better to do. I wonder what sort of face I was making. Grimacing, I suppose, the corners of my mouth turned down in revulsion. I also deciphered the names of four or five publishing houses: Scribe and Co.... Calligrapher Press... New Batala Editions... Day After Tomorrow Limited... Le Papyrus... Timekiller Books...

After a while Céline lost patience:

"Well, come on, are you going to make up your mind or aren't you? I hope it's not going to take you another six months to send the thing off!"

"Well, I don't see..."

"We're all getting so sick of you!"

And as she spat out this anathema, she picked up another book from the floor and slammed it down on the table. It landed on top of the others, raising a small cloud of dust. I picked up the volume, its front cover half torn off and hanging loose. It was a science-fiction novel, with a cheap hand-drawn illustration on the cover. The author's name was as unknown to me as the grandfather of the great-grandfather of the great-great-grandfather of the mother-in-law I never had. And then, at the bottom, in small type, *Gastinel Editions, Paris.*

"Well, how about this one?" I sighed wearily, after paging through the horrible thing for a few seconds (the typography was a mess, and I'd already spotted two or three typos spattering the text like specks of fly shit).

"The crap you've got in your library!" I said, flabbergasted. "You didn't really read this thing, did you?"

"No . . . It's Odette's . . . She's keeping a few of her books on my shelf. She ran out of room when she inherited her sister's linens. I think she brought that one back from the market in Uzerche, along with some others. A little handful of worthless secondhand books. I don't suppose she ever read them . . . She hardly reads at all anymore, actually, she's got troubles with her eyes . . ."

"Gastinel Editions," I read again.

I opened it up. I located the address facing the title page: 22, Rue du Pressoir, 75020 Paris. The copyright was recent: 1991.

"Let's go with that one," I said.

"This is such a terrible waste, Jean-Rémi. Imagine giving *Brown Java* to a publisher who probably doesn't even have two pairs of boots and four shirts in his closet . . . But if you're going to insist, I won't stand in your way. Maybe you'll regret it one day. This guy's going to give you a pathetically small advance, I can tell you that from the start."

"Oh, I . . ."

"I know. You're not in it for the money, just the glory. As you wish, big boy."

The meeting with the publisher Gastinel—Charles Gastinel—took place on Monday, May 29th, 1995. I have to tell you about that, one of those things you don't forget, a major event in my dumpy little existence. And then I'll let you go back to "enjoying" the story.

On Sunday the 28th, I got myself ready to head for Limoges and catch the TGV. I was more or less presentably dressed for the big city, my shoes polished, a dab of goo in my hair. Céline didn't help me do my tie—a brand-new bordeaux number I'd picked up in

Brive a few days before—but she came close. She did try to stick a handkerchief in my breast pocket, but I shooed her away. I was as nervous as could be, and that would only get worse till after the interview—which wasn't exactly an interview, in the end, because my first contact with Gastinel was amazingly brief—the next day. I locked up the manuscript and the photocopy of the typescript in the suitcase that never leaves my room, then put the publisher's copy in my overnight bag and headed downstairs. At the front door, I kissed Céline on both cheeks.

"We're all with you, my boy. Courage."

Céline, Odette, and Camille accompanied me—the cats too, tails in the air—to the front gate, where the old Citroën was waiting. Two customers, not knowing what exactly was up but sensing that this was a historic moment, an important departure—for whom, and why? who can say!—came to join the three ladies of the house: a begoitered, chess-playing math teacher from Vesoul and an over-weight Marseillais who'd showed up that morning (he'd had some difficulty finding La Halte, poor guy, and must have spent the night in his Mini-Cooper with a Thermos of coffee and a goose-rillettes sandwich as his only companions, not exactly diet food, but clearly he'd long since given up checking his weight at the drugstore).

They all waved me a hearty goodbye, and I climbed behind the wheel.

I headed off to Limoges, my hands shaking, driving like a little old lady, twenty-five miles an hour, royally pissing off the people behind me when I came to a curve—I don't know if you've ever driven the D16. I boarded the TGV. Looked through the manuscript a little in the train, feeling more and more nervous, apprehension constricting my throat like I'd come down with diphtheria. In Paris, not wanting to waste any time looking for a hotel, I made for the one I'd stayed in before, just by the Gare d'Austerlitz, on the Boulevard de l'Hôpital, nothing grand about it, far from it, but I have my little habits. The owner recognized me immediately and graced me with a smile. It wasn't till I got to my room that I made the decision to reread *Brown Java*. Cover to cover. I'd never really read the whole typescript, just little bits here and there. It was going to take some courage, but I thought it had to be done before I handed the thing over to a publisher. So I reread it from first word to last. God, what a chore! I started about three in the afternoon (all I'd had to eat was a little chocolate croissant in the train station) and finished a little after three in the morning, with just one short pause around eight o'clock for some roast beef and fries in a restaurant on the Rue Poliveau (taking the monster with me, of course, no way I was going to leave it lying around a hotel room). This rereading was a kind of feat, both physically and mentally, so mediocre—and even so downright bad—did I find the prose I'd churned out over the past four and a half years. My fresh tumble into the manuscript did nothing to change my mind, and Céline's enthusiasm continued to puzzle me. Why had I struggled so hard to write all this crap? Had my years as a down-and-outer left me a little cracked in the head? Maybe if I'd chosen to tell my life story as a homeless man on the streets . . . but no, I had to write a work of fiction, and one set during the Occupation, to boot!

All the same, I did my best not to skip a single line. Apart from those few little changes Céline urged on me while she was typing it all up, nothing had changed. Nothing new to see. Still as shitty as ever.

Tucking myself into bed at 3:15, I realized I wasn't going to be very bright-eyed the next day—or rather later that same day—when I met with the publisher in Belleville. I'll try to sleep till ten, I told myself, maybe then I won't be in such bad shape, and most importantly not too groggy. I didn't want to show up at Gastinel's all drowsy and slow.

Amazingly, I did manage to sleep till ten, without too much tossing and turning. Calculating in my head while I washed my face, I figured I could be at the publisher's office by around 11:30, a decent hour to go calling. I hadn't let him know I was coming, but surely a publisher that minor wouldn't be drowning in meetings. Besides, it would all probably go pretty fast, it doesn't take an eternity to drop off a manuscript. It's only later, once he's read it, that the negotiations start up, and sometimes drag on endlessly (the text, the contract, all the usual questions). But I was ready to bet the farm that my opus would end up being turned down.

I took the subway to Couronnes. The Rue du Pressoir was close by. I was early, as anxious people always are, and seeing that it was only ten to eleven when I came out of the subway, I headed for a café on the Boulevard de Belleville. I hadn't eaten any breakfast, I already had a stomach full of butterflies. I sat down at a table in back. The place was almost empty. I put the manuscript on the table and asked for a large black coffee and croissants. I was getting jumpier all the time, and I caught my hand trembling as I paged through the manuscript. What had to happen happened. I shifted awkwardly in my seat, and my elbow hit the cup, spilling half the coffee all over the table. A fine mess, which immediately sent an unpleasant river of sweat running down my back. My page 192 was ruined, drenched in a great big brown puddle. Totally unpresentable. Like an imbecile, I tried to mop it up with my crumpled napkin. Some bitch sat watching me from across the room, snickering. Probably a hooker, her vagina chock-full of AIDS and the clap and all the most fashionable microbes. She was almost laughing out loud, seeing me trying to wipe off the stain like an idiot. No luck. Finally it dried, but the page was one-quarter white and three-quarters light brown. What was I supposed to do now? No way to redo the damn thing. Where? How? Too bad: the publisher would just have to deal with it. Anyway, it really wasn't that big a thing. You could still read the words through the brown blot. Perfectly legible. These things happen, I told myself. Why shouldn't a writer spill something, anything—coffee in my case, but also Pernod, whiskey, even the juice from a slice of rare roast beef, maybe not the contents of his chamberpot, of course, let's be serious—on a page of his manuscript? I had nothing to apologize for, I'd hand over the manuscript as is, and if by some miracle the publisher got to page 192, well then he'd see what had happened, it wasn't going to hurt him. If *Brown Java* really was a masterpiece, why should anyone mind that one of its pages is a little dirty?

I was getting more and more worked up, my legs limp, my hands clammy. Finally, at 11:25, I stood up, tucked the manuscript under my arm, and headed for Gastinel's offices. Like a moron, I hadn't even drunk my coffee, or what was left of it.

Before leaving La Halte, still racked by doubt—oh, my writing was so limp and lifeless!—I'd told "mommy" Céline of my fears . . . for instance, that the publisher would insist on bringing in a rewriter.

"No danger of that, sweetie," she assured me. "First of all, it's magnificently written and well constructed. They won't dare touch a word. Second, you have to understand that a little two-bit publisher like this Whatsisnel hardly has the wherewithal to hire a rewriter. Only the big boys can afford an overhaul like that, and only when the author's written something completely generic, interchangeable, devoid of personal style . . . In short, real writers are spared that kind of surgery, except in their earliest days, maybe, especially if they didn't graduate from one of the better schools. If it's too much of a mess, there'll be no talk of saving it. The guy will hand your monster back to you, and that'll be that. He won't even suggest you rework it yourself. But look at you, still all mired in gloom! A few days from now, you'll be the one dancing the java, Jean-Rémi. At long last, you'll be saying bye-bye to all your little fears and doubts. And, then, I promise, we'll celebrate like there's no tomorrow!"

His offices were on the ground floor of what had to have been an old storefront. A horsemeat shop, evidently, because a horse's head was still sticking out of the wall above the front door, a bit dingy now, but probably gilded in the old days. Now the horseflesh had been replaced by dusty books, but the letters of the old sign were still there, or some of them: HOR EME T. So this was the home of Gastinel Editions. None too promising, but better than an old funeral home or medical-supply shop—rubber hygienic wear, trusses, enema bulbs, filth like that—and I wasn't going to start quibbling now, because after all I was the one who wanted to aim low, to approach only the bottommost man on the publishing world's totem pole.

No grand entryway, no staircase. You got in by joggling a door handle just like you'd find in a butter-and-eggs shop or a coal merchant's. There were books all over the place, stacked up in impressive piles. I saw some science fiction numbers, some porn, some little sentimental love stories no thicker than a shoesole, like Simenon used to crank out before he hit it big. Who the hell read this stuff? They've got the 8:30 TV movie for people like that nowadays. But anyway, if it sold, good for him.

Watch out for the stacks of books on your way in—you had to wriggle along to keep from knocking them over. Not much in the way of elbowroom, kind of like a gully through a gorge. Dark, too, and smelly. The office was at the far end of a hallway. The glass pane in the door had GASTINEL EDITIONS painted on it. I was shaking like a sapling in a thunderstorm.

The publisher, a three-hundred-pound giant in suspenders, his shirt unbuttoned down to his tits, gives the visitor a genteel welcome. The behemoth's voice is like a small child's, strangely soft and gentle. Dochin immediately finds him approachable and unintimidating.

"Say, now, that's a big one!" the giant laughs, accepting the well-stuffed red folder. "And you're the one who wrote all this?" (He undoes the folder's elastic strap, opens the monster, pages through it.) "Well, how about that? *Dancing the Brown Java.* Not a bad title, I must say. So you'd be Jean-Rémi Dochin, then?"

"Yes."

"Your real name, or an alias?"

"My real name."

The mountain of flesh (stinking slightly of sweat, that friendly pile of blubber, but after all, it happens, and sweat's better than smelly feet) pages through it a little longer, distractedly, his look jovial (his eyes are small and reddish, like a rat's, though a rat's can sometimes be expressive and benevolent). The ex-puppeteer flips through the pages, his gaze harpooning a word here, a phrase there. Dochin is still standing in front of the desk. The publisher hasn't offered him a seat, for the excellent reason that they're all taken up by books, galley proofs, files, even manuscripts. There are books piled on the floor in every corner of the room. They've even invaded the little hallway connecting the office to the former shop, stacked up along the walls. The floor is littered with crumpled newspapers, two or three camp stoves, empty beer cans, half-drained liquor bottles, dirty plates set on crates or boxes, still laden with olive pits or sausage casings, ashtrays advertising Byrrh or Martini or Pelforth, overflowing with butts, primarily cigar or cigarillo. As for the gray smoke hanging in the air, it bears a certain resemblance to the Concarneau fog on a November morning. And indeed, the publisher has just stuck a cigarillo in his mouth. He lights it with a quick match.

"I'll have this read in seventy-two hours at most," the giant promised, vigorously shaking—and half crushing—Dochin's delicate intellectual's hand. "And trust me, my friend, I won't skip so much as a comma. No skimming here! We take our work very seriously—we respect our writers far too much for that. And thanks for thinking of Gastinel Editions. I hope I've finally found a winning horse here. I suppose I'm the first?"

"The first what? I'm sorry . . ."

"The first publisher you've tried, for goodness' sake!"

"It's true, you're the first."

The giant let out a huge laugh.

"That's what they all say! Don't try to tell me you haven't already been to Furne or Gallim's or Hetzel . . . you know, the usual crowd."

"As a matter of fact, no. I assure you, I haven't."

"Doesn't matter. It's not serious. They've overlooked more good books than you can count. Fortunately we're here, we little presses, we rank-and-filers, to stop—I won't say the drowned man—but the tasty fish before it goes over the dam. Ha ha! Don't worry your head about it, none of that matters. This is all that counts." (He gives the manuscript a hearty swat.) "The rest . . . Good-bye, monsieur. I don't mean to chase you away, but I'm a little busy here. My secretary has the mumps. I won't see you out, you know the way. Turn left at the end of the hall, after the sci-fi remainders. That way you don't have to go through the shop, you'll come right out into the courtyard. Ah! one second. You've written your address on the manuscript, I hope? Ah yes, here it is. La Halte du Bon Accueil. In the Corrèze! Say, you've come a long way, haven't you? You didn't come up to Paris just for this, did you? After all, we've got a very fine postal service in France, you know!"

"I had some business to take care of in Paris . . ."

"Good, good."

"I also wrote the address of my hotel here in town. I'll be staying on a few days . . . and the phone number too . . ."

"Very good. Boulevard de l'Hôpital . . . 43 36 01 09. By the way, you do have a second copy, don't you?"

"Of course."

"Perfect. I'll give you a call as soon as I've got news. Well, good day to you, dear Monsieur Dochin. And don't stop writing! This world needs more beautiful books."

24 Some Kind of Wonder

Piloting his Mercedes toward Poitiers, returning Dochin to the Corrèze—we're back where we started, they've just been on TV, etc.—Charles Gastinel turned his mind back five months and let it wander at will. Not a peep out of Dochin, no doubt lost in his own thoughts. Five months now since Dochin first showed up at his offices on the Rue du Pressoir. What might this thing be worth? he'd wondered at the time, once the author had turned tail and gone on his way. Not a fig, of course. No need to tell me. It's a real epidemic these days, everybody's convinced they've got a book in them, a vast horde of bugwits all itching to bare their innermost souls! Usually not for the pleasure of writing, oh no, they just want to get on TV! Scowling, he hefted the massive manuscript again, telling himself the author clearly had all the trappings of a first-class retard. These writers and their little dreams! he mused, opening a can of beer. He'd tried his own hand at writing, but nothing had come of it. Instead, for what would soon be seven years, he'd been publishing all kinds of unter-literature, eighth-rate graphic novels, half-assed sci-fi, even a real book now and then, written by Jean Q. Nobody and submitted only after all the others had turned it down. And even then, he inevitably imposed the cruel, piratical law of the authorial subvention. Inane little dribbles of nothing, that's what he published. Not to mention that he was in debt up to his double chin, the printers and distributors forever badgering him for cash . . . along with the occasional slavering wannabe with whom he'd consented to sign a normal contract . . . promising to publish his work . . . His *work*, so called! Two or three of these losers had even come to shriek vilifications at him right there in his offices, and he'd had to threaten them with a good swift kick in the behind, one hand already clutching his blackjack. His business was circling the drain. High time he turned things around in the wallet department, or else he'd be back to hawking *Le Réverbère* on the street corners, and him sixty-two years old! This was in May '95. Oh, how he missed his beloved marionettes! The sound of children's laughter was like a balm for his soul, a solace for his heavy heart. He'd been forced to give it up because of the weight he'd put on, some kind of protein he was missing. According to the news, it was starting to look like obesity might one day be conquered at last, now that a scientist was claiming he'd managed to slim down some overweight mice by injecting them with a fat-eating protein—a neat little trick that just might work on human beings as well. So much the better: labor on, you gentlemen of science, because all things considered I'd rather be a Laurel than a Hardy.

Thus, he was sitting at the head of a tottering publishing house, set up in a former horse butcher's, at the edge of the abyss as it were, when suddenly this little hick from the Limousin comes along with a book fatter than *Wuthering Heights*. Just what he needed!

Interrupting this train of thought, Gastinel glanced once again at the little hick sitting beside him. He seemed to be sleeping. Millions of francs were about to come flooding into his pockets—he'd already got a tidy little check, his first royalties—and even now all the critics were praising him to the heavens—him and Gastinel, of course. Glory was his. Hilarious!

The car rolled on through the night, now lashed by falling rain.

He'd cracked open the manuscript. *Dancing the Brown Java.* Well, what do you think of that? Should I read it? he'd asked himself. Give it a quick look, or not?

It was lunchtime. Closing up his shop so as not to be disturbed, he set out a napkin and had a quick bite to eat: sausage on bread, two or three pieces of fruit . . .

Swallowing the last mouthful, he wiped his soiled fingers on a Kleenex and dove into the manuscript that had ended up in his hands late that morning. With no great conviction, at first. But as he pressed on . . . Utterly engrossed in his reading, he soon took the phone off the hook, even forgot to drink beer and smoke.

The interjections started to fly around page thirty-five, Gastinel's avid eyes never leaving the page, the words and sentences vying for his attention and sweeping him along—such at least was his impression—like the glimmerings of some limpid, sun-dappled torrent . . .

"Holy sow! Suppurating catfish!"

And his reading went on . . .

"Holy tit! Swinedog! I do believe I've found myself a real writer!"

The Occupation. Gastinel's completely enchanted. Over the moon, as they say. So masterfully depicted! It's all there. Like the tiles and cobblestones and little windowpanes in an Utrillo! All present and accounted for. What a panorama! A dazzling klieg light on that whole filthy scene! Fascinating! What a riot of images in those pages! A cavalcade of words!

"Oh, the turd! Oh, the cow flop!"

Page 65 . . . pages 72, 73, 74, 75 . . . 85, 90 . . .

It raced along. A toboggan! Such a pace! Wait for me, I can't keep up! Stunning! Oh! that piece of filth! Hell on wheels! It can't be true! And this passage here! I'd like to slip it off the page and preserve it under glass. Unheard-of! I'll reread it. Astonishing! It nearly levi-tates! The words fairly dance! Dazzling! Ye gods, what a journey! Next to this one, every other writer out there seems as dusty and dry as an old geezer's ballsack! Tip top! Oh, my stars and garters! Oh my cock! What a talent! What, am I dreaming? Oh, those jackasses! Oh, those toads! Always telling us there are no good books left! No more real writers! Oh, but our little Napoleons of the publishing world are going to be beating their beastly breasts with rage! Why not us? Why shouldn't we get the great manuscript for once? The *Java*! Look at them dance, the dupes! All those big shots, always stealing the good stuff away from us! Vampires! And I'm the one who ends up with this! Me! A nobody! Oh! I bet I know how this miracle manu-script landed in my mitts! By Gad! Cocksucker chickened out at the last minute, that's got to be it! Don't stick your neck out! Lie low! Not Gallim's! Not Furne! None of them! Find some little nonen-tity! Some little joke! Slink along, keep your head down! Oh! you devil! Oh! still waters! So unassuming, but under all that . . . Would you look at these sentences! Rejoice, paper! Rejoice at the words you've been graced with! Now you shine! Such a fine raiment! So stylish! Oh! you rotter! Oh! mutthole! Oh! by all the bidet water in France! If only I could have written like that! Oh! turdlet, oh! toilet-scrape! It can't be true! I'm dreaming! Manuscript, tell me you're not real . . . tell me you're going to turn to dust in my hands . . . tell me you're just made of meaningless words . . .

In his exaltation, he even forgot to go to dinner. He paused in his reading around nine o'clock, ecstatic, joyous. He sat breathless, his face clammy. Mopping his brow with a handkerchief, he reached for his first cigarette since late morning. Then he began to think. Suppose this was another *Journey to the End of the Night* I've been handed? he wondered.

"Let's not get carried away, Charles! Don't forget that old song: 'Baby, baby, you've got it all wrong' . . ."

Ten minutes later, with the manuscript in his briefcase—he'd stuck the pages into a sturdier folder, of stiff reinforced cardboard—he locked up the former horsemeat shop and its back rooms—his "publishing house"—and walked to his apartment, a few blocks away on the Rue Ramponneau, two rooms plus kitchen, running water, toilets on the landing, up on the top floor of a decrepit old hulk of a building, greedily eyed by the squatters and destined for demolition.

Back in his humble abode, he planted his buttocks on a caned dining chair and reopened the manuscript. A scowl briefly ruffled his features on encountering page 192, covered with brown stains, probably coffee, a godawful mess. He gave it a quick glance and set it aside. What, did that asshole put his leaky coffee pot down on it or something? Still, he went on reading the massive tome, turning the pages one by one with eagerness and curiosity, his eye racing over the lines like a flame along a Bickford fuse. Still as good as ever. What class! Oh! the clod! Incredible! Swear to God, I never would have believed it! Oh yes, I was wary at first. I had my doubts. Quite a surprise, I must admit. A bolt out of the blue! Tremble, you phonies, here's a real book! Motherfuck, what a style! What colors! Streamers! Rockets! Shooting stars! Palaces! Intoxications! Piss off, the lot of you! Oh, incandescent sentences, take pity on my poor eyes! Oh! that marvel! Oh! that dirty rare bird! The majesty of the story! Oh, shivers! Oh, rapture! I'm coming! Hold me back! I'm flying! I'm going to scream! With joy! I'm losing it! And this passage here! A vein of pure gold! Diamond dust! Such beauties! Such talent, where's it been sleeping all this time? What an awakening! Finesse! Lightness! What a poem! *Dead Souls* has a successor!

Hosanna! An avalanche of glorious words! Songs! Grace! Ah! What a wonderment! Oh! pus-flower! What's happening to me?

Tirelessly he turned the pages, marveling, his fat fingers excavating pickled herrings from a nearby tin can.

Around 11:00 he went to bed with the manuscript he'd been clutching since early that afternoon. He dove back into his reading, still lambasting the author with his peculiar insults elicited by a mix of amazement and jealousy, but which were also, at the same time, expressions of joy. From time to time he let out a great belly laugh. My God, there's humor too, the dogsquat! And it was true, little by little a sort of jealousy—almost a loathing, like every true, fine, potent jealousy (that bitch could stir up a revolution all on her own, if she wanted to)—a sort of jealousy took hold of him, as if some foul and treacherous beast had been lurking just beneath his fat-laden heart all this time, awaiting its moment. It first poked out its nose around page 170 . . . Made its presence felt a little more strongly a bit further on . . . At page 250, the scene in the Versailles whorehouse between Desbés, the former socialist, a character likely inspired by Marcel Déat, and Lafaurie, Bosquet's stool-pigeon—just a few lines, half a page, a scene he'd found perfectly masterful—his jealousy erupted in full fury. Now, rage. Reading a superb manuscript like this when you're a failed writer yourself, oh, what a torment! Frustration and spite had him by the throat. The sense, now crystal clear, of not standing knee-high to a dog turd . . . Not one drab little poem had he ever squeezed out, not even a simple short story devoid of charm or originality . . . Reading, yes, he loved that. Reading had replaced the cinema early on in his life. He'd avoided movie theaters like the plague ever since that day long ago when he'd escaped from a burning cinema in Dieppe, unlike his unlucky parents, who'd ended up being burned to two crisps.

Besides, movies hurt his eyes, like television, which he gladly did without, and which he'd never looked at for more than five minutes at a time, so to speak, since at age twenty he'd come down with a bad case of retinitis, complicated by photophobia (which had furthermore earned him an exemption from military service). He'd always loved to read, he was a regular at the public libraries back when he didn't have a sou to his name. And all the books he'd stolen from the shops! Cratefuls of them. But for writing, no, not a lick of talent, not a word, sitting there like he had chilblained fingers and the Eiffel Tower up his ass, the virgin page before him hell-bent on staying that way, crying "Keep your filthy nib off of me, you brute!" Oh! That piece of shit! What a treat! Superb! Oh! what ass-fuckery! That bubo! What a talent! Amazing! Oh, the torrent is carrying me off! Sublime sentences, let me go, I'm drowning!

Around 1:30 in the morning—he was now on page 316—sleep came along with a come-hither look and a beckoning finger, but in the end Morpheus went on his way, saying, "Oh, all right, if it means that much to you." Gastinel was still glued to the text, which, even as it stirred up his senses, also pierced his head and his heart with the nefarious pickax of jealousy . . . he who had never managed to make himself a writer!

Then his enthusiasm waned a little.

At page 434, he dropped the manuscript. Day was breaking, a wan light filtering through the Venetian blinds. Indecisive, he began vigorously rubbing his jaw. He sat there in his bed, spent, mulling over everything he'd just read, staring vaguely into the distance like some poor sap who's been knocked on the head and can't summon the presence of mind to react. He stayed that way for some time.

"Suppose I've got it all wrong?" he murmured after a few minutes. "Why exactly did I find this so good? I've been mistaken so many times! Why was I—or why did I think I was—so knocked out by this thing?"

He picked up the pile and began to reread, first the beginning, then a page here and there from the first third of the book.

"Is it just my imagination, or . . . ? I don't like it so much now that I'm rereading it . . . I'm not sure what to think anymore. Still, what a sock in the face when you read those first pages! But now . . ."

Like the book was some kind of chameleon!

Caught up in his reading, he'd let a number of pages slip over the side of his bed. They littered the floor like a carpet of chestnut leaves in mid-November.

Charles Gastinel, a guy with a jinx up his ass since earliest childhood, a guy who's always wanted to be a writer but who has no ideas and takes two hours to cobble a sentence together that can more or less stand up to scrutiny—as long as it's got crutches—Charles Gastinel gazes down upon those scattered pages and wonders whether he'd been reading with stars in his eyes, or if this really is one of those manuscripts that comes along only five or six times in a century. Less than that, even. Since 1900, he said to himself, here on our shores: *Remembrance of Things Past, Journey to . . .* and *Death on . . . Molloy,* two or three by Giono, Aymé's short stories, and after that you can ring down the curtain, all the rest belongs in airports and train stations. Oh yes, let's not forget old man Gracq. And Aragon's *Residential Quarter.*

Let's see, how much more to read? A little more than two hundred pages. Turning into an uphill climb, he's running out of steam, Lord, what a mountain! But you've got to get through it, come on, show some fortitude! I really do have to finish it, after all, he told himself.

In his nightshirt, out of his bed, on all fours, nose to the ground, elephantine posterior pointing howitzer-like toward the ceiling, he gathers the scattered pages. Then, sitting in an armchair, he puts it all back together, sheet by sheet, moistening his thumb, back like he found it. A sip of coffee, a splash of water on the thick layer of blubber that is his glistening face, then let's throw on some clothes and get back to our reading.

At twenty past noon, he closed up the manuscript, now read through to the end. He sat slumped in his armchair for ten minutes, stunned, pensive, dumbfounded, shaken.

"What do I do?" he wondered, looking at the clock. "Let's go have a bite to eat, first of all. That'll help us think."

He shaved and set off with the manuscript in his briefcase, downed a Morteau sausage with red beans in a little restaurant on the Rue Jean-Pierre-Timbaud, just a stone's throw from home, then came back again. He still hadn't made his mind up about *Dancing the Brown Java*. He paged through it once more, reading a snatch here and there, less and less able to decide if it was brilliant, adequate, perfectly ordinary, or moronic. He just didn't know.

Holding the pile on his knees, he sat for another long while in his armchair, wondering, befuddled, certain scenes of the novel still running through his mind.

"What do I do?"

In any case, he thought, I don't have the dough to put out a doorstop like this. And then it'd need a big-time distribution . . . and the media would have to be brought onboard! A book like this has to be launched. One thing's clear from the start, they won't be inviting me on the radio or TV, I'm nobody, no way I can compete with the big dogs in the business, out of the game, not easy being a tiny turd in a great big world. No, no way to put this thing out. You're too little,

Charles! Besides, I really don't know how good it is. It says "End of Volume One" on the last page. So does that mean there's going to be a sequel? Who knows? No. I know what I'm going to do. I'm going to ask Malgodin what he thinks. Malgodin's on firmer footing than me. Down in the cellar of the publishing world, it's true, but still a notch or two above Gastinel. He's put out some decent novels. But mostly I just want his opinion. Malgodin used to be a big literary critic. Okay, that was twenty years ago, it's true, and he had to bid farewell to that trade—that art!—owing to his fondness for the bottle, but still, he discovered five or six young authors who managed to make something of themselves. I've heard he has a real nose for a good book. Is it still as keen as ever? We'll see. I'm going to have him read this thing. Supposedly—this is all hearsay, I know, but all the same—supposedly the big boys still seek out his advice. What the hell, I'm going to give it to him. If he likes it, then I imagine it's a sure thing, and then—but only then—I'll get my fat ass to work.

Yes, let's go with Malgodin, Gastinel told himself, back in his office on the Rue du Pressoir, the manuscript on his desk. With some agitation, he dialed the number of the CEO of Le Papyrus, a small publishing house with offices near the Porte d'Ivry. Of course, he's still hitting the bottle pretty hard, Gastinel remembered, but maybe I'll get lucky and catch him sober.

"Hello, Malgodin. Gastinel. Tell me, dear friend, I don't want to disturb you—" (It's looking good, the fatso told himself, he sounds fairly clearheaded. Not plastered yet. Of course, it's only two in the afternoon . . .) "—but I have a manuscript here that looks interesting. The thing is, and this is completely absurd, but I find myself having doubts . . . A great many doubts, as a matter of fact. I'm completely lost, in other words. Yes, that's right, I'd be most grateful for your opinion, dear friend. No, don't move. I'll bring it to you myself. See you in a bit. Excuse me? Very fat? Uh . . . yes. A little more than six hundred pages. Be right over."

He hung up and started to think again, nibbling at his thumb. An idea had sprouted in his mind. Or rather in the back of his mind. He opened the manuscript and pulled out the first sheet, with *Jean-Rémi Dochin* at the top and DANCING THE BROWN JAVA in the middle. He crumpled that page and dropped it in the wastebasket. He then took a clean sheet from his desk, picked up a red felt-tip, and wrote DANCING THE BROWN JAVA, *A Novel* in large letters. No author's name.

His sausage-like fingers anxiously massaging the glistening little roast beef that was his heavy chin, he thought again, sitting for almost five minutes in deep meditation. Let's see . . . What did I tell that asshole on the phone? "I've got a manuscript here that looks interesting . . ." Fine. "I'm having doubts . . ." Nothing compromising, in short. An author can have doubts, can't he? And he can certainly find his work interesting . . . without feeling too sure—that's what they call doubts, by God—of its quality. Isn't that right? We'll see what Malgodin has to say. It's never a bad idea to think ahead. If he finds it brilliant . . . But the more I think about it, the more I'm convinced I just got carried away . . . It's understandable, people send me such a lot of worthless crap year after year that I took this thing for some kind of wonder, when it might be perfectly average. It's just the contrast!

"Who's the author?" asked Euloge Malgodin, a generic-looking man of about sixty, more than a few white hairs on his slightly oblong skull, the flushed face and fat red nose of a veteran alcoholic, piercing blue-green eyes, a somewhat wary demeanor, but always dressed to the nines, very presentable, nice white stiff-collared shirt and big cufflinks, smart bowtie, elegant little touches like that, a well-tailored light-gray suit. The office isn't bad either. And five or six employees—pardon me, colleagues—two or three of them nice-looking girls. A small press, to be sure, but a fairly serious one, it seemed, nothing like that seedy dump on the Rue du Pressoir.

He opened the manuscript that Gastinel had just brought to his offices on the Avenue d'Ivry. The bulging folder lay on his desk, next to a copy of a book he'd just put out: *Suburbs: Home of the Wanking Class*, a brilliant sociological study that, to his great satisfaction, had caused a bit of a stir among the reading public, bringing him some free publicity and some much-needed cash.

"I won't say till you're done with it," Gastinel answered, doing his best to look mysterious. "Just read it. It'll be a surprise."

Malgodin gave a hint of a smile; his thin, unsentimental lips sketched a fine slit into his features, then froze, rictus-like:

"It's not you, is it?"

"Read it . . . We'll talk later."

"You know the author's name?"

"Read it, Malgodin."

"Pretty damn thick, I have to say . . . You'll give me a week?"

"Of course."

"But at least tell me who it's by. Come on, Gastinel, don't play games with me. You're handing me a big fat—excuse me—well yes, a big fat line of bullshit! I know you. You've got the real title page back at your place, and you wrote up a new one with no author's name. Am I wrong?"

"Just read it, Malgodin . . . You'll be doing me a great favor."

"Okay, okay," the publisher sighed. "If you won't tell me . . . We'll talk about it later. That is . . . assuming this thing happens to interest me. But don't tell me you're the . . . I know you've tried before . . . a couple of poems . . . two or three unfinished short stories, too . . . That's what you told me, right? I can't remember when . . . That time we had dinner with the babe from *Paris Qui Lit*, I think . . . But a real book like this!"

"Sometimes people reveal their true personality late in life, all of a sudden, just like that . . ." said Gastinel. "It's been known to happen. But I'm not going to tell you a thing."

"Sly devil. You'll be hearing from me."

"Thanks, Malgodin."

"You have another copy, I hope?"

"Of course. See you soon."

No sooner was Gastinel out of the office than Malgodin opened a drawer and took out a bottle of whiskey, little matter what brand. His afternoon bottle. Early afternoon bottle, to be precise.

25 Malgodin, A New Denoël

Many sheets to the wind, comfortably ensconced in his little house in L'Haÿ-les-Roses, just outside Paris, Malgodin launched into page 180 of the manuscript on the stroke of two in the morning. He'd been doing some celebrating, in honor of the not-too-shabby sales figures for *Home of the Wanking Class*—finally, a minor success, after a four-year drought! He'd spent the early evening trolling the streets of Montparnasse for a likely piece of young flesh (he'd long since stopped sleeping with his assistant, too much moaning about his bad breath). Tucked under his arm in an oversized envelope was the manuscript of *Brown Java*, which he'd begun reading at the office. From four to seven, the staff, his assistant, and the press officer had heard him crying out in enthusiasm, but no one was overly alarmed, as they knew the boss was usually half drunk by 3:30. Just a month earlier they'd heard him howling in ecstasy—fueled by gin and Munich beer mixed with vodka, the good old Germano-Russian entente—as he read through the manuscript of a novel that, when later perused by his sober colleagues, proved perfectly mediocre and utterly unpublishable.

A bit after eight, then, wanting to celebrate the modest success of *Home of the Wanking Class*, the publisher had headed off to stroll the streets around La Coupole, the manuscript under his arm, with a bookmark to remind him where he'd left off.

He preferred the old-school approach to picking up beautiful women. To every such creature he met in the street, he gave a deep, unambiguous stare. They almost always laughed and wiggled their bottoms, unless a guy was with them, of course, in which case they watched their steps. He finally found a taker on the Rue Delambre, a former stewardess turned mail-order umbrella merchant, who made ends meet by the grace of what nature was kind enough to place below her navel. He took her out for some couscous, then moved on to one of those cabarets where for a hundred sous an hour you sit there bored stiff, dutifully laughing it up all the same . . . one of the last such places to be found in the City of Light. Three-quarters gone, he never did manage to screw her, a condom's not always as easy to pull on as a sock, and your lady isn't always overjoyed to watch you spend ten or twelve minutes playing slingshot with the thing. He sent her on her way in front of the Miramar a little before two in the morning; then—his mind not sufficiently clear to go get his car, which he'd left he didn't quite remember where, maybe in a garage near Saint-Germain-des-Prés, a bit far for someone who tends to walk backwards—he hailed a taxi and got himself delivered back to L'Haÿ-les-Roses. A rather full night, but he'd managed to keep hold of the manuscript. No doubt taking it for the new edition of the phone book her swain had picked up from the post office on his way over, the girl hadn't gone poking her nose into it. Back at home, another bottle of whiskey, the seventh or eighth of the day. Alcohol was getting the upper hand again. He'd cut it out a year and a half before, on the advice of the TV show *All About Health*, but now it was all starting up anew. Alcohol had cost him his job as a literary critic many long years ago, when he'd taken to penning encomiums for beach books, novelized TV shows, and other such turkeys, while simultaneously, in his muddled way, blasting and lambasting Hemingway, Restif de la Bretonne, Maupassant's stories, Gabriel Chevallier's *Fear*, the latest Faulkner, Jarry, and others, cruelly skewering Raymond Roussel, holding Gogol up to ridicule, and trying to prove—via six long articles in the *Figaro Littéraire* and *Arts-Spectacles*—that Madame Hanska was Balzac's ghost writer for the last three years of his life.

Foregoing his bed, he lolled on his living-room carpet, racing feverishly through the manuscript, expressing his admiration in onomatopoetic bellows. On reaching page 516, thoroughly drunk, he staggered painfully to his feet. He fell back to the floor, summoned his resolve, and crawled across the room to rest his head on a cushion that had slipped off a sofa. Having accomplished this feat, he realized that for some time he'd been reading not *Dancing the Brown Java* but Céline's *Rigadoon*—not quite the same dance: three beats to the measure in one, just two in the other—which his frolicsome arm, aiming for a fresh bottle of wine, must have knocked off a bookshelf. Realizing his error, he spat out a vulgarity, sent the Céline flying, and wriggled back across the floor to the manuscript, arm outstretched; but, with his eyes mulishly refusing to focus, it was Léon Bloy's *Le Désespéré* that his fingers now snagged. He opened the book and read a few paragraphs, hiccupping, before realizing it didn't sound quite like the novel Gastinel had given him. Finally he succeeded in getting hold of the manuscript, found his place, and went back to reading. Just to be sure, he looked at the first page and read the title scrawled out by the behemoth. Very good, he said to himself, let's continue. *Rigadoon* wasn't too bad, I read that a long time ago and don't remember it very well, but this too, this *Java*, is really quite remarkable. Let's read on . . .

A few more hiccups, a few more little cries marking the pleasure of a reader who's finally found something worth reading and thoroughly enjoys it even if he's had a bit too much to drink; then, at around five in the morning, leaving the manuscript aside, he dragged himself to his study and took his old .33 from a desk drawer.

A few minutes after five, his neighbors, a retired couple, were brutally wrenched from their slumbers by a series of gunshots fired into the garden. Knowing Malgo as they did, they were aware of his habit of celebrating his editorial pleasures and triumphs—when he discovered a good manuscript, for example, or when he'd got wind of some especially promising sales figures—by firing a gun, just as Gaston Leroux did each time he finished a book. The neighbors, Monsieur and Madame Poindrot, both of them retired from the world of education, weren't, therefore, particularly alarmed. No point calling the police. Nothing serious. No rowdies to fear, no brigands. Besides, the gunshots stopped almost immediately, just one quick little salvo, scarcely more than a backfiring motorcycle. There were only three bullets in Malgodin's weapon. Oh yes: he'd fired the other nine a few weeks before, on seeing the first sales figures for *Home of the Wanking Class*. "He must have found a good writer," said Monsieur Poindrot, who'd taken up reading when he began watching *Apostrophes*. "Maybe a new *Jalna*, who knows. Good for him!" "Well, personally, I think he went a little too far, with his *Home of the* . . . you know what," grumbled his wife.

Thoroughly bombed, Malgodin closed the window and staggered back to the living room, seeing rats and scorpions in every corner. He collapsed into an armchair and picked up the manuscript again.

"Ah, no," he mumbled three minutes later, "that's the illustrated edition of *The Little Prince*."

He'd only realized this on encountering the first pictures, after a few pages of unbroken print. He located the manuscript again and tried to read the last thirty or forty pages without his glasses—he must have lost them in the hallway as he was creeping into the study.

"Superb!" he hiccupped. "Pure class! U-*hic!*-nique! Hic! Bril-*hic!*-liant! And all those details on-*hic!*-on the Oc-*hic!*-cu-*hic!*-pa-tion! Wow! Diabol-*hic!*-al! But why didn't that imbecile . . ."

As if semi-paralyzed, he worked his way into the kitchen on his elbows, miraculously opened the fridge without toppling back-wards, and fished out a cold Tuborg. He set the manuscript on the Formica table and tried to sit down before it, his legs rubbery, his buttocks very nearly missing the seat. He labored to decipher the next pages. His pupils were refusing to converge again. He couldn't understand a word—or at least not many words—but this wasn't new: he'd been more or less in a stupor since page 200, when the whiskey began to take hold. Not very professional, reading a man-uscript in this state, he'd told himself in a brief flash of lucidity. Pages 593, 594 . . . 597 . . .

"Shit! I must have skipped 595 and 596, yes I did! *Hic!* Where'd they go? Ah! here they are!"

The letters were whirling and dipping before his eyes; somehow the pages seemed to have mutated into the planks of a dance floor.

"Jesus, it's like a remake of *They Shoot Horses, Don't They?* Come on, let's get back to it . . . But why didn't that imbecile author—who's a genius, let's not lose sight of the facts! I may be plastered, but I can see that clearly enough—why didn't that imbecile author submit this to Gallim's or Charpentier, Furne or Ollendorff, *hic*? Why me? Could this be some kind of trap? It's true, all Gastinel wanted was my opinion . . . he didn't ask me to publish the thing. He can't re-ally be the author, can he? Unreal! But if I go to him squealing with enthusiasm, he'll . . . No, he hasn't got the cash to publish this. Out of the question. It's mine! If he refuses, I'll put a slug in him! That'll give Le Papyrus some badly needed publicity!"

Around 5:45 he attempted to take a cold shower, which sobered him up a bit, then successfully brewed some very strong coffee and called Gastinel. It was two minutes to six. Pulled from his bed, the blimp scratched his buttocks through his nightshirt as Malgodin raved that he finally knew how Robert Denoël must have felt on that memorable night in April 1932 when he first plunged into the manuscript of Céline's *Journey*.

"A discovery of the same order," Malgodin affirmed thickly. "And I say that with all the friendly sincerity you inspire in me, dear friend."

"It's true, then? You're sure you're not mistaken? You're not just trying to make me happy?" exclaimed Gastinel, breathless.

"I'm choosing my words carefully, Gast-*hic!*-nel. It's a . . . *hic!* masterpiece. And believe me, it's best this be published by a small press . . . I know . . . *hic!* some big-time publishers who . . . *hic!* might very well . . . *hic!* shoot it down . . . put it away in the . . . *hic!* drawer . . . for fear of displeasing some. . . *hic!* of their . . . *hic!* big stars. You've no . . . *hic!* idea of the kind of things that . . . *hic!* go on in this fucked-up . . . *hic!* publishi-*hic!*-ng game! I've seen it . . . *hic!* all!"

"No, not quite all, I bet," thought Gastinel, chuckling and faintly terrified.

"I give you my . . . *hic!* word . . . hand on . . . *hic!* heart."

"Shit, he's got the damn hiccups again," thought the flesh-mountain. "Not exactly reassuring. I got Malgodin the world-class lush for a reader, not Malgodin the serious publisher. Oh, well . . . I'm going to go for it all the same. Let's hope he had a few clear-headed moments somewhere in there, at least."

"And now, would you be so kind as to tell me whose it is?" begged Malgodin.

"Whose it is?"

"You know what I mean! Who wrote it!"

"Well . . ."

Gastinel hesitated. Now he had to act fast. Double-cross Dochin, quick-smart, bundle him up and put him in the trunk and take him for a good, long ride . . . And hope it would be the start of the literary scoop of the century.

"Well?" Malgodin cried. "What's the matter, lost your voice?"

"We have to meet," said Gastinel.

"Look, who wrote this goddamn mother of a manuscript? Are you going to tell me or aren't you?" the addled, exasperated publisher hissed.

"I'm going to piss him off if I keep this up too long," Gastinel realized.

"The thing is . . . There are two authors," he said calmly. "And I'm one of them."

"What is this, some kind of joke?"

"Not at all, Malgodin."

"What, a real-life collaborator? Your book's full of them, after all!"

"No. He hadn't even been born when the Germans came in."

"Who?"

"My collaborator."

"What you're telling me is about as clear as your manuscript."

"Where can I find you, Malgodin?"

"Let's meet . . . I don't know . . . at the offices of Le Papyrus?"

"As soon as possible, Malgodin."

"Right away. I'll see you in an hour. We'll have the place to ourselves, the staff won't be in yet."

Malgodin put up a furious struggle when Gastinel tried to take the manuscript from his hands. Pages went flying all over the room, and the two men had to get down on all fours to gather them up and put them back in order.

"I'm warning you!" bawled the drunken publisher. "You're not giving this to anyone else! To some son of a bitch who'll try and cut it by a quarter, who'll lose his nerve about all the Occupation stuff! I know it's good! I know it! You hear me? Because at one point I opened it up and for three or four minutes thought I was still reading Céline!"

"Excuse me?"

Exhausted, the blimp had dropped into an armchair.

"*Rigadoon,*" said Malgodin.

"Oh come on, what are you talking about? Are you drunk? Uh . . . no, excuse me, that's not what I meant to say . . . What's the matter, didn't you sleep well last night?"

"Sleep, with *Brown Java* right there in front of me? Blasphemy! No . . . See, I'd dipped into Céline's last book without realizing it, and for a while I thought I was reading *Brown Java,* and then when I went back to the manuscript I forgot I wasn't reading *Rigadoon* anymore, that I'd changed books, kind of like a sleepwalker gets out of bed and winds up in his living room without realizing it. You follow me? So obviously *Brown Java* is the work of a great writer."

"I don't understand a word you're saying," said Gastinel, who was nonetheless giving some thought to the publisher's remark. Indeed, was that confusion—*Rigadoon / Brown Java*—not a sort of proof that, despite the alcoholic fog clouding his brain, Malgodin had sensed he was reading something very unusual, something out of the ordinary, no doubt a truly great novel?

"This book is for Le Papyrus!" Malgodin thundered.

"Calm down, Malgodin. Yes, it's yours, I give you my word. But I need to think about all this, and I want to reread my work."

"Your work? You've got to be kidding! Come on, you didn't write this."

"We did it together, the two of us. Tirelessly, I'll have you know. That's how it is. Nothing you can do about it. There are two authors. Me and . . . you'll know the other name soon enough. I want you to calm down and show some faith in me. Don't worry, you'll be the publisher of *Dancing the Brown Java*."

"And who's the other guy? Is he famous?"

"N . . . no. He's an unknown."

"Not a ghost writer, I hope?"

"Not at all. This was a team effort, plain and simple. Like Erckmann and Chatrian . . . The Rosny Brothers . . . You get it? Give me a few days, Malgodin. I promise, the book is yours."

"Listen, you bastard! If you're screwing with me, you'll be sorry. Believe me, I'm capable of anything. If a book like this gets snatched out from under me, things are going to go very hard for you, my dear Gastinel. I'm half-dead from alcohol, as you know . . . my liver rotted away, this far from being a slab of hamburger . . . I'm sixty-five years old, and I don't have much left to lose. I pity you if this thing ends up going to somebody else!"

"Come on, Malgodin, calm down. As a modest businessman and a disinterested publisher, I give you my word: you'll get the manuscript. For Le Papyrus. But I have to talk it over with my friend, after all, don't you think? What'll he say if I agree without asking him? Suppose he refused to sign the contract you're going to offer us? Hmm? How'd you like that?"

"For the contract, we'll . . ."

"Hang on. We'll see about that when the time comes. We're not there yet. First of all, I have to meet with my co-author."

"But why isn't he out flogging the book for himself? Or at least doing his share?"

"He . . . he lives a long way from Paris. It's hard for him to get out."

"Is he sick?"

"Not at all. But since I'm here in Paris, we thought it made more sense if I . . . In short, I'm the one doing the legwork."

"And you haven't given it to anyone else?"

"But it's brand-new, Malgodin. Fresh off the vine. Just been typed up. You're the first, I swear. Besides, I never asked you to publish it, you must admit. I just wanted your opinion. But since you got back to me so quickly, and since you think so highly of our work, it would be a pretty low trick if I . . . if I turned around and offered it to one of the big boys. I'm very fond of you, Malgodin, oh yes I am, I am . . . *Dancing the Brown Java* is all yours. I'm sure you'll go the extra mile for this book . . . Euloge."

"Thanks, Charles. I have to tell you, hand on heart, in all my years in the game, I've never read anything like it. Not even when I was the great critic you remember me as—so feared, so influential, so respected. Nothing close. This is going to make a splash as big as the *Journey*. Believe me, all those alcoholic vapors made a sort of prism in my brain, allowing me to see in color—in color, I say!—what was already a pure wonder in black and white. I had before me, my dear Gastinel, at once a book and a film. Amazing! Alcohol is sometimes a brother to art."

But here Gastinel was forced to abandon certain of his illusions. He'd just realized that Malgodin, appearances to the contrary, was still in the grips of the vast quantities of rotgut he'd downed in the last twenty-four hours. A word about those appearances. One sometimes witnesses such miracles; it's rare, but—in the case of truly world-class alcoholics—not unheard-of. Having drunk their fill and more, they can sometimes put up a surprisingly good front, often with some brio, creating the illusion of perfect lucidity. They can keep this up for an hour or two, sometimes more, their posture upright, their speech coherent. Such was Malgodin's case, from the beginning of his tête-à-tête with Gastinel at Le Papyrus. But a rope stretched too far always breaks in the end, and so it is, too, with the fleeting sobriety of a dipsomaniac still sodden with whiskey, gin, Pernod, or rough, dark Corbières. Having repeated, "This is going to make a splash as big as the *Journey*," and adding, "I assure you I read the whole thing," Malgodin abruptly slumped forward and somersaulted onto the carpet, dead to the world (it should be said that after showering and ingesting some strong coffee he'd succumbed to temptation and cracked open a bottle of Smirnoff). Discouraged, the former tripe butcher shoved the inanimate rummy aside with one foot, stowed the manuscript under his arm, and hurried out of the publishing house—reflecting that Malgodin probably would have been happier running a bar . . .

26   Gastinel's Designs

Gastinel entered his office at 22 Rue du Pressoir and began building castles in Spain. No question about it, Malgodin's pottedness notwithstanding, his doubts had now been swept thoroughly away, and he was firmly convinced *Brown Java* had the makings of a massive hit. As promised, Malgodin would take over as publisher.

With the manuscript in front of him, the behemoth began to reflect, twisting his little nose—an exceedingly cute little nose, like a nonpareil atop a gargantuan cake, quite a contrast with the monstrous bulk of his person, martyrized as he was by the unrelenting assaults of a merciless adiposity. He'd read the thing himself, after all, and by God he knew how to tell good books from bad! If he'd asked for Malgodin's opinion, it was essentially to confirm what he already knew. Now he was going to have to play his cards very carefully. First of all, reread the book from start to finish and get it thoroughly drilled into his head—for now his mind was made up: he was going to palm himself off as the co-author. Leap aboard that gravy train and set sail for parts unknown!

He opened the manuscript and began to read through it again. He reread very quickly; his eyes hit the last line around seven that evening. Start to finish, at one go. Sustained only by a bit of beer and two or three Nescafés. Now his brain was overheating, and his belly furiously growling. That raft of pages was as good as gold. Watch your step, now, no slip-ups. It's true, a little press like Malgodin's was better, was preferable. Too risky going with the big boys. They always try to dig up all possible info on the author before they start throwing their money around, and then if the book's a hit you've got the publicists and reporters on your ass, each more curious than the last, all asking the same indiscreet questions, up to and including who shares your bed. And he didn't want anyone getting the idea he was just some interloper who hadn't written one line of the thing. A little one-and-a-half-bit press like Malgodin's wouldn't be so inquisitive, wouldn't go sticking their nose where it doesn't belong, we're delighted to accept your manuscript, here's your check, good-bye monsieur, and good day to you. Later on, if there were TV shows and other promotional stunts to be done, Gastinel would just have to watch himself, use his brains, brazen it out to the end. With a big publisher you feel less free, more constrained, a whole bunch of people making you their personal concern, and then what chance have you got of eluding the exclusive contract, you become the big book magnates' plaything, their prey, they shepherd you, they own you, very gently, it's true, with all the trimmings, but still you're tied down with no hope of escape, it's just like being married, they take you to dinner in chic little restaurants, sometimes they even want you to be their pals, not just business partners but friends, in short, good-bye to your incognito. Malgodin was ideal, no question. That was a damn smart move, asking him for his take on the manuscript. He could more or less count on some breathing room with a nobody like that, who, furthermore, would now owe him—him and Dochin, because Dochin was going to stay in the picture, of course, no question of dropping him, don't make me laugh!—who would now owe him virtually everything: fame, money, success . . . A big publisher has other steeds in his stable, all perfectly capable of hitting the jackpot on their own, and even if you're an absolute ace, he never has to rely solely on you. Whereas with a small-timer like Malgodin . . .

"I can do with him what I will," the gargantuan Gastinel told himself.

At 9:00, Gastinel tucks the manuscript under his arm and goes out for a bite to eat. For a good, hard think too. You can never think hard enough when you're planning a dirty trick, he told himself, especially one that looks suspiciously like the dirty trick of a lifetime.

He walks through the streets of Paris. May is nearing its end. What a pleasure to inhale the not-too-polluted air, a delight to bask in the unusually balmy spring temperatures. He walks confidently, almost gracefully, a sort of colossal balloon being wafted over the sand by a very slight sea breeze—the kind they have at Cabourg, for instance. A fat man full of joie de vivre, as certain passersby observed, a lover of fine books who's discovered a doozy and knows just what he's going to do with it. He advances ever onward, his stomach extending prow-like before him . . . The Canal Saint-Martin . . . the Place de la République . . . the Grands Boulevards . . . the Place de la Bourse . . . Ever onward he walks, waddling slightly, like a corpulent duck, his dainty—for his feet are in fact surprisingly small—his dainty light-brown pointed shoes hammering the asphalt, his voluminous trousers—almost wide enough to hold two Morris columns—flapping like twin gonfalons around his hamlike legs . . . Here's the Palais-Royal . . . He crosses the Seine by the Pont du Carrousel, and soon, lost in thought, his gait still as carefree as ever, he winds up in the Latin Quarter. It's nearing half past ten. He enters a packed trattoria on the Boul' Mich'. A handful of diners look on as he sits down, squeezing his fat stomach behind the table with some difficulty, he pays them no mind, he's used to it, fat people never go unnoticed in public places, often all eyes are glued to their improbable rotundity, and now, downing his osso-buco à la milanaise, he once again pores over the manuscript, picking out passages at random, singling out a sentence that leaves him gurgling with delight. Oh! the hellcat! What a style! He thinks some more, chewing his spiced veal, and then, having mopped his plate with a piece of bread till it fairly gleamed, having licked the sauce from his plump fingers, waste not want not, he lights a cigarillo and resumes his Machiavellian ruminations. Nothing to do for the moment but wait. Not a word to Dochin. He's got to lay the groundwork. Indispensable. You can't just spring something like that on a person, or there's no telling what might come of it. No, for the moment, just wait. He'd promised Dochin a quick answer. Still, it's not unusual for a publisher to leave you hanging for months and months, all his assurances notwithstanding. Dochin will just have to wait, it won't kill him. Should Dochin call, lose patience, and become a problem, he could be told something like, "I'm very hesitant, my friend . . . I asked my concierge and my butcher to read it, and they liked it well enough, but said neither yes nor no, so I gave it to my neighbor the night before last. Don't worry, these are very solid people . . . more or less old-fashioned, you see, not entirely acquainted with contemporary mores . . . Don't worry, your manuscript's in no danger."

He sinks his little spoon into the rum baba just set before him by the waiter, and continues his imaginary chat with Dochin: ". . . your manuscript is in absolutely no danger . . . but you see, dear friend, the Gastinel method is to seek the advice of the man in the street . . . poll the average reader before giving the author a response . . . not like the big publishers do . . . Go ask Furne or Gallim's if they bother with that!"

He knocks back an espresso, tucks his briefcase under one arm, and goes out for a stroll on the boulevard, heading toward the Place Maubert, a nice tranquil spot after nightfall. Keep thinking, don't stop now. Let's see. How to turn this book to our advantage? And little by little—he can't help it, even after that lovely dinner—his belly once again begins churning with rancor, like a savage tempest tossing a tiny lifeboat this way and that. A cold rage boils up inside him, climbs right up to his throat. Jealousy. Yes, he's jealous of the author. For doing something he himself never could. So yes, jump aboard that train and hold on for all you're worth. If there's success to be had, then yes, damn it all! be a part of it! don't dither! He glimpses the opportunity of a lifetime. If he doesn't act, he'll always be a failure, a nobody. So it's decided.

Walking alongside the fence of the Jardin des Plantes, he thinks of the perfect solution. Wild beasts on one side of the iron bars, and a beast of a very particular sort—Gastinel—on the other. On one side of the bars, growls and roars; on the other, deep concentration. And like the true man of action he is—no flabby bottom, no bulging belly can hold back Charles Gastinel!—he makes up his mind, doesn't waffle, doesn't go on chewing it over. He's got a little plan all ready, and it's just the ticket. Good thing he's such a perfect nonentity in the literary world. There may be some who'll know he's a publisher—a flea-bitten two-bit waste-of-space publisher, granted, but a publisher all the same—but nobody knows him as a writer . . . for the excellent reason that he's never written a word, he doesn't have a shred of talent. So he's never sent in so much as a single submission. No old reader's reports in any file cabinet anywhere on a certain Gastinel. He's an unknown. He likes it that way, oh so very much, because wouldn't some people find it a bit odd if a guy who's spent years submitting illegible piles of tripe to all the publishers in Paris suddenly, just like that, miraculously, published something . . . well, let's say something a little better? The idea keeps coursing through his head. A no-talent well known to the editorial boards who suddenly . . . Extraordinary, my dear Watson! Whereas an unknown, an author who's never published a line, who's never written . . . he might just . . . well, appear, all of a sudden . . . burst onto the scene . . . that could work, that's perfectly plausible. A very simple man turning to literature at the age of sixty-three, well now! that's a beautiful thing, isn't it, after all? Why shouldn't merit go hand in hand with age, just this once? Especially if it's the merit of a real writer! A beginner, a brand new man, not a trace of compromising ink in his past.

It's in the bag, our blimp told himself with a smile, starting across the Pont de Sully to hail a taxi somewhere near Bastille.

27　The Murder

October '95. Back to square one again, after *Book Culture* and the blow-up by the Panthéon. Gastinel's Mercedes is still racing down the highway toward Poitiers, ferrying Dochin back to the Corrèze and the Halte du Bon Accueil. As the hulk drives, he replays the next step in the process that would spring the trap on the chump who'd brought him his manuscript that Monday, May 29, 1995. He can see it all. Like it was yesterday! Oh, did he put one over on old Dochin! Five months ago! My, oh my! And how fast it all happened!

The back-alley publisher owns a small farmhouse outside Carrouges, in Normandy, not far from the Forest of Écouves, inherited from a paternal aunt and currently being remodeled. A vacation home, just like a bourgeois. Wasting no time, he invites Dochin out for the weekend. A pleasant, quiet spot to talk over the manuscript, out in the fresh country air, the pastoral tranquility, and nature is so lovely in the middle of spring . . . We'll have a nice relaxed chat.

After a protracted phone conversation concerning his tottering publishing business and a few questions of a private nature, the tiny-nosed behemoth telephoned Dochin at his hotel to give him his "yes" on *Dancing the Brown Java*.

"Oh yes, yes, dear friend, I assure you, this is no joke, I'm telling you straight out, you've written an extraordinary book here. Do you know" (here he's stealing Malgodin's idea), "for a few seconds, as I lay in bed devouring your book, I took myself for Robert Denoël on that great night in April 1932, lost in the manuscript of *Journey to the End of the Night*, which is assuredly the novel of the century. Don't take it amiss, dear Dochin, if I place yours just a little lower than that . . . but all the same, that's a hell of a place to be, you must agree! A discovery of the same order" (he remembers the words of Malgo-the-elbow-bender with admirable clarity), "and I say that with all the friendly sincerity you inspire in me, dear friend."

On the other end of the line, Dochin, incredulous, his stupefaction mingled with joy—but nevertheless remembering, in deepest befuddlement, Urbain Langillier's verdict—accepted the blimp's invitation at once.

"I'll pick you up at your hotel Saturday morning. Nine o'clock sharp. Will that work? Perfect. My car's seen better days, but we'll make it there all right."

On Friday night, Gastinel sets his deeply immoral plan into motion.

But first let's get back to Dochin. No sooner had he learned the good news—Gastinel's acceptance of the manuscript—than he called Céline, who'd asked him to let her know the moment he heard.

On the phone, the motel owner sounded positively radiant:

"This is a great day for you, kid. But you know, I'm not surprised. You're wrong to get yourself so worked up. As you see! Just like I told you! Old Céline knows what she's talking about, doesn't she now? And what about those tarot cards? I'm telling you, those little darlings never lie! So, you're going to stick around Paris a while?"

"Well, yes . . . I have to . . . How's business at La Halte?"

"Not much going on at the moment. We do have one couple, they showed up night before last. From Lille. Getting on in years.

Very upstanding people. He's a *notaire*. Poor man suffers from meteorism, and has to keep the windows wide open at all times. They noticed that right away at the Grand Cerf Royal in Guéret. So is this Gastinel nice?"

"He seems like a *bon vivant*. Say, Céline . . ."

"What is it, lamb? Why, my little sheep sounds so worried all of a sudden . . ."

"I've been thinking about something, Céline. I wonder if it wouldn't have been better to give it to a big publisher after all. Charpentier, Furne, or Gallim's . . . It's true, in the end . . . If Gastinel thought it was so great . . . Maybe there's still time, I mean, I haven't signed anything yet. What do you think?"

"Out of the question, my boy. It's just not done. In business, you've got to mind your manners. Otherwise it'll come back and bite you in the behind. You can't do that to this man, as long as he's been fair with you. In the first place, it's too late, Jean-Rémi. You've found a taker, you can't let him go. A bird in the hand, my friend. Suppose—it doesn't seem likely, but they can be hard to figure sometimes—suppose Gallim's or one of the other big houses said no, wouldn't you look like a perfect fool going back to see Gastinel, announcing you've changed your mind? Let's not forget how Benjamin Crémieux turned up his nose at *Journey*! Imagine people making the same face at your *Brown Java*, my son. No, no, my boy, stick with this one. If the book really is good, it'll sell, even if it's put out by a minor press. Now, what about the contract? When do you get it? Did he say? Careful now, don't sign just anything."

"He mentioned it, vaguely . . . Oh! just two words . . . I have to wait a few more days. I think he wants us to talk it all over, somewhere we won't be disturbed. He invited me out to his house in Normandy for a nice, long chat. What do you think?"

"Go ahead, sweetie . . . The fresh air will do you good. Don't ever say no to your publisher."

"Your tarot cards don't see me going on *Apostrophes,* by any chance, do they? I mean . . . on *Book Culture.*"

"We'll come to that when we come to it, billy goat. That's not the most important thing."

"Except for the critics. So they can see what kind of guy I am."

"Do as you like, but you know, real critics never trouble themselves with the author, they only care about what he's written. The text, and nothing but the text!"

"My parents would be so happy to see me on TV. And the neighbors! They'd finally realize I'm not such a loser after all."

"I understand, my little bear cub. But don't forget, the great ones never show themselves . . ."

"The great what?"

"The great writers, for heaven's sake! Because that's what you are, lamb, like it or not. No, the great writers never show themselves. Their work's all they need, and they know it. Look at Gracq. And Beckett . . . Félicien Marceau . . . Anouilh . . . Marcel Aymé . . . They never felt the need to go making a spectacle of themselves on TV . . . Or Montherlant or Genet either. And old André Dhôtel must have got lost in the corridors. Writers of that scale don't have to go blowing hot air into the cameras. And I'm sure a Mirbeau or a Poe or a Barbey D'Aurevilly wouldn't have either. Balzac would have . . . he was the social type. As for Dochin, he'll do as he pleases. It's up to him whether he wants to show his pretty little fox face to the public. In any case, hats off, duck!"

"For what?"

"Boy, you really didn't sleep well, did you? Hats off for your book, of course, your success! I told you they'd like it. Like I said, they'd damn well better!"

Dochin felt a strange sensation on hearing these words, and once again saw his protectress's face, her almost terrifying demeanor as she spat out that semi-threat, just before reading his tarot—"And if by chance they don't like it, they'll be kicking themselves. Black and blue!"—along with those other words he'd found so peculiar, those words like a viper's hiss: ". . . Death's not in the cards . . . At least . . . not for you." What was she up to? he wondered. How far was she planning to go to defend him? "Hats off for your success!" She could be so weirdly fanatical, with her endless compliments, so utterly over the top at times, for in spite of everything that had just landed in his lap he still didn't quite believe in his book; his doubts came flooding back after that first flush of overjoyed surprise, which was even now beginning to fade. And now here comes that insidious black dog of doubt once again . . . Could this hand, his hand, really have written a novel that other people considered a great book? Was it possible that a man as intelligent, as serious, as competent as Urbain Langillier had got it so wrong? And wasn't this Gastinel just a cut-rate publisher of the lowest magnitude? Did he really have the talent, the indispensable sixth sense required to judge a work of fiction with some degree of certainty? Where was this all going to lead?

Dochin finally shrugged his shoulders: after all, what did it matter? If they want to publish *Dancing the Brown Java,* let them publish it. Was he going to be struck dead on the spot just because one more shitty book happened to show up in the shops, even if he did write the damn thing? He was never going to be a writer who really matters, so what did he have to lose?

"Come back quick to La Halte, sweetie, and we'll have a nice celebration . . ."

Crazy old woman! Nutcases, all of them. Céline . . . Odette . . . Gastinel . . . What have I got myself into? he wondered.

"A great big party, Jean-Rémi. A blowout! Odette will make us a nice little old-fashioned beef burgundy like only she knows how . . . She uses Cahors wine . . . You'll love it. Hugs and kisses from your mommy, pirate. Keep me informed. Hickies all over your little Balzacian hands."

That woman is clearly going out of her gourd, he thought as he hung up the phone.

Friday night, Gastinel sets his deranged plan into motion. Now that he's decided how to work it, he hasn't a moment to lose. Henceforth, time is of the essence. On the phone Dochin had assured him, without being asked, that nobody else had seen the manuscript, no other publisher. "You're the first," he told him proudly, probably aiming to make a good impression. He's a coward, that one, a real solid-gold yellowbelly, thought Gastinel, no way would he have given it to anyone else, not Charpentier, not Gallim's, not Hetzel, not anybody . . . You don't need a little bird to tell you that . . . He's like putty, and I've got him in the palm of my hand, one little squeeze and he'll cave, become anything I please . . . "Have you ever written anything before, Monsieur Dochin? Anything publishable, I mean?" "Oh! A crime novel . . . nothing to write home about. *Mayhem in Les Minguettes.*" "Long ago?" "Seven, eight years." "Under your own name?" "No, I used a pseudonym: Jean Rem." "Who put it out?" "It was part of a little collection called *Suburban Jungle.* Black Hand Press. They're not around anymore." On Friday night, then, Gastinel sets his plan into motion. He heads for a dance at the Salle Cadet, frequented primarily by serving girls. Without difficulty, he picks up a fourteen-year-old Breton lass, Maryvonne Le Goff. A charming little creature, auburn hair, eyes full of merriment, face sprinkled with freckles, the sort of girl you might see on TV doing commercials for Ireland and its fine Irish beer, very sweet, not the slightest bit difficult. He makes quite an impression. It's true, he has a big belly and a drooping derrière, but luckily he's got an oversize personality, too. A gift of the gab like his opens many doors, and besides he's dressed just *comme il faut*, vestimentarily correct, nice and refined, no feather in his ass, just a carnation in his buttonhole. He almost looked like that old terrorist Carlos, something of the TV personality about him, it did something for the girls at the ball, they liked that, he noticed it straight off, it got them going, and then sometimes it's useful not to be too prepossessing a physical specimen, people kind of take pity on you, they want to treat you nice, try to convince you you're just like everyone else, show you they're not going to reject you, today's young people are very kind that way, very humane, it wasn't like that at all in his day, he who was born in '32, in short, young Maryvonne fell almost swooning into his arms, easy as pie, to the sound of the accordion, all thanks to my big mouth and my flab, he told himself. And then the sweet talk started up. "You look a little like Mathilda May . . . I love Brittany . . . the menhirs . . . the buckwheat crêpes . . . the Morlaix viaduct . . . What do you like on TV? I'll bet you're crazy about Narcy and Foucaud, I'm partial to Mireille Dumas myself . . ." etc., a little more bullshit like that and the deal is done.

Discreetly, he leaves with the kid—who got off the bus in Paris only ten days before—after assuring himself she'd come to the dance alone, without friends or chaperone. Just as easily, he lures her up to his apartment on the Rue Ramponneau and very gently has his way with her, don't think the man can't fuck just because he's got a king-size paunch, people always find a way. The next morning, Saturday, he invites Maryvonne into his slightly shaky old Talbot

Murena, heads for the Gare d'Austerlitz, and picks up the Limousin joker in front of his hotel. And then it's off to Carrouges. He quickly handles the introductions: "Monsieur Dochin, a writer friend of mine. Maryvonne, the angel of my life." The kid will be spending the weekend with them. Or part of the weekend, at least. Gastinel's hoodwinked her good, she takes him for some sort of showbiz pooh-bah, thinks he's going to give her her big break, just a naïve kid from the sticks, there are still a few of those left, fortunately for swine like me, thought our wily blimp, who, for all his blubber, had displayed not the slightest awkwardness in the Salle Cadet as he danced the waltz, tangoing as lithely as a South American Michelin man in spite of his sumo-wrestler loins and the many pounds of lard jiggling on his abdomen.

The house lies at some distance from Carrouges, secluded, nestled up against a little woods of white birch trees, no obligation to be sociable, you can live there like hermits. The only neighbors are blackbirds. Perfect. The girl's absence from Paris? No problem. Her parents live in Rosporden, where her father's a mason. She has a little place on the Avenue Mozart, lives alone, isn't scheduled to be back at work till Tuesday at noon, her bosses are a couple of industrialists. It all works out very neatly. Saturday night, Gastinel pours Dochin drink after drink, talking literature all the while . . . Turgenev . . . Mallarmé . . . Eugène Brieux . . . Daniel d'Arthez . . . and so on . . . Drink after drink after drink . . . Merrily they celebrate the acceptance of the manuscript of the decade. Naturally delicate in his constitution, the writer's already feeling a bit woozy. Gastinel knocks them back right along with him, but he can hold it a bit better. He's not afraid of downing a few—a few quarts, that is. He picked up the knack in the tripe business, lot of boozing in that guild. They encourage the girl to keep up with them (meantime, in keeping with the spirit of the occasion, she's kindly consented to make them some dinner: chicken chasseur with girolle mushrooms). The booze flows freely. Wine, and not the cheap who-knows-where-it-came-from stuff either, no, the real thing. Whiskey. Cider. Vodka. Calvados. Almost like being in Malgodin's office. A fiesta. A great lovefest between the author, his publisher, and the serving girl, in the spirit of fraternity between intellectuals and laborers, all workers together, the only thing missing was a union organizer to keep score.

The wine flows, the spirits . . . The chicken is now cooked well beyond perfection, but they'll get to that later.

Glass after glass is drained.

And here begins a night of pure hell.

"The things you have to do to become a writer!" thought Gastinel as the "festivities" wore on.

The girl's dead drunk. They strip her bare. Gastinel takes her once again. No condom. But AIDS is the least of her worries. Such a sweet little thing. Dochin doesn't hold back. Who would have thought a constipated twat like him could manage it? He took the fat man's place, still warm. And look at him go! Ramrod stiff, snootful or no. "What the fuck am I doing here?" was, at one point in the evening, his favorite sentence, a real broken record . . .

And so on, into the night.

"Aren't you going the Châteauroux way?" asked Dochin.

Lost in his thoughts, the driver makes no reply. The Mercedes speeds toward Châtelleraut and Poitiers, where it will pick up the highway to Limoges.

Ye gods, what a night! And all that just to go play show and tell with Eyebrows, as if going on the tube somehow made you smarter!

Naturally, just as the publisher hoped, the vile festivities in Carrouges soon degenerated into a most sordid circus. Pure shock porn. Broken, panting, the young servant succumbs to a nervous fit; sobbing, half-naked, she flees through the sleeping countryside. She sets off in the wrong direction, strays into a cul-de-sac, and hurries back toward the main road, giving Gastinel time to react. The two men hurriedly pull on their trousers. Gastinel pushes the brilliant novelist along from behind. The two losers climb into the Talbot, the three-hundred pounder at the wheel. They give chase, tracking the girl like a wild boar. And here things take a horrific turn. Rolling along at twenty-five miles an hour with its high beams on, the car pins the adolescent against the wall of an outbuilding on Gastinel's farm. A wrenching cry. No neighbors close by, the village is almost a half mile away, all the better. Two or three more screams . . . Moans, really . . . Seeing the girl still moving, the driver violently throws his vehicle into reverse, then floors it and roars forward again. Rams the wall a second time. Another cry. A shriek that rips through the night. Reverse again. Forward again. A great jolt rattles the Talbot. Another cry. Muffled this time, just a whimper. Then nothing more. Silence once again reigns over the deserted countryside. No movement now from Maryvonne, or what used to be Maryvonne. Then, little by little, she begins to slide toward the ground, slower than a slug, a trickle, it's painful to watch, she's virtually glued to the wall. As if to finish the job, Gastinel once more shifts the Talbot into reverse and lurches forward again, straight toward the wall, like a battering ram. One last jolt. The first and second time, Dochin nearly smacked into the windshield, but this time he's braced himself, his hands flat against the dashboard.

A crime without witnesses. Suddenly cold sober, Dochin climbs out of the car and stares at the gray-white wall and the flattened, bloodied, half-shapeless thing at his feet. Pedal to the floor, without the slightest attempt to brake, the heavy car had crushed the fleeing girl just around the waist. Her head remains turned to one side, as at the moment of the first impact. Her face is untouched. Numb with shock, Dochin awkwardly unsticks the child from the wall, stupidly takes her in his arms, turns her over. On one side pallid and wan, red as a freshly butchered carcass on the other. The writer's hands and clothes are covered with blood. The headlights illuminate the scene: Jean-Rémi Dochin, soon to stand at the pinnacle of literary success, hailed by seasoned critics as the Alexandre Dumas of the Occupation, as the bleakly humorous portraitist of Paris's sorrows beneath the German boot, now deathly pale, his gaze dulled with horror, clutching the girl's body, her angelic face turned to the Talbot Murena, eyes wide open.

Resourceful soul that he is, Gastinel leaps out of the sedan, and, swift and sure as a veteran filmmaker, turns on his video camera, heretofore concealed in a bag beneath the driver's seat. It all happened in record time. An eighty-one second clip, horrific and in the worst sort of taste, but thanks to which he's got Dochin caught like a rat in a trap.

The rest of that night of June 3, 1995 will be put to good use: spitting on their hands, wielding their shovels like born gravediggers, the two accomplices will bury their victim's corpse in a field of clover just behind the farmhouse, still clad in the few clothes she was wearing when she took flight. With bucket after bucket of water, Gastinel will wash the blood from his car. As for the slightly dented bumper and crumpled hood—oh, but you'd need a magnifying glass to see the damage—well, should anyone ask, they'd blame it on a minor fender-bender in Paris, unless they simply sent the nosy bastard packing with a swift kick to the behind. As for the damage to the wall where the girl was flattened from mid-back to mid-thigh, they wouldn't touch it. Who would ever suspect that those few little cracks might be evidence of . . . ? The wall was already half crumbling anyway. And the blood stains, still visible an hour after the events—they looked more like mildew than anything else—posed no problem either, two little rain showers and they'd be gone for good. Finally, in the kitchen, the writer will conscientiously wash away the few brown spots still soiling his shirt and pants.

They ate the chicken all the same. Or part of it, at least. Gastinel took a thigh, Dochin a wing and a breast. Although this latter had some difficulty choking it down. And besides, it really was badly overcooked, and the shallots were burned.

Just like I told him, thought Gastinel, sucking the white wine sauce from his fat fingers. As long as it's done carefully, with no slipups, and especially without leaving any inconvenient clues behind, a murder's a very simple thing—people are crazy to make such a big deal of it. Just a few rough minutes to get through. Especially for the victim, of course.

"So, Monsieur Writer? Don't make that face! What's the matter? Incidentally, I think it's high time we started calling each other *tu*, don't you agree? A touch more Margaux to wash down the chicken?"

And then that fantastically corpulent man, who didn't seem to give a damn about any of this, suddenly broke into song:

> "Hey ho! Don't you fret! We'll get through it okay!
> Cause that's the good old French waaaay!"

28 Boileau, Narcejac, Erckmann, Chatrian, and the Others

Returning to Paris on the N12 that Sunday night, the two accomplices ran into a police checkpoint just after Mortagne, whereupon Dochin discovered he'd misplaced his papers. He begged the officer's indulgence, respectfully assuring him he must have left them at home. The cop—thinking nothing whatever of the Talbot's slightly crumpled hood—let it slide, and waved the driver on.

"Your mind was on other things," Gastinel told him a little while later, Dochin still anxiously rifling through his pockets. "I swiped them while you were plastered. They're in the kid's jacket pocket."

The writer sat in silence, as if stunned by a massive blow to the head.

"Should the cops happen to dig her up . . ." the fatso went on, driving serenely, not too fast, keeping to the slow lane like a good boy. "Even two or three years from now . . . Don't make that face! What are the odds? One in a thousand. How do you expect them to catch on to us?"

"Where did you find that girl?"

"At a dance . . . in the Salle Cadet . . . But there's no cause for alarm, nobody saw us. First of all, she was alone . . ."

"Suppose they print her picture in the papers . . . You're assuming no one else at the dance ever noticed her? You must be dreaming!"

"Shut your face. I don't much care for that belligerent tone you're taking. I'm telling you, the place was packed . . . Nobody would have paid that kid any mind. No one saw me snag her. They were all dancing, staring deep into each other's eyes, the assholes. And she never told anyone she was going to the hop. Didn't know a soul in Paris. Just got off the bus a few days ago. And nobody noticed when we snuck off to my place either. Anyway, no little chickie's going to get her picture in the paper or her puss on TV just because she's gone missing. Three hundred of them disappear every day! If they knew she'd been killed, that'd be different . . . But otherwise, no. She'll just go on being a missing person. Not a murder victim. There's a difference. How do you expect the cops to find her body? Don't get all agitated over nothing, it's not good for you."

"But what about my papers? Why did you put them in her pocket?"

"Oh . . . just an idea I had . . . for the cops. If by some miracle they find the kid. Her skeleton, I mean. Well . . ."

The blimp drove on a bit longer in silence.

"Well what?" Dochin finally asked, his voice a mere terrified peep.

"Well, to begin with, they'll find her papers. You know, those police labs are really something these days. Look at this genius! He's the crime novelist, and I'm the one who has to explain all this! Along with the papers, there'll be the remains to identify. They've got this thing they call PCR—you following me? They can analyze tiny fragments of bone and find the genetic imprint. That puts them on the trail, you understand. So they'll see that the papers do indeed belong to the skeleton. And then there'll be your papers too, get it?"

"Well, no, actually, I don't get it at all," hiccupped the "new Céline," his face ashen.

"It was a British professor who invented that PCR thing, a really sharp tack. A guy called Jeffreys, from the University of Leicester. Take it from me, anyone who tries to tell you the Brits are all bugwits has his head up his ass!"

"I still don't understand . . . about my papers," stammered he who had "shed a whole new light" on the Occupation.

"Oh come on, it's easy. Add all those troublesome details to the little home movie I shot last night . . ."

"And?"

"Don't worry yourself about it. I'll keep the tape in a nice, safe place. Someone might steal my balls while I'm sleeping . . . but not that cassette, never. That's one piece of plastic no one's ever going to lay hands on."

"What are you planning to do with it?" the writer croaked, every syllable shaken by tremolos.

"We're bound together for life, Jean-Rémi . . ."

"You piece of shit!" cried Dochin, livid.

"A crime like that will get you thirty-five or forty years in the slammer for sure. No parole. Oh, you'll be nice and rested when you get out—in the pink! I'll be, what, ninety-eight years old? And you eighty. Just a kid! But a kid without much of a future, especially if the unemployment situation hasn't improved, which seems highly likely . . . if there hasn't been a Third World War in the meantime. You still following me? And all that's assuming we get arrested tomorrow morning, of course. But don't work yourself into a lather. I repeat: who's ever going to go looking for that poor girl in the clover field behind my house? Don't worry, there must be loads of corpses like that scattered all over our lovely land. So many people vanish without leaving a forwarding address! The missing persons bureau is swamped, they get fifty cases a day. Don't tell me some of them didn't end up quietly buried in some godforsaken spot. Just you try and find them! Happy hunting!"

"You were the one who rammed into her! It was you, you bastard!"

"Well, you could have done something to stop me, couldn't you? Any eight-year-old can pull an emergency brake. Or else you could have forced me to swerve to one side. You've got hands. The steering wheel wasn't exactly a mile away, now was it? Maybe you were admiring the scenery? Jesus, what a dolt! Writes like a god and reasons like a retard! Admit it, you didn't show much initiative for someone hell-bent on preventing an accident!"

"I was drunk . . . You were pouring liquor into me all night long . . ."

"Try telling that to the cops. A bit late for the exonerating Breathalyzer test! And then try and convince them I was the one at the wheel! I've got you, my boy. I know all sorts of things about you. For instance, that you have—or had, at least, because now it's in our late friend's pocket—a driver's license. And here's another little challenge for you: try proving to the cops I was even there at all. Oh, that's going to be tricky."

"So supposedly I came out to your shack all on my own?"

"The whole thing happened outside, boyo. Not in the house. Any drifter can find his way into the field . . . What a sucker you are! In any case, you could easily have done your little deed without my being there, and without my knowing. Just because we're acquainted, that doesn't mean . . . In short, you get my drift."

"So who would have filmed me, then?"

"Oh, you'll come up with something . . . maybe say an owl hunter was hanging around . . . and thought he might make himself a little souvenir, just for fun . . . No, there's not the teensiest fart of evidence to suggest it was yours truly behind the camera."

"So how am I supposed to get new papers made up?"

"You'll have to find a way. Tell them you dropped them in the river. It'll take some time, but our beloved bureaucrats—those champions of the rubber stamp—will be only too happy to make you a new set. All you did was lose your ID, that doesn't make you a murderer. Stop getting all worked up over nothing."

"I was drunk . . ." Dochin said again, utterly stymied.

"Well, you didn't exactly turn up your nose when it came time to stick it in, did you, Mr. Asswipe? Hmm? Didn't look too out of it at that point! Rock hard! Those TV swine could almost have used you for one of their condom commercials."

Outraged, Dochin tried to throw himself on Gastinel. The car swerved. Disturbing, when you're doing sixty miles an hour. The hulk righted the vehicle just in time and called Dochin a cocksucker. With this, the writer calmed down. A bit after Houdan, their progress slowed by misty rain and the Pentecost-weekend traffic, Gastinel said:

"Suppose we talk a little about your manuscript, buddy? That's some kind of populist epic you've tossed off there. Magnificently written, to boot. What a style! From now on people who want to sing an author's praises won't say 'He writes like Céline,' but 'He's another Dochin.'"

"More flattery," Dochin snickered, bitterly.

"It's true, it's true . . . It's magic, that thing of yours . . ."

"Quit spewing at me, will you? It's a piece of shit. All these endless compliments . . . this weird fervor . . . Now I get it. An act! All that just to drag me into this murder . . . I don't know why yet, but . . ."

"You'll see, you're going to end up liking that book of yours. 'It's a piece of shit, I tell you!' Get a load of this guy! So Monsieur likes to play modest! Make like a nobody! . . . That thing's really well written, I tell you. Written to the hilt! We'll just have to wait and see what the critics have to say, then we'll find out what's what."

"Shall we make a little bet on it? It's a sure thing. Either they'll say nothing at all or they'll rip it to shreds."

"Listen to this cowflop!"

"I write like a seven-year-old . . . I know it perfectly well. I might look like an imbecile, but, honestly . . . What the hell . . . ? I churn out one flea-bitten thriller that goes straight to the trash heap where it belongs . . . and now, three or four years later, I've suddenly tossed off a masterpiece? Jesus, what's with all you people?"

"So why did you submit it, if it's so worthless?"

"I don't know anymore . . . Oh, fuck it all!"

"What a pussy! Monsieur is afraid of success. That's the living end! Or is it that poor little corpse you're afraid of, you worm? You'll see, the media types won't bite. Stop shitting your pants just because you've finally been discovered by people who actually know what they're doing! God, it never ends with you!"

"The only reason I wrote all those pages . . . used up all that paper . . . is because it gave me a place to stay . . . with someone who was willing to put me up . . . and feed me . . . There's your explanation. Nothing glorious about it. And since that someone was also—it must be contagious—ecstatic over my fucked-up little prose, my little sub-shit writing . . . well, I went on trying to please her—to take advantage of her—by filling up page after page like a dope . . . The days went by . . . and I went on living it up in my nice, comfy nest. That's what *Dancing the Brown Java* is: a sick little ploy to keep my belly full and my sorry ass off the windy streets and out of the Salvation Army. Nothing more."

"I can't believe I'm listening to this bullshit! Every writer, every real writer, will tell you there was some motive, some ulterior motive, behind their great books. Every one of them. Love . . . Fear of exile . . . Even hate. Or the need to escape some kind of situation, family stuff, whatever . . . Political ideas, sometimes. In your case, it was dough. Nothing to blush about there. It's as good a motive as any other. Your novel is a great book, I say it again, cross my heart and hope to die. And remember, I know a thing or two. I've got no reason to throw you candy hearts, do I? A real book by a real writer. And believe me, I've read my share of books!"

Only at the gates of Paris, on the Périphérique, creeping along with the rest of the steel magma flowing by fits and starts into the Saint-Cloud tunnel, did the blimp reveal that the monster had been read and greatly admired by the publisher Malgodin, and that it was he, whose financial health was a bit sounder than his own, who'd be publishing *Brown Java*. Simultaneously, Gastinel brought up the idea of a literary partnership for the first time, musing that there would surely be enough space on the cover to put "Gastinel" next to "Dochin," perhaps in smaller characters, he wasn't asking for the moon.

"You've heard of Boileau-Narcejac, haven't you? And Erckmann-Chatrian? Two Alsacians who made a whole bunch of dough. You've read those guys, haven't you? No?"

The "neo-Célinian" novelist—his face transformed into a white sheet bearing the mingled stigmata of despair and dazed incomprehension—shrunk back into his seat, mouth agape, jaw trembling, speechless. The Norman told himself it was a done deal.

29   A Great Writer Gone Senile

Dochin stayed in Paris a few days longer, waiting to sign the contract. He called Céline to let her know, wondering what on earth he could say to her in the wake of the murder. Not a word about that atrocity, of course. He just told her Gastinel wouldn't be publishing *Brown Java* after all, he didn't have the wherewithal for a project of that scale, since this wasn't just any old book, it was a great novel. Rather, the task would be taken on by one of Gastinel's friends, not terribly well known, perhaps, but very professional: Eugène Malgodin, the director of Le Papyrus. Not the first novel he's put out. Apparently Céline found nothing to gripe about in all this.

"Gastinel or Malgodin, what's the difference?" she answered. "You wanted a small press . . . now your wish is granted. Let's just hope he'll make a decent job of it, that's all we ask. But hang on: Malgodin, that rings a bell. He used to be a literary critic. A pretty big one, too. I believe the man knows how to spot a good book. He wrote in *Comœdia*, if I remember . . . well thought-of, influential . . ."

Dochin chose not to reveal that the publisher in question had a certain fondness for strong drink. No point complicating things.

The novelist stopped by the Rue du Pressoir to see what Gastinel was up to. And also—especially—to tell him he'd . . . Oh God, what a mess! What a nightmare his life had become! "No, for pity's sake, wake me up!" he moaned inwardly. "Wake me up!"

Receiving Dochin in his smoke-filled, paper-strewn office, the potbellied assassin announced that the contracts would be coming any day now. Malgodin was just drawing them up.

The behemoth poured a couple of glasses of beer. Dochin didn't touch his.

"Malgo wants to get the book out as soon as possible," said Gastinel. "Probably around mid-September. Three short months' wait, and then glory, champagne, and willing young ladies will be yours—I mean ours."

"Oh, shove it!"

"What's the matter? If you could see your face! Is it the contract that's bugging you? It's no problem, we'll go fifty-fifty. That's what we decided, right?"

"It's not that . . ."

"I can't believe you're looking so down in the dumps! You've just learned—what was it? four days ago! am I right?—you've just learned you're a writer like they don't make anymore, a one-time-only deal—I mean *we* are—and here you are pulling a face like somebody's trying to stuff a box of dominoes up your ass, one by one . . . Or like some mug on the Goncourt list who knows he's going to be cut two or three weeks before the big day. Come on, for Christ's sake, how about a smile?"

"But I keep telling you, it's not that . . . I wish I could make you understand how thoroughly I do not give a fuck about the contract!"

"Fifty-fifty, that was our deal, right? Malgodin thought that sounded just fine. That's how Erckmann and Chatrian handled it . . . Allain and Souvestre too . . . probably the same for Boileau and Narcejac. What's the matter with you? You have diarrhea?"

"So you told Malgodin you'd written the book with me?"

"What a question! Of course I did. He has to draw up the contracts, doesn't he? And the title page . . . with our two names on it . . . Come on, get your head out of your ass!"

"And? What did he say?"

"About what?"

"Well, about the two of us writing that thing . . ."

"Nothing much. That it was a most fruitful collaboration, that we make a first-class team . . . a couple of crack writers . . . in short, a whole heap of compliments. And he wasn't even smashed at the time! Why, what did you expect him to say?"

"Nothing, nothing . . . it's just that . . ."

"Well come on, spit it out, for Christ's sake! What is it now? What, has the memory of that poor little corpse got you all worked up again?"

"No, no . . . Although . . . No, but . . ."

Dochin had long wondered what to tell him. In the end, rather than reveal that he'd met with a well-known journalist about the manuscript, he decided to feint, to pretend he'd acted on his earlier idea, thinking Gastinel would find that less alarming:

"Here's the thing. I had Galice read the manuscript."

"Galice? Why not Julien Gracq and Jean Dutourd, while you're at it? Don't tell me you've gone and made an ass of yourself with Galice . . . like a young Proust, timidly ringing Anatole France's doorbell with his first manuscript under his arm!"

"As a matter of fact that's exactly what I did."

"When?"

"Oh . . . back in March, sometime around then . . . I hadn't quite finished it at the time."

"What got into you?"

"Oh, you know, it's always the same deal . . . I just couldn't work up any faith in that book, and I . . . A . . . a friend of mine was virtually squealing with enthusiasm when she read it . . . swooning over my words. . ."

"Our words, bucko. Let's get that straight once and for all."

"Right, well . . . It was my manuscript, wasn't it, for Christ's sake?"

"Don't get all hot under the collar, Docho. So?"

"Well, the friend in question happens to know a thing or two about literature . . ."

"This is the one who's putting you up? . . . and filling your belly . . .? That deal you were telling me about on the way back from Carrouges?"

"That's right. Yes, I sleep at her place. Now you know everything. Her opinion means a lot more than some serving girl's or some . . . Anyway, she knows what she's talking about."

"And? Was she wild about it?"

"Pretty much, yes. But I thought she was just trying to make me happy, sort of keep me from sinking into despair. After all, when you like a guy, you don't go telling him he's a dumbfuck. It's true she's a little love-struck, got kind of a thing for me . . . Supposedly I look like her late brother . . ."

"Careful now, let's not go getting dames mixed up in our affairs."

"So since I couldn't feel any confidence in my lame-ass prose, well . . . I thought she was praising me out of . . . I wouldn't say charity . . . or love, no . . . But something sort of like that, all the same."

"Oh yeah, a woman in love will find all sorts of qualities in a guy, that's well known. 'My lame-ass prose.' Listen to our timid little flower! Pretty soon they'll be calling you Céline number two—you and me both, that is . . . shit! I keep forgetting I'm in on this thing too—anyway, Céline number two, and here you are comparing yourself to Georges Ohnet!"

"No, no . . . But still, I know what my writing's like, I'm not that dumb. That's why I can't figure how come Malgodin's so excited about it. He stayed up all night reading my book, for Christ's sake!"

"Our book, kid. Ours. You've got to get that through your head. But it'll come in time."

"I just can't figure it, see?"

"So you're thinking a guy as thoroughly drenched in sordid self-interest as Malgodin—oh yeah, I know *him*!—a guy whose cupidity has few rivals on this earth, would sink a load of dough—a whole stinking shitload of dough—into a book that was only good for toilet paper? Just come out and admit it, will you? You're afraid of success! Admit it! You're scared shitless. What's the matter, can't you hear your 'little music' anymore? Gone deaf, have you? It plays through every line of the manuscript, just like an orchestral score! And here's this great clod shrugging in disbelief!"

No escaping them, Langillier's words kept playing over and over in Dochin's head: "I'm sure that like a big boy you'll launch right back into it and fix everything that needs fixing . . . many passages that might need some revision . . . Might even need to be rewritten entirely . . ." Not to mention that "Oh yes, yes, I read it through to the end. The end works rather better, now that you mention it," still echoing in his mind, like the coup de grâce.

"Now I've heard everything," said Gastinel. "Galice. So you wanted the opinion of a literary master, is that it, smart boy?"

"Well, yes . . . I . . . I went back and forth for a while, then I decided to go for it."

"And how'd it work out?"

"Oh . . ."

Hurriedly, Dochin—so he did have some imagination after all!—invented and described the fictive encounter:

"On the phone—it was a miracle, I managed to get hold of him right away—Galice was very friendly. 'Send me your manuscript, or leave it with my concierge,' he said. 'I'm always eager to read a young writer's work. I'll tell you very frankly what I think of your novel.'"

"With his concierge? Strange . . . Galice doesn't have one, he lives in a château out by Montfort-l'Amaury."

"I don't remember his exact words. Maybe he said 'house-keeper' . . . something like that . . ."

"And?"

"Well, that was that. He promised to tell me straight out what he thought."

"What a moron!"

"Who, Galice?"

"No, limpdick, you! Don't you know senile old writers are always cribbing ideas from youngsters starting out in this harebrained trade?"

"Galice steal my ideas? What are you, nuts? He's as honest as they come. Honesty and generosity personified. That's like saying Giono or Marcel Aymé would have swiped my ideas, just as ridiculous. So anyway, I didn't waste any time, I left the manuscript at his place, out by Montfort-l'Amaury, as you say . . ."

"So then what happened? He thought it was brilliant, I hope?"

"Three days later, I called him . . ."

"And did you get him in person?"

"Nope. Just a secretary."

"Danielle Fiorentini, I'll bet. The broad who fixes all his spelling mistakes. So?"

"Well . . . she sounded just a bit cool. She didn't exactly blow me off, no . . . But oh boy, was she distant! Long story short, she gave me to understand that Galice didn't have time to waste on . . ."

"Take it easy, now . . ."

"In short, she gave me this whole long spiel that stank to high heaven of the polite rebuff. She suggested I pick up the manuscript from the housekeeper . . . then hung up in my face. Not even a 'good-bye.' So I figured he must have read two or three pages, and . . ."

"You sound bitter . . . outraged . . . all bent out of shape . . . Simmer down, boy. Galice is a doddering old duffer. Everybody knows that. Either he never read a word—and if he told you he did it was only to make you happy, just to be nice—or else he's gone flighty, and changed his mind after the fact. Unless old lady Fiorentini didn't think much of the whole business and just kept the book away from him. That happens a lot. The old fart probably never even had your pages in his hands. Women like that can be a real menace. They get to thinking they're the brains behind their boss's books. So wipe that glum look off your face. And what about Malgodin, anyway? Doesn't his opinion count for anything?"

"You told me he's almost always drunk off his ass . . ."

"Well, then, what about me? Your beloved Charles?

"You . . ."

"What, me? Oh, come on, out with it, whatever it is."

"Wait . . . I haven't told you everything."

Gastinel having proven entirely unimpressed by the "Galice version" of the events, Dochin now decided to reveal the whole truth and bring up Langillier.

"What is it now?" said Gastinel. "You give our book to somebody else?"

"Yes, a journalist. A guy I met back when I was living in the street. He was doing a story for *Le Figaro* . . . on society's castoffs . . . on people who've 'fallen through the cracks,' as assholes who don't know what it's like always say . . . Probity personified, that guy, and enormously kind."

"Him too? Gee, what a wonderful world you live in!"

"He was an editorial advisor for ten years or something. At Poulet-Malassis, I think. In the sixties."

"And?"

"He couldn't even finish it. And what a dressing-down he gave me on the phone! Oh, sure, it was all wrapped up in thoughtful little encouragements . . . plenty of tact, that guy . . . But it was worse than if he'd just come out and called me a loser to my face. In short, to hear him tell it, almost the whole thing had to be redone."

"So he didn't read it through to the end?"

"Yeah, well, what he did read must have been enough for him."

"Another jerk-off. One more journalist who thinks he's God's gift. Must have felt like he was back at his old publishing house, playing judge and jury over some poor hopeful sap's manuscript. Big mistake, going to see that guy. But don't make a tragedy out of it. This world's full of petty jealousies. Plenty of assholes panned *Journey*, or *Tropic of Cancer*, or *For Whom the Bell Tolls*, isn't that right? That's where greatness will get you, my friend. But what are you driving at with all this?"

"Well, it's just that . . . Galice and the journalist, I didn't tell them . . ."

"Didn't tell them what? You got a fish-bone stuck in your throat or something?"

"And there was my lady friend too . . . who thinks so highly of *Brown Java* . . . They all think there's just the one author. When they hear . . ."

An amused puff of wind escaped Gastinel's lips:

"Ah! So that's it? You told them you'd written it all by yourself? That you were the only author?"

"Let's leave my lady friend out of this, for the moment . . . As for Galice and the journalist, no, I didn't tell them a thing. I didn't give them any details, but I imagine they would have assumed . . . What am I supposed to tell them now? What am I going to look like when the book comes out with our two names on it?"

"What a worm this guy is! To think he'll have a seat in the Académie in twenty or thirty years! So that's it, you little slug, you've got the screaming meemies just because your pinhead pals are going to see two names on the cover?"

"Well . . . well, yes. Put yourself in my place."

"But it's all very simple, Monsieur No-Balls. You're getting all in a tizzy over trivialities that wouldn't even worry a little brat scribbling with his crayons. Jeez, I almost feel sorry for you. And of all the jerks in this world, this is the one I team up with! Thanks for nothing, Dame Fortune!"

"What, that wouldn't make you just a little uncomfortable? Don't you think they're going to say to themselves, 'So his book needed a rewrite, and the rewriter wanted his name on the cover'?"

"Listen here, my dear asswipe—one of two things will happen. Either they found your—our—book genuinely piss-poor, unpublishable, in which case, seeing the same text in print, they'll have to grant that there's been no more rewriting than they have butter coming out of their buttholes. Or else, if they find themselves liking it once it's been published, that'll prove they never even read a half-line of your manuscript, and they were handing you a load of grade-A bull."

"None of which answers the question. Why did I make them think it was all my own work?"

"Oh! You slay me, with those scruples of yours. It's really sort of sinister, if you think about it. In the first place, you never told them a thing. Was your name written above the title?"

"Well, no, it's true . . . All I put was *Dancing the Brown Java*."

"Very good. So you never told them a thing. And they'll realize there were two authors and that's all there is to it, you just didn't think it was worth troubling them with that little detail, that's all. It's not like we were going to come strolling in arm in arm to bring them the manuscript, right?"

"Maybe so."

"Anyway, to hell with them. If Monsieur Galice only read a few lines of your . . . of our book, he's got no right to get up on his high horse. As for the newspaperman, he'll just realize there are two authors. That's not going to change his opinion, of course, but who gives a fuck about that?"

"I'll give him a quick call all the same."

"If I were you, my boy, I'd let sleeping dogs lie."

"I'll see . . . But then, that's not the worst of it . . . There's my lady friend . . . The woman I was telling you about . . . The one I live with . . . She saw me write most of the book with her own eyes . . . I wouldn't want her to think . . . to assume I was pulling a fast one on her . . ."

"In what way?"

"I mean . . . if there were two of us writing the thing . . ."

"Well, that one you're going to have to handle on your own."

"I'll try to talk to her."

"I can't believe you're getting so worked up about this. Listen. There's a surefire solution. Put your hand on her ass and everything else will take care of itself, you'll see."

"You know, if there was some way to weigh all the shit-brained ideas you come up with, you'd seem like a wispy little waif in comparison."

"In any case—and now I'm being serious—don't be a dumbass. We wrote *Brown Java* together, and don't you forget it. That's what matters."

With a stern look and a tinge of menace in his voice, Gastinel added:

"Don't fuck this up, Jean-Rémi. Watch yourself. There's only one critic who can do us in, and it isn't any of those bozos who write in the papers . . . It's our little friend in the ground."

Dochin fell silent, ashen, and swallowed hard twice.

30   The Contract

In the end, Dochin never did find the nerve to call Langillier. "Let's just wait and see," he told himself.

The contract was signed a few days later, on Friday, June 9. The book's title would be simply *Dancing the Brown Java*. No subtitle. Dochin had suggested *Volume One: Max and Mimile*, but Malgodin was against it, on the grounds that the two kids weren't important enough to the plot. So just plain *Dancing the Brown Java*, and on the last page, "End of volume one," suggesting a sequel to come.

With the papers duly signed, Dochin and Gastinel paid a call at Le Papyrus. Already half-drunk, Malgodin invited them out for a bouillabaisse lunch at Le Varois de Coeur, on the Avenue des Gobelins.

Dazed and befogged, Dochin listened with one ear as the publisher droned on and on about print runs, publicity, jacket copy, etc., and several times declared he was aiming to get the book out in mid-September. The authors would receive the proofs toward the beginning of August.

At some point, though, Dochin felt duty-bound to open his mouth without cramming fish into it, and so came the first stammered words of what promised to be a long-running charade, whose conceit was that he'd written *Dancing the Brown Java* in collaboration with Charles Gastinel. It was all rather painful and difficult, he was continually pausing like an actor who's forgotten his lines and doesn't know how to improvise. More than once the blimp had to come to his rescue, pulling him back from the edge of the abyss with his great gift for blather.

"Two champions, that's what you are," Malgodin concluded, "working as one single man."

Then, with a great laugh enlivened by the Provence rosé and the pre-lunch apéritifs (as well as the glasses of whiskey knocked back that morning and the swigs of white wine on arising):

"We'll tell them the left-hand pages are Dochin's, and the rest Gastinel's."

"Ha! Ha! Ha!" the fat man bellowed, causing several nearby diners to turn around, while the author of *Dancing the Brown Java* sat in stony silence, somewhat hard put to see the humor. Visibly, the literary side of things interested their publisher far less than the cash he stood to rake in. He scarcely said a word about the novel itself, just two or three imbecilities like "Oh! your Max and Mimile! So true to life!" or "You really got the Occupation years dead to rights! Hats off!"

Dochin and Gastinel parted ways early that afternoon. As if in a stupor, the rat-trapped writer trudged back to his hotel on the Boulevard de l'Hôpital. He called La Halte to let Céline know he'd be back sometime the next day, a Saturday. She asked if everything had gone well.

"It's all done, the contract is signed."

"What about the advance?"

"Thirty thou. Half on signature, half on publication."

"Not exactly putting himself out for you, is he? Furne or Gallim's would have given you a damn sight more. Thirty thousand francs for a book like that!"

"Don't forget, we're . . . I'm just an unknown. A beginner."

"Never mind. The money will come rolling in soon enough, my angel. But you'll show me the contract all the same, won't you?"

"Well, the thing is . . ." said Dochin, uncomfortable beyond all expression, remembering what it said at the top of the contract's first page:

> *The undersigned, Monsieur Jean-Rémi Dochin, La Halte du Bon Accueil, La Petite Saulée, 19260 Térignac*
> *and*
> *Monsieur Charles Gastinel, 8, Rue Ramponneau, 75020 Paris, henceforth known as the Co-Authors,*
> *and the privately owned company Le Papyrus, publishers, located in Paris, henceforth known as "The Publisher," represented by its General Director, Monsieur Euloge Malgodin, hereby agree that . . . etc.*

"Say, you don't sound quite like yourself."

"Oh yes, I'm fine, I'm fine . . ."

"I'll bet you're starting to worry again. You'll see, Jean-Rémi, they're going to love it. Anyone who doesn't like *Dancing the Brown Java*, well . . ."

"Well what?"

"Well, good luck to him."

31   In His Sleep

At 7:45, Dochin went off to dinner in a restaurant on the Boulevard de la Bastille, just across the Seine. A TV was on. In the middle of the news, the anchor announced:

"I've just been handed a bulletin announcing the death of Léon Galice. The great writer was said to be in perfect health, and planning to celebrate his eighty-sixth birthday a few days from now. He passed away in his sleep at his residence, 'Les Mesnuls,' on the outskirts of Paris. Léon Galice, born Léon Georges, who prided himself on having only a sixth-grade education, son of a humble railway crossing guard in the eastern Pyrénées, first became known to the public in 1935 with a resounding critique of Léon Daudet in *L'Intransigeant*, after the appearance of his own fifth novel, *The Shrew-Mouse*, published by Michel Lévy. Galice will be particularly missed by the Disadvantaged Children's Fund, of which he was a founder, and to which he donated generously. Galice chose to accept no decorations or honors during his lifetime. Our network will broadcast a tribute tomorrow evening, hosted by . . ."

Dochin returned to his hotel, still shocked by this news, distressed at having used Galice's name to deceive Gastinel, Galice being a writer he greatly respected. Galice, whom he'd never contacted, never met. He found himself in the grips of a sort of moral discomfort, which soon evolved into a superstitious terror.

He called Gastinel. The lard-ass was still in his office on the Rue du Pressoir.

"Listen, I know it's stupid . . . but I just heard Galice is dead . . ."

"Yeah, I heard that too, on the radio. But they talk so fast I could only make out a quarter of what they were saying. Something happen to him?"

"I told you, he's dead."

"Well, I got that, but . . ."

The mountain of flesh in (more or less) human form guffawed:

"From the way you were talking, I thought maybe it was because he didn't like *Brown Java* . . ."

"What do you mean?"

"Well, that's what you said, isn't it? He read it, and he didn't like it one bit. Don't you remember?"

"I don't see the connection . . ." said Dochin, on guard and suddenly ill at ease, overcome by a strange sensation, his mind ringing with Céline's words: "If by chance they don't like it, they'll be kicking themselves . . ."

"It's just that when you told me Galice hadn't thought much of your thing, there was something about you . . . I don't know, a sort of rage . . . something menacing in your voice . . ."

"Menacing? Me?"

"Don't get upset!"

"I'm not upset."

"You seem all prickly . . . Like a rooster when somebody tries to pinch its crest! If it bothers you that much, forget I even said it. But . . ."

"What, 'but'? What are you trying to say?"

"Nothing at all. You're the one who called me. I was just on my way out. What do you want?"

"As a matter of fact, I wanted to tell you . . . I was stupid, but . . ."

"But what?"

"Well, all that stuff about Galice was a lie. I never did call him. Never, you hear?"

"Is that right? Well, well."

"So he could never have read a single line of *Brown Java*. I made the whole thing up."

"No kidding. But why? What a joker! All that crap about Galice not liking *Brown Java* . . . What got into you? And what about the journalist? Was that a con job as well?"

"Oh no, not him. In his case, it was true. He really did read the manuscript."

"So that's why you called me?"

"Well, yes . . . I was feeling sort of guilty, about Galice."

"Guilty? Hmm. But why?"

"No reason . . . Just because . . . A feeling . . ."

"You've really got too much time on your hands tonight. Go find a hooker, that'll take your mind off things. Anyway, the dead will keep. Let's get back to our own affairs. You're still leaving tomorrow?"

"Yeah, nothing's changed."

"Well then, bon voyage, Monsieur Dochin."

And with this the giant abruptly hung up.

32 Céline, We Need to Talk . . .

I headed home to La Halte, and two days passed by. I'd found a way out of showing Céline the contract (of which there were two copies, one for me, one for the fat-ass). She wanted to see it, but to save time I'd thought up a story in advance, just like a little kid trying to protect his guilty behind: I'd asked an employee at Le Papyrus to be so kind, when she had a minute, as to make me a photocopy of the contract, but then—too late, I was already on the train—realized I'd completely forgotten to go pick it up. So I'd called the lady from Limoges and asked her to mail the contract and the photocopy off to La Halte. Céline seemed to swallow that without choking. Which gave me a reprieve of three or four days, in the course of which I was hoping to find some way out of this profoundly fucked-up situation. I was going to have to show it to her sooner or later, otherwise who knows what she might think. If only—I told myself that Saturday night before I fell asleep—if only I had a sheet of letterhead from Le Papyrus, then I could make up a fake contract without Gastinel's name and Céline would be none the wiser . . . but I ended up ditching that idea, because Gastinel might very well call me at La Halte, or Malgodin for that matter, and give me away to Céline, who never missed a thing. Then I'd really be in for it. Furthermore, it was in no way impossible that Gastinel, that great swine, who I knew to be capable of anything, might show up unexpectedly at La Halte. And then, oh, what larks! Jesus, what a mess I was in . . .

As soon as I got back to the motel, sort of to get my mind off all this, I buckled down to start volume two, *Rage Beneath the Cagoule* (I'd come up with that title while I was writing the last pages of volume one). Céline had already cleared my desk of its papers and bric-a-brac, then given it a good waxing and set out a nice ream of blank paper, ready and waiting to receive my exquisite handwriting, the inkwells neatly lined up, the dictionaries arranged in a perfect stack, and then, on one side, a brand-new blotter from the stationer in Térignac, Madame Ducasse, with a color illustration from La Fontaine's "The Tortoise and the Hare": in short, my desk was welcoming me with open arms, and urging me to get back to work.

As for the crime that I would now forever have on my conscience—in collaboration with Monsieur Flab, like "our" novel—I was doing my best not to think about it. Not easy, as you can imagine.

That Tuesday morning, unable to bear it any longer—I'd hardly slept a wink thanks to all these things (the contract with the two names, the murder) bobbing around in my head, like shit floating to the surface of a lake—I went to see Céline. My heart was in my boots, and that's no lie. I must have looked like a little kid with some great big boo-boo on his conscience. I wasn't exactly walking along with my head bent toward the ground, but close enough . . . a penitential sort of gait.

She was in the kitchen, shelling peas with Camille.

"What's the matter with you, my little calf? Why, my lamb seems all out of sorts. Did you do some good writing? How many lines this morning, my little freeloader?"

Now that that bastard Gastinel had leapt aboard my train, I was going to have to rethink my approach, find some way out of the deeply unappetizing brown substance into which I'd been plunged up to the neck . . . My throat was bone dry. How was she going to take this?

"Céline, we need to talk . . ."

Seeing the look on my face—that of a man impaled: I caught a glimpse of myself in the mirror—she realized this was important.

"Excuse us, Camille," she said. "You can start on the two back rooms, 13 and 14. I just got a call from a little lady from Commercy, she has two kids with Down syndrome. I'm expecting her tonight. She was here last year. Poor thing decided not to try her luck in the hotels again."

"We'll put the kids in 13?"

"That's perfect. They'll like the view of the river. Give them pillows. Madame Laurière too. Give her a couple. She gets dizzy when her head's too low down. I imagine they'll be staying two or three days. They're going to a fair for the handicapped in Langon."

Camille went out, wiping her hands on her flowered apron and wiggling her hips. Céline once again planted her friendly but analytical gaze on my face:

"Well, hen, I'm listening."

"It's about my book, Céline."

"Volume two, you mean?"

"No . . . well, yes . . . that too . . . But mostly I mean the one I just handed in to Le Papyrus."

"What about it?"

She seemed more than a little intrigued. I pulled up a chair and plunked down like I had a sack of lead strapped to my ass.

"I have to tell you . . . It's stupid, I know . . . That contract I signed . . . Friday . . . There were two signatures."

"Two?"

She didn't seem to understand. She seemed completely lost, as a matter of fact, and I could have sworn she sort of jumped in her seat, exactly like someone had given her a good, hard pinch on the butt. I wanted to sink into the earth and disappear forever.

"The thing is . . . You see, there are two authors . . ."

Surprise painted itself on her features, and even bewilderment.

"Two authors?"

"The other one's Charles Gastinel. We collaborated."

Her incomprehension jumped up a notch:

"What do you mean? You're trying to tell me . . . that *Dancing the Brown Java* isn't yours alone?"

"That's right."

"I . . . I don't know what to say!"

"Yes, I . . . I should have told you sooner . . . just my stupid, foolish pride . . . It's ridiculous, I know . . . childish . . ."

"But . . . Gastinel . . . Gastinel, the publisher?"

"Right."

"But then . . . why did you say you wanted to give him the manuscript?"

"Well, I . . . It's simple. It's simple and it isn't . . ."

Was I ever going to get out of this?

"Here's the thing. Remember when you showed me all those books so I could pick out a publisher? Imagine my surprise when I saw one put out by . . . by Charles. So I said, 'Let's go with this one.' It sort of came at the right time, if you like. I knew Gastinel was going to find us a publisher with some cash to burn. Which he did. Once I told you I was going with Gastinel Editions, I didn't dare let on that . . . well, that . . . you know, that things were the way they were."

"I'm not following you, Jean-Rémi. What's the matter, are you tired? You want to wait a while before you get down to volume two?"

She seemed all shaken up—and, worse than that, full of pity. She looked at me like I was a sick man, a sick man in extremis.

"I'm not following you," she said again.

I launched into a crazy story: my collaborator Gastinel had fallen seriously ill, and I stupidly told myself he might not be too long for this world . . . in which case I could sign the book all by myself, since none of his acquaintances—or mine—knew we'd been working together. Completely idiotic, but that was the best I could do.

"And today your Gastinel's in good health again. Fully recovered."

Now she was smiling. Without a trace of irony. With kindness, even understanding. I told myself I'd pulled it off. I'd come right up to the edge of a deep, deadly ravine. To my great relief, she didn't seem the least bit upset. No, more than anything, she seemed sort of amused. Her second smile told me that. I was extricating myself fairly well. None of the shock, the dismay, the howls of rage I was dreading when I first came into the kitchen.

"But I don't quite understand," she said a few seconds later.

The smile had faded, but her face was still calm, serene . . . no resemblance to a harpy about to leap on me with all her claws bared.

"There's one thing I don't quite understand," she repeated.

A disagreeable little shiver strolled down my nape. Had I forgotten something? For want of a nail, as they say. Was some little detail going to bring this whole thing crashing down around me?

"All those pages you showed me when you first came to La Halte, all that stuff I typed up . . . Your tiny writing, all those sentences, those crossed-out words . . . Well, after all, it was your handwriting. The manuscript's still here . . . the one you wrote out by hand, I mean, with all the additions and changes. I don't quite understand."

"It's very simple," I said, inspiration suddenly pulling my head out of the water, like some miraculous life preserver. "For that part of the book I was mostly using Gastinel's notes . . . He'd jot down these notes, see, then pass them on to me to work up . . . Not just a couple of lines here and there, mind you . . . sometimes two or three pages, front and back . . . Funny old Charles, that's how he liked to work. He's not like me, you know. That's just how he is . . . not so big on details . . . sort of a force of nature . . . Not much of a pen-pusher . . . Not the type to sit at a desk for hours on end . . ."

"And where are these notes?"

I hope this isn't going to turn into the old third degree, I thought, my back once again bathed in a cold sweat.

"I threw them away as soon as I was done with them . . . Don't forget, I was living on the street . . . homeless . . . So as for carefully filing away a raft of jumbled old pages . . ."

"That's true," she conceded.

"I only had so many pockets. Oh, and my bag full of tattered rags and little scraps of food. Not much room there! Where was I supposed to put all that paper?"

"I understand, lamb. You recopied it all . . ."

Bravo for me if I was still her lamb! It was working. Little by little I was making my way out of the danger zone, without so much as a scratch. She hadn't shot me a withering glare, hadn't called me a filthy liar, a shameless plagiarist . . .

"I see . . . You incorporated your friend's work into your text . . ."

"Right. Pretty much like that. And then sometimes he talked . . . sort of dictated, if you like . . . He improvised, off the cuff . . . I can picture us now, sitting side by side for hours on end in the Jardin du Luxembourg . . . or by the lake in the Bois de Boulogne . . . He talked and talked . . . Ideas just poured out of him! Meanwhile, my pen or pencil was racing over the paper . . ."

"I see . . . you took it all down . . . you transcribed . . ."

"Right. That's more or less how we worked . . . I should have told you, of course . . . I'm just a poor fool, Céline. I was wrong to . . . I acted like an idiot . . ."

"No, don't say that. So, in short, your talent . . . it's a shared talent."

"Well, yes . . . Disappointed?"

"Not at all! That doesn't take away anything from you, ducks . . . So this . . . what's his name again?"

"Gastinel. Charles Gastinel. The cover will say Dochin-Gastinel. Like Boileau-Narcejac or Erckmann-Chatrian, say."

"Yes, I understand. But . . . there's something else I don't get . . ."

Oh, shit! What now? My imagination was starting to run dry. What was she going to ask? I stood by, at the ready, but not without apprehension, I'll admit.

"All that work you put in here at La Halte . . . Almost three-quarters of the book, after all . . . So that part you wrote without this Gastinel, is that it?"

"Not exactly!" I shrieked, my voice choking with terror . . . but I got hold of myself just in time. "Not exactly."

"You still had some of his notes with you?"

She could easily have rummaged through my papers while I was away . . . Who knows? No telling, with women . . . Ixnay, then, on the imaginary notes still in my possession.

"I . . . No. But Charles's health was going downhill fast, so I . . . I worked mainly from memory, if you like . . . stuff he'd told me before . . ."

I kept sinking in deeper and deeper. This was starting to suck but good.

"I still had it all in my head, you understand . . . We'd talked so much about that book . . . and for so long! Day after day! Sort of like it was printed in there, you see what I mean?" (I gave my sorry skull two or three taps.) "And then, you know, we also met up from time to time . . . Remember how I used to take the car out to the lake? . . . or the Audouze tower or Ventadour or the Roman ruins by Pérols? Sometimes I was going to meet Charles. We talked. Once his health started to come back, he tried to get away whenever he could."

"I see. Funny you never mentioned him, though . . . your coauthor . . ."

"I told you, Céline, I thought he was done for. His heart . . . He's very heavy, his heart is encased in fat . . . He's got other problems too, something about his stomach, I don't know what . . . serious health issues . . ."

"Well, aren't you the sly one!" she said with a smile. "In short, once your friend kicked the bucket, you were planning to pass yourself off as the sole author of *Brown Java*?"

"Pretty crummy, I know, but . . ."

"Crummy, yes. Still, it's no crime."

That word made me jump.

"All the same," she concluded, "it's not exactly honest. But anyway! Now it's fine, since you've confessed."

"I just couldn't put it off any longer, Céline . . . If you'd seen the book, printed and published and everything, with two names on the cover, I . . . what would I have looked like?"

I threw myself on the mercy of the court, posture fully submissive.

"Don't get all worked up about it, lamb. But let me tell you, that's just about the last thing I expected to hear! Still . . . I'll get used to the idea. So your buddy's on the mend?"

"Back in the pink, yeah. And I'm very happy about that, you understand."

Oh I was, was I? Jesus, if only he *would* kick off!

"How old is he?"

"Quite a bit older than me. Sixty-three."

"And you met where?"

"Well . . ."

She was starting to bug me. How was this ridiculous little game going to end?

"Um . . . I can't quite remember . . . Oh yes. It's coming back to me now. In a homeless shelter . . . in Paris . . . He's seen some rough times, you know . . . We talked literature . . . and since we had the same tastes . . . Céline . . . Genet . . . Bukowski . . . Nerval . . . Baudelaire . . . All the outcasts . . . the *poètes maudits* . . . our brothers, in a way . . ."

"You think you could have gone on by yourself if something had happened to your pal?"

"Well, I . . ."

There I sat like a dingus, weighing the pros and cons. Calmly, serenely, she'd gone back to shelling her peas. Should I say "yes," even if it meant looking like a pretentious jerk, or "no," and play it all humble and modest?

"Oh, well, I would have tried," I stammered, choosing the happy medium—so often the remedy for even the shittiest situation . . .

There she had me, the cow, throwing out a sarcastic:

"You would have remembered everything he told you, all those hundreds of notes . . . you knew them by heart . . ."

"No, I . . . You're ragging me, Céline."

"It's true, I was just teasing, my little sugarlump. Don't get yourself into a state. I understand. Writers are always complicated. You have to know how to deal with them . . . tame them . . ."

All of a sudden she seemed thoughtful.

"But tell me . . ."

"What?"

I'd almost barked out an enraged, "What is it now?," but I held back.

"This volume two . . . that you've begun . . . So you're not writing it alone, then?"

"I . . . I started it on my own, yes . . . But . . . Charles and I will be getting together one of these days."

Alas. Three times alas!

"Yeah, we'll be meeting before too long. And meanwhile, he's working too, on his end."

"Oh, I see. And then you're going to sort of meld your two texts together?"

"More or less, yes."

"So he's writing now?"

"Who?"

"'Who'! Not the pope. Your Gastinel, obviously!"

"What do you mean, 'he's writing'?"

"Well yes, you tell me he works mostly by notes, which he then sends on to you . . . or else he does it out loud . . . orally . . ."

"He used to work that way. But for volume two he's decided to try writing himself."

"I see. Out with the tongue, in with the pen."

I thought I detected a slight whiff of sarcasm there. Did she believe me? Nothing was certain, all told.

"And I'm supposed to wait till you've got all that put together before I can start typing it up."

"I don't know . . . No. I'll just use what he's written on his end. They'll be something like notes . . . Our way of working won't have changed all that much, really . . ."

When was this going to end? I hoped to God she wasn't going to ask to see the blimp's nonexistent jottings. For pity's sake! What had I got myself into? Still, I was feeling more or less relieved, in spite of everything . . . when all of a sudden, point-blank, she gave me a "You're hiding something from me, Jean-Rémi, and that's not very nice"—which whipped me in the face like a gout of cold rain.

"Not at all, Céline . . . I've told you everything, I promise. I've been sort of vague about it, I know, but . . ."

"Try to remember what I once told you, Jean-Rémi . . . You hadn't been here even an hour . . ."

"What? What about?"

"About your manuscript, damn it! I told you—and believe me, I know what I'm talking about—I told you a boy your age, who never saw a blessed moment of the Occupation, couldn't possibly write about it except like an ignoramus."

"And?"

"Well, admit it: your book's background, the setting, the atmosphere—life in Paris under the Germans—that's all Gastinel's doing, isn't it? Admit it! It's no crime not to have lived through those filthy days, and if you didn't, there's no way to recreate them in writing. Admit it, you beast!"

So that was all it was . . . It came at just the right time. I grasped the opportunity like you'd catch a fly in your clenched fist:

"Well yes, that's exactly right. You got it. You've seen right through me."

"I've got a nose for these things, you know!"

"It was all Gastinel. Because, after all, he was born in '32, so he turned eight in 1940. From eight to twelve, a kid can take in a whole lot![2] Especially one who got around like he did."

---

2   Very true. (Author's note.)

"Well, I must say, that friend of yours has a real eye. It's all there . . . the whole ambiance of Occupation-era Paris . . . brought back to life . . . a real tour de force! Give him my compliments."

"I won't forget, Céline. He'll be happy."

That fat fucker would be waiting on her compliments for a long time to come, because the authentic verdigris ambiance was my work and nobody else's—and no, I wasn't around at the time, just a gleam in my father's eye. That's how it was, and that's all there is to it—contrary to the ludicrous, mush-brained claims of Madame Céline Ferdinaud.

"You see, Jean-Rémi . . . The whole time I was reading—devouring—and typing your manuscript, there was something beneath my enthusiasm . . . How to say it? Something that bothered me . . . needled me . . . something I couldn't quite swallow . . ."

"What was it?"

"I didn't want to hurt you, but . . ."

"But what?"

"Well, it was that early-'40s atmosphere . . . the whole 'Occupation' angle, if you like . . . I tried and tried to tell myself you came up with all that, but I just couldn't see it. I spent those years in Paris myself, you know. I was twenty-two in 1940. My husband and I ran that bookstore from 1937 to 1946. So you can bet I saw my share of Krauts and Pétainists, sometimes up close and personal . . . We even had Ernst Jünger in our little shop a few times! A very amiable man, as a matter of fact. And some of his officer pals who liked books . . . Oh my! Never let it be said they didn't behave like perfect gentlemen. And so clean! Not like our own French slobs, with their clothes all askew and their unshaven chins and their red noses and fat stomachs and big mouths! Mind you, it's not like Jean—that's my husband—like Jean and I were Kraut-lovers. Unlike a lot of the big Paris booksellers . . . I won't name any names. Anyway, to get back to *Brown Java* . . . it's amazingly true to life, that has to be said. Full of authenticity. And obviously, that couldn't have come from you."

Well, as a matter of fact, my dear lady, it *does* come from me, and you're just going to have to accept it. Oh, what am I saying? She'll never accept it, because . . . because now that diabolical blimp has sauntered onto my stage—without crashing through the floorboards, amazingly enough. So no one will ever see my remarkable talent, my gift for describing days gone by, for recreating ambiances I've never known and never experienced. Say what you like about the rest of the book, but there, clearly, I'd scored, and no one would ever know it. No one. All that because of a murdered teenager. Crime doesn't pay—any asshole can tell you that. But this particular crime tops them all, if you don't mind my saying . . .

"Something just didn't fit, Jean-Rémi, I could spot it right off the bat. Those descriptions were just too true to life to be real. But I didn't dare breathe a word of that to you. Writers can be so touchy! And then, there was the rest of it . . . Such an extraordinary book . . . Why quibble? All the same, it made me wonder, I have to tell you. Now I finally understand. This Gastinel's quite a writer, isn't he? Such mastery in his touch—yours and his, I mean! Really something. You don't have to read more than half a page to see it's in a whole other class from most of what they put out today. I mean the usual sort of stuff . . . all those twits parading around on TV . . . As if being on-camera gave you talent! Of course, nobody gives a crap about talent nowadays. Nobody cares about that. Does anybody even know what it is anymore, with all the tripe we get fed on the tube? It's all about money nowadays. As for art, well . . . Look at sports, look at what they've turned into. A money-grubbing racket!

And all those chuckleheads watching it . . . eating it up . . . Say, my lamb, you're going to have to introduce me to this friend of yours."

That's it, here we go, I said to myself. Needless to say, I was resolved to do everything in my power to make sure no such thing ever happened.

"Oh, he can't stand the countryside . . ." I stammered. "The pollen . . . all that . . . it gives him hay fever . . ."

"We'll see about that later. Maybe when summer comes, he'll want to come out and pay us a call."

Oh, you can bet on it!

"And summer's not so far away, Jean-Rémi."

33   Céline Number Three

A few days later the fat man in my life—and my nightmares—gave me a call. I happened to be alone in the front office.

"Started in on volume two yet, kid?" he asked, in a breezy sort of tone.

Keeping an eye on my progress, the turd. Somehow he'd got it into his head that my stupid book—extolled by a madwoman, adulated by a drunk, and praised to the heavens by a thick-headed brute, a former tripe man without the faintest idea what he was spouting about, but judged a worthless pile of crap by someone, Langillier, who'd once been a literary figure without peer—that my pointless book was going to set a bunch of new sales records, so he was already thinking about a sequel. No, "our" book was already as good as dead and buried!

"I've begun, yes . . . Maybe ten pages . . . but it's not coming along too terribly well, at the moment . . ."

"So? Did you talk to your girlfriend?"

"About us? About the book?"

"Well, yes, of course. What did she say? She didn't hit the ceiling, did she?"

"No . . . No . . . She understood. She took it just fine . . ."

"What about the journalist? Did you call him?"

"No, I haven't done anything there."

"Good for you. Fuck him. How did you explain all this to your little friend?"

"All very simply. I'll tell you when I see you. We're not going to talk about it on the phone."

"You did tell her there were two of us?"

"Of course . . . Besides, she's going to see the book in September."

"She didn't show any particular interest in me?"

Here my guard went up. With a swine like this, you had to be ready for anything.

"What do you mean, 'interest'?"

"Well, after all . . . Since she's drooling with admiration for you . . . so you said . . . for *Brown Java* . . . Now that she knows there were two of us holding the . . . I almost said 'the steering wheel' . . . holding the pen . . . I was thinking the lady might like to get to know Céline number two . . . number three, I mean . . . maybe offer her congratulations . . ."

"No," I told him. "She didn't seem that interested . . . changed the subject . . . This stuff doesn't mean that much to her, you know. Listen . . . if you don't mind . . . I'd just as soon you didn't call me from now on. I'll call you. Not from here, maybe from Tulle or Uzerche . . ."

He snickered:

"Afraid of the little lady?"

"Just to be on the safe side . . ."

I was alone in the office, but I'd lowered my voice all the same.

"You told me yourself, we shouldn't get women mixed up in all this. You understand . . . One little mistake . . . Let slip one word too many, it can happen just like that . . . suppose she's standing there breathing down my neck . . . I don't know . . . suppose she hears something . . . You don't think it's a little dangerous?"

"Dangerous? Oh! I see . . ."

He let out a loud, devastating laugh—a truly assholic laugh:

"I understand! Monsieur is thinking of our late little friend!"

I'd hardly hung up when Céline burst into the office. I could almost feel the cannonball whistling past my head. She was accompanied by a customer, a dropsy case who probably needed a periscope to see his shoes, Monsieur Legendre. We'd had the pleasure of hosting him two or three times before. His olive-green Opel Senator was parked in the front drive. Legendre ran a lighting shop in Paris. He was even fatter than last time, his stomach stuck out like the hood of a 4x4.

"Still no luck in the hotels, Monsieur Legendre?" Céline sympathized.

She'd thrown out two glances on her way past, one at me, the other at the phone.

"I'll give you your usual room," she said, her nose in the register. "Our Vézère is particularly beautiful in June . . ."

"Stupid of me to keep trying the hotels, I know . . . It's not that your nice little motel doesn't please me, Madame Ferdinaud, but . . ."

Odette extracted two suitcases from the Opel's trunk and carried one of them into the office, the other being lugged by a petite brunette in glasses and sporty clothes.

"Just think, my daughter-in-law and I were actually planning to spend the night in a field somewhere!" the customer complained.

He collapsed into a chair:

"Really, these hotel owners can be most unkind."

He wiped his forehead with his handkerchief.

"Four hotels we tried," said the petite young woman. "My father-in-law's sixty-three years old, he's starting to get tired . . ."

"For Pete's sake!" cried the dropsical one. "I'm not asking for charity! There's no civic spirit these days! At the Relais Royal in Montluçon I even offered to take my meals in my room. They wouldn't hear of it. They told me I'd block traffic in the hallways. And that they've got a whole big busload of Dutch tourists coming. And that their elevator's been acting up. I'll never get used to this. Good Lord! We're all Frenchmen, aren't we?"

"All Frenchmen, all Frenchmen . . ." said Céline. "That's the tragedy. Frenchmen can't stomach each other to save their lives. Take the bags up to 8 and 9, Odette. Let her take your suitcase, Madame Legendre . . ."

"Madame Fruitier," the short lady corrected her, smiling.

"My daughter-in-law's just been granted a divorce, and she's gone back to her maiden name," Legendre explained amiably.

"Odette, take Madame's suitcase," Céline ordered. "Until lunchtime, my friends . . . we have a delicious coq au vin waiting for us . . ."

Odette, Legendre, and his daughter-in-law set off down the book-lined hallway toward the stairs, the gentleman's belly repeatedly colliding with the furnishings.

"Odette told me you were in here," Céline said to me. "Making a phone call?"

"Well, yes . . . Is that not allowed?"

"Not allowed? Did I ever say that?"

"No . . . It's just your look . . ."

"What about my look?"

"The way you were looking at me, I felt like I'd been caught doing something wrong."

"You're not accusing me of spying on you?"

"I never said that."

"Did I even ask who you were calling? It's just that you seemed so flustered when I came in, that's all."

"It's no secret. I was talking to Gastinel."

"What did he want with you?"

"Nothing. Just wondering how I was getting along."

"You didn't tell him you're feeling a little lonely writing volume two all on your own?"

"I already told you, he's working on it too. And then we'll meet."

"You're planning to go to Paris again?"

"No, not at all . . . Gastinel can come down here . . ."

"Yes, tell him to stop by and see us. We won't bite. It's got to be better than meeting in the middle of the Plateau de Millevaches or the banks of Lake Vassivière, with the chilly wind blowing."

"I . . . I'll talk to him about that, of course . . ."

Terrified, I imagined the moment when I would have to invite the butterball to La Halte. What would happen? Céline would bombard him with questions. How would that dangerous creature react? Would we not then witness firsthand all the merry adventures of a bull elephant in a china shop? And the worst thing wasn't that Céline might find out Gastinel hadn't written a single line of *Brown Java* . . . that was small, absolutely miniscule potatoes . . . No, the real landmine was the other secret: the murder! What a cesspool I'd stumbled into! In the end, this was all the French hotel industry's fault: if they hadn't ostracized me for my inelegant getup, I never would have wound up at La Halte du Bon Accueil, and I don't imagine I would ever have met Gastinel, since I would never have dreamed of approaching that unwholesome specimen if my protectress hadn't shown me that book he'd put out. Would I even have finished my novel? No, without Céline egging me on, I bet I would have brought that sad little narrative to a well-deserved, hasty end. Today, I'd probably be a failed writer—the streets are full of them, it's no tragedy—but not a murderer. Having nothing obscene on your conscience is worth a lot more—a whole hell of a lot more—than any royalties you might get from a book at the top of the bestseller list.

Céline could say what she liked, insist all she pleased, I was still firmly resolved to keep Gastinel the hell out of La Halte.

"Incidentally, Jean-Rémi, what's happening with your ID?"

"It's all done, I've got the new papers. They were very nice down at the police station, and very quick about it."

"What a thing to do, losing your wallet in the métro! Only you could manage that. I'll bet you didn't lose it at all. You got your pocket picked, that's what it was, and nothing will ever make me think otherwise."

34 The Proofs

To my great surprise and my no less great relief, after Céline had browbeaten me on multiple occasions to get my co-author to come out for a day at La Halte, Gastinel finally declined the invitation, pretty brusquely as a matter of fact, and I realized he had no desire to find himself face to face with Céline. The prospect of a tête-à-tête with "the old lady who fed and bedded you," as he said, seemed to spook him. I called him a gutless wonder, he answered with a rude word, and that's how things stayed. I couldn't have been happier, and, you'll understand, I had no intention of asking again.

So I had no reason to worry he might show up unannounced at La Halte—one thing, at least, I didn't have to be afraid of. He wasn't going to set foot in this place, probably terrified he might blurt out some compromising detail about our literary pseudo-collaboration or the murder of Maryvonne Le Goff. Furthermore, he knew the motel owner was an expert on literature, with a long career as a big bookseller behind her; I'd told him all about her, and that seemed to intimidate him, seemed to inspire him to tread carefully, to avoid laying himself open to all sorts of insidious questions—literary ones, above all—that he might have some difficulty answering. I can guess what he was thinking: mixed up in a rambling conversation on topics well beyond the ken of the publisher of literary detritus that he was, he might just see his writer disguise suddenly crumple and fall at his feet. For the same reason, wary of the potential traps—for all his poise and his ready supply of hot air—he showed no great eagerness to show his fat face on TV or broadcast his blathering voice on the radio, once the novel came out, knowing he ran the risk of slipping up and being unmasked by someone sharper than him, and to tell you the truth I didn't much relish that idea myself, because who knows how he might react? If he got confused, the blimp might very well lose his cool and decide—if only to hurt me, purely out of jealousy and an urge to destroy—decide to launch all our shit toward the ever-ready fan and tell everyone what happened in Carrouges on the night of June 3. So for pity's sake, leave the fat man alone! Don't go trying to delve into his inner recesses or anything!

Thus, with a mind unclouded by dread, I sat down to correct the proofs of my novel in the first days of August.

Camille brought them in from the mailbox. The hulk had called me a week before to let me know they'd be coming. He'd heard this from Malgodin's assistant. Monsieur Jumbo would receive a separate set, and then we'd each sign the "Authorization to Print" form on the top of our own stack.

Wanting to leave me in peace, Céline had gone off to spend a few days with her niece in Bordeaux.

I reread the whole thing—quickly, but without skipping a line. I liked it less and less. Nothing had changed. Still crap. Clearly the proofreader hadn't exactly put himself out, because I spotted a number of syntactic screw-ups that hadn't been touched, little slips I hadn't seen while I was writing, when I was tired or thinking of something else, that's a very common thing, try writing a big fat book like this sometime and you'll see. Although I had no particular respect for my work, I corrected them all. There were also some missing words here and there (for example, on page 23: "Max and Mimile crossed tracks of the train station of and headed for the signal box," or, on page 129: "He picked up his hat, put it on his, and went out into street"), along with two or three typos, for instance on page 136, "Rain had begun to fall, and in the street the umbrellas were opining," not to mention the appearance of a Renault 5 in 1942! It's murder, cranking out more than six hundred pages like that, I really should have taken a break between chapters . . . And the bloopers just kept on coming, till finally I realized the thing hadn't been proofread at all. World-class skinflint that he was, Malgodin had handed my manuscript straight to the printer. Gastinel was right: no danger of anyone messing with my work! Well, if they liked that kind of writing, good for them, but frankly I didn't share their tastes. Just about every last sentence of *Brown Java* limps along like a mud-coated slug—I won't bore you with the whole long list of nasty adjectives I'd have to use to demonstrate that obvious point. A lot of work for nothing, pissing into the wind—throw down your pen, my lad, you'd be better off trawling the brothels or hunting winkles on the beach. I was still utterly nonplussed by what was happening to me. Why keep poking at the rump of such a tragic, broken-down mare (by which I mean my beloved novel)? Who knows what strange things go on in a publisher's stables? Beats me. Still, Céline isn't just some silly, uncultivated woman, I told myself again. How could she find anything remarkable in my deeply mediocre prose? How could she possibly admire my glutinous sentences, oozing all over the page? How could she see what she said she saw in a book that could have been drooled out by any blithering boob on the street? That's what really killed me. Deep down, I knew Céline was no nutjob. So what was the deal? And then Malgodin, dumping a load of dough into the thing, all but slavering to sink his money into such an empty-headed, ham-handed, flat-footed book! As for the fatso, who claimed to have been so dazzled by it . . . All I had to do was to think of the tenth-rate science fiction and the brainless comic books he'd published in his horse-butchers'-turned-novel-mill to wonder what exactly that alarming lard-ass had in mind, getting the two of us mixed up in a murder just for the privilege of becoming my Chatrian (I say "my Chatrian" because apparently it was mostly Erckmann who worked the pen) . . .

No, honestly, I gave up trying to understand. Maybe enlightenment would come when the book hit the shelves—a day I was now eager to see. After all, only three people, so far—not counting the printers, the various whosits who'd set the pages and so on—only three people had read my novel: Céline, the blimp, and the drunk. No editorial board at Le Papyrus, it was all up to the boss. Hard to believe the thing would ever have gotten its foot in the door at Gallim's or Furne or Alphonse Lemerre or Lacroix and Verboeckhoven! They all had their own literary advisors, their editorial boards, well-stocked with professional, serious-minded people . . . Whereas in this case . . . Leaving aside Céline's rather bizarre fervor . . . Only two people had actually deemed *Brown Java* a great book: on the one hand, a former tripemonger and one-time puppeteer who—if you needed any further proof that he wasn't really quite right in the head—had led me into the perpetration of a murder; and, on the other, a lush who'd proved incapable of saying three coherent words on the supposed literary qualities of my work, merely proclaiming, amid great peals of laughter that owed more than a little to the bottle, that I was—or rather that we were, the fatso and me—true champions, showering us with adulation, the whole spiel liberally seasoned with dithyrambic interjections and an endless tattoo of slaps on the back, behavior that for a time seemed to me highly redolent of flimflammery.

So now all I had to do was wait. No doubt the book's debut would lift the veil on this mystery. And if there was one thing I was still entirely certain of, it was this: *Brown Java* was either going to be blasted or totally ignored by the press—though, since a scathing review can still bring good publicity, I was betting on indifference—and then disappear posthaste into the same pit of oblivion as the hundreds of other gray little books that come out every year. Then we'd see how my tiny crowd of well-wishers would react. Brought down to earth with a nice, hearty thud! Alas, one thing that would never vanish into the pit of oblivion was the murder that Big Belly and I had on our consciences. Regardless: I was no longer dreading the day the book went on sale. On the contrary, I yearned for it—I couldn't wait. Come on, mid-September! Six weeks to go.

All of a sudden, rereading the proofs—in my admittedly half-assed way, because it was really tedious work—I hit . . . Hey, page 111. Which got me to thinking about page 111 of the manuscript I'd given to Langillier, which he'd misplaced somewhere and later sent back to me. Page 111 of the manuscript must be something like page 90 in the printed text. I'd already reread the passage in question, but paid it no mind, probably thinking of something else at the time. I went back to it. There it was. It straddled pages 92 and 93 of the proofs. The passage—which hadn't changed, but why the hell would it have changed?—where Max and Mimile are trying to steal eggs from a henhouse on a Norman farm. A scene where absolutely nothing significant happens, distressingly flat, crushingly vacuous . . . but which, in terms of quality, was surely every bit the equal of the rest of the book, or let's say nine-tenths of the book, because in all honesty, it had to be said, there were some amusing bits in there, every now and then, they don't last long, it's true, but still . . .

All that to help you understand why I now got back to thinking about Langillier. About Langillier's verdict. And how I got the idea of giving him a call, remembering how decent he'd been to me when we first met.

I dithered for five full minutes, then shrugged. What would be the point? And what would I say to him? But I stood firm in my mind: nothing would ever convince me Langillier hadn't seen things just the way they were. No way that guy could have been wrong. And so my impatience—for it all to be over, to see the book in the shops—immediately jumped a notch. Just a notch? Shot straight up into the stratosphere, more like!

But, I wondered . . . Wasn't there a chance that this lunacy would drag me into a nightmare even more horrible than what had happened in Carrouges at the beginning of June?

And even as I used that noun "nightmare" and that adjective "horrible," I still didn't realize what feeble euphemisms they were . . . how far short of the mark I still was.

It was just before noon when I signed the Authorization to Print form. Whew! That was done, at least. And I had no desire to reread that mess a second time. I stuffed the proofs into a big padded envelope. I was hungry. I'd heard from Odette there'd be pig's feet and stuffed cabbage for lunch.

We had a few guests at the motel, among them Fredo-la-Casquette, an aged Northerner, an ex-foreman in the coalmines, disfigured in an explosion, poor guy. Not having the wherewithal to get his mug rebuilt, he'd been walking around with a face like something out of *Phantom of the Opera* since he was thirty-nine. Needless to say, he was given a pretty cool reception in the swanky hotels. Now he was retired, and to kill time he drove all over France in his old clunker, just him and his accordion. He'd probably be playing us a little song at some point. We also had a Japanese teacher with a clubfoot, a Parkinson's case and his wife, a guy in a wheelchair accompanied by his daughter, and two or three other misshapen folks, *personae non gratae* in both pretentious palatial hotels and low-class dumps trying to put on airs. I'd eat my lunch with them. I was about to leave my room in the little house when Odette appeared.

"Lunchtime?" I asked.

"No, not for another hour, Monsieur Jean-Rémi. I was coming to get you, you're wanted on the telephone. A very polite gentleman. He didn't say his name."

My three-hundred-pound friend, I presume. Very polite, I don't doubt it—with everyone but me, the swine! I hurried out, holding the proofs in their envelope—I was planning to head to Tulle right after lunch and mail them off—and rushed into the office ahead of Odette. Yes, of course it was the fatso. I'd asked the slob not to call me here—waste of breath.

"You started correcting the proofs?" he asked (not even a "hello"—not exactly a model of Norman thoughtfulness and discretion and goodwill).

"Well, come on, are you going to answer me?"

"I just finished, I signed the approval form. I was getting so sick of that thing, I can't tell you . . ."

"I'm only up to page 60 myself. I think I can finish by tomorrow night. Do you want me to send you my set so you can compare my corrections to yours?"

"Hell, no! What did I just say? I'm sick of the whole thing. I'm not going to go reading that goddamn manuscript all over again! I've wasted enough time as it is!"

"Listen to the way this asshole talks about the new *Journey to the End of the Night*! I was just asking . . ."

"God fucking damn it, will you listen! Just leave me alone! You're the co-author of *Brown Java*, that's what you wanted, right? So what else do you need? You want me to give you a paid vacation?"

"Don't lose your temper, Jean-Rémi. Listen, if you don't feel like comparing the two sets, then just send me yours and I'll deal with it. You understand, Malgodin's a serious publisher, and I don't want to give them a bunch of sloppy, half-finished proofs. What would they think of us?"

"Fine, if that's what you want, I'll get my set right off to you. Re-read to your heart's content, and then just send the whole thing to the book man. See you!"

I hung up. Malgodin a serious publisher! Seriously alcoholic, maybe.

Alongside the guests—who were delighted with their lunch—I dug in to Odette's inspired bacon-stuffed cabbage and pig's feet in *sauce ravigote*. Fredo-la-Casquette played us a few tunes on his accordion. All very nice. Then, swallowing the last mouthful, I took the sedan and headed to Tulle to mail off the proofs, crossing out Malgodin's name and address and replacing them with that reeking lardbelly's. Then, just for a change of scenery, I took a little drive out to Lake Ruffaut, but the ghost of that kid Maryvonne was following me, no way to shake her, and as I clutched the steering wheel of that broken-down Citroën I kept thinking I was holding the other one, the one in the pachyderm's Talbot Murena, the lethal weapon.

35   The Cream of the Critics

That Monday evening, August 21, it was party time at La Halte, champagne and celebration—some of the guests even joined in. I wasn't really in the mood for festivities, myself. Less than a month to go—the book was supposed to be out around September 15—and I didn't know how to feel. Malgodin had sent galleys out to all the important literary critics. The big boys. The ones whose reviews, articles, chronicles, or columns could launch a new author, or confirm one who'd already published a little, or crown and canonize a veteran—or, conversely, the ones with the power to level an established reputation, bring down a star of the literary firmament (sometimes with no more than three cruel lines), or send a newcomer with a naively optimistic publisher backing him straight to the black hole of Calcutta. That is, all the critics who struck terror into the hearts of mere mortals—the inescapable ones, the great judges: often feared, sometimes reviled, always un-do-without-able . . . The persnickety ones, like Hector Desbrestières of *La Nouvelle Rive Gauche* or Chauffier-Delamotte of the *Figaro Méridional*, the merciless ones, like Loïc la Briançais (probably the most important of the bunch, who wrote for one daily paper, two weeklies, and several literary revues), the semiautomatic annihilators, like Marcel Cuzenat of the *Francilien Républicain*, the assassins, like Oscar Davidovitch of *L'Intransigeant* or Jérôme Herbelet of the *Capitaliste Social Rénové*. Not to mention the fierce, ever-splenetic Planche of the *Petit National*, whose hobby seemed to be sawing off the legs of young colts to keep them out of the running for big literary prizes—Planche who didn't much care for the younger generation and swore by Julien Green and other old-timers, people with thirty, forty, or fifty books behind them, who, said Planche, were now finally learning their trade. And let's not forget the sinister Brice Écoffard, a newcomer at *Paris-Midi* but already responsible for the suicides of two novelists just out of their teens (he'd drowned them in seven columns of caustic ink, just when they had one foot in the door at the Restaurant Drouant, where the Académie Goncourt meets), nor André Alvernias and Eude Beaumélou, the Siamese twins of the literary firing squad, specialists in the snuffing-out of authors about to be thrust center stage by an advertising campaign a little too raucous for their tastes, the former eighty-seven years old—his first literary massacres dating back to the twenties, at the same paper too, *Le Globe*, having filled a whole cemetery with novelists cut down after the appearance of their first book, but having erected some fine, glorious statues as well, two or three of them still standing—the latter publishing a monthly column in *Le Nouveau Messager du Livre* that was more like Sniper Alley than a little patch of newsprint. And those two were more than just killers: they were guardians of the writer's trade, banishing anyone who didn't try hard enough to be even a little bit like one of the three *B*s: Balzac, Bloy, Bernanos, their gods—both of them, of course, copiously despised by anyone trying to make a place for himself in the republic of letters. Oh, and also that Émilienne Tessy-Harcourt, she of the melodious voice (her domain was mostly the radio). There were those who considered her quite mad, owing to her odd penchant for confusing authors with ducks on a carnival firing range and the rabid invective she unleashed when a novelist's work had displeased her. This lady had an imitator, too: her colleague Esther Lebeuf, who was also her daughter-in-law—Lebeuf was a pseudonym—and whom she'd carefully mentored, instilling in her protégé her own loathing for the awkwardly written and the sloppily constructed, a high-profile bluestocking who penned a biweekly column in *Les Nouvelles Littéraires* and occupied a gun turret at *Info-Matin*. But it would have been terribly imprudent for any novelist or short-story writer to neglect the new kid on the block—he'd only been a critic for a year—Sven Pélissard, already nicknamed The Critic Sadistic, who wrote for the *Panorama des Lettres, des Sciences, et des Techniques*, a monthly read all over Europe. His peculiar trait was to heap praise on the author and the book under review, showing the utmost benevolence, feigning profound interest . . . in short, convincing the author that all was well—but in fact only toying with his prey, like a cat with a mouse, because, then, pow! in the last eight or ten lines, suddenly he'd unsheathe his saber, and in the ensuing carnage everything he'd just written, all the kindliness, the simpering compliments—sixty, eighty lines, sometimes more, of fulsome praise—was instantly swept aside to make way for a final, sometimes witheringly acid assault that cast everything in a whole new light, to the point where almost everyone whose work he reviewed—only the greenhorns were taken in by that trick—habitually started reading his articles ten lines from the end. If you were lucky enough not to find the customary axe there, still bloody from leaving your book headless, or else the three or four devastating remarks apt to rattle even the most indifferent reader, or else, finally, some fierce jack-hammer wallop capable of sending any somewhat sensitive writer into a dead, twitching faint, then you felt relieved, everything was okay, you could breathe again, and then go back and read from the beginning. They're a gang, that critical syndicate, a merciless mafia. Or, at least, so said those who envied them, those not allowed to join in the fun (who nevertheless would have gladly picked up the machine-gun themselves). And, of course, so said more than a few authors, shot down on their very first flight, never to rise again.

Gastinel called a little before four P.M. with the news—he was spluttering with emotion, the moron—that Desbrestières, old lady Tessy-Harcourt, and Oscar Davidovitch of *L'Intransigeant* were all atwitter about the book, and calling it a literary accomplishment of a sort unseen since Marcel Aymé's *The Miraculous Barber*. With those three on your side, you've got 100,000 copies as good as sold! He'd heard this, of course, from Malgodin—an ecstatic Malgodin, apparently—who'd called around two, not yet completely drunk, preferring to deliver this news to Gastinel rather than me, since the blimp lived in Paris.

36   A Triumph

The lard-ass called again at 4:30 with a fourth name for our list of admirers: Georges-Michel Folenfant, the last word in blasé jadedness, was calling our book a breathtaking triumph, a massive event, and promising a five-column review in *Le Cabinet de Lecture*.

"The news is spreading all over Paris," the fathead told me. "Two major authors are born. A couple of heavyweights!"

"You joking?"

"I assure you I'm not, Jean-Rémi. We're going to hit it big. That book we wrote . . ."

"That book *I* wrote."

"Careful now, not too loud, or . . . You know, I've still got that video."

"You'll go down with me."

"I'm not so sure, my friend. I've already explained all that, haven't I? What's going on, are you backing out on our little deal?"

"I never said that."

"So what's the problem? Maybe you're starting to feel a little faith in the book?"

"Not at all, I still think it's as putrid as ever. All this acclaim . . . something doesn't add up, and I swear, I'm going to find out what it is."

"In any case, that makes four names—four big names—on our side."

Another call came in around six, adding to that quartet the unpredictable Sven Pélissard and—the ultimate! the brass ring!—the toughest critic in Paris: Loïc La Briançais.

"You can't do better than that, kid," the blimp insisted, on cloud nine.

To hear him tell it, the word-of-mouth on *Brown Java* was roaring through Paris like a tidal wave, flooding Saint-Germain and the whole Odéon neighborhood, home to all the major publishers, all the big names, Gallim's, Furne, Lacroix et Verboeckhoven, Conard, etc., etc. Everyone was trying to figure out why these two guys, Duchin and Rastinel—the names were almost always mutilated, sometimes willfully, probably out of jealousy, just to make sure we interlopers understood we were rank unknowns—why those two had submitted their work to a publisher known only for blurred type and missing pages, and an inveterate drunkard to boot, a nameless mess of a man. Never had two neophyte novelists been so ill-advised, they said.

At 6:45, the filthy fart delivered up another name: Laroche-Beaulieu of the *Méridional Littéraire*—he who'd been friends with Pagnol, he who'd discovered the Mauriol woman, now on the jury for the Prix Femina.

"I'm hoping word will come from other critics tonight, Jean-Rémi. Can I call you, if I hear more? I asked Malgodin to go ahead and wake me up if there's news."

"No, don't do that," I said, wearily. "I can never get back to sleep again. But where's Malgo hearing all this?"

"Well, you know, in the bars. He's flitting from one to the next, he's already hit a dozen of them all around Saint-Germain."

"Stewed to the gills, of course."

"Not completely. Strangely, joy seems to sober him up. Good-bye for now, Jean-Rémi."

He called again two days later. Four more new newspapers were with us. Surprise, excitement, delight. Some in the literary milieu were already clamoring to meet the authors, desperate to make their acquaintance. Politely but firmly, Malgo held them off.

"Not till the book comes out, friends. And even then, my colts are more the stay-at-home type, you know . . . Not at all into the social scene . . . They don't go to cocktail parties and all that . . ."

"You're sure they weren't stoned out of their gourds when they read that thing?" I asked the colossus.

37   Dinner at the Brasserie Lipp

Things went a little awry on the evening of August 28. We were still at the dinner table. It was around 9:30. I remember we had stewed veal shanks and fricasseed coulemelle mushrooms on the menu, just after the lamb-brain fritters (Odette was a little out of sorts, she'd been slaving over the stove almost all day long). We were sitting with an elderly couple from Nancy who'd been turned away from all the hotels, her a former trapeze artist whose career was cut short by a fall that almost landed her in a steel corset and a wheelchair, him afflicted with sialorrhea, which can be quite a nuisance in restaurants—charming people, her very cultivated, him a great reader of Conrad and Jack London, but not of Dochin-Gastinel, no thanks.

Anyway, I heard the phone jangling in the front office, so I got up and pulled the napkin off my neck, my mouth still full, anticipating that my beloved pain-in-the-ass partner was at it again. He'd been calling for days now, jamming the line. Apparently enchanted beyond words by our glittering success, Céline scurried in on my heels.

"I've finally got what I wanted! Finally, my dream has come true! Now I can die in peace!" she'd exclaimed several times over the last few delirious days. The poor thing was awash in delight, that's a fact, and all for a louse like me.

My benefactress picked up the phone's second earpiece to listen in. This time the news didn't seem so good. Things had changed. Gastinel's voice sounded husky, and a good deal less joyous than before:

"Cuzenat of the *Francilien Républicain* and Folenfant of *Le Cabinet de Lecture* were dining together at the Brasserie Lipp a while ago. They're great friends, you know."

To stave off potential disaster, I muttered an aside to Céline, so my son-of-a-bitch collaborator would know she was listening in and wouldn't make the mistake of bringing up the murder. Like I said, with this guy you had to be ready for anything. He read me loud and clear, and gave me a reassuring, "Don't worry, kid."

"Why would you be worried?" Céline asked me.

"Nothing, nothing . . . He's always afraid I'll go to pieces about the reviews . . ."

So Cuzenat and Folenfant had had dinner together.

These were two heavyweight critics. Cuzenat was widely considered a full-time demolition man, and Folenfant a blasé, seen-it-all type, but according to Gastinel the latter had taken quite a shine to *Brown Java*, had in fact displayed an enthusiasm at least comparable to Léon Daudet's on encountering *Journey to the End of the Night* nearly sixty-five years before. With just ten positive lines in his column, Folenfant—like La Briançais—could send ten thousand people scurrying into a dozen Parisian bookstores in less than an hour: one word from him, and the cash registers clicked into overdrive. A bon vivant, a connoisseur of fine foods . . . if his belly had only been a little roomier he could have dined out with eager publishers fifteen times a week, in joints where you need never have your view polluted by the sight of some blue-color slob or office worker . . .

"What's going on, Charles? You sound all keyed up."

"Well yeah, like I was telling you, Folenfant and Cuzenat just had a cozy little dinner at the Lipp."

"And? What, was the soup too hot or something?"

Céline kept the spare earpiece glued to her head, looking like she was listening to Radio London the day before D-day.

"Nizier, of the *Constitutionnel Libéré*, was eating a plate of *choucroute* two tables away, and overheard part of their conversation. And believe you me, Nizier got an earful . . ."

"And who is this Nizier?" I asked, never having set foot in a newspaper office or a cocktail party or the Brasserie Lipp. "We haven't been introduced."

"A small-time critic," Céline whispered, up on everything as always, even after forty-plus years in this godforsaken backwater. "Still, he has to be handled with care. Kind of a gossip columnist, if you like."

"Nizier's a walking rumor-mill," the blimp confirmed. "But dishing dirt isn't all he does. He's got to the bottom of some real literary mysteries."

"So?" I said. "Are you going to tell me what they ordered, too? What are you getting at? Sit down and catch your breath, if you're too winded to talk."

"I *am* sitting down. Jesus, what a pain you can be! This is important stuff I'm trying to tell you here. Folenfant's crazy about the book, like I said. Wants to give it a full-page spread in *Le Cabinet de Lecture*, a rag as highbrow as the late, lamented *Arts*. I'm telling you that because I'm sure you wouldn't know, you who read only *True Detective* and *The World in Pictures*. With Folenfant on our side, we'll be translated into ten civilized languages for sure. But there's a hitch."

"What's that?" Céline yelped, upset and alarmed—even a little menacing, I thought. She snatched the receiver out of my hand and spat:

"Speak, Monsieur Gastinel. I'm Céline Ferdinaud, Jean-Rémi's mo . . . friend. Very pleased to make your acquaintance, and all my congratulations while I've got your ear. You know, we would have loved to have you down to La Halte as our guest . . . We drink in your words, believe me, and out here it's been nothing but joy and celebration for the past week!"

I grabbed back the receiver:

"Well come on, out with it. What's up?"

"Here's the thing. Folenfant is ecstatic, yes, but Cuzenat's flat out against it. And Cuzenat's reviews can do a great deal of damage. They're nasty and vindictive, and they cling to you like a badge of shame for years afterward. Some call him the purger of the editorial boards. Not even afraid of slander, Cuzenat. And he's completely opposed to letting a book slip by in silence. He wants to grind *Brown Java* into the dust, he said so."

"What doesn't he like about it?"

"He must be out of his mind," said Céline.

"A whole bunch of stuff . . . I'm not going to give you a list . . . The important thing is, he hates it. And to make matters worse, Cuzenat's one of the gatekeepers of the Académie Française. Without his gracious consent, we might never get in! Left out in the cold!"

"What the fuck does that matter? You're not seriously aiming for a seat in the Académie, are you? Which glorious predecessors are you going to cite in your inaugural address, butcher boy? Chateaubriand? Hamburger?"

"Oh, shut your hole, will you? Anyway, that's not all, my dear dipshit. Cuzenat's spent the past few months adding new keys to his ring, and now he also reigns over the Restaurant Drouant and the salons of the Prix Femina. He thinks our book is contrived . . . and badly written, and duller than dishwater . . ."

"Impossible," said Céline, her lips twisted into an almost vicious sneer. "He must have been paid off by some rival of yours. Already jealous of your success, before the book's even come out."

"Like who?" I asked.

"Another writer, who do you think?" she said. "Seats in the Académie aren't easy to come by, you know. Use your imagination! I can hear them now: 'Who are these two assholes trying to worm their way into our little enclave? We can't have that. As if old man Céline didn't give us enough trouble, now here come two more just like him. What's this world coming to?'"

"No, Madame Ferdinaud, I'm sure it's not that," my beloved Gastinel intervened, overhearing her. "Cuzenat's well known for his intellectual integrity. And financial too. He's a man of faith, a practicing Catholic, very upstanding, father of eight, he's no operator. He just doesn't like the book, that's all. And he wants to rip it apart. His mind is made up. Six columns in *Le Francilien Week-End*, the biggest literary paper of them all. Malgodin's tearing his hair out. Everyone knows a Cuzenat review packs more punch than a Folenfant, although he's nothing to sneeze at in himself. I'm telling you, we just have to accept it: this is the kiss of death!"

Two days later, on Wednesday, August 30, we were listening to the news on the radio—several of us huddled up against the receiver to catch the newsreader's machine-gun delivery (afterwards we reconstituted the gist of the bulletin, each of us having managed to grasp a few snatches) and heard the following: "The body of Marcel Cuzenat has been found in Lake Neuf, in the Forest of Rambouillet, outside Paris. Early this morning, a passing cyclist spotted the swollen corpse afloat in the water and alerted the gendarmes in Gambais. No one can say at present if his death resulted from an accident, suicide, or murder. The widely respected literary critic Marcel Cuzenat, aged fifty-two, is known to have had a violent argument with his colleague Georges-Michel Folenfant, of *Le Cabinet de Lecture*, two nights ago in the Brasserie Lipp. Witnesses report that the dispute very nearly came to blows. The two critics left the brasserie a little after 8:45; according to the coroner, death by drowning occurred sometime around 11:00 on the night of Monday, August 28. The public prosecutor of Versailles has opened an investigation."

Two days later, on Friday, September 1, we read the following in *La Montagne* (just a few lines at the bottom of the last page):

> *No sign of violence having been detected on the body of the literary critic Marcel Cuzenat, who drowned four days ago in a lake in the forest of Rambouillet, the investigators of the Regional Crime Squad of Versailles have ruled out foul play, and are now operating on the theory that the critic died either by accident or by his own hand. How the victim found his way so far into the forest has not been determined. No taxi driver has come forward with information. Barring the discovery of further evidence, Judge Boichoux, charged with overseeing the investigation, is reportedly preparing to close the case.*

As Céline had so lucidly predicted, Cuzenat must have ended up kicking himself for not liking *Dancing the Brown Java*. Unless he never even had time.

The good news kept pouring in. Almost every critic who matters admired the novel, and defended it with all the means at their disposal. People were hailing the birth of a sort of new Céline, hoping, however, that in years to come, the authors would not follow the regrettable course that was Doctor Destouches's after 1936–37 (in the words of the critic Firmaine de Saint-Gelbraut, in the *Moniteur Littéraire*).

38   A Quarrel over a Novel

Sitting at his desk, his lamp lit—it was only 5:30 in the afternoon, but the thunderstorm threatening Paris that Monday (September 4, 1995) had darkened the skies and dimmed rooms and apartments all over town—the great literary critic Loïc La Briançais, whose articles had opened the gates of success to more than one novelist (including several unknowns, entirely without connections), and banished more still to the literary ergastula, who wielded his pen like a sort of scalpel, like a razor-sharp blade, and who had long been the terror of the entire literary world . . . Loïc La Briançais wrote the following lines:

> *With a sickening stench seeping from its style—yes, we'll call it a "style," for lack of a better word—far more pungent than the emanations of any sewer at the height of the summer heat, this novel takes the form of a blustering rant that I dare not call Ubuesque, lest I ruffle the admirers of Alfred Jarry. No, I shall call it simply ridiculous. Clearly, the authors are aiming to ape Céline. So these, apparently, are the wan spurts of saliva that have sent some of my colleagues into swoons of delight!—but this comes as little surprise, in an age when vulgarity, mediocrity, sitcomery, and slapdashery— those great friends of the masses—all lurk in every roadside grove, fingering their blackjacks, waiting for Art to happen*

along. I refer of course to the writing of Messieurs Dochin and Gastinel, two accomplices from the more sordid suburbs of literature. With their absurd histrionics, aimed at a readership of the most hypothetical sort (whom I sincerely pity, should the authors manage to find them), they reveal themselves as indigent clowns, purveyors of the badly-written, the badly constructed, the wholly unreadable—their laborious act falling flat from the very first lines of this Brown Java, *which no music would ever consent to accompany. The book is more than six hundred pages long—let us pity this poor paper! decency forbids me to cite the substance that it would no doubt have preferred to be smeared with, rather than these ridiculous waves of incongruity!—the volume, as I was saying, contains more than six hundred pages, such that I was forced to place an urgent call to my podiatrist this morning, so gravely swollen was the foot on which that doorstop happened to land, when I finally let it fall . . .*

This wasn't the opening of the article. There were fifteen or twenty lines of the same flavor above it. A withering attack, brutal and merciless, intended to cut the legs out from under two novelists just taking their very first steps.

La Briançais smiled as he wrote. The man—in jabot, embroidered smoking jacket, impeccable white sleeves—seemed to be delighting in his cruelty.

"I thought you loved that book! You've been shouting about it in every literary café and restaurant for the past week—no one could get a word in edgewise! You were just rhapsodizing about it to Raphaël Sorin in the Deux Magots night before last. That Borowski woman from Furne said you were drooling with enthusiasm!"

La Briançais sighed, stopped his pen in mid-flight, and looked up:

"Are you still here? I hope you're not planning to put down roots?" He affected an expression of surprise, his lower lip sarcastically curled. "I thought you wanted to take all your dollies and go home."

Margaux, his mistress, his concubine for the past five years—ever since he'd demolished her work in the journal that published his column, his dreaded critiques, so mortally feared by publishers and authors alike: his long, influential analyses, unfailingly punctilious, detailed, sharp, sound, intelligent, and constructive—Margaux, his girlfriend ever since he'd demolished her first novel, her only novel in fact, stood peering over his shoulder, reading the first lines of his article. Finding herself blown to bits by the formidable critic in September 1990, just when she was picturing herself on the Goncourt lists, she'd hatched an ingenious plan: to get close to him . . . very close . . . in short, to become his special friend, so that the bully might prove a little more amiable, a bit more gallant, when Hetzel published her second book.

Margaux Mongolfiaud was a very beautiful woman—a superb creature, still modeling for Patouil at the time—and her plan met with immediate success. A confirmed bachelor of sixty, Loïc La Briançais had not lost his eye for the ladies. Loïc and Margaux met at a cocktail party in the salons of the publisher Ladvocat and immediately settled their differences. "That's not exactly what I meant, my dear woman . . . *The Sawtooth Perimeter* is not, strictly speaking, a mediocre novel, and surely would not have been out of place on the short list for the Goncourt, but you see . . ." "I know you weren't intending to be cruel, dear La Briançais, and if I wanted to make sure and tell you that in this work I was above all seeking to create a synthesis of the heroine's abstract interiority and her irrational desire for an exarchate state, it's simply because . . ." "Tell me, my dear, what are you doing tomorrow evening? I've looked through *TV Week*, and there's nothing much on. Perhaps we could dine together. At La Méditerranée, for instance, where they make a superb veal scallop with sorrel." But for Margaux, that second novel never came. La Briançais firmly dissuaded her—after several rolls in the hay, of course—from ever again trying her hand at that arduous, frustrating craft, in which the French language is little more than an inextricable tangle of traps. After a brief bout of tears, Margaux gave in. "Try to become an anchor on the eight-o'clock news—apparently they're looking for good people," he'd suggested. To console herself on finding the gates of literary glory slammed shut in her face, the ex-model went to work for our fearless slayer of bad writers, even giving her opinion now and again on some new release placed in the light—occasionally warm and illuminating, more often incendiary and withering—of her friend and lover's gaze. And he sometimes took these opinions quite seriously, for the young woman had a smattering of good judgment.

But now the spell had been broken. Not only was their affair coming to an end—oh, it's true, anything can happen! Mademoiselle Mongolfiaud was actually dumping her revered critic and lover!—but the former model and failed authoress had let out cries of delight as she read through the galleys of *Dancing the Brown Java*, which she'd discovered in a drawer of her illustrious mentor's desk.

And so, since everything was now finished between them, he'd kindly suggested she gather her things, pack her bags, disappear, and take care never again to set foot in his spacious apartment on the Boulevard Raspail, its walls lined with canvases by the great masters—the critic having won a great sum in the lottery ten years before.

"You still here?" La Briançais repeated. "I thought your new guy was waiting downstairs in his Porsche. Don't forget to wear your little hat or you might catch cold, it's been raining, and there's a nip in the air. Such a lovely little head . . . so full of clever ideas . . . Ha ha ha ha ha!"

The young woman was shocked by the brilliant journalist's cackle.

"Don't mock me, Loïc. I may have spent more than four years with a freak like you, but still, I'm no fool!"

La Briançais inserted a Camel into his cigarette holder.

"Shove off," he said curtly. "I've seen enough of you."

Peering over the shoulder of this scourge of overpraised mediocrities, she read the first lines of the review. It wasn't due for another three or four weeks, but he'd started it early, in a sudden fit of inspiration.

"Just like I thought, he's going to tear it apart, the rat!" she spat out, furious, her eyes welling over. "It's horrible! I've never seen you write anything like this . . . so cruel . . . so spiteful . . . so unjust!"

"*Dancing the Brown Java* is shit," he said matter-of-factly. "It's obviously been gathering dust in publishers' offices all over Paris . . . Furne, Gallim's, your old friends Hetzel, Charpentier, pretty much everywhere, I'd wager . . . I'll have to look into that. A turkey of this magnitude was predestined to end up with a bottom-feeder like Malgodin. Someone who belongs in the backwoods of Borneo, publishing photo-novels in pidgin."

Margaux idolized this book, had even reread it twice over; her anger swelled, and her eye turned cruel, stripping her of some of her beauty, as ill humor nearly always does . . .

"So what was that you were spouting to all your highbrow friends in the cafés? You said it was brilliant, you said nothing so fine and so new had come down the pike since Céline's first book! Oh! You people and your precious Céline, forever comparing some new writer's work to his . . . how would you ever manage without him?"

"Why, we'd use Proust . . . Zola . . . And why not Aragon? Not Marcel Aymé, though: he's incomparable. Maybe he'll produce an heir someday . . . maybe in a hundred years . . . phenomena like that don't come along every day . . . At any rate, I was only saying all those things to draw out my colleagues, to see where I stood. Imbeciles, every one of them! All on the wrong side of the fence! They love the damn thing! Except poor Cuzenat, of course: he couldn't stand it. I wonder what could have moved a happy, healthy guy like that to commit suicide . . . or to go bobbing for ducks in that lake . . . and at such an ungodly hour. Anyway. As I was saying, all those halfwits are praising the book to the heavens. Well, not me, I'm not going to play along. This pointless book . . . by two unknowns . . . Where'd they come from? You have to wonder. They say Gastinel . . . unless it was Dochin, I can't remember . . . wrote and published a crime novel five or six years ago. Straight out of the ghetto, in short. But if I choose to demolish these two nonentities and their slipshod style, it's simply because they've written a dreadful book, not worth a fistful of used Kleenex. And that's that."

"You change your mind like it was a pair of underwear. You're nothing but a bastard!" shrieked Margaux, furious.

Sensing she was about to crumple or rip up the pages on his leather-topped desk, the man of letters leapt to his feet and tried to immobilize the young woman, roughly clasping her arms behind her back. But, thrusting her head forward in the manner of an enraged ram—she was an Aries, as it happens—she gave his nose a good, hard bite, as if ripping into an unusually tough link of dried sausage. Blood began to flow. She was wriggling like a lunatic who'd been throwing her tranquilizers down the toilet and whose caretakers were struggling to push into a cold shower. Writhing like a spider dropped onto a hot frying pan. The critic lost his toupee in the skirmish, a tuft of false silvery-blond hair that she now set about trampling underfoot like a doormat. Finally breaking free, the ex-model scratched savagely at the critic's face, hands, and neck, with all the rage of a partisan of the white party ripping down the posters of the red party, or vice versa. The aristocrat riposted with a fierce volley of slaps, whipping her pretty, doll-like face back and forth till tears flowed from the charming blue eyes that had so bewitched him a few years before. An all-out brawl was brewing, the bloodied lovers rolling over the carpet, limbs intertwined, Margaux howling like a Fury, her skirt hitched up to her waist, kicking for all she was worth. They rose to their feet, looking daggers at each other. Blows began to rain down again. A few more good jabs. The girl had a shiner. Unidentified objects flew across the room, shattering an aquarium to bits.

"Slut!"

"Asshole!"

"Little guttersnipe!"

"Big bastard!"

"Know-nothing!"

"Long live Dochin and Gastinel!" Margaux cried, raging and vengeful. "Long live *Dancing the Brown Java*!"

"Little idiot! Little tart! Go read your TV-show novelizations!"

"Put your rug back on, or a hen will come sit on you!"

They stood for a moment face to face, panting, machine-gunning each other with their eyes. She held an Oriental vase in one hand, ready to throw it in his face. He'd picked up his letter-opener, almost as long as a samurai's sword.

"You're only panning *Brown Java* because I like it!" she hissed, breathless, beside herself with anger. "Just to be mean!"

"You know, baby, it's not really so unusual for someone to write a bad review not so much because they want to demolish the author as because they're hoping to bug someone else who's big on him, someone whom he, the critic, can't abide. Cruelty by proxy, if you like. The opposite works too, actually. You might shower praises on X's book even if you're not all that keen on it, primarily to exasperate Y, who can't stand X—Y whom you, the critic, consider a filthy swine. Are you following all this, or do you need a compass?"

"Just say it: you're doing this to get at me! An underhanded way—oh, so brave!—of reminding me I'm just an airhead, a philistine, a fan of soap operas and photo-novels!"

"That's about the size of it, yes . . . Let's say it all fits together . . . I've always thought you had something of the serving-girl about you."

"Cad!"

"But the underlying reason for my aversion to this small-town-train-station novel is entirely different, of course. I'm known for my intellectual honesty. That's what gives my column such an impact on sales . . . and non-sales, of course. No, if I choose to lay into *Brown Java*, it's because it's a bad book, plain and simple. Because I despise it."

And here, raising his voice, enunciating like an actor at the Comédie Française in the days of Mounet-Sully, La Briançais shouted square in the face of his former beloved:

"I LOATHE *DANCING THE BROWN JAVA* BY MESSIEURS DOCHIN AND GASTINEL! Let's get that straight. And I'll say so in black and white when the thing shows up in the bookstores a few weeks from now!"

Margaux conscientiously cleaned out her ears each and every morning, and so heard all this quite clearly. As did the plumber, who wasn't really listening, but was just next door in the bathroom. Hearing raised voices, he'd paused in his labors, clasping his wrench in one hand and wondering what was up. "Sounds like it's getting a little rough in there," he told himself. He realized this wasn't exactly a classic lover's tiff, there was something else behind it. They seemed to be quarreling over a movie or a TV show, or maybe a book. He was leaning toward the latter, as the gentleman worked for the papers, giving grades to novels, or something like that. The title of the book was *Dancing the Brown Java*, even a deaf man with no hearing aid could have told you that, the way they kept braying those words in particular, louder than the rest . . . sort of like how the radio always gets louder whenever an ad comes on.

39 In the Vavin Station

The next day, the newspapers, the radio, and the small screen announced:

> *Loïc La Briançais is dead. The great literary critic, he who discovered Babette Balazier, Pierre-Augustin Chavaillard, and Mamadou Bételgrain, he who denied the Goncourt to so many young novelists, well-connected or otherwise, fell onto the tracks of the Vavin métro station at around 6:30 yesterday evening, in the middle of rush hour, just as a train was pulling in. The platform was filled to capacity, and investigators have yet to determine whether the critic slipped or was pushed, either deliberately or by a surge of the crowd as the train entered the station. Métro traffic from the Porte de Clignancourt to the Porte d'Orléans was immediately suspended. On the arrival of paramedics, Loïc La Briançais, half-decapitated, one leg severed, had already succumbed to his wounds.*

This news sent a shock through the entire literary world, but particularly through the offices of Le Papyrus, where Malgodin had been expecting a rave review from that critical titan—wrongly, it seems, since before long a rumor propagated by the journalist's ex-girlfriend began making the rounds of the press rooms and publishing offices: La Briançais hadn't liked *Dancing the Brown Java* at all. To many this came as a great surprise, for on several occasions the critic had publicly lauded the book, with great warmth and at considerable volume. Had he perhaps changed his mind at the last minute, possibly after a second reading? Conjecture was heaped upon conjecture.

At La Halte, dismay ruled the day. Hadn't Gastinel called Dochin on August 21 to tell him La Briançais had gone gaga over *Brown Java*? And that a rave review from the critic of *Le Temps* was now guaranteed?

"It's just like you said, Céline," Dochin mused. "Anyone who doesn't like it . . ."

"Some things you can just see right away, my boy . . . if you've got any sense, that is. Some things are just blindingly obvious, that's all. Take the tarot, for instance, one example among many: don't go trying to tell me those cards don't know what they're talking about!"

"But La Briançais . . . You think . . . ?"

"If he changed his mind at the last minute, then that's just too bad for him," Céline shot back in an odd, unfamiliar voice, and with an equally queer look in her eyes.

"What do you mean?" asked Dochin, his features taut with anxiety, a spoonful of watercress soup hovering two inches away from his mouth.

"Nothing. I don't mean anything in particular."

"You said: 'That's just too bad for him.'"

"Really? I said 'That's just too bad for him'? How very strange."

"I assure you, my dear Céline, you said 'That's just too bad for him.'"

"If I said that, then it's really just too bad . . ."

"You don't think it's particularly too bad for me and Gastinel? So much for our big review in *Le Temps*!"

"Don't let it get to you. There are other critics, thank God. Big ones, too, influential and everything."

"There was Cuzenat. But now he's bought it too."

"Gastinel found out right away Cuzenat was against it. That's what he told you, isn't it? And he's always up on the latest dirt."

"You're right, Cuzenat didn't like it," Dochin murmured, increasingly troubled.

"Seems like that didn't exactly bring him good luck," said Céline, once again fixing her protégé with that ambiguous stare.

"What do you mean?"

"Me? Nothing. I don't mean anything."

"You said not liking *Brown Java* didn't exactly bring Cuzenat good luck."

"Really? I said it didn't exactly bring him good luck? How extraordinary."

"I assure you, my dear Céline, you said . . ."

"Come on, eat your soup, Monsieur Jean-Rémi," Odette intervened. "I'll be bringing out the main course in a minute. We've got chicken with garlic and golden clavaria, and onion-and-saffron rice on the side. You don't want it going cold."

"Finish up, my fine fellow," said Céline. "And don't make that face. Paris is full of critics who love your book, you're not going to have to go hunting for them high and low. So there are two or three quibblers in the bunch! No point going to pieces over a little thing like that."

She flashed that fierce, owl-like look at me, the light from the overhead lamp accenting the gaudiness of her overdone makeup, her carnival mask.

"You'll see, they're all going to love it! Remember what I'm telling you. Imagine anyone not liking *Dancing the Brown Java*! . . . They'd have to be out of their minds!"

And this book everyone was going on and on about . . . was mine! How was all this going to end? They were all trying to push me along somewhere, I could feel it. Like any idiot who might have written a great book but surely hadn't invented the wheel, I saw myself for a moment—a ridiculous image, I'll grant you—with a cloak on my back, green as the springtime undergrowth, the little sword, the bicorner hat . . . The raiment of the Académie! Like in a dream!

"Get this through your thick skull: they're going to love it, I promise!" repeated Céline. And as she spoke she picked up the big carving knife and planted it brutally in the spluttering-hot chicken that Odette had just brought out: not so much as though she were pinning a butterfly as—just a thought that flashed through my head, not terribly perceptive, I know—like she was skewering some hard-to-please critic of *Brown Java*.

40　A Critic on the Hot Seat

Partial transcript of the interrogation of Monsieur Georges-Michel Folenfant, literary critic at Le Cabinet de Lecture, *by the Versailles Regional Crime Squad, dated Wednesday, August 30, 1995.*

VRCS: Monsieur Folenfant, you are the last person to have seen Monsieur Marcel Cuzenat alive. Our witnesses tell us the two of you dined at the Brasserie Lipp the day before yesterday, the evening of August 28, between 7:30 and approximately 9:00 P.M.

GMF: That's right. We often dined or lunched together. Cuzenat was a friend. And an excellent colleague.

VRCS: You are a literary critic for *Le Cabinet de Lecture* and *La Nouvelle Pensée Française.*

GMF: Yes, since 1977.

VRCS: And prior to that, editorial advisor for Lacroix and Verboeckhoven Editions.

GMF: Yes indeed, for thirteen years, June '64 to March '77.

VRCS: Our witnesses speak of a violent dispute that broke out between Monsieur Cuzenat and yourself at the Lipp. During the latter half of the meal.

GMF: Just after the escarole with croutons, herbs, hard-boiled eggs, and gambas. We were about to start in on the cabbage hotpot.

VRCS: Other diners seated in your vicinity were in fact greatly disturbed by your quarrel, and Monsieur Bourgnasse, the *maître d'hôtel,* was about to ask the owner to call the police. Apparently a group of Australian tourists were becoming particularly upset.

GMF: Yes, it was quite an animated discussion. Nothing more than a professional disagreement, though. Our voices were raised, I admit, and some particularly sharp, even spiteful words were exchanged. None of which diminished our reciprocal friendship one iota, of course.

VRCS: Still according to witnesses, this . . . fracas—let's call it what it is—lasted nearly three-quarters of an hour, and one of the waiters, Raoul, tells us you very nearly came to blows.

GMF: It's all perfectly ridiculous, I know.

VRCS: Witnesses further report that your unusually lively discussion concerned the publication . . . or rather the announcement of the publication . . . of a novel entitled *Dancing the Brown Java,* to appear shortly under the aegis of a small Parisian press, Le Papyrus, headed by Monsieur Euloge Malgodin, himself a former literary critic at the *Parisien Français.*

GMF: Yes. We'd read it in galleys. That's not unusual, when the publisher thinks a book's going to make a big splash, and it's virtually standard practice if the author's well known . . . or has a good sales record, at least. The novel should be out in the second half of September.

VRCS: It seems the author, or rather the authors, since there are two of them, are newcomers to the literary scene.

GMF: They are. Two unknowns. They're not exactly young, one of them in particular, I'm not sure if it's Dochin or Gastinel, I don't quite remember the press release, but we can still, justifiably, call them beginners. I was greatly impressed by their book. Let me say it flat out: it's a masterpiece. I'm sure it'll have the same impact as

Journey to the End of the Night in 1932. A tremendous book—and the debut of two remarkable writers. A wholly unique style, haunting, powerful, like nothing we've seen before . . . two extremely compelling talents. I'm planning to publish a most enthusiastic review in *Le Cabinet de Lecture* in mid-September. It's only natural—that's my job, after all.

VRCS: The publisher and the authors will be delighted, given your great influence as a critic. You're what they call a maker of great novelists.

GMF: Let's not exaggerate. I've delivered six Goncourt prizes, two Renaudots, and seven Feminas, that's all. Sainte-Beuve and Edmond Jaloux had many more notches on their belts than I.

VRCS: And Monsieur Cuzenat condemned your . . . infatuation for this work.

GMF: It's true, Cuzenat was adamantly opposed to it. One of the very few critics who didn't like it, actually . . .

VRCS: Monsieur Cuzenat criticized you quite sharply.

GMF: Quite violently, you mean . . . Up to and including personal attacks! I hardly recognized him. I had to strike back. What could I do? I've got a short fuse . . . Things were heating up all through the second half of the meal. By the cheese course—Munster without cumin, as I recall—a kind of hatred had crept into our remarks. Entirely inappropriate, to be sure, if only because of the other diners around us . . .

VRCS: Monsieur Cuzenat seized you by the necktie, apparently preparing to rise to his feet, and . . .

GMF: And I slapped him, it's true. What do you expect . . . he had every right not to like *Dancing the Brown Java*—and it's clear he didn't like it at all . . . a sort of contempt for the authors, I don't know what to tell you . . . but I was within my rights, too, to protest.

When I like a book—which doesn't happen often, ask anyone, but when it does—well then, I defend it to the last.

VRCS: Was it the book's little revelations concerning certain people who apparently flirted with the Vichy régime . . . and sometimes more than that . . . people who—in some cases, at least—are today in prominent positions and rather comfortable, financially, perhaps a little too comfortable . . . was that what made . . . ?

GMF: What made Cuzenat want to pan it in *Le Francilien*? Not at all. Cuzenat couldn't have cared less about that. No, his reasons were essentially literary. The political side of things interested him very little, hardly at all . . . Besides, those so-called revelations really don't add up to much, it's the same kind of gossip you might hear from your concierge, by no means the book's greatest asset. It's true that two or three of the characters suggest they'll have more shattering disclosures to give us in volume two. Hard to know what to think of that. It could just be the authors trying to drum up some more interest. Although the publisher claims it's a warning to be taken very seriously, that the next book might well be naming names, or only lightly disguising them, if that . . . might be fingering a number of real bastards who once wore the Vichy Francisque pin in their lapels, then decided it might be time to change jackets . . . when they saw what was coming . . . right after Stalingrad, for instance, or the landing in Algeria. Some of those wise guys are big shots today. I can well imagine that such people have something to fear . . . certain revelations they'd rather didn't see the light of day . . . It's true that Cuzenat condemned the authors as stool pigeons. But it was essentially the book itself, its purely literary content, that he despised.

VRCS: An autopsy is currently being conducted on Monsieur Cuzenat's body. For the moment, we don't know if we're dealing with an accident, a suicide, or a murder. Suppose it was murder. Do you believe some supporter of this novel, for purely political reasons—for the sake of those so-called revelations—having learned of Monsieur Cuzenat's aversion for the book, might have decided to derail this attempt to torpedo two writers fighting for transparency and justice?

GMF: Good night! That's pushing it a bit too far, don't you think? First of all, I told you: Cuzenat's objections were of a strictly literary nature. Second, *Brown Java*'s would-be revelations are just idle tittle-tattle, they lead nowhere . . . everyone agrees about that part, it's nothing we haven't heard thirty-six times before . . . And third, I simply can't see Cuzenat setting out to demolish two writers just because they've attacked a bunch of former collaborators who got off scot-free. On the contrary. Didn't he praise—and rather vociferously, too—Jean-Louis Huntz's book on the details behind the Fontanet assassination? And just a few months ago he did the same thing for Marie-Thérèse Chantrel de Villedieu's book, published by Furne, which brought to light the truth—or at least *a* truth—concerning the seedy financial underbelly of (a) the Moon sect, and (b) Greenpeace, as well as the true motives of that organization . . . whose leaders are all unelected, let me just say that in passing . . . No, that . . . let's call it that "righter of wrongs" aspect would only have earned my late colleague's esteem had he not felt obliged to denounce the authors as ill-informed gossipmongers . . . and especially had he not so thoroughly disapproved of the book's prose and its construction, and had he not judged the role of the two kids, Max and Mimile, so painfully hollow—so pointless, as he said—a position I strongly contested. No, gentlemen, I don't believe we need seek any farfetched political or parapolitical motive for Cuzenat's dislike of Dochin-Gastinel's book. In any case, it's true that we were scrapping like a couple of drunken sailors in defense of our positions, our very firm positions, on that work. But this in no way implies . . .

VRCS: In any case—to return to this point—you are the last person to have seen Monsieur Cuzenat alive.

GMF: If you say so . . .

VRCS: The margin of error is extremely slim. The last person we've been able to track down, at any rate. You parted ways after dinner, a little before nine o'clock. Following a more than heated discussion . . .

GMF: Around nine o'clock, that's right. But we calmed down as soon as we got out of the restaurant. The cool evening air must have done us some good. We immediately went our separate ways. Cuzenat had to make an urgent trip to Meaux.

VRCS: He did, and we know why.

GMF: His ninety-one-year-old father had fallen dangerously ill. Cuzenat's car was in the shop, and he was in a great hurry, so he asked if I wouldn't mind lending him mine.

VRCS: A red Ford Fiesta.

GMF: Right. I was only too happy to help, so I immediately handed over the key. I had an engagement not far from the Lipp, just a short walk, ten minutes at most.

VRCS: And where exactly did you part ways?

GMF: Just in front of the Lipp. Cuzenat walked off toward the Saint-Germain-des-Prés parking garage, where, as I'd told him, my car was waiting on the fourth level down, to the right, on the Rue du Dragon side.

VRCS: In front of the Lipp . . . almost exactly where Mehdi Ben Barka was kidnapped.

GMF: True. But I don't see the connection.

VRCS: Neither do we.

GMF: So Cuzenat set off for the garage, and I turned down the Rue de Rennes. And that was that.

VRCS: Marcel Cuzenat never took your car. It stayed just where you'd left it.

GMF: That's true.

VRCS: The key was found in the drowned man's jacket. In short, Monsieur Cuzenat never went to the garage. The coroner tells us he drowned in Lake Neuf a few hours later, between 11:00 and midnight. Where did you spend the rest of the night, Monsieur Folenfant?

GMF: You're not trying to suggest . . .

VRCS: We're not suggesting anything at all, Monsieur Folenfant. It's a routine question, standard procedure in an investigation of this sort. Surely you're not unaware of that?

GMF: Fine, fine. Well, I spent the rest of the evening at the home of the Baroness de Palindré, on the Rue d'Assas. She and some friends were just finishing dinner when I arrived. The Baroness is the principal shareholder of the journal *Le Mercure à Plume*. She's an old friend, a delightful woman. We chatted about literature. In fact, we discussed *Brown Java*, which everyone was talking about. Madame de Palindré was eager to read it. I left a little before one in the morning.

VRCS: We'll have to verify that.

GMF: That's your job. Go right ahead.

41 The Plumber

Partial transcript of the interrogation of Monsieur Fernand Gé-déon, plumber, by the Criminal Brigade of the Judicial Police, dated Wednesday, 6 September 1995.

CBJP: Monsieur Gédéon, you are the sole witness to a violent argument between Monsieur Loïc La Briançais, literary critic at *Le Temps*, deceased under the wheels of a moving train on Monday, 4 September at 6:45 in the Vavin métro station, and his ex-girlfriend. We know that these two live-in lovers were on the verge of separating. They had a falling-out shortly before the tragic accident that cost Monsieur La Briançais his life. We call it an accident, but it may have been murder.

FG: Yes, I was working in the bathroom of Monsieur La Briançais's apartment on the Boulevard Raspail. The door was half-open, so I could hear an earsplitting argument going on—not that I was listening, mind—with all sorts of shrieking and cater-wauling.

CBJP: The dispute concerned the imminent separation of Monsieur La Briançais and Mademoiselle Montgolfiaud. Neighbors speak of hearing raised voices.

FG: Well, mostly it had to do with a book. It almost turned physical . . . I got the impression there were things flying through the air, in both directions . . . On my way out, I saw that Monsieur La Briançais had scratches all over his cheeks and chin.

CBJP: Was the Mongolfiaud woman still in the apartment at that time?

FG: No. She must have left ten or fifteen minutes before. I heard the front door slam . . . And then everything went quiet, of course.

CBJP: Did she threaten her ex-lover in any way?

FG: I didn't hear anything like that. No, they were arguing—but it sounded more like a pancratium, the way they were whaling on each other—they were arguing about a book. The lady was wild about it, but not Monsieur La Briançais. I understood he'd started a review, and he was really tearing it down. Monsieur La Briançais was paid to give his opinion on books when they came out. Apparently he had lots of enemies.

CBJP: Who told you that?

FG: The concierge, when I came downstairs. I told her a little about the fight, and that was when she said the tenant on the fourth floor front had lots of enemies, because of the mean things he wrote about novels he didn't like. I think it was a book that got them fighting. It got very violent, you know.

CBJP: Do you remember the title of the work?

FG: No, I don't recall. I think it was something about a dance . . .

CBJP: *Dancing the Brown Java*, wasn't that it?

FG: Oh yeah, maybe that's it. Something like that. The lady liked it and he didn't. The lady said he was going to shoot it down just because she thought it was interesting. Just to needle her, you see. At least that's what I could work out. Thing is, to hear the lady tell it, the guy'd been mouthing off all over the place about how much he loved it. So she thought if he'd suddenly changed his mind, it must have been just to piss her off. You know, when people get sick of each other . . . Couples, I mean . . . My wife and

I have been married twenty-six years, and never a voice raised in anger, all sweetness and light. We plumbers have simple ideas, it's true . . .

CBJP: Once the woman was gone . . .

FG: With her suitcases, everything, her two fur coats, she was clearing out for good.

CBJP: Thanks, we knew that much already. As we were saying: once the woman was gone, did Monsieur La Briançais do anything unusual? Did he say anything odd to you?

FG: Why, no.

CBJP: You were alone with him in the apartment?

FG: From what I could see, yes. Apart from the kitty-cat . . . Ah! I remember: Monsieur La Briançais called someone. I heard the whole thing, because I'd finished my job and come into the living room to give him the bill.

CBJP: And what was that phone call about, generally speaking?

FG: I'm not sure. He seemed in a hurry. He was supposed to go out to the Porte de Montreuil for dinner with his sister, I think . . . Something like that.

CBJP: That's exactly right. We've already looked into it.

FG: He said he'd be taking the métro . . . and he'd probably be there around 7:30.

CBJP: Perfect. That all checks out. La Briançais always got around by bus or métro, in Paris at least. He hated driving. He didn't own a car, in fact.

FG: You think somebody pushed him onto the tracks?

CBJP: We have no idea. Maybe the autopsy will clear that up.

FG: Apparently the platform was jam-packed because of an anti-nuclear demonstration going on in front of the Tour Montparnasse.

CBJP: We know, we know . . . And now, Monsieur Gédéon, we have a very important question for you. We ask you to think carefully before answering.

FG: Anything you say.

CBJP: Here it is. Apart from Mademoiselle Mongolfiaud, who apparently wouldn't have had time—assuming she had the intention—to spread the word (that La Briançais no longer liked and in fact despised *Dancing the Brown Java*, that is), you are, barring some further last-minute revelation, the only person who knew that this immensely renowned literary critic was planning to give the novel some rough treatment in the press over the next few days . . .

FG: Oh . . . you think so?

CBJP: You understand, when La Briançais's change of heart came to be known in the literary milieu, no one took it seriously. He adored that book. His plan to demolish it was no doubt simply an act he put on to infuriate his girlfriend. It seems a fairly safe bet that he never intended to publish the excoriating article we found on his desk, that the review he was going to turn in to the paper would have been far more sympathetic. So, the question, Monsieur Gédéon, is: between the time you left the apartment on Boulevard Raspail, which is to say around 6:15, and the moment of Loïc La Briançais's demise, did you inform anyone that he disliked the novel *Dancing the Brown Java*?

FG: I mentioned it to the concierge . . . Just making small talk, you know . . .

CBJP: We've questioned her. Madame Oliviera-Gonçalves is adamant: she kept that information strictly to herself. Anyone else?

FG: Well, as a matter of fact I did go into a phone booth on the Boulevard Montparnasse on my way out of his building. I wanted to call the boss and tell her I was on my way home.

CBJP: Your wife?

FG: Yes. We did chat for a few minutes, it's true. And yes, I sort of told her what'd happened, how the gentleman whose bathtub drain I'd just fixed—she knew who I meant because she'd looked at my appointment book for the day, so she knew my last customer would be that book critic—anyway, I told her things had got hot between the customer and his ladyfriend, all because the guy couldn't stand a book that was about to come out: *Blue Java*. Or *Brown*. And that's about it, really.

CBJP: Do you know if your wife told anyone?

FG: Told them what?

CBJP: That La Briançais didn't like *Dancing the Brown Java*.

FG: Yes, at the butcher's this morning, she must have told Madame Betty, who runs the cash register at A la Royale Pièce de Boeuf on the Rue Caulaincourt, she's very fond of literature, watches *Apostrophes*. My wife must have thought Madame Betty knew about the book . . . So she told her about it, and . . .

CBJP: How well do you know this Madame Betty?

INTERVENTION OF THE CHIEF OF POLICE: No point pursuing this line of questioning any further, Salicetti. La Briançais would have been dead for twenty-four hours by the time the lady at the butcher's shop heard.

SALICETTI: Oh, quite right, sir, that's true. Well, we thank you, Monsieur Gédéon. We appreciate your cooperation. You're free to go.

FG: Thank you, gentlemen. Good day to you.

CONCLUSIONS OF THE CBJP: Only the plumber and the woman being dumped—or doing the dumping, rather—knew that La Briançais no longer liked *Dancing the Brown Java* and was planning to tear it to shreds. The plumber has been cleared. The girl has an alibi: at the moment her ex-sweetheart was waiting in the métro station, she was getting a quick set at her hairdressers' on the Rue de Rennes, having previously stopped by a pharmacy to deal with her black eye. She would not have had time to concoct any sort of plot—to hire a hit man, for instance, the old standby. Furthermore, she could not have known that the critic was going to be taking the subway. Nor what station he would have been at, since there are three almost adjacent stops in the neighborhood. We are thus most likely dealing with an accident. La Briançais didn't give a damn about being dumped, and he was in excellent health. We can thus rule out suicide. The victim must have been pushed onto the tracks by an involuntary surge in the crowd as the train was pulling in. This would not be the first such mishap. The autopsy will in all likelihood confirm this hypothesis: neither murder nor suicide. No witness has come forward to report seeing the critic jump onto the tracks. Nevertheless, this makes two eminent literary critics in less than a week who have come to a mysterious end: Cuzenat in Lake Neuf, and La Briançais under the wheels of a subway train.

"Two critics who didn't like that book . . . Very strange . . . very strange indeed . . ."

"It is indeed, particularly because Internal Intelligence's arts-and-literature branch says most of the critics are crazy about it."

"Not the chief. He got hold of the galleys. Couldn't follow the thing to save his life, and he was yawning all the way through. His tastes run more to San Antonio and *SAS*, anyway . . ."

"If he didn't like it, it might be in his best interests to . . ."

"To what?"

"Well . . . to keep it to himself."

On the last page of the September 8 issue of *La Montagne*, we read:

> *After an exhaustive investigation, the criminal brigade of the judicial police has concluded that the death of Monsieur Loïc La Briançais, literary critic for* Le Temps, *crushed by a subway train in the Vavin station on Monday, September 4, was purely accidental in nature. Standing at the edge of the platform, the victim evidently lost his balance, perhaps owing to a dizzy spell, just as the train was entering the station. An Officer in the Order of Arts and Letters, Loïc La Briançais liked to say that a novel must be judged as attentively and thoughtfully as if the author's life depended on it. He will be sadly missed by the entire publishing world.*

42   Walk, Don't Run

Dancing the Brown Java hit the Paris shops on Thursday, September 21, 1995, and the rest of France and the French-speaking world over the following week. The first review appeared in *Paris-Midi* on the day of the book's release, a veritable cry of wonderment from Brice Ecoffard, who for once had the human decency to refrain from ripping the author(s) limb from limb. Then came the fireworks, a rousing critical ovation; glowing, delirious, dithyrambic reviews rained down from September 23 to October 8. No doubt these glorious salvoes would keep up well into December. Even before the book's publication, the question of publicity had raised its head, and, with the news of this exceptional literary discovery spreading like wildfire, the two authors were invited to offer themselves up to the public gaze. Having jointly refused a two-or-three-minute appearance at the end of the evening news on TV—Gastinel more reluctant than Dochin—they nevertheless consented to hold forth on a major radio station in mid-September, while the book was still at the printers'. The interview was a disaster, a deplorable, unbroken gush of gibberish. The literary journalist Louise-Émilienne Tessy-Harcourt, who thought the novel superb, asked them a number of questions. In spite of their reticence, the co-signers of *Dancing the Brown Java* had grudgingly accepted this mercantile ordeal, which had nothing, absolutely nothing, to do with the difficult art that is literary writing, Euloge Malgodin having insisted that they submit to the mounting media frenzy. They maundered shambolically before the mike, nowhere near up to the challenge, absolutely devoid of media savvy—like all great writers, as the sagacious Desbrestières noted in *La Nouvelle Rive Gauche*—Gastinel wholly repellent, revealing not only his puppeteer past but also his long years in the tripe business, adopting a vulgar, brutal, peremptory tone in hopes of overcoming his own (somewhat unexpected) timidity, Dochin virtually wordless or incoherent (lots of "uh"s . . .). The Tessy-Harcourt woman nevertheless thanked them with a broad smile and proclaimed that all of France was eagerly awaiting *Brown Java*'s appearance in the bookshops.

As fate would have it, Urbain Langillier was in Paris on Tuesday, September 26, when the first sensational reviews were beginning to appear.

The journalist, ex-literary advisor for Poulet-Malassis, had just read the notoriously harsh Georges-Michel Folenfant's ebullient review of *Dancing the Brown Java* in the Sunday, September 24 issue of *Le Cabinet de Lecture*.

"Unbelievable, unimaginable," Langillier murmured, dumbfounded, setting the newspaper aside. "Have they all gone out of their minds? I've got to get to the bottom of this before I go around the bend myself."

Bewildered, he stared at the newspapers lying open on his desktop: *Le Figaro d'Outre-Mer*, *La Nouvelle Dépêche des Deux Mondes*, *Le Petit Républicain du Centre-Droit*, *Le Moniteur National*, *Les Nouvelles Littéraires*, *L'Heure Matinale*, *Info-Matin*, and also *Le Temps*, in which, absent La Briançais, the novelist Alexis Duchet-Méliancourt, whose candidacy for the Académie Française had just gone down in defeat—in vain had he campaigned for the seat of the late Monseigneur Feltout (garnering only two votes)—inaugurated his tenure as a literary columnist by trumpeting his limitless admiration for *Dancing the Brown Java*, pleased that his first published review should herald the triumph of two authors whose names it would be a grave error to forget: Dochin and Gastinel.

Langillier had spent a part of the morning reading those reviews (and then incredulously rereading them).

"Are they nuts?"

His Ethiopian maid Titi was in the room with him, doing the housework.

"Bad news, Monsieu La Gilié?"

"I'm just wondering what's going on with the critics," Langillier said. He hadn't forgotten Dochin's manuscript, that supremely unacceptable text, that disaster, badly written, bungled, incompetent beyond imagining, unpublishable, unrewritable.

"What's wrong, Uncle? Troubles?"

The young woman who'd just entered the room had the habit of calling Langillier "Uncle," though she was in fact his great-niece. Tracy Le Cardonnel, eighteen, recently hired by a private detective agency, wild about American crime novels and the works of Léo Malet, was the daughter of the obstetrician Serge Le Cardonnel, who practiced in Broussais, himself the son of Amélie Le Cardonnel née Langillier, the great reporter's elder sister. That morning, Tracy had left her little room on the Cours de Vincennes to call on her uncle, who was all too rarely in Paris.

Langillier slapped the pile of unfolded newspapers:

"A great gale of madness appears to be blowing through the world of French literary criticism. Or else I'm still in bed, dreaming. Please, my dear, pinch me."

"What's going on?" asked Tracy, astonished, refusing to deliver the requested pinch. (She perched on a stool before a set of tall bookshelves and began to reorder her great-uncle's library, left in some disarray by a workman hanging new wallpaper.)

"It's about this novel . . . *Dancing the Brown Java.*"

"Everyone's talking about it. What is it?"

"Pure tripe. A beach book for mental defectives, my dear; I urge you not to read a single page. Not only has it been published, which is mysterious enough in itself, but—and here's the second mystery—they're all calling it a . . . No, it's just too ludicrous. I've got to figure this out."

"*Dancing the Brown Java,*" said the girl. "I heard two or three words about it on the radio. I thought it was a movie."

"Well, now that you mention it . . . Yes, it could well be a movie, in any case it's an obvious plagiarism of several movies, I remember that much. Furthermore, Dochin never told me he'd written it with someone else. Better and better: all of a sudden it turns out there were two authors! If that doesn't beat all!"

"Is he the one who asked you to read his manuscript? That ex-homeless guy?" asked Tracy, a green-eyed redhead, petite and a bit plump, her manner lively, her voice spirited.

"Yes, that's him . . . Must have been back in . . . in March, something like that, when I got home from my assignment in Cambodia."

Suddenly, Titi remembered the manuscript page she'd found and left on the desk. She'd been doing the housework, straightening up Monsieu La Gilié's desk. She'd moved the papers to do some dusting, picked up the manuscript, opened it . . . She'd completely forgotten to tell him about that page. She'd started a note, but something must have interrupted her, maybe someone ringing the doorbell, she couldn't remember, and then the whole thing slipped her mind.

"Monsieu, I never tolja, I found a page a that manuscript."

"Good God!" Langillier cried, thumping his forehead. "I'd completely forgotten! The missing page . . . THE PAGE! Oh, Lord!"

Tracy gazed aghast at her great-uncle's bulging eyes. Unky Urbain seemed almost terrified.

"My God, the page!" Langillier repeated more quietly, as if in a state of shock.

"What page?" asked Tracy.

In her halting French, Titi explained that she'd picked up the fallen page from the carpet and put it back on the desk among the journalist's other papers.

"I forgot tell Monsieu bout that."

"But I found it, Titi," said the journalist. "And I sent it right back to Dochin. I never heard from him again, so he must have got it. But that page . . . I remember reading it . . . Oh God! I wasn't dreaming, I know it!"

He bounded toward his raincoat (it was drizzling outside).

"Where are you rushing off to, Uncle?" Tracy inquired, surprised and a little alarmed.

Uncle seemed quite unnerved—pursued by a pack of ghosts.

Equally taken aback by her boss's behavior, Titi wondered, "Monsieu, where you goin?"

"The lost page, for God's sake! The lost page!" exclaimed Langillier, as if gravely disturbed by a memory he'd have preferred to push aside, or perhaps erase altogether. "I can see why Dochin never asked me to do a review!" he barked, frantically struggling with his raincoat, his arms flailing wildly, like the masts of a tempest-tossed sailboat.

Tracy and Titi came to his rescue.

"He never sent you his book?" asked the great-niece.

"Certainly not! After all, I'd told him it wasn't worth a toss! Perfectly understandable. Maybe he was put out with me. I mean, I was very polite about it, it was all done with kid gloves. But the brute understood me, that's for sure."

"They've already sent out the review copies?" Tracy inquired.

"Of course, they must have by now, since the book's in the shops. I imagine the critics read it in galleys . . . As for the other VIPs . . . either they've already got the book in the mail or they will soon. But Dochin never sent me a thing. I'd be amazed if he had. When I say Dochin, of course . . . I mean him and the other one."

He was already out the door, rushing downstairs, beside himself. In his haste he almost missed a step, nearly tumbled forward and skidded to the landing on his stomach, but he caught himself just in time.

"Be careful, Uncle!" Tracy shouted, leaning over the banister.

"Careful, Monsieu La Gilié!" the maid seconded.

"Be right back, ladies!" Langillier cried.

"What's all this about a missing page?" Tracy Le Cardonnel asked the maid as they turned back into the apartment.

"Well it's like this, Mamzelle Técy . . . Monsieu La Gilié was away, and I was just tidyin up when . . ."

The door closed behind them. They were back inside the apartment.

Langillier sprinted across the Rue de La Tombe-Issoire, which intersects with the Avenue René-Coty—not using the crosswalk, as it happens. The Dormeur du Val bookstore was just across the street, a big shop where well-known or well-connected writers sometimes held signings, complete with petits-fours and all the trimmings. And indeed, before he was halfway across the street,

Langillier spied *Brown Java* in the shopwindow, lovingly displayed in the place of honor.

"I've got to get to the bottom of this! Damn and blast and curse it all!"

The massive Renault van was racing along at fifty-five miles an hour. Right in the middle of town! It struck Langillier full force. He bounced onto the hood, flew through the air like a child's toy, and landed on his back with an unwholesome *plotch*.

The vehicle was already long gone.

A crowd of gawkers immediately gathered around the victim, vilifying the maniac at the wheel. Sprawled on the pavement, face heavenward, eyes wide open, arms outstretched, the journalist lay motionless. Blood was flowing from his bruised and swollen right temple.

It was the owner of the Dormeur du Val who called the ambulance.

Hoping to catch sight of her uncle in the street, Tracy Le Cardonnel had opened the door to the balcony. Titi had just come to join her. Shocked, their faces contorted with anguish, the two girls gazed on the scene of the tragedy from the third floor of Langillier's building.

"Son of a bitch never even slowed down," said a street sweeper.

"I couldn't see the driver, he was going too fast," said another guy. "A Renault van, I think."

43   The Road Sign

God, what a shock! Like a big bolt of lightning, zigging right down to my toes. I'd just called Gastinel. I was still back at La Halte, of course. Sure, all the literary honchos in Paris were talking about me—me and the blimp—but that was no reason to leave dear old Céline's side. As for the radio and TV shows, all those tedious obligations you just can't get out of, well, for that I'd drag myself onto the TGV, which is for us provincials more or less what the brand-new métro was for the Parisians of 1900–1905. Our first appearance in the media—on the radio, before the book had even come out—was a disaster. We swore up and down we weren't going to do that again, but Malgodin had a fit and harangued us: "Buck up, my boys! Look at all these pretentious assholes you always see on the box! You're no dumber than they are, for Christ's sake! Besides, let's make no mistake, at eight o'clock at night your average TV-head has his nose buried in his soup, he's not going to waste his time eyeballing the likes of you, and the guy who asks the questions won't bite, I promise."

So I'd just called the hippo to ask what the hell was going on at Le Papyrus. The book had been on sale in some bookstores for two or three days, and I still hadn't even seen it. The critics had already got the galleys, and in a few days they'd be getting their copies signed and dedicated by the authors, and same thing for the chosen ones, the VIPs who get their books for free, Monsieur de

Whatsisname and Madame de Gimme-Gimme, all that crowd. We were supposed to show up at Le Papyrus and do the signings on Thursday, September 28, two days from then.

Chaos was the order of the day at Le Papyrus. Small-time sub-pulp publisher that he was, Malgodin was sort of lost when it came to launching a real book. At Furne or Hetzel or Gallim's they know the score by heart: (a) the manuscript goes to the proofreader; (b) the manuscript goes to the printer; (c) the proofs go to the author; (d) the thing gets printed and bound, the cover gets chosen, and all that; (e) the galleys get sent to the major critics; (f) the authors sign dedicated copes for the journalists and VIPs; (g) right after that, sometimes simultaneously, the thing goes on sale in the bookstores. But at Malgo's joint, with no one much to help out, a tiny little staff—badly paid, to boot, so not likely to give a flying fuck—and where the whole affair was more or less dumped in the lap of his secretary and ex-mistress, there was a certain chicken-with-its-head-cut-off quality to the proceedings. I'd sent the manuscript to Gastinel on May 29, and the blimp passed it straight on to Malgo. The printer—Cossé and Villarot, a family business since 1843, offices in Laval and Mayenne—got the manuscript (apparently never entrusted to the loving hands of a proofreader) around June 15. Fatty and I got the proofs at the beginning of August. All the critics that matter got the galleys not long after. We'd started hearing their reactions around August 20. Given that the book had gone on sale the next-to-last week of September, the pachyderm and I should have been signing the VIPs' copies on the 22nd at the latest. But no, it was going to be the 28th instead. Like Céline told me, nobody was going to get all steamed up about that, the main thing was to get the book to the critics before anybody else, something like six weeks before it came out, more or less, you've got to give them time to discover the thing, to read it, maybe even reread it, get out their fine-tooth combs . . .

Gastinel and I did our best to get out of the signing-and-dedicating chores. It sounded like no fun at all, and besides we had no idea what to write over our signatures. Gastinel whined that nobody gave a damn about that stuff, claimed the secondhand bookstalls were loaded with signed first editions, complete with a quick little personal remark, gracious or sycophantic, none of which, clearly, had meant more than a rat's ass to their esteemed addressees.

"All this so I can find a *Java* in a cheap *bouquiniste*'s stand three years from now, complete with my compliments and my signature!" he'd objected. "No thanks!"

"This is just how it's done, that's all," Malgodin told him. "People might be miffed if they get a copy with nothing written inside."

"What do you mean, 'nothing written inside'?" the blimp grumbled, that bastard, he who hadn't written so much as a line—"What about the story? That's a bit more than two or three polite little remarks and a signature! What else do they want? Aragon's *The Century was Young* under the same cover, and then the phone book too to round it all out?"

Anyway, I'd called Gastinel, but not about that, though he did say straight off:

"So it's still a go for the signing, day after tomorrow, two o'clock, at Le Papyrus?"

"Okay, okay, I'll be there, keep your shirt on. I'll jump on a train tomorrow morning and be in Paris by noon."

"Is that what you called about?"

"Not exactly, no. It's about our ten free copies, the author's copies. Complimentary, like the contract says. You get yours yet?"

"Not yet, no. You either, I suppose."

"As a matter of fact no. And Céline's getting on me about it . . . she can't wait to see them."

"Give her a good poke in the ass, that'll take her mind off books for a while."

"Still as foul-mouthed as ever, I see. You'd do well to mind your vocabulary, now that you're a writer. Better watch your pie-hole and talk properly when we go on TV or back on the radio."

"Quit riding my ass, will you? What do you want, anyway?"

"I told you. I wanted to know what was going on with our author's copies. Some of the stores already have it in stock, and we haven't even got our own yet."

"Business first, my boy. But they're coming. I heard yesterday afternoon. I wanted to call you, but you know how it is . . ."

"And?"

"The chick at Le Papyrus told me they were all wrapped up and ready to go. Ten free copies. Ten for yours truly, ten for Monsieur Dochin."

"I can't wait to see it."

"I saw a copy at Malgo's. And also yesterday at La Hune, the bookstore, by Saint-Germ'. You'll see, it's a thing of beauty. Doesn't anybody sell books down in that burg? Geez, you really are in the boondocks, aren't you? It's got our names in great big letters, just like famous writers, orange against a dark blue background, and there's a picture of a Kraut soldier from behind, walking down the Rue de Rivoli, you can see the arcades and everything, and then at the end of the street there are flags with swastikas hanging from a government building. *Dancing the Brown Java*, it says, and then underneath, smaller, *A Novel*. And down at the very bottom: *Le Papyrus*. But it's what's inside that counts, don't you think? Oh, by the way, get a copy of this morning's *L'Aurore-Le Pays*, there's a review by . . . I forget his name, but he compares us to the Malraux of *Man's Fate*."

"So now it's Malraux? They're out of their skulls."

"And what does your Céline have to say about all this?"

"What do you think? She's over the moon. Can you imagine, she's speechless. Mute with joy. A new old woman, almost. It kind of scares me, how happy she is. So you say I'll get my copies in a few days?"

"Before the end of the week, bucko, Malgo's assistant was sure. So long, kid. See you soon. Incidentally, Malgo told me the first printing would run 7,000. But don't you worry, that number's going to go up fast. Ciao."

So I hung up, and that was when I heard the news. Camille was out straightening up in the hallway, where Céline keeps her books. She'd put her transistor radio on a pile of *L'Illustration*s sitting on the floor, and I heard the bulletin: "We've just learned that the great reporter Urbain Langillier was mowed down this morning by a reckless driver in front of his home on the Rue de La Tombe-Issoire, in the 14th arrondissement of Paris. The noted journalist was crossing the street when he was struck head-on by a speeding van, which continued on its way as if nothing had happened. Passersby were unable to make out the vehicle's license-plate number. Urbain Langillier was transported to Cochin Hospital. At last report, his condition is described as extremely grave."

I collapsed onto a stool, like all the strength had drained out of me at once. And all the blood out of my face too, I'll bet.

"Oh, shit . . ."

Langillier . . . who hadn't cared for *Brown Java*, not one little bit.

"Oh God, oh shit," I repeated, nervously running my hand through my hair.

"Well now, does my little lamb have worries on his mind?"

Céline had come into the office, trailed by a tall, skeletal beanpole of a man—just like Valentin le Désossé—with a cheery face and jug ears. I couldn't quite figure what infirmity had earned him the ostracism of our local hotel owners. He was wearing a mauve bowler and a too-tight pinstriped suit, like Gilles Margaritis in *L'Atalante*, and carrying a little patched-up suitcase in one hand. Such a select crowd we got at La Halte! What next? Maybe a pair of Siamese twins? Or some joker doing the Tour de France on his ass?

"This is Monsieur Larmory," said Céline. "A longtime customer. Used to be a hotel thief. He did seven years in the pen. He's been blacklisted from almost all the hotels—not the casinos, mind, but most definitely from the hotels—so he came straight to us."

"Give me room 2, Mâme Ferdinaud," the sprightly skeleton requested. "The view over your glorious Pisarro-colored orchards always brightens my spirits."

"Where are you off too?" my protectress asked me.

I was already outside. I needed some air. Langillier! What the hell did all this mean? Was it a crime not to like my wretched little book, that sheaf of toilet paper for illiterate shits?

Next day at lunch—a purée of chestnuts like they just don't make anymore, plus kidneys in Madeira sauce, Odette-style, not the snooty-restaurant kind, there's a big difference—Céline thought I wasn't looking too good.

"You have to get the blush back in your cheeks, my boy. Don't forget, you've got two TV shows next week. Including the ten-o'clock news with Catherine Matouche."

"I'd just as soon Gastinel went on by himself, I'm telling you," I sighed. "Paris just doesn't do much for me anymore—if you only knew! So many terrible memories . . . You ever notice how everybody in the street has a big scowl on his face?

"And why were you looking so spooked when I came in with Monsieur Larmory?"

"Your hotel thief?"

"That's the one."

"I was looking spooked?"

"Like you didn't have a drop of blood left in your body, my boy."

"It's nothing, it's nothing . . . I'm just a little tired."

"Success is wearing you down?"

"Maybe that's it, I just can't get my head around it. I mean, come on . . . you saw it, you read it, that thing I wrote, you were the one who typed it up . . ."

"Yes, and? You're not going to start that again, are you? You still down on that book of yours?"

"Well, you saw how I write . . . right? Pure dime-store crap, like a serial in an old-time hick newspaper, back before the war. I know my limits, I'm not that dumb."

"So why do you bother to write at all, if you think you stink so bad?"

"I don't know . . . It keeps me busy . . . And also I like it, in spite of everything . . . it's irresistible . . . There must be something wrong with me . . . with my head . . . something off . . ."

"Listen to this! My, you do seem tired, that's a fact. You need a break. A nice, long rest . . . Not in the country, that's where you are now! Maybe in a convalescent home."

"Oh, yeah! With the head cases! Better and better!"

"Listen to yourself, my dear, you come up with the strangest ideas . . . If I didn't know you better, I'd think you really *were* soft in the head! It's badly written, blah blah blah, nya nya nya . . . it's this, it's that . . . Enough! Who do you think the newspapers hire to write those reviews? Idiots? Mushbrains? Addlepates? Retards? Literature is a very serious thing, my boy."

"I'm not backing down, Céline. I write like a pig. And it's for *that*, that mess, for *Dancing the Brown Java*, that all the bookstores are packed with slavering crowds waving their money in the air? What the hell? God, when I think of that book! Maybe the end holds up a little better—I'll grant you that—but there are passages that really need to be rewritten . . . almost all of them, as a matter of fact . . ."

Langillier's little remark was still trotting around under my bonnet. Absolutely impossible to doubt that guy's judgment. Unless he'd come down with some kind of brain damage.

"I just can't see it, Céline. Just you wait, it's going to be a massive flop! Fall flat on its face! I have no hopes whatsoever for that damn book. You'll see."

"In any case, you can't tell me you didn't look like a man condemned when I came into the office. What were you doing there to begin with? You'd just got off the phone?"

"Yes, I called Gastinel. About our free copies."

"Yes, come to mention it, is that Malgodin of yours ever going to send you your books? I hope he's not planning on screwing you over! Ten copies, it's not like you're asking for all the gold in Peru. What a tightwad! Ten measly copies of *Brown Java*, when I've already promised one to almost all the shopkeepers in Térignac, and even some in Uzerche! What's he up to, anyway? He doesn't expect us to buy them off him, I hope? The little Sigaudel sisters asked me for one, too. And Tuviaud wants one for his daughter-in-law. And Colard the pharmacist, for his twin nieces. I can't very well ask them to go out and buy a copy! They'd never forgive me! I've been doing business with these people for almost thirty years. La

Rigaudie, at the garage, he wants one. He never reads—not even the newspaper—but that doesn't matter, he told me, he just wants to put it on his mantelpiece next to his in-laws' photo. I can't say no to these people, they've sort of become like friends over the years. Let me remind you, Jean-Rémi, we're in the provinces. This isn't Montmartre or Mouffetard or Grenelle. And anyway, they couldn't buy a copy if they wanted to. The bookstores in Brive and Tulle won't get it for at least another two weeks, Paris always comes first, and I don't suppose that's going to change anytime soon. Imagine them seeing the book on TV and still not having a copy to call their own! I'll spare you the sharp little remarks they might make to me or Odette on shopping day. Our butcher Dézargnac might very well discover he doesn't have a scrap of meat left to sell us. I know him!"

"Those people never read anyway."

"And you suppose people who get a copy of the latest Goncourt winner for Christmas ever read it? Most of them, anyway? What are you getting at?"

"The publishers don't give a damn. As long as the book sells . . ."

"Still, doesn't the author look like a twat? Oh, I'm king of the of the world on my way in to pick up my prize, with all the cameras flashing, but you can crown me king of the boobs when it turns out my book ends up being used to prop up the two or three best photos from somebody's last vacation."

"That's what all the sore losers say."

"If you only knew where most books end up, my poor boy! I used to sell them, don't forget. There are more uncut first editions than spiderwebs in your average French attic. Ten copies! And let's not forget Félibut. He wants two. He told me again just this morning. The poor man can hardly even read, it's not really his fault, the oldest of eleven kids and his father a worthless poacher. Not to mention a mother who drank. She ended up in the home in Brive. He gets *L'Humanité*—but only reads the headlines. Two copies he wants. One for his wife, one for his schoolteacher brother-in-law."

She was starting to chafe my earholes with all her plans to hand out these—I almost said "prizes," but no—these books, whose contents weren't worth a tin sou. I was still thinking of what I'd just heard, still stunned by the news. But no way was I going to tell Céline about Langillier's accident. I didn't want to give her ideas. I'd never told her I asked a journalist to read my book—and a highly respected one at that. No reason to go stirring up trouble. If I told her now, she'd immediately want to know why this, why that, pester me with shitloads of questions. And furthermore . . . imagine telling her Langillier hadn't liked it? She'd come right back with her night-owl cackle: "Didn't you tell him he'd be sorry if he decided not to like it?"

"You really aren't looking well," she said again when we got to the cheese course. "You know what you ought to do? You ought to take the old clunker out for a spin. Not too fast, now, lamb, because I have to say, you're looking mighty on edge . . ."

Excellent idea. No need to tell me twice. At two o'clock I stood up from the table and sat down behind the wheel of the old sedan.

"Try heading over toward Le-Suc-au-May. It's wonderful in late September, the forest around the Monédières mountains is turning all red and gold . . ."

So I headed off in the direction of Chaumeil. After a quarter of an hour, not far from Veix and the druidic ruins at the Puy Pantout, the road started to wind its way through the Mondédières, up and down, twist and turn . . . Five minutes later I saw a temporary sign by the side of the road: "Danger—Falling Rocks." On and on, with those sheer cliffs towering over me. Then all of a sudden I had to put on the brakes, because the road was blocked by a broken-down car, hitched up to a decrepit old camper. Right in the middle of the road, without so much as a safety triangle! A guy in a beret and blue coveralls was hunched over the engine, sucking on a cigarette butt. I got out and walked over with my hands in my pockets. I didn't get far, because just like the sign said, there were falling rocks. The road was covered with them—just pebbles, not paving-stones. Still, the one that landed on my skull must have been at least as big as a cinderblock, because I went down for the count without further ado. No way to tell you who picked me up.

I'm going to have to leave you for a while, because they tell me I spent a pretty long time in a deep coma, just next door to death, perfect peace and quiet, totally ignorant of the shit going on in the wide world around me—in the wide world, but also nearby. My book was just going on sale, but I myself was starting down a tunnel darker than all the cheap ink I'd wasted writing that thing.

See you soon, maybe.

44 Dismay at Le Papyrus

Back at the offices of Le Papyrus, in a little salon reserved for the signing of new publications, a salon enlivened by a potted plant enormous enough to cast a shadow, Gastinel was beginning to weary. Three hours he'd been sitting there, twiddling his thumbs, bored out of his skull. Early that afternoon, the secretary had brought in four or five stacks of brand-new *Brown Java*s, with that nice just-off-the-press smell, ready to be signed and sent off to friends of the publisher and other VIPs. But here it was nearly five o'clock, and still no sign of Dochin. Malgodin was on pins and needles, pacing from his office to the salon, from the salon through the workroom, past his woolgathering colleagues, then into the storeroom, then back, then to the bistro next door, then out again with a couple of drinks in his belly, then quickly on to the tavern thirty meters further up the Avenue d'Ivry, then lightning-fast back to his offices, then starting all over again. This had been going on since three.

"Where the hell is Dochin? Is he standing us up? What's he thinking? Oh! I know you both hate having to sign all these books! But I'm not going to put up with this nonsense, I promise you!"

"Believe me, Malgo, we don't mind signing the books at all. Not me, anyway. But you must understand, I can't sign without Jean-Rémi. What, just one signature? It'd look like I was the only author! And after all, my buddy did do his share of the work. It just wouldn't look right."

"I know, I know! So did you reach that hotel where he usually stays?"

"I called ten minutes ago. No Dochin at the Hôtel des Voyageurs. He never checked in."

"Maybe there was a TGV accident?"

"Nothing on the news, boss," said Ida Salembert, the assistant, striding in, tugging at her girdle, clearly very put out herself.

"What about his place back in the Limousin?" asked the lush. "Maybe he's out mushroom-hunting?"

"No answer there, I called twice," said Gastinel.

"Try again."

"Fine, but . . ." sighed the monster, struggling to his feet and heading for the phone, involuntarily jostling the table with his belly. The stacked books tumbled to the floor, and Ida hurried to pick them up. But the phone rang just as Gastinel was reaching for the receiver, and it was an anxious Malgodin who answered.

"Hello? Oh it's you, Madame Dochin . . . Excuse me, I mean Madame Ferdinaud. Yes, that's right, Malgodin. No! It can't be! You say . . ."

As if struck dumb, white as a sheet (apart from his nose), the publisher dropped into an armchair, the receiver still in his hand. Gastinel and Ida Salembert looked on, curious, concerned.

"I'm shattered, dear Madame," said Malgodin, after a long, attentive silence. "Wish him a swift recovery for me. Oh I see . . . of course, if he's not conscious . . . Well then, the moment he comes to—because he will come to, I'm sure of that. That little guy doesn't seem like much, but believe me—you must know this already—he's a real fighter. Please know that all of us here at Le Papyrus are deeply saddened by this turn of events, dear Madame. We're all very fond of him, you know. We'll be thinking of him, and if I don't ask you what his favorite flowers might be, it's only because I know he'll pull through, I assure you. I'll give Gastinel the news at once. What a disaster . . . I hope the book won't suffer for it. Good-bye, dear Madame. Of course, I'll see what I can find out, and I'll call you the moment I've got news. Good day to you in spite of all this."

"What's going on?" asked Gastinel as the distraught publisher hung up the phone and began frantically mopping his neck and temples with a handkerchief.

"Dochin went out for a little drive yesterday afternoon . . . He stopped at the foot of a sort of cliff and got out of his car. There was a bus or something stopped in the road . . . I'll spare you the details. But it's a place where they often have falling rocks. Can you believe it, one of them hit our poor friend square on the head, and not a little pebble either. Fortunately there was a motorist right there, his car had broken down . . . I didn't catch the whole thing. Anyway, he called for an ambulance at once. Dochin was taken to a clinic in Brive. They consider his condition critical."

"Is he conscious?" asked the secretary.

"Alas, no. And it's been twenty-four hours now since the accident. It's horrifying to say this, but . . . this is what Madame Ferdinaud told me, anyway . . . the poor woman seemed completely overcome . . . apparently Dochin's in a coma."

To steady himself, the publisher went to his desk and pulled out a bottle of gin, then came back with a glass in his other hand. He poured himself a generous drink, drained it, and slumped back into his armchair:

"What a blow! Not even a week after the book went on sale! And the day before he was supposed to do the signings. It's a catastrophe!"

"What are we going to do?" asked the Salembert woman.

Malgodin seemed overcome with exhaustion.

"I don't know . . . Shit, shit, shit! This sort of thing only happens to me! A brand-new author who everyone's calling another Céline! And then pow! My old jinx, coming back to haunt me!"

"In any case, there's no question of my signing without Jean-Rémi," said Gastinel. "The most basic principles of solidarity and friendship compel me to . . ."

"I understand, Gastinel, I understand," sighed Malgodin peevishly, pacing the room in a fixed orbit. "I know you're a very decent guy. Ida, you'll have to make up some inserts for the book. Something like 'Owing to Monsieur Jean-Rémi Dochin's regrettable accident,' etc. Come up with something . . . Some elegant turn of phrase . . . You'll manage . . . Anyway. But not fake-sounding, we don't want anyone thinking this is some diplomatic little excuse . . . that it bugged him having to sign the things, and . . ."

"Don't worry, I'll deal with it," Ida said.

"And then get the books sent off right away. My poor Gastinel, I don't know what to say . . ."

"In any case, same deal for the TV and radio spots we had planned. Don't count on me if my friend Dochin can't be there. We support each other, you understand."

"I understand, dear friend. Too bad. But I imagine the book's going to sell very nicely all the same, with all these ecstatic reviews . . ."

As these words were being spoken, Dochin lay in a deep coma in room 2 of Dr. Crespiaud's private clinic in Brive, his head swollen by almost a third, so massive was the stone that had landed on it. The most urgent phase of his treatment was over, but the doctor's prognosis encouraged no sighs of relief. The first, anxious sentence addressed by the sawbones to his assistant was:

"I fear that this poor man might hover between life and death for quite some while. Give him camphor. A bit of codeine, too. One shot every eight hours. And I've got something else for you, too. Come into the lab . . ."

Was it simply a vague manifestation of the sexual harassment so common in our fair hexagonal land, or because she was in fact already his mistress, that Dr. Crespiaud now placed his hand on his assistant's buttocks?

They made their way into the lab.

Early that evening, one or two radio stations—not the TV, there was soccer on one channel and a show about con artists on the other—briefly mentioned Dochin's accident. He wasn't exactly a well-known public figure as yet, but since everyone was talking about his book, well . . . The prognosis remained uncertain.

The radio also reported, but at greater length, the death of the great journalist Urbain Langillier in Cochin Hospital, victim of a hit-and-run driver. The police had not succeeded in locating the vehicle, and no doubt the search to apprehend the criminal would be a long and difficult one.

Tracy Le Cardonnel, the journalist's great-niece, had remained by his bedside and witnessed his final moments. Briefly regaining consciousness just before he succumbed, Langillier had managed to whisper a few words in her ear. Tracy was left in a state of shock, doubly so because she was already shocked by the state of her relative, shocked and stunned, almost overwhelmed.

"Promise you'll get to the bottom of this, my dear, or at least try . . ." the dying man had murmured.

"How could I not? That missing page . . . it's all just too strange," Tracy replied. Such dark enigmas must be brought out into the full light of day—however implacable that light may be.

Gastinel was still at Le Papyrus when news of Langillier's death came over the radio. Malgodin had kept him there for some time to discuss the contract for volume two, not yet written, but which, said the blimp, would certainly be done in six months, at the end of winter. It had to be! Gastinel was firmly convinced Dochin would pull through and once again take up his pen. They also talked print runs. And something else: Malgodin, who by contract had secured right of first refusal for the authors' next two titles, now wanted to emend that clause to cover the next fifteen. For his part, Gastinel demanded an enormous advance for volume two, and even a supplemental advance for volume one, on top of the money already paid out, a colossal sum, well into the six figures. Their discussions dragged on and on.

A transistor radio having been turned on in the office next door, and the door left ajar, Gastinel and Malgodin heard the announcement of Langillier's death.

"Wow, tough luck," said the fat man. "That guy had everything going for him."

"He was literary advisor at Poulet-Malassis once," Maldogin noted. "He directed a literary revue as well . . . Mostly poetry, I think . . . He was the one who discovered young Archambaud. But I didn't know him personally . . ."

"There's a guy who would have loved *Brown Java*," said the one-time puppeteer. "I'd stake my life on it."

"Oh, a connoisseur like him, absolutely . . . Another drop of port, dear friend?"

"No thanks, I find port a bit heavy . . . But I'd gladly have a touch of that . . . I can't quite tell what it is, I can't make out the label, back there, there . . . that bottle."

"Which one? The vodka or the Pernod?"

"No . . . behind those . . . the sixth bottle behind the two next to the Courvoisier. Just next to the plum brandy and the magnum of Champagne."

"Ah yes, very good . . . if I can just get it out without knocking over the others . . . There we are . . . I'll pour, my friend. Where will you be dining this evening?"

"Well, to tell you the truth, I've sort of lost my appetite. What with everything that's happened to us."

"To Dochin, mostly, wouldn't you say?

"Yes, that's true . . ."

"We could go to Brussonnier's on the Rue de Dantzig, they've got food from the Rouergue. The best place in Paris, not the least bit fussy or snooty, no need for advertisements and rave reviews, they're perfectly happy with just the few connoisseurs. At Brussonnier's you can really eat. Simple as that. No tra-la-la in the décor. Just a table. No 'look-at-me-aren't-I-wonderful's sitting all around you, no curtsies and obeisances from the maître d'hôtel. It's all about what's on the plate. The real thing, the best grub in Paris, and the owner doesn't come sticking his nose in, wanting to know what you think. You can eat with your fingers, if you like. Just good honest casseroles. No chef who's going to go on TV and tell his life story."

"That's it, poor Malgo's already soused," thought Gastinel. "Best thing would be to leave right away and go tuck into an andouillette with fries at the café downstairs from my place."

Repeating that he wasn't hungry—he was in a hurry to get out of there—the author withdrew, leaving behind a Malgodin already three-quarters gone, slumped in an armchair and beginning to gnaw at his fingernails. The lush's assistant had given Gastinel his ten author's copies, neatly bundled up. And Dochin's as well.

"I'll get them to him," he promised. "Poor guy! Thanks on his behalf."

He decided to send the package to La Halte and let Céline Ferdinaud take it from there.

45   Mad with Joy

Gastinel sent Dochin's books off the next day. Céline took the package from the postman's hands and eagerly ripped it open. Delighted, she marveled at the ten copies of *Dancing the Brown Java* stacked on her bedroom table. She picked up a volume, settled cozily into an armchair, and plunged into the book, having asked Odette and Camille to leave her to her reading all afternoon long. All she wanted was a little tray with something to nibble on at around one, a couple of hard-boiled eggs, a bit of pâté or a piece of Roquefort, some grapes, and something to drink, say a glass of red wine. She reread *Brown Java* from cover to cover, finally closing the book at around 7:30 that evening, moved, elated, mad with joy, her eyes shining, a great wave of jubilation washing over her, and she murmured:

"I don't think any book has ever hit me in the guts the way this one does."

So was this the real definition of happiness? Hour after hour in a comfortable armchair, rambling through the pages of a good book, a great book, a book that's almost a friend! "Oh, I'm all aquiver! You don't need a microscope to see that," she told herself, welling over with emotion. She sat for a moment, cradling the volume like a baby freshly extracted from the womb, her eyes riveted to the cover, reflecting on this whole long affair. Thinking of Jean-Rémi, the shabby drifter she'd taken under her wing. She reread the cover from top to bottom. *Dochin-Gastinel. Dancing the Brown Java. A Novel. Le Papyrus.* And there it is! she thought. It's come to pass! Incredible! That damn novel's finally seen the light of day! Thank you, my little Jean-Rémi. Poor kid! Lying there in the clinic . . . Knocked out . . . But just wait, lamb, when you come to, when you get out of that clinic, I promise you, crazy old Céline might just have a nice long talk with you . . . It's true, some secrets don't want to come out . . . always stalling, taking detours . . . like they're afraid to cross over your lips . . . They come right up into your mouth, and then whoops! they make a U-turn. "No, let's wait a while, we'll try again later." It's got to happen someday, though. Poor lamb! He really should have been able to see it. Oh, he's not the brightest boy in the class, that one . . . Secrets like these . . . Well, I mean, really!

Now the books would have to be handed out—but she'd keep one for herself, all the same—to everyone she'd promised a copy. Or some of them, at least. They wouldn't all get to partake. Once Jean-Rémi was back on his feet, they'd have to convince Malgodin to send off some more, at a discount of course, because the author would surely be wanting some for himself, it's only right. She'd pay for them herself if need be, five or six copies, out of her own pocket. The least she could do for the poor boy. Still, he wouldn't be needing a ton of them, who would he give them to? He didn't have any friends, didn't really know anyone apart from his parents. But clearly he wasn't going to be walking out of that clinic anytime soon, so she might as well go ahead and start doling them out. Some of the shopkeepers had even asked after Dochin, Odette having brought word of the accident to Térignac as she made her daily rounds: Dochin knocked flat by a rock . . . in a coma . . . at Doctor Crespiaud's Bellevue Clinic, in Brive . . .

"I'll start tomorrow," she decided. Few of the ones who wanted a copy ever read books—almost none of them, in fact—but in this case they'd make an exception, given that the author was a local, and especially if he was going to be on TV. "Very interesting," they'd all call it, those readers-for-a-day. They'd be expecting dedications. Maybe a little ceremony was in order, say at Margnoux's, the village's main café. Jean-Rémi could sign their books, and then there'd be a modest reception, full of what they call convivial bonhomie. The mayor would come. And then the signed copies would find a place in their homes, a place of honor, maybe on the mantelpiece, a place in a house otherwise without books, save perhaps two almanacs and a medical dictionary.

Céline thought it a shame to waste books like that, giving them away to people who wouldn't understand a word, whose only distraction in life involved a TV set. But what could she do? She'd worked damn hard to earn a decent reputation around there—what with all the weird people she put up!—and she wasn't about to ruin it just for the sake of a few books. "No, that wouldn't be the thing to do, not now," she told herself.

Odette knocked and came in to say they were waiting for her downstairs at dinner. There would be watercress soup, then pâté en croûte stuffed with duck gizzards, perch meunière, pan-fried potatoes with parsley for those who might want them, artichokes in mustard sauce, the great tray of cheeses, and a blueberry cake. Larmory, the one they called the hotel thief, a longtime regular at La Halte, almost a friend, would be seated at her table.

46   Visiting Hours

I didn't come around till the next-to-last week in October. Almost a month in a coma. Absolutely nothing goes on in there, let me tell you. Total blackness, like after you die or before you're conceived. All kind of sister-states, if you will. My head had completely deflated. I'd come back from the brink. Doctor Crespiaud, who was looking after me—nice guy, looked like Erich von Stroheim—was very pleased. Every three minutes he kept saying how he'd snatched me out of the grim reaper's clutches. I was myself again. First thing I thought of was my book. *Dancing the Brown Java* had been out for a little more than a month. How was it doing?

But I had visitors, so the sawbones discreetly slipped out.

They'd been there for five minutes, clustered around my bed. Céline among them, of course. She'd put on a chic little going-out hat, the one she always wore for her trips to Bordeaux. Her whole outfit was pretty smart, for that matter, still a Parisian after all these years, nothing of the hayseed about her. She had a big grocery bag full of who knows what sitting on one of the chairs, she looked like she'd just been to market. Malgodin was there too, half sloshed, but what else do you expect at three in the afternoon? The blimp rounded out the trio. So my protectress and him must have met. As Céline immediately informed me, in fact.

"I had the pleasure of making Monsieur Gastinel's acquaintance only this morning. He came straight out to La Halte as soon as he heard you were doing better. We had lunch together, and now here we are with our beloved little lamb, who's finally recovered and who'll very soon be getting right back to work, I just know it."

"Give me some time to rest up," I pleaded.

"Oh, the pig! He's been lazing around in bed for a month, and here he is claiming to be tired!" the blob guffawed.

I'd scribbled down some notes on a pad once I came out of the fog, maybe just to check that the writerly gears were still working, some thoughts for the sequel to my book . . . Max and Mimile were going to meet up with a guy who raised hamsters . . . A dancer in love with the sculptor Arno Breker was going to be kidnapped . . . two or three other things . . . little brainstorms like that . . . Gastinel grabbed the pad from the nightstand, gave it a quick look, and congratulated me on having recovered the fruitful imagination he so admired, and on having the force of character to pick up the pen so soon after my mishap.

I noticed he was wearing a brand-new suit, and those shoes must have cost more than a thousand francs. Cashwise, things seemed to be humming.

Malgodin was in an exultant mood:

"Five hundred thousand copies sold already, my dear little Dochin. I can't even remember what printing we're at, I've lost count."

"And fourteen translations on the horizon, my little colt," added Céline. "A scintillating success. You're all they've been talking about in the book pages for the past month. You and Monsieur Gastinel, of course."

"What about my book? I'd love to see a copy, just once."

"Our book," the blimp quietly corrected, shooting me a dark glance.

"Poor lamb, you're going to be cross with me," said Céline. "I gave them all away . . . What can you do? The shopkeepers had been waiting for weeks. I just kept one for myself. But Monsieur Malgodin has promised us more."

"I wanted to wait till you got out of that awful coma, Dochin," the publisher chimed in. "But now that you're all better, you'll get them all right. I've given the orders. Fifteen copies. Will that do?"

"That'll do, I think, yes."

"If you're in a hurry, my boy, we can go pick one up in Tulle or Uzerche, or at Cloquard's in Brive," said my "mother."

"Don't bother, Madame Ferdinaud. I'll call in the shipping order this evening."

"Incidentally, here's your check," said the blimp. "Our revered publisher was as good as his word, he's a great guy, honest down to his fingertips, a veritable saint of literature. I've already put mine away, as you might well suspect. We each get our own sweet little slip of paper."

I took the check, drawn on the Crédit du Nord. A hundred fifteen decagrands. One million one hundred fifty thousand francs, if you prefer. Took me three tries to decipher the thing. It made my eyes tired.

"And that's just for starters," Malgodin smiled, jubilant on my behalf, apparently. "A little advance, that's all. Wait till next spring, our coffers will be overflowing. And we've got Gaumont and four other producers eyeing the film rights. I'm stalling them to drive up the price . . . In January Le Papyrus will be moving to Saint-Germain des Prés, just like the big boys. Plenty of lovely cafés around there, too. Gallim's, Furne, Hetzel and company are all furious with me. And all because I landed the manuscript of *Brown Java.*"

"Hurry up and get better, Jean Rémi," said the lardbucket. "Our little volume two has to grow up."

"Imagine my impatience, dear friend," said Malgodin. "And the readers are even more eager than me!"

Céline opened her grocery bag and took out a big pile of newspapers, magazines, and literary revues from all over the place, Paris, the provinces, Belgium, Canada, Pamplona. She sat down by the bed and read out a few snatches, picking the rags up one by one, opening them, then carefully folding them again. A breathtaking symphony of praise, almost uncomfortable to hear. I wondered if maybe I was still off in slumberland, under assault from the battering ram of some bad dream . . .

"Almost everyone loved it," the behemoth exulted.

"Just two or three naysayers," Malgo added. "Cuzenat and La Briançais."

"And they won't be badmouthing your work anymore, they're both dead," murmured Céline, almost in my ear, sending a shiver the length of my spine. She had that hard look in her eye again.

"We never really found out if La Briançais loved it or hated it," said Malgodin. "At first, he was telling everyone he was for it . . . then his ex-girlfriend started saying he didn't like it after all, and was planning to pan it to pieces."

"Didn't exactly bring him luck," Céline said again.

She folded her papers and stuffed them back into the bag.

"Three or four didn't review it at all," she said. "Wait-and-see types, presumably . . . Everybody knows there's going to be a volume two, so might as well sit back and see what transpires, not take any chances . . . Not a blessed word from Archibald Ranfolin of *L'Européen du Jeudi*, to our great surprise."

"Oh! That guy's such a phony," exclaimed Malgodin malevolently. "And not exactly the bravest man you're likely to meet. If he didn't care for *Brown Java*, I'll bet he was too scared to come out and say so in print."

"Very wise of him," my protectress smiled.

She looked me square in the face.

"You're a great man now," she said, clearly delighted with her little protégé—either that or she was a terrifically good actress.

"I'm out of the publishing game for good," the blimp informed me. "The old horsemeat shop got snatched up by a pooch groomer. So long to the stinking sci-fi crap that's been poisoning my life for the past seven years! Now that we've got Crichton, everything else seems sort of creaky anyway."

"Well, nobody ever did better in that line than Barjavel," said Céline.

"I've just bought an apartment near the Eiffel Tower," the fat one continued. "Just a few little renovations and it's ready to go. House-warming at Christmas. A fancy jalopy, too. A Mercedes. E 280. Two hundred fifty grand. Makes quite an impression, believe you me. I like to go cruising down the Champs-Elysées at five miles per hour, all the sweet young things eyeing me longingly . . ."

"And now I bet this old rogue will be wanting to move out of La Halte himself, now that he's rich," Céline threw out, watching for my reaction.

"Oh no, Céline," I protested. "I owe you so much . . . Sure, I can afford a little pied-à-terre in Paris, but that's not going to change the way I live. Besides, I'm in no hurry."

"I knew it, my colt. And in any case the fresh air of the Limousin is good for your writing. I'll bet the smoggy skies of Paris wouldn't do much for you, inspiration-wise."

"It's true," said the fatso, "some of the critics found the first quarter of the book excellent, but not quite up to the level of the rest, all the same. So you see, Jean-Rémi, what you . . . what we wrote back in Paris is a little less captivating than what you . . . what we wrote here in the countryside."

"But you were still writing in Paris, weren't you, Monsieur Gastinel?" Céline observed. "Your notes, all that, where did you write them?"

"What notes?"

I gave the pachyderm a look fit to pierce his fat flesh and drain him of all his blood—which would have taken a while, it's true. He must have understood, because he started simpering and screwing up his face in classic Oliver Hardy fashion, wiggling his fat ass for all he was worth and pawing at his chin like it was a piece of fruit he feared might not be quite ripe:

"Well, it's true . . . I can come up with ideas pretty much any-where . . . in an elevator . . . a taxi . . . under the boughs in the Bois de Boulogne . . . What matters most is that Jean-Rémi have a nice comfy nest in the quiet of the country, since he's the one who writes it all up."

"And what about the radio and the TV and all that stuff?" I asked. "What did you end up doing, Charles?"

"What do you think? I canceled. No way am I going to go strutting around on the screen without my old pal Dochin, I told them. Oh! they understood perfectly, in the end. A couple of reporters made some discreet inquiries, and what do you know? Turned out you really were laid up here, just like I said."

"Apparently there was a paparazzo skulking around the clinic at one point," said Céline. "But he didn't manage to get your picture."

"Speaking of TV, I've got some good news," said Malgodin. "I didn't want to say anything until we were all together with our dear Jean-Rémi. You might have a chance at a spot on *Book Culture*. A little late, I know—the book's been out for a month, after all—but that's nothing serious. Now hang on . . . it's not quite certain yet. I'm waiting for confirmation from Eyebrows. What with Jean-Rémi's incapacitation, you know . . . Say, you don't seem very happy to hear it."

I wasn't too thrilled, it's true. The fatso was looking deeply peeved. Even Céline was almost scowling.

"Oh, I know it's a drag, having to deal with the media!" our Malgo exclaimed. "But what can you do . . . If Eyebrows insists, I don't think it would be nice to say no. Best to stay on good terms with him."

"Wouldn't we be better off waiting till volume two comes out?" Céline wondered. "Jean-Rémi's still sort of punch-drunk."

"Well, we'll see."

Malgo didn't look too happy:

"But I'll tell you one thing: I've been working my ass off for weeks trying to land you that spot. So don't go all prima donna on me, okay?"

"We don't need that garbage," the fatty groaned. "We sold five hundred thousand copies with no help from those assholes. Same thing for the Goncourt, they can keep it! Give it to some well-connected young dandy . . ."

"When would we be going on?" I asked, not at all in love with the idea.

"Oh, certainly not for a few weeks. But I repeat, nothing's for sure."

I fingered my skull. "In any case, I still don't see how I could have spent a month in a coma just from a knock on the head."

"But you had severe cranial trauma, my boy, with water on the brain," Céline answered. "That's no laughing matter, you know. They fed you on serum . . . Drop by drop . . . You just lay there, quiet as a mouse, no idea what was happening. For a while the doctor was even thinking of trepanning you. Which would have been a bit of a nuisance for someone who lives by his pen . . ."

Malgodin had an appointment with someone or other, and went on his way. Poor man hadn't had a moment's peace since *Brown*

Java hit, Céline told me, invitations everywhere, people pulling him this way and that, and with that everlasting thirst of his I was afraid it wouldn't be long before cirrhosis came calling, along with the three or four big publishing houses that were after him, hoping to absorb Le Papyrus.

"When do you get out, buddy?" asked the blimp.

"Wednesday, supposedly, the day after tomorrow. They want to keep me under observation just a little bit longer, another forty-eight hours . . ."

"I'll come pick you up," Céline promised. "Maybe with Odette. Your desk will be ready and waiting, with everything you need, pens and inkwells. I bought you some paper."

So it was all going to start up again, just like before. I remembered the unadulterated mediocrity of my book, and Langillier's unshakeable, unappealable thumbs down. I was completely at a loss. I'd found my way out of that coma all right, but not yet out of the mystery hanging over my putrid, botched mess of a novel.

47   Such a Well-Behaved Patient

Two days later I was back on my feet and ready to go. My last day in the clinic. I was waiting for Céline in the hallway, my nostrils under assault from various medicinal odors. The doc and his assistant bade me a fond farewell, smiling nonstop—I almost thought they were going to give me flowers.

That Wednesday, October 25, Céline found the promised fifteen copies of *Dancing the Brown Java* in the morning mail. Brand-new, just off the press. She put them on an already overloaded shelf in the hallway, just off the front office. At long last, Jean-Rémi was going to see his book, she told herself. High time. The novel was out, the money was rolling in . . . now maybe she'd finally work up the nerve to talk to him. Would he understand? She thought she might pull it off. But little by little, as the morning wore on, panic began to grip her by the throat and shoulders, like an oncoming flu. Wouldn't it be better to wait just a tiny bit longer? The poor kid had so little faith in his work. She'd read his tarot. Was she right to tell him the cards promised that anyone who didn't like the novel would be calling down a jinx on himself? It's true, of course, that . . .

At two o'clock I was ready to leave Bellevue clinic at last. As I said, Doctor Crespiaud and his assistant gave me a long, drawn-out, but very kind good-bye.

"You were such a well-behaved patient, so quiet, we'd almost like to keep you a little while longer," smiled that excellent practitioner with the Erich von Stroheim skull.

"All right, that'll do, that's enough good-byes for now," Céline interrupted, sounding a mite snappish—she'd been waiting almost five minutes. "We need him back at La Halte. Besides, he's got to get writing again."

She took my arm, and we headed for the front door. In the little lobby, the receptionist had a book lying open on her desk. I stepped forward and lifted it up to look at the cover. It was *mine*! First one I'd seen.

"Nice-looking book, huh?" asked Céline, with a smile. "Come on, we've got loads of them back home. Malgodin kept his promise. They just came this morning."

She asked the receptionist what she thought of it.

"Oh, Madame, it's entrancing."

Then Céline tugged at my arm:

"Hurry up now, Félibut's got to take delivery of some wine casks."

I could tell she was eager to delight in the spectacle of my joy. Good old irreplaceable Céline.

The 2CV was waiting on the Quai de Tourny, right in front of the clinic, with Félibut at the wheel. He greeted me, half raising his filthy beret:

"A very good day to you, Monsieur Jean-Rémi." He held out his fat, callused hand. "What a pleasure to see you up and about again."

And then off to La Halte. Félibut drove at full speed, tires squealing on the curves, Céline and me sliding into each other every few seconds.

"He's in a hurry to sign for the casks. Cordelier's got quite a temper, and he doesn't like to be kept waiting."

"Why didn't you drive yourself?"

"I'm too overcome with emotion, seeing you again, my lamb. Too drunk with joy to handle the wheel."

Poor Félibut was terrified of trucks, so he stuck to the back roads.

Now we were racing past the Puy de Pauliac. I couldn't wait to open my book, turn the pages, smell the freshly printed letters. But there was still one thing I couldn't get out of my head. How could so many critics have been won over by anything as richly substandard as my worthless, pointless prose? They're all serious, well-informed people, mostly, so what gives? And then I thought of the ones who didn't like it at all, that little handful, that unhappy few, now bathed in a sort of sinister twilight glow: Langillier . . . What happened to him, anyway? Did he pull through? Not the slightest idea—I'd gone off for a spin in that miserable jalopy right after his accident. Céline must have seen it in the paper or heard about it on the radio, but no way was I going to ask her. She'd want to know why I cared, and then the questions would never end. Langillier. And Cuzenat . . . One got run over by a speeding van, the other drowned in a lake. Coincidence? I remembered the tarot. No, that's a bunch of bullshit.

"Why are you shrugging like that?" Céline asked.

"I was shrugging?"

"I'll say. Like you had a wasp stuck under your shirt collar."

"Oh, it's nothing . . . I was just thinking about this whole thing."

"What whole thing?"

"You know, the book, for Christ's sake! That piece of shit . . ."

"He's at it again! Are you joking? What more do you want? All the reviewers are crazy about it. Almost all, anyway . . . I hope you're not planning to go tell them they're out of their minds!"

A volcano of reprimand seemed to erupt in her eyes as she spoke. Come on! If I started hating *Brown Java* myself, what would happen then? Growling, her eyes flashing like the glint from a newly sharpened scythe, she reminded me:

"You saw how all those people who didn't like it ended up."

"What do you mean? That's just it, Céline, I'd like to talk to you about that."

"About what?"

"Which way shall I go, Madame Céline, through Seilhac or Saint-Salvadour?" asked Félibut, like he was driving a taxi—but at least he wasn't bombarding us with indiscreet questions, so that's one point in his favor.

"Whichever you like, Félibut."

"I'll go the Seilhac way. That'll save us five minutes. Cordelier's probably already waiting at La Halte."

The 2CV picked up speed, now following the Corrèze.

"What did you want to talk to me about, Jean-Rémi?"

"Well, about that . . . about those critics who didn't like it, and . . ."

"Cuzenat . . . and the other one . . . What was his name? La Briançais?"

"Your tarot cards said something like that . . ."

"And?"

"You don't think it's just a little bit odd?"

"Well, big boy, if it bothers you that much, you'll just have to ask the tarot about it."

"People don't like *Brown Java*, and then bang, something happens to them, just like the cards said."

"And not just any old thing!" my protectress chuckled with a kind of savagery in her eyes, her face turning almost ugly. "A little something that only happens to you once!"

I jumped in my seat. There was also Galice. I'd just remembered. Galice never read my novel, but I'd given the blimp the impression he had, and hadn't much cared for it. Later I changed my story, but . . . all the same . . . The blimp must have blabbed it all over Paris, and who knows who might have been listening? "Do you know, I recently had an author in my office who'd given his manuscript to Galice, and . . ." etc. That sort of thing. No, it's ridiculous. Pure coincidence, and nothing but. For one thing, the guy was eighty-six years old. About time he was shuffling along anyway. No, no connection. He never got a chance to pan my book, because he'd never had it in front of him. Still, that's not what the fatso thought, at least for a while . . . That idea kept running through my head, like a song you can't shake. And then there was La Briançais. That guy was the blow-hot-and-cold type. I love it! I hate it! Two steps forward, two steps back. That's not the java, that's the tango. Apparently his girl was telling everybody he . . .

"Stop saying you don't like *Brown Java*, Jean-Rémi. It might end up giving you grief."

She said that in a serious voice, so serious it gave me goose bumps.

"Why?" I stammered like an idiot.

"No reason."

Her "no reason" felt like two little pieces of ice that someone had slipped under my collar. I would have preferred a wasp.

48 Kidnapped

A big fancy gunmetal-gray car was parked by the front door of La Halte, in front of the waiting wineman's truck. I didn't even have time to catch my breath. After a minute I realized it was the blimp's new heap. He and Malgodin were standing beside it, the pachyderm nervously puffing at a little cigar. A lady was sitting in the backseat. After a moment I recognized Ida Salembert, the rummy's assistant. The gentlemen were visibly impatient. What the hell were they doing here? We never even got a chance to go inside. No sooner had I climbed out of the 2CV with Céline—Félibut hadn't yet slid out from behind the wheel—than the two specimens rushed forward and collared me.

"We're kidnapping him!" Malgodin announced merrily.

"What's going on?" asked Céline, intrigued.

The two assholes were all over me, clutching at me like I was going to fly away. I was still a little limp, still sort of out of it, so I didn't put up much of a fight. Besides, what was I supposed to do, with that brute dragging me toward his car, a brand new Mercedes—but covered with grime, they'd obviously done some driving—like some oversize, unwieldy package?

"Don't worry! Nothing sinister!" the fatso declared to all and sundry, with a great laugh.

He shoved me into the backseat, next to the skank, who gave me a smile and scooted over to make room. I deduced that Madame had patched things up with old Malgodin, all that money pouring in must have made her forget his bad breath. Malgo joined us and sat down on the left, with Ida between us. The fatso was already at the wheel.

I saw people standing around in the garden, probably customers waiting for Céline. Odette and Camille showed up as well. Everybody was staring wide-eyed at the car, looking startled by all the commotion.

Céline was holding the driver's-side door open, refusing to let go:

"Can't I at least know what's happening?"

"I had to break the speed limit to get here in time," Gastinel told her.

"Oh yeah! We were roaring along!" the publisher exclaimed. "As if he didn't have enough points on his driver's license already! You could almost hear the poor little thing whimpering for its life!"

"Dochin and Gastinel are going on *Book Culture* tonight," the assistant announced.

"A last-minute deal!" Malgodin tossed out. (He was sober, no time to stop off at the bars along the way, I guess.)

"Eyebrows called me last night, a little before midnight," Malgodin explained. "The Minister of Culture was going to be on, but something came up . . . I don't know what . . . something important. Maybe some health thing, I can't say. Eyebrows asked if we could come on in his place. As you can imagine, I said yes."

"Right then and there," said the fatty. "Malgo calls me straightaway, I pick him up at his place with Mademoiselle Salembert, and we hightail it right to La Halte. We don't have a minute to lose. Come on, let's get going."

"On TV?" asked Céline, looking anxious. "But have you seen the state Jean-Rémi's in? He can hardly stand on his own feet!"

"Besides, what am I going to say on TV?" I stammered, my knees almost knocking.

"I'll give you some tips on the way, Jean-Rémi," said Malgodin.

"Don't worry, no one's going to eat you," said Ida.

"The main thing," said Malgodin, "is for people to see you on the show. I didn't want to pass up this opportunity, I'm sure that's not hard to figure out."

"All you have to do is keep your trap shut," the ex-tripemonger advised me. "I'll do the talking. You'll see, it'll all go swimmingly."

"You know, nobody really cares what an author says," Malgo told me. "They just want to see his face. The stuff in the book, fine, that might interest some people. But mostly they just want to see what he's like, that's all. The public doesn't really give a shit about what people write. Nobody reads anymore."

Gastinel started up the engine.

"Really, you're taking him away from me?" Céline wailed. She seemed completely distraught. "He hasn't even seen his book!"

"You're kidding!" said the hulk.

"I most certainly am not."

"He'll see it on the show."

"Can't you even give him a chance to get his wits together?" Céline whined.

She skewered the blimp with a furious stare. They glared at each other like that for a full minute, right in the whites of their eyes. Finally the colossus gave her an understanding nod.

"Don't worry, Madame Ferdinaud," he said. "We won't damage your little Jean-Rémi. We'll bring him back right after the show, good as new."

The car had already started off. It immediately picked up speed. Now it was roaring down the road to Meymac.

"I'll get on the highway at Clermont," said Gastinel. "It'll be faster that way."

"It's already three o'clock," said Malgo. "We've got to get to the studio by ten at the latest."

He was cruising along at 110 miles an hour. What the hell was I going to say on TV? My mind was going blank, like I was headed to a driver's license test, or my baccalaureate. And let's not forget my physical condition . . . just don't expect too much from me, that's all. I still reeked of the sickhouse—excuse me, the clinic. My legs were still rubbery—a month on my back!—my hands all clammy, still a little stiff in the neck . . .

49   Back to Square One

Two men sat center stage on the *Book Culture* set that night, flanked by a panel of supporting guests culled from the world of fine writing: they were the two guests of honor, the stars of the show, the now-famed duo known as Dochin-Gastinel. Two names to be reckoned with, names with a ring to rival the illustrious Erckmann-Chatrian, Allain and Souvestre, or Boileau-Narcejac: the authors of *Dancing the Brown Java,* an epic novel published six weeks before, etc.

■

Now the mighty vehicle had merged onto the autoroute, traffic-free at this late hour. They sped through the night in the left-hand lane . . .

"Suppose you decided to talk . . ." the obese one resumed. "Suppose you were to tell everyone I can't handle a pen. Let's imagine. What happens? I head right off to the police and hand over the evidence of our dirty little crime."

"Oh, you make me want to puke! Blackmail! How spineless! How slimy! Revolting beyond belief!"

"Writers aren't always saints, you know."

"Get a load of this louse! He didn't write one single line of *Brown Java* and he calls himself a writer!"

Gastinel merely snickered into his double chin. Then silence. The giant drove for some time without opening his mouth. The illuminated highway signs heralded Artenay, Orléans, and the turnoff to Blois. The radio was quietly emitting South American tunes.

■

We drove all night, interminable stretches of road without speaking a word, the radio turned down low, almost inaudible. There was a film showing in my head, a revival, everything that had happened in my worthless existence over the past several years, a real horror picture! That goddamn projectionist—what a bringdown! Shit upon shit upon shit! How I longed to forget it all!

We'd taken the autoroute to Poitiers, and now we were speeding toward Limoges. The blimp was still clammed up tight. At least he was taking me back to La Halte, that was something, anyway. Our shouting match by the Pantheon had left its mark. A certain coolness had insinuated itself between us.

We weren't far from Térignac. Day was breaking. Slowly, the trees were emerging from the dark. Not much fog. Just a few little wisps, looking like they wanted to play with the branches.

"I was thinking . . . Suppose Céline found out about all this?" I finally asked.

"All what?"

"Well, you know, that we're criminals."

"What should she care? All she's thinking about is the book. She doesn't give a shit about anything else. But anyway, why should she find out? Nobody knows a thing. The video, that's the only thing that could . . . So, whatever happens, I'd advise you to treat me nice."

"Where's the tape?"

"Somewhere."

"Oh, sweet Jesus!"

"Look, stop agonizing, will you? We're rich now. And this is just the beginning. Volume two's going to be a beaut, and everything will turn out just fine. Have you seen how they're all slavering for our sequel? All sorts of revelations about the Occupation's dirtiest double-crossers . . . Heads are really going to roll! Most of them are still alive, senile old geezers though they may be. And of course there are their descendants too . . . who may well not enjoy the attention, particularly if they're the in-the-public-eye type. 'Wow! So-and-so wore the Francisque? I never would have believed it.' Ha ha! That'll be a big bloody thorn in the side for a bunch of irreproachable patriots living the high life in their pishy-posh houses! Not to mention the little art-dealers . . . the kindly old antiquarians . . . who ratted out rich Jews to the Krauts so they could get their hands on their paintings . . . Oh, it's going to be a lot of fun! Of course, the rats in question ended up doing pretty well for themselves! . . ."[3]

"Where did you come up with all that? You know what I'm going to write before I've even started? More of your gold-plated bullshit. This is the day for it, that's for sure."

"I'm giving you subjects, that's all . . . All you have to do is get your ass in gear and do some research, fill in the details . . ."

"Oh, that's right, I'm going to piss off a great big horde of assholes just to make Monsieur happy! What sort of revelations did you have in mind, anyway? Any ideas? You're just trying to drum up publicity. And in the meantime, I still haven't seen my book."

---

3 On this point, see Hector Féliciano's *Le Musée Disparu: Enquête sur le Pillage des Oeuvres d'Art en France par les Nazis* (Éditions Austral). (Author's note.)

"Come on! It was right in front of your face the whole time on the show! What, do you want to reread it?"

"Why not? Is that a problem?"

"I couldn't even finish it, myself."

"You mean the manuscript?"

"Not the manuscript, shithead! How do you expect me to have fallen in love with the thing without reading the manuscript? No, I'm talking about the published text, you know, the book."

"You couldn't finish it?"

"No."

"You didn't write a line . . ."

"Listen, Dochebag, you're not going to start that up again, are you? You don't think that routine's getting a little old?"

"Céline's pretty much the only one who's crazy about it . . ."

"Céline, yes, and the critics. And what about the readers? What are they, chopped liver? A whole big honking mob of them. So *Brown Java* isn't a massive hit, eh? You got the brain rot or something? Too much playing with yourself?"

"Nothing's going to change my mind: that book is shit through and through."

Once again Langillier's image flashed through my head. Once more his devastating words echoed in my ears. And in spite of all that, the critics were going gaga, the book was selling like hot crêpes, and I'd just gone on *Book Culture*. Up to my neck in surrealism. I felt like I was lost in a labyrinth. And then there was that other little sentence, still tickling my eardrums: "I pity anyone who doesn't like it." What was all that about? People were supposed to lose their minds over a novel in which, according to Langillier, everything or nearly everything needed rewriting—or else some sort of curse was going to descend on them? A new way to sell books:

"You'd *better* like it, or else . . ." Literary terrorism. The author's inkwell brimming with a particularly deadly magic philter . . .

"Look, cut it out about not liking *Brown Java,* Jean-Rémi," the blimp told me, very earnest all of a sudden, like a village priest doling out sage advice. "I'm serious. Here we get a plum spot on *Book Culture,* and you just sit there sulking the whole time! At one point I even thought you were going to chime in with your vomitous little opinion, go public with those bizarre qualms you've been inflicting on us for lo these many weeks. These many months! If you don't like the book, at least think of the dough. Royalties almost as kingly as Agatha Christie's or Simenon's, all coming our way!"

"That's what I can't understand."

"Don't try to understand. Myself, I just take the cash, and never mind the rest . . ."

"Yeah, and all without having written a word."

"Shut your face. Change the channel. You were dumb enough to get taken, so kindly dismount from your high horse and show some humility. Charlot Gastinel screwed you good, one two three, easy as pie. Am I right or am I wrong? So if you don't want to hail and revere the fine writer that I am not, at least have the good sense and decency to tip your hat to a rogue who managed to pull off a sweet little murder that's going to bring him a fortune. You think I was sure *Brown Java* was going to make me a bundle when I plastered that kid to the wall? That was a shot in the dark, pal, pure and simple. No idea how it was going to turn out. I was just taking a chance. Like in poker. Suppose *Brown Java* had flopped like the latest books of those four other assholes on the show last night: who would have landed flat on his face then, hmm? Why, a certain Gastinel, I do believe. And you too, come to think of it. So I'm telling you: at least show a little respect for the guy who had the finesse to put together a lucrative scheme like this. Why should I go spilling the beans? You keep quiet, I keep quiet, everybody's happy."

For five minutes now the great hog had been yawning uncontrollably, wide enough to dislocate his jaw and his chins along with it, spewing this crap all the while.

"I'm bushed," he said. "Paris to La Halte. La Halte to Paris. And now Paris-Térignac again. Eight hundred miles in less than twenty-four hours. I must be out of my mind. And all that just to pick up Monsieur and deliver him back home again. God, am I beat! I think I'm going to stick around your neck of the woods for a while and rest up."

"You're planning to find a hotel?"

"Absolutely not. I bet Céline will be delighted to give me a room."

"It'll be like getting a visit from the Michelin man."

"Please don't make fun of my weight, you fucking little twat. If there's one thing that outweighs all my surplus flesh, it's your own assholic stupidity. For—allow me to inform you, dear Monsieur—you are as dumb as half a post. And you haven't seen anything yet. Let me tell you, when you figure this whole thing out, the blazing sun of the Sahara's going to seem like a pallid little ray of moonlight in a Watteau painting."

50 The Letter to Bordeaux, and the Truth Right in the Kisser

We got to La Halte around breakfast time. The air was filled with the smell of strong coffee. And hot chocolate, too—for Camille. A glorious autumn day in the works. Bright sunshine, soft and sweet, the way it can be in France. All the trees behind the motel and around the little house had gone yellow and gold, good luck finding colors like that any other time of the year.

The blimp seemed a little unsteady when he climbed out of the Mercedes, he was staggering around like a sleepwalker. He knocked back a cup of coffee, then went up and locked himself away in room 1. Céline was happy to put him up, no problem. Monsieur even closed the shutters.

"I'm going to take a three-hour nap, and then I'll be on my way," he'd said. "You think it went okay on TV last night, Madame Ferdinaud?"

"Odette and I went and watched you in Margnoux's café. It was perfect. You seemed a little sleepy, Jean-Rémi, but with everything you've been through . . . You see? Nobody bit you. You were wrong to get so clutched up about it. In the end, you didn't talk much about the book, though, did you? They were more interested in your life stories. As if that was what really mattered! What a bunch of asses! They can't get it through their heads that the only thing that counts with a writer—a real one, at least—is what's going on inside."

"It all went wonderfully," the fatso echoed, dragging himself off to beddie-bye.

A little handful of guests were hanging around. The people I'd seen in the garden, I suppose, just before Gastinel and Malgodin hauled me off to Paris.

Céline and I were still standing in the doorway to the little office. A few early-rising guests came over and—as they hadn't had a chance to do the day before, when we got back from the clinic—congratulated me on finally getting back on my feet. Some of them were misshapen, and there was a sort of grungy-looking weirdo with a Mongol-style face and a big straw hat like they wear on banana plantations. I remembered this guy. He'd been here once or twice before over the past three years. Shaking my hand, he launched into a sob story about being kicked out of La Rochelle by the champagne-socialist mayor (his words, not mine), who didn't much care for panhandlers, and told me how happy he was to be taken in at La Halte. There was also a cripple who didn't seem to get on too well with his crutches, and an amputee wheeled around in a sort of special stroller by a fat old lady in a floral dress—the classic 1930s concierge look. All fine people, but not particularly attractive for a real hotel owner, or at least for his guests, most of them northern Europeans longing for beauty and nothing else—so sad sacks and sorry specimens need not apply. Fortunately for this crowd, there was La Halte. In theory, Céline never sent anyone away. In all the time I'd been living here, I'd only seen her turn down two or three especially shady-looking vagrants, criminals on the run, by the look of them, and also, I'd never understood why, one or two perfectly decent-looking guys, well dressed, normal in every way, the go-getter type, middle-management, maybe even better than middle, who'd introduced themselves as traveling salesmen. Maybe she just wasn't too crazy about normal people. She'd sent them off to the nearby hotels, very nice places, she'd assured them, where they'd be taken in with no problem, places that didn't hesitate to give the bum's rush to anyone who didn't fit the norm, anyone who might send a collective shudder through the dining room when they made their big entrance . . .

So I had five or six guests clustered around me, among them the beggar expelled by the so-called champagne socialists in La Rochelle, all of them cheering my recovery despite never having laid eyes on me before. Apparently the good ladies of La Halte had told them all about me. I was touched by their kindness. Soon they were joined by the stringbean I'd met a little before my accident, that Larmory guy, the one Céline had introduced as a friend. He seemed to be making himself right at home, because once he'd welcomed me back he went straight off to help Félibut prune the peach trees at the far end of the orchard. I don't know why, but there was something about that guy I didn't like, and I hoped he wasn't planning on putting down roots at La Halte, which I'd more or less come to see as my own private nook.

Céline thanked them all for the hearty welcome, and then she and I went into the office. Odette and Camille came in from the kitchen, all smiles, their aprons covered with carrot peelings, and gave me friendly hello.

"We'll have a lovely little veal à la bonne femme at noon," Céline told me. "You'll be joining us, I hope?"

"I'm worn out . . . all that driving . . . I'm going to try to get some sleep. I don't know, we'll see. Right now I'm not hungry."

"Wouldn't you like some coffee? Gastinel had a cup."

"Later on . . . Let me get settled in . . ."

The two servants went on their way, and I was about to ask Céline if I could see my book when I spotted a stamped envelope at the top of a stack on the counter. The outgoing mail, presumably.

"You want to have a look at your old study?" Céline asked me. "Like I told you, it's all . . ."

"Oh, enough about the study! What's the hurry, anyway?"

"Well, now you can get back to work, right?"

"Let it go, will you? Come on, Céline, give me a break. Get off my back about the book."

"I bought you a fancy new typewriter. You'll have to get used to writing that way, just like Simenon. You told me you knew how to type."

"Yes, yes . . ."

"Think about volume two, my boy. You've got to finish it, the quicker the better. Malgodin's waiting. You heard how Eyebrows was talking about it last night . . ."

"Gastinel too, I suppose?" I snickered. "And here he is snoozing away! Our fat friend couldn't care less about volume two. He's off sawing wood."

"Well, there, my boy . . . You'll have to work that out for your-selves . . . It's not up to me to . . . The main thing is that we all do our job and get volume two finished."

And then I sort of blew up:

"Now, listen, Céline! Let me catch my breath! Yesterday I get home from the clinic and those two assholes are all over me! And now this morning *you* start riding my ass! It's *my* book, isn't it?"

"Butt out, is that what you're saying?"

"No, I didn't say that, but . . ."

It was mostly that letter on the counter that was needling me. It caught my eye the moment I came into the office. There was some-thing written on it I just couldn't get out of my head.

"Is this your niece," I asked, "this Feuhant person?"

She realized I'd seen the letter.

"Why?"

I ran two joined fingers over the envelope.

"It's going to Bordeaux. Mademoiselle Colette Feuhant, 37 Rue Furtado, Bordeaux."

"So?"

I noticed she was looking sort of tensed up.

"I can know other people in Bordeaux, can't I?"

"Other Colettes?"

"Why not?"

Seeing me look so suspicious—which I was, my face must have given me away—she decided to drop the act:

"Yes, that's her. That's Colette."

Céline usually just picked up the phone when she wanted to talk to her niece, or anyone else. But now, for some reason, she'd written a letter. The name and address were in her handwriting. Maybe the schoolteacher was out of town, and having her mail forwarded . . . yes, that must be it . . .

"You've turned so suspicious lately, my dear Jean-Rémi . . . What's up with you?"

"Well, I can't have been very suspicious from September 27 to three or four days ago, now can I?"

"Is it my fault you got conked on the head? What are you getting at? What's the big deal about this letter? So now I don't have the right to send off a letter if I feel like it?"

"Isn't your niece named Ferdinaud? That's what you told me . . . Isn't she your brother Hubert's daughter? Your brother I'm supposed to look so much like?

"Yes . . . well . . . You know, that's a private matter. She got married. To a man named Feuhant, as it happens."

Feuhant . . . Feuhant . . . That name was familiar. I couldn't say why, exactly. Just a vague memory. Something I'd heard in a movie, maybe. Yes, that had to be it. But what movie? I could have sworn I'd heard that name in a movie theater somewhere . . . Or was it on TV? No point trying to remember. It was gone.

"The divorce was never made final. She doesn't want people to know, you see. It's her business."

"Why?"

"I'm telling you, that's her business. Does my niece really interest you that much? I must say, that's news to me."

"Listen, why don't you show me my book and let's forget about it. I've been here almost twenty minutes now, and I still haven't seen my copies."

She seemed hesitant. "Didn't you see your book on the show?"

"Eyebrows was holding it . . . I wasn't going to stand up and walk over . . ."

"Didn't you sign a copy for him?"

"Just quickly . . . The blimp was in such a hurry to get out of there . . . You can't tell much from the flyleaf."

"Oh! If that's what you mean . . . They didn't change anything, you know. Anyway, you saw the proofs."

"Probably would have been for the best if they'd changed everything," I snorted.

"Oh, we're back to that again. Really, now . . . So all these compliments you've been getting from everyone, those are just farts in the wind? You're not even just a little bit moved . . ."

"Look, instead of arguing with me, why don't you just show me the books?"

"They're out here in the hallway . . . I got them yesterday morning. Malgodin sent them right away."

So we started down the long hallway, the walls lined with columns of books squeezed in so tight they seemed to meld into some weird amalgam, almost right up to the ceiling, a great big jumble of books, their spines a riot of colors, titles, authors, publishers . . .

"Here they are."

There was something gloomy and dejected in her voice, like we were standing not by a bookshelf but by a tomb where these "They" were resting . . . like this hallway was some sort of graveyard—and it's true, there were a lot of dead people there, lucky writers who'd never had to do their routine on TV: Balzac . . . Céline . . . Maupassant . . . Charles-Louis Philippe . . . Zola . . . Poe . . . Mark Twain . . . Villiers de L'Isle-Adam . . . Turgenev . . . Camus . . . Verlaine . . . and yet all of them still alive, in a sense, in spite of it all. Not one of them ever showed his face on the tube, but that didn't stop people from reading them! Lucky corpses, who'd never have to face that idiotic question, "What were you trying to say in your book?" But who knows? With this fixation on hauling writers up in front of the cameras, maybe one day we'd see some Eyebrows of the future discussing *The Red Lily* or *Les Misérables* with a little pile of bones . . .

I picked up one of my books, opened it, and once again discovered my pointless prose, my thick-headed wordplay, my malformed sentences trudging painfully over the page, my shallow, police-report behaviorism, my inane descriptions, my lovely syntactical screw-ups poking out here and there like weeds, my dialogue straight out of a dimestore novel or a TV series . . . Line after miserable line . . . I paged through the book, a strange weariness coming over me. The flatness of the thing hit me square in the face, just like a cream pie, only some joker had replaced the custard with cement. Talk about empty intellectual calories! I was already sure of it, and now the book in my hands made it clear as day: this was the best I could hope for, I'd never do better, never rise above this ocean of blather, this mountain of commonplaces, this forest of clichés. I pictured myself struggling to churn out those wretched sentences . . .

I put the book back on the shelf with the others. My hands were shaking. And then, all of a sudden, I understood why everyone was so wild about *Dancing the Brown Java*. And I realized I had only to make one little move, just one little move, to get the truth right in the kisser. But did I dare make that move?

"Well, what's the matter, my fine fellow? Still down on that book of yours? What's wrong with it?"

I jumped. Céline was wearing that half-teasing, half-hateful smile of hers. A smile that was hers alone, and seemed to laugh in the face of the whole wide world.

"All the shopkeepers loved it. Madame Jutier, the baker, she was telling me just the day before yesterday, she . . . And Farrand, the harness-maker . . . This is a guy who hasn't read a word since his army days . . . And he's seventy-six years old, the animal! You've got some real money in the bank now, my boy. Pretty soon you'll be rich. What have you got to complain about? Listen . . . There's one thing I have to tell you, though, Jean-Rémi . . ."

Make a move . . . Just one move . . . And then I'll bet everything would be clear.

51   The Paparazzi

After my talk with Céline, I realized I had no choice. I had to go on. Still, it was a very different man who now sat down before his ream of paper and picked up his pen in that little house amid the brambles.

So back to work I went. What she'd told me had really . . . How to put it? To say it had shaken me up would be a euphemism to rival the claim that the events in Tokyo in 1923 or in San Francisco on April 18, 1906 involved nothing more than five or six pebbles being rattled around with some vigor.

I never would have thought . . .

Here I was just back at La Halte, and already a paparazzo was trying to slither through the underbrush on the other side of the garden, facing the house. I don't know how he'd made it there without going through the front gates—had he rowed across the river in a little boat? swum it?—but there he was all the same, slinking along, head down, doing his best to blend into the greenery, playing cowboys and Indians, the jackass.

It was still warm for fall, and I had my window wide open. My mysterious disappearance, my abrupt exit from the stage just as *Brown Java* was going on sale, my unlikely accident—the chance encounter of a good-size stone and a human noodle, pretty rare in itself, and all the more so when you consider that a writer's most valued tool is his head—and then my long stay in the clinic for simple cranial trauma: all that, Céline told me, had greatly intrigued the ladies and gentlemen of the press. Not the critics, no—they'd already done their job—but the chroniclers, the columnists, the recorders of strange or amusing little events. A book comes out, makes an enormous splash, everybody's talking about it, and then all of a sudden one of the authors gets knocked silly and goes down for the count. As peculiar as it is bizarre, wouldn't you say? And what about Gastinel? Were the paparazzi trying to find out what he was up to as well? Apparently not. Nobody disturbing the fat man's peace and quiet.

"No, you're the one they're after," Céline told me. "They want to see you at work, for goodness' sake!"

There'd been some rumors making the rounds . . . What with his head injury and three or four weeks in a coma, Jean-Rémi Dochin will never write again . . . Or at least not more than ten or fifteen minutes a day, say his doctors . . . Which meant that *Rage Beneath the Cagoule*, the sequel to *Brown Java*, wouldn't be in the shops for . . . for years!

"According to Gastinel it was Malgodin's rivals who started spreading those stories . . . other publishers, who hadn't had the good fortune to get their hands on *Brown Java*!" Céline told me. "Don't you worry about it, my boy. Don't hide yourself away. Write with your window wide open, let the cretins see you're back on the scene . . ."

Two or three of these paparazzi had apparently come prowling around La Halte when I was snoozing away back in Brive. Supposedly some of them had even come plying their trade at the clinic, or at least just in front of the clinic, searching every little window for signs of activity, their telephoto lenses aimed and loaded for bear. Those guys have way too much time on their hands. I mean, come on, I'm not exactly another Françoise Sagan or Minou Drouet, now am I?

52   The Curiosity of Tracy Le Cardonnel

The days went by . . . November . . . December . . . Little by little, *Brown Java* was fading from the public eye. Two or three final reviews by laggardly critics as winter set in—excellent reviews, as it happens—and then the overseas Francophone press, and then it was over, and everything went quiet.

But we'd done it. The book was a hit. Copies were still being sold, and the translations were coming along.

Gastinel, now a full-time author—he was through with publishing for good—had moved into a great big apartment overlooking the Champ-de-Mars. Myself, I decided I'd wait for volume two to come out before getting my own place in Paris. Just a little pied-à-terre. I was thinking of something around Auteuil, near the race track or the Bois de Boulogne, just a vague idea as yet, nothing specific. We'd see about that in due time.

My parents finally read the book, and of course they didn't believe I'd actually written it. But now that my bank account was bulging, they'd have to get used to the idea.

I thought of Langillier again. I'd finally heard he was dead. I'd made a discreet call to his house, from Uzerche, so Céline wouldn't go asking questions. I ended up talking to a young-sounding person who introduced herself as his great-niece. She told me he'd died just twenty-four hours after the accident, there was nothing the surgeons could do. The driver was never found. She'd moved into his old apartment on the Avenue René-Coty.

"I must see you, Monsieur Dochin," she said, in an insistent little voice that struck me as odd. "Would it be too much trouble?"

At that moment all my senses went on the alert, I remember it well. Something was up, I realized . . . something dangerous, maybe.

"What do you want with me?"

"I just want to talk to you . . . My uncle read your manuscript."

"Yes, that's right . . . And?"

All of a sudden, I don't know why (or rather I do!), I remembered the missing page Langillier had sent back to me, the page I'd reread and found nothing funny about, absolutely nothing at all, nothing compromising or . . . well, weird. Max and Mimile were trying to steal eggs from a henhouse on a Norman farm, the farmer came running, but instead of yelling at them he brought them into the kitchen for quick swig of cider. The farmer's wife showed up, and didn't seem too happy to see the two kids. It ended there. An amazingly insignificant little passage, extraordinarily uninteresting . . .

But now I saw that page—no way around it, since for the past few weeks, starting when Céline talked to me, I'd become a different man—now I saw that page in an entirely new light.

And Langillier had read that lost page . . .

All at once, talking to her on the phone, I felt an urgent need to shield myself from the curiosity of this young Tracy Le Cardonnel. No matter what it took, I was going to have to keep her at bay till she gave up on the idea of meeting me. Of talking to me, as she put it. Langillier—but how could I have seen that at the time?—knew far too much about this whole affair. Was that why he'd ended up lying bloodied and battered in the street?

"I'm very busy at the moment, Mademoiselle Le Cardonnel," I told the girl on the phone. "Please don't take offense if I say no. Later on, maybe . . . Much later . . ."

When? I wondered. When this whole nightmare was over, when I finally woke up?

But wasn't *Dancing the Brown Java* now slated to go on for several more volumes?

And what about the little video that could have sent me straight to the slammer? Where had the blimp hidden it?

53 Céline's Birthday

The days went by. Raced by, even. It was all going very fast. Gastinel was still living in Paris, in his new apartment on the Avenue de Suffren, near the Eiffel Tower. To be sure, the publisher's promise of juicy disclosures—fresh dirt on the big and little wheels of the Occupation, the many minions orbiting the Vichy régime—had gone unfulfilled, but the book was still selling all the same. It was now understood that the publisher's enticing predictions were pure puffery. But those much-vaunted scoops were coming, don't you worry. Only a matter of time. Just wait till volume two hits the shelves, then we would see what we would see. Such was Malgodin's promise, and he swore the new book would bear it out. And indeed, toward the end of *Dancing the Brown Java*, one of the main characters, a close associate of Doriot and Bousquet, had kindly let it be known—a wink in the reader's direction—that he'd soon be speaking out, soon be spilling some interesting names, soon be fishing some pretty little things up out of the cesspool.

With his newfound riches, Gastinel had begun buying fine art—he didn't know squat about painting, it was just an investment, as any dealer in pigs or concrete or bankrupt businesses might indulge in—and gambling as well: poker, baccarat, the works. He haunted the racetracks and casinos, he picked up beautiful women, life was good, he played the role of the rich writer to the hilt and beyond, but most of all he blew hot air right and left, no one ever really saw him write, he went on a couple of TV game shows and even a roundtable on AIDS, where he contributed two or three imbecilities worthy of a writer of sentimental twaddle or beach potboilers, thereby incurring the wrath of Malgodin, who, now that Le Papyrus had offices at Saint-Germain-des-Prés, was eager to come off as a serious publisher—without renouncing the bottle, of course—and forget everything he'd published back on the Avenue d'Ivry, including *Suburbs: Home of the Wanking Class*, which had proven a pretty sweet coup, all the same, a good little seller, nothing to sneeze at, but for him only *Dancing the Brown Java* counted henceforth.

As for Dochin, he stayed out of sight, hunkered down at La Halte du Bon Accueil. Paris was no fun for him anymore. He liked the countryside, the peace and quiet. Also, he wanted to stick with Céline. He spent hour after hour at his desk. Gone were the pencils and pens. Now, at Céline's suggestion, he worked at the typewriter. He'd taken to it well enough; no longer did he emerge from his study at the end of the day with his fingers all covered in ink. Sometimes he kept at it for ten hours at a stretch, hammering away on the fancy electric Underwood his protectress had bought him in Tulle.

The paparazzi never returned. Dochin had clearly gone back to work; no truth to those tales of grave repercussions from the blow to his head. The newsmen and gossips had found other targets.

Dochin was giving it all he had, as Malgodin was eagerly awaiting volume two.

From time to time Gastinel came to La Halte in his big-shot jalopy, but only to make an appearance, he never stuck around long, just a quick stop to see how the work was progressing. Spending his days doing nothing, frittering away the time, living it up, he'd accumulated still more excess lard; he was now solidly steatopygic, his derrière like a forty-gallon drum, damn hard to drag around, tits right out of a Pirelli calendar, tough luck for the shock absorbers in his Mercedes. He bent over Dochin's shoulder, read a few sentences of the novel in progress, exulted in some particularly elegant turn of phrase, chortled with joy over a bit of dialogue; then, after absentmindedly massaging Dochin's nape with his fat, puffy—and now ring-bedecked—fingers, he hauled himself off, eager to get back to Paris where there were ladies waiting to do the java with him. Perfectly oblivious to the absurdity of the idea, he feared there might be a pack of curious journalists on his tail, and so did what he could to play the co-author of the season's hit novel. Once, when a paparazzo—one of the last to come crawling through the brambles, thank God . . . it never happened again—had managed to get near Dochin's house, the blimp glimpsed the lurking photographer and hastily struck the pose of someone handing his pseudo-collaborator a pile of pages pulled from his pocket—phony notes, imaginary, simply a handful of paper he'd had time to snatch up from the desktop. Dochin mimed a feverish reading of those torn pages, nodding meaningfully, approvingly, this whole Marx Brothersesque scene played before the open window for the benefit of the spy's telephoto lens. A little later, the picture was published in *Paris-Match*, with this caption: "Dochin and Gastinel, the literary heroes of the autumn, in full creative flight." The mob simply had to go on believing that *Dancing the Brown Java* was co-written with the former tripeman turned puppeteer, and that's all there was to it!

On December 27, 1995, Céline celebrated her seventy-seventh birthday. This called for a little dinner *en famille* at La Halte. Gastinel couldn't make it, but a few of the motel's regulars came along to join in the festivities: the ex-coal-miner Fredo-la-Casquette, the stringbean Larmory—whom Dochin still couldn't stomach—Monsieur

Jouffroy (the potbellied little man with the naïve look who sold candy in Charleville, now without his pit-bull but with his wife), even good old Doctor Crespiaud and his assistant Marie-Jo. The Northerner with the patched-up face hadn't forgotten his accordion, and he played them a java, a real java, the one by Fréhel. And in chorus they sang:

> *It's the blue java, my dear*
> *Oh, it's swell*
> *How it casts its spell*
> *When you hold your partner near*

and Doctor Crespiaud danced with Céline, who clung to him for all she was worth, blissful, half-swooning, still quite nicely put-together for her age, not a trace of cellulite, slim-waisted, lithe and lively as any teenager. A lovely evening, cheery and convivial, "far from the asshole crowd," as the accordionist put it. But Dochin, alas, couldn't seem to enter into the spirit of the thing. He was frowning all evening long. Something was bothering him, nagging at him. Visibly, his mind was on other things. No surprise! What he'd learned two months before, after the clinic and that stint on TV! What he now knew! Enough to put you in a pensive mood for a good long time. Crespiaud's friend Marie Jo even asked if he was sick.

54   Rage Beneath the Cagoule

In an interview published in *Lire* in late January 1996, Dochin and Gastinel announced that volume two of *Dancing the Brown Java* would appear sooner than planned. Probably April or May. A second volume markedly thinner than the first. This was Céline's idea. Since *Rage Beneath the Cagoule* was a long way from done, and probably wouldn't be before November or December, she thought it might be wise to go ahead and publish the 150 or 160 pages that had already been written. To further stoke their devotees' ardent impatience, they'd tell them the much-vaunted revelations would finally surface in volume three, for which they'd already found a title: *If These Francisques Could Talk*. At the same time, this tactic would bring in some ready cash, for they'd charge nearly as much for that diminutive second volume as for the first. No reader would balk at that little swindle, of course: after all, the authors were now famous men.

Malgodin thought this a brilliant idea, and the decision to proceed was made.

The manuscript was turned in to the boozehound at the beginning of March. It really was going to be a very slight little tome, but its cover would bear the co-authors' names in gigantic type.

Around March 25, Gastinel and Dochin received their proofs to correct. Dochin didn't want to touch his. He was disgusted, nauseated, by the entire affair. Now that he knew the score, he'd lost all interest in his literary career. The whole thing stunk to high heaven, in his estimation. Céline gladly took on the task herself.

A little before mid-April, Malgodin sent the galleys out to the top ten or fifteen critics.

Here and there, in cafés near the main publishing houses, at cocktail parties, in radio studios before a book show, in Left Bank restaurants for gastronomically inclined writers or publishers, words were being exchanged, mostly between critics, most often in hushed tones and with anxious faces, concerning the strange deaths of *Brown Java*'s disparagers at the end of the previous summer. Cuzenat . . . La Briançais . . . There were nervous whispers . . . perplexed expressions . . . hesitations . . . Was this an attempt, as Oscar Davidovitch of *L'Intransigeant* suggested—a highly distasteful maneuver, a reprehensible tactic—to break their will, to coerce them into liking the book? Was this all meant as some sort of indirect threat? But in the end, to everyone's great relief, the phrase "absurd coincidence" carried the day, and so, cradling a nice glass of wine, they blithely turned to other subjects, without a care in the world. "What would become of us if we started going to pieces every time some silly rumor like this came along?" exclaimed old man Planche of the *Petit National*, who, though only halfway through the galleys, found volume two well superior to its predecessor. Already acclaiming the authors' genius to all comers, he had absolutely nothing to fear.

"Quite agree, my dear Planche," concurred the venerable Alvernias of *Le Globe*, with his son-in-law—the drama critic La Motte Gambriac—looming over his shoulders, guiding his wheelchair. (Criticism was practically a family business for these people, a trade passed down from father to son, Alvernias's great-great uncle had spent years trying to topple Balzac, and that ancestor's maternal grandfather, Anatole-Gédéon Ricoeur, panned Charles Nodier's *Smarra ou les Démons de la Nuit* so violently in 1821 that a duel nearly ensued.) "Quite agree, my dear Planche. Not since Bernanos have I read anything so fine, so grand, so rich. There's absolutely no point in intimidating us."

"Of course, there'll probably still be some troublemakers," complained Esther Lebeuf of *Les Nouvelles Littéraires*, who'd been swooning over Dochin-Gastinel's "extraordinary transcendence," their "neo-paroxysmic sublimity," almost at the expense of her dignity. "Just the other day at the Café Procope, Ranfolin was telling Desbrestières and his wife how much he loathed that book, he was calling it a tedious sub-Schopenhauerian exercise, and claiming he's going to blast it to bits in his column. And remember, when he isn't busy transmuting a book he adores into precious metal, Ranfolin can be more devastating than a smoldering cigarette butt in a public library . . . In other words, there may be grounds for concern."

"Ranfolin's the only one turning up his nose," said the aged Planche. "I've heard nothing but raves. Everyone who knows how to read a book is cheering loud enough to bring down the house. Even at Gallim's, even at Furne, at Charpentier, at Conart, where no one can stand Malgodin."

"They say Alphonse Lemerre's trying to buy him out."

"I heard the same thing last Monday at Vagenende . . ."

Sitting discreetly among them in that literary bistro, alone at a corner table, nursing a green drink, perhaps crème de menthe, a mysterious, insignificant little personage, like a simple notary's clerk from the provinces—from the provinces of Balzac's time, of course, not today's—seemed to be drinking in not only the contents of his glass but also these critics' words, leaning his ear in their direction with such assiduity that it seemed to want to hang itself on the coat rack.

"Ranfolin never reviewed volume one," recalled little Pélissard, the Critic Sadistic, the one who could kill a book dead with one savage swipe of his claws in the last seven lines of his column, after starting out with a great display of affection for the author and reverence for his work. "Our good colleague couldn't stand the thing, but these were first-time novelists, after all, so on reflection he decided to be charitable and keep quiet."

"And he's damn lucky he did, if you ask me!" guffawed the wheelchair-bound but still robust octogenarian—almost nonagenarian—that was André Alvernias, critic at *Le Globe* since 1926, who had, over the years, not without *maestria*, armed only with a pen, assembled the largest cemetery of failed writers the world has even known.

55 Monsieur and Madame Ranfolin

Archibald Ranfolin's ears must have been aflame, so vigorously was his name being bandied about every corner of central Paris. He was home, in his four-room, courtyard-facing apartment on the Rue de Crimée, in the 19th arrondissement, dining with his wife Georgette, the TV turned on but the sound off, a common practice in many French households. The galleys of volume two of *Dancing the Brown Java* lay on the TV set, bound by a rubber band.

For several days running, in all the book world's principal watering holes, he'd trumpeted his disdain for *Brown Java*, and particularly for that execrable volume two, never thinking to keep his opinions to himself. But now, as for the past forty-eight hours, he who had long signed the most eagerly awaited and tremblingly feared column in *L'Européen du Jeudi* found himself needled by a vague apprehension, the sense of having wagged his tongue a bit too freely, of having committed an imprudence by openly declaring his aversion for Dochin-Gastinel's work.

Oh! his wife saw it all too well, anxiety was gnawing at her life-long companion.

"Aren't you going to eat your dinner, Archie? Not hungry? Do you want me to cut the fat off your ham? You hardly touched the blanquette last night. And you love it so!"

"I'll just have some potatoes with bacon . . . to make you happy, my dear."

"Oh! I know perfectly well what's bothering you! You're thinking of those two who died last summer. The one in the lake and the other in the subway. You don't think you were being a little rash, telling everyone how little you thought of that book?"

"Is it my fault if the thing is unreadable, utterly hollow, dull beyond telling?"

"Well, all your critic friends thought it was wonderful."

"Maybe they're right. But I just don't like it, and I'm not going to back down. There's nothing there. Pure concierge style. Page after page of clichés and platitudes . . . That's how I feel. What do you expect me to do? And this time I'm going to say so out loud. Enough is enough. I was very charitable when volume one came out, not doing a review . . . I thought the authors would understand, and quietly file away the sequel to their tedious little novel. But no. Malgodin won't see sense, he's going to publish the damn thing! What can I do? They've got my dander up! Is it my fault I like good books?"

"Listen, Archie . . . about your review for *L'Européen* . . ."

"Yes? Say, pass the wine, would you?"

"Couldn't you just lie? Just this once?"

"What, you mean write a good review? Make the readers think I like the thing?"

"Well, yes . . . It won't kill you."

"Fake it, eh? For the first time in my twenty-seven-year career in the service of good writing? Georgette, can you imagine what would happen? People would think my palm had been greased! Like a soccer player, like a referee, a boxer, a tennis player! The shame of it all! The vulgarity! I'm here to serve Art, Georgette, not athletics!"

"Do it for me, Archie. I'm worried to death about you. I can't sleep at night. When I think of La Briançais . . . that great thinker . . . sliced to bits by that subway train . . . And poor Cuzenat all ballooned up in that lake, he who discovered Ridiano and Georges Jissande!"

"Oh, you're a funny one! How could I possibly pull it off? It's a worthless novel, beyond repair, I wouldn't even give it to a ministry bureaucrat or a desk-jockey at the Brussels Commission to make paper airplanes out of! That'll tell you how much I loathe it."

"You could just copy the articles you did on *The Charterhouse of Parma* or *Cousin Pons*, your favorite novels. Doctor them up a little, change the characters' names, but keep all the flattering adjectives, all the praise, the acclaim, it wouldn't be much, just some quick grammatical gymnastics. Would you mind?"

Starting out as a young critic, Archibald Ranfolin had—simply for the sake of it, for his own pleasure, more or less as practice—written some dozen reviews of novels he particularly loved, and still loved today, novels he'd enshrined in his own private pantheon. These articles were never published, of course, undertaken as they were solely as an induction into his difficult trade, and he'd stowed them away in a drawer.

"Oh, I'll see," he finally conceded. "It's true, if I could adapt one of those, that would make things a lot easier for me."

"Sort of like a man making love to a frumpy woman, Archie. If his get-up-and-go needs a shot in the arm, he just closes his eyes and thinks hard about a beautiful lover he had years before."

"You're right . . . It just might work . . . I'll have to reread my piece on *The Lily of the Valley* or *Sentimental Education* . . . I imagine

I could say some wonderful things about Dochin while I was thinking of Balzac, and about Gastinel while I was thinking of Flaubert . . . Unless Barbey d'Aurevilly and Montherlant would work better . . . I'll see."

"Just don't get the names mixed up. Would you like some salad? I put in some garlic-rubbed croutons and tarragon and little pieces of horseradish. You remember? Your Aunt Zulma's recipe."

Making the best of a bad situation and purely for safety's sake, Archibald Ranfolin finally penned a review of *Rage Beneath the Cagoule*, volume two of *Dancing the Brown Java*, a wildly laudatory piece, almost deranged in its intensity, a delirious dithyramb.

On Monday, April 15, 1996, he submitted the text to his editor in the offices of *L'Européen du Jeudi*, on the Boulevard de Bonne-Nouvelle. He'd ended up lifting whole passages from a review of *Nausea* he'd written in 1961, back when he was a mere stripling aspiring to become the Sainte-Beuve of this latter half of the twentieth century. Needless to say, he'd made a few changes, emending the proper names, rewording certain points of the argument, the introduction, the plot summary . . . A fairly simple task, on the whole, just a few strokes of the pen, costing him only a bit of his Sunday, the essential elements of the review staying just as they were, its panegyric effusions above all.

Word of Ranfolin's stunning about-face raced through the newsrooms, the literary cafés, the big publishing houses, and soon Malgodin was rubbing his hands in glee. Before long, anyone who was anyone—anyone who could read, that is—knew that Archibald Ranfolin now revered volume two of *Brown Java*, and was going to publish an extraordinarily enthusiastic review, once again, as was his wont, transmuting the base metal of a book he admired into gold.

Needless to say, this came as something of a surprise, and even a deep, bewildering shock, to many who'd witnessed his earlier fulminations against Dochin-Gastinel's book. Dark whisperings began to circulate, among them that Ranfolin—needing some cash for an overhaul of his dim, well-nigh uninhabitable apartment on the Rue de Crimée—had accepted a payoff from Le Papyrus. Corruption and fraud, those twin plagues imported to our shores from America, lately flourishing in the world of sports, of TV game shows, of business, of politics, in certain town halls, in medicine, banking, commerce, unions, government—had they now infected even the world of publishing, heretofore blissfully spared their ravages?

But all ill-feeling toward Ranfolin faded at once on Saturday, April 20th, when the anchor of the eight-o'clock news made following announcement: "I've just been handed a bulletin reporting the death of Archibald Ranfolin, the highly respected literary critic at *L'Européen du Jeudi*. Out for an early-afternoon stroll through the Parc des Buttes-Chaumont, in Paris, the journalist was crossing the so-called 'Suicide Bridge' when he inexplicably tumbled over the side. A homeless person who was relaxing on a nearby lawn claims to have seen two individuals of indeterminate appearance seize the critic and toss him over the guardrail. The police have categorically dismissed this account, terming it an outlandish fabrication, the witness being in an advanced stage of alcoholism. On to sports. After turbulent discussions at the Union of European Football Associations, Monaco FC will be matched with . . ."

"Those imbeciles at *L'Européen*! Why couldn't they have published his piece right away?" Georgette Ranfolin lamented between two sobs, as she identified the body at the morgue. "They could have saved Archie's life. Why did those bastards wait? I'll bet I know why: that fat old Pajol's been after his job for twelve years!"

56   The Interview

Rage Beneath the Cagoule appeared as scheduled in mid-May 1996, to instant critical and commercial success. Record sales. A second printing was undertaken at the end of the month, in numbers to make any author or publisher drool.

Back at La Halte, Dochin still sat glued to his typewriter. Volume three was coming along. Gastinel was promising that this third installment of *Dancing the Brown Java* would finally bring the long-awaited revelations. Curiously, Dochin was saying nothing. He seemed to have dropped out of the whole affair, his mind elsewhere. In a mid-June interview with *Info-Matin*, the blimp had declared that the disclosures in question would primarily involve bigwigs in the Vichy regime who remodeled themselves post-Liberation, having had the good sense to jump on the bandwagon just after Stalingrad or the American landing in North Africa, when everyone with any foresight or judiciousness or ambition realized that the brown-clad hordes' goose was cooked, and that it would be most unwise to go on playing ball with them. Volume three would also raise some interesting questions concerning the Nazi pillage of France's pictorial treasures, questions that might well prove troublesome for certain French antiquarians (or at least for their memory, or their heirs . . .), who'd served as informers for Goering's or Rosenberg's emissaries, helping them help themselves to various masterworks owned by Jewish collectors, in exchange—of course, everything has its price—for a nice little Matisse, or maybe that lovely Renoir over there, which the German gentlemen might be willing to forget to bring back to Monsieur Goering for his Carinhall. Oh! Such a dark time in our nation's history! Were they right, in the end, to publish their *Brown Java*, perhaps running the risk of making waves in what, after so many years, were now inoffensive, still waters?

"After this third and no doubt final volume," the erstwhile tripemonger announced in the interview, "we promise to stop inconveniencing certain of our fellow citizens who chose to . . . Isn't it high time we French made our peace with each other once and for all, after all our many tribulations? The Commune, the Front Populaire, the Occupation, the Liberation, the Purge, May '68, the Social Security reforms, etc., etc.? Once we finish *If These Francisques Could Talk*, Dochin and I plan to take a brief vacation, first of all, and then move on to other things. Perhaps a love story. But in the meantime we have that explosive third volume to get out. And just you wait! Things are going to heat up!"

These dire threats were proffered by a Gastinel grown monstrously misshapen, a Gastinel who, had he applied at one of our fine employment agencies, would no doubt have been pointed straight toward the freak show of some country fair.

"I'd wager some of our fellow Frenchmen—who shall remain nameless, of course—might be getting a tiny bit antsy just now," the obese personage added. "Jean-Rémi and I have almost finished work on that volume three, and believe me, it's going to make a lot of noise. Just a few last-minute touchups and we're done. It should be out in November."

"Could you be more specific, Charles Gastinel? Perhaps tell us a bit more, something more explicit, about the shattering revelations that, as you said at the start of this interview, might well reopen the rift dividing the French on that sad chapter in our history?"

"You'll see, you'll see . . . I can tell you nothing more for the moment. We have to preserve the suspense, just like in a good crime novel. You might be surprised, that's all I can say."

"Will you be naming these people by their names?"

"Of course not. Dochin and I don't have the time to deal with a lot of libel suits—which we'd win, no doubt about that, but they might drag on forever, and interfere with our creative process. But the names will be perfectly clear. You've already seen a number of disagreeable characters in volumes one and two: Abel Panard . . . Darqueue de Pellepouze . . . Darnuche . . . Hérold-Paquet . . . Philippe Horion . . . Brunon . . . Buquart . . . Picheu the Guillotiner, and I could name many more, scum that they are."

"Yes, but those were the worst of the worst. In their case, and others like them, we learned very little that we didn't already know . . . The imprisoned patriots . . . the torture . . . the executions . . . the deportations . . . the informers . . . France bound and gagged . . . the sweeps . . . little children arrested . . . and more besides. We already knew those people stood with Laval and the ex-socialist Déat against the Gaullists, against the Communists, the Jews, the Freemasons, the anarchists, the FTP, the German and Spanish refugees, the printers who made up false papers, the . . . in short, against almost all of France."

"Yes, but don't worry, the barely-disguised names you'll find in *If These Francisques Could Talk* belong to people who never appeared center stage on the Vichy or collaborationist scene. Which doesn't mean they weren't part of the gang, or that some of them didn't join in on some pretty filthy business, often solely for the sake of filling their pockets."

"Isn't this just another ploy of the sort Monsieur Malgodin has already inflicted on us more than once? Come on, Charles Gastinel, play fair, tell us the truth."

"Oh, no, this is no cheap publicity stunt. You'll see, our book's going to kick up a whole lot of dust. You'll be hearing some wailing and gnashing of teeth, I promise you that."

"But where did you and Dochin dig up all these secrets?"

"Well, we already talked about that on *Book Culture* last October. By way of certain archives placed under lock and key in 1944, which we managed to get at all the same. Also by carefully reading between the lines of lots of private correspondence. And so on and so forth. We're not going to keep repeating that forever. In certain respects, the novelist's sources are much like a reporter's. Discretion is of the essence."

"Are some of the people in your sights still living today?"

"I can't answer for all of them. But some are, yes indeed. The youngest were born around 1920. So . . . do the math. You'll find that the truth—ofttimes disturbing—will out, and that the classic little excuse for the behavior of X, Y, or Z—'Yes, it's true, he did some absolutely appalling things, but he was also quite helpful to the Resistance' (and this should always be carefully looked into, mind), which is to say, 'With my right hand I help fill the Vélodrome d'Hiver with innocent victims, and with my left I give a friendly little wave to the Croix de Lorraine, and if I had three hands I'd probably go tickle the Commies' mustaches'—that classic little excuse just won't hold water."

"In volume three, will you be showing us former members of the Cagoule, as you did in volume two? Perhaps some of those decadent or backward young bourgeois who brayed 'Down with Halfbreeds!' on the boulevards of the Latin Quarter in 1934?"

"A little of that, yes. There'll be some surprises. You'll even witness a few cases of spontaneous Semitophilia, generally dating from the fall of '44."

"Can you tell us, Charles Gastinel—since Dochin doesn't seem particularly eager to speak, at the moment—can you tell us what exactly inspired you to write *Dancing the Brown Java*? Stylistically speaking, it's clearly the work of an immensely talented writer—forgive me, two immensely talented writers—but where exactly did it come from?"

"Well, it was mostly a single sentence. Just one little sentence, from Philippe Aziz's book *Tu Trahiras sans Vergogne*:[4] 'And don't forget, many members of the "French Gestapo" are still alive to this day. Some of them are in business. Others were never found or arrested, having successfully concealed their existence for many years . . . etc.'"

"Thank you, Dochin and Gastinel. And thanks, too, for your patriotic spirit."

Tracy Le Cardonnel, still working at the private detective agency Le Guetteur—offices at 9, Rue Delambre, in Montparnasse, directed by Monsieur Chignard, former commissioner-in-chief at the Internal Intelligence Agency, now semi-retired—read the Dochin-Gastinel interview in *Info-Matin*. Early in July, still unable to forget Urbain Langillier's dying words, she telephoned Dochin at La Halte du Bon Accueil.

Alarmed by this call, the Mayennais immediately thought of the manuscript page Langillier had sent back in March or April of the previous year. An ice-cold geyser erupting just behind his back wouldn't have chilled him more.

---

4   Published by Éditions Fayard. (Author's note.)

"I'm sorry, Mademoiselle. It's absolutely impossible for me to meet you. Please be so good as not to insist. I have a great deal of work to do, you know."

"I can't believe it."

"Why, may I ask, this insistence on meeting me? You're not a journalist, as far as I know."

"It's about your manuscript . . . *Dancing the Brown Java* . . . Monsieur Langillier read it . . . or at least part of it . . ."

Not knowing how to respond, on the verge of blind panic, Dochin rudely slammed down the phone.

PART IV   Curiouser and Injuriouser

57 Another Flashback
(The Excursion to the Ile d'Yeu)

We drove all night after that stint on *Book Culture*, interminable stretches of road without speaking a word, the radio turned down low.

That worm Dochebag sat beside me, sulking in silence. Nothing. Not even a fart. Probably lost in thought, the halfwit.

As was I, for that matter.

Roaring down the highway toward Poitiers, I gave my memories free rein to wander at will. Back to the recent past. A little film playing in my head. Scene one: the day I made Céline's acquaintance. Or rather a little before.

I'd had to face facts, my puppeteer days were over. I'd grown grossly overweight, not so much from stuffing my face as from some glandular misfire, or some protein thing, I heard about that once on the radio, and another time a sawbones tried to tell me how it works, sort of like what happened to Max Dalban, one of Jean Renoir's favorite actors before he got hit with this thing. Too fat to move around in the cramped little shack I called my marionette theater. I'd made some good dough out of that thing, but now . . . I walked away and never looked back. Left the key under the mat. I was scared stiff of ending up homeless again. Here I was, almost fifty-five years old! Another disaster like that and I'd be bound straight for the boneyard. Still, I managed to keep body and soul together for a little over two years, eating nothing but beans, not exactly the high life, living on the modest nest egg I'd built up from my kiddie shows. My dream was to open a business, but I didn't have near enough cash to get anything off the ground. This weird little idea had been rolling around in my head for a while: go into publishing, set up shop and start putting out books. Don't get me wrong, not some arty-farty kind of deal, no, just an ordinary little joint to sell cheap literary trash, stroke books, low-rent comics—everybody and his brother's putting that stuff out, so there've got to be some rejects I could pick up—cut-rate science fiction, crap like that, and then, well, if things went okay, maybe a few normal novels that Furne and Charpentier and Gallim's and all the others had turned down, nowadays even the most benighted dipshit wants to write his own novel—I tried it myself, but after eight pages I dropped my pen, my complete lack of talent staring me in the face.

It was from Malgodin that Gastinel had contracted the idea of becoming a publisher. They'd met back when he was doing his marionette shows. Euloge Malgodin had worked as a literary critic for years, but eventually he started hitting the bottle, got laid off, and went into publishing. Oh! nothing ambitious. A no-name little press. But two or three of his authors had written sketches or playlets for Gastinel's theater, and so their paths necessarily crossed. Though never really becoming friends, they saw each other from time to time (Gastinel tended to keep his distance, as the perpetually sloshed publisher made disagreeable company). But then Gastinel conceived the idea of imitating him, in professional terms at least. He didn't have the money to go into business in any serious way, but he'd spotted an old shop in Belleville, a former horse-butcher's, whose two or three back rooms, once the owners' apartment, might well serve as his office. Lacking the capital to buy the place, Gastinel had appealed to one of his uncles, Lucas Pernochot, his mother's brother, who'd made a name for himself in the food industry via a line of canned ham and corned beef available in almost any supermarket.

In July '88, the blimp screwed up his courage and placed a call to that uncle. The first time in decades he'd tried to make contact. Luckily, Pernochot was by nature a jovial man, and greeted him without a scintilla of rancor:

"Oh! Of course I remember you, Charles! I can picture you now in your uncle Adrien's tripe shop by the Porte de Pantin. You were just a little kid. Must have been back during the Occupation."

Gastinel remembered. Uncle Lucas had pulled some odd stunts between 1940 and 1944, resulting in a five-year term in Fresnes Prison. Youthful indiscretions, the canning magnate inevitably called them: first he'd joined the collaborationist militia, and then he'd volunteered to head to the Eastern Front with Bucard's boys and fight off the Bolsheviks.

"Listen, my dear Charles. I'd be happy to lend you a hand, but we'll have to talk all this over. Besides, I'd love to see you again. You must be how old nowadays?"

"Fifty-six, uncle."

"And I'm sixty-nine. We're not getting any younger!"

"You were Mama's favorite little brother . . ."

"I can see your parents now. You still remember that movie-house fire in Dieppe?"

"I try not to think of that anymore. I haven't for years. It was so long ago!"

"I never see anyone these days, with my business to look after. What about you, Charlot? You're holding up well?"

"I . . . uh . . . I've put on some weight."

"Not letting life's little tribulations get you down, eh? We'll talk about that."

"Anyway, about getting together . . . shall I come out to your place?"

Pernochot lived in a little Norman manor house near Louviers.

"I'm afraid that won't be possible, my boy. Not anytime soon, at least. I'm just off to the Limousin to meet up with some old friends. If you could wait a little while . . ."

Gastinel was in no mood to wait. He had his moneyed uncle in his grasp, and he wasn't going to let him slip away. Pernochot thus named a spot where they might meet, the evening of July 21 or the next morning before ten: the Hôtel de la Cuiller d'Or, in Brive.

"Don't come after that, there probably won't be anyone around. I'm part of a group. We sleep at the hotel—the owner's a friend—and then we take a hired bus to the Ile d'Yeu. We have to be there on the 23rd. It's a sort of pilgrimage. The thirty-seventh anniversary of Pétain's death. We're going to put flowers on his grave. We do it every year. As you probably know, I've remained a faithful admirer of the late Marshal."

Gastinel realized the former militiaman's politics hadn't changed a bit.

"But uncle, if we meet there, I'll just be in the way . . . With all your friends around . . ."

"Don't worry about that. Why don't you come with us? Are you a Pétainist, too?"

"I'm not big on politics, uncle. Besides, I was too young in those days . . ."

"Well, it doesn't matter. Come along anyway, that'll give us a chance to talk over your plans."

From the Limousin to the Ile d'Yeu . . . Pretty long trip, Gastinel thought to himself.

I'll ditch them along the way, the ex-puppeteer finally decided. As soon as Uncle says he's willing to front me the cash, I'll head back to Paris. I'm sure I can find some excuse. What the hell would I be doing at Pétain's grave? Why not Napoleon's tomb, while we're at it? Or maybe the last resting place of Jean-Jacques Rousseau on the Ile des Peupliers at Ermenonville (not that I'd find him at home anyway, now that he's taken up digs at the Panthéon)?

What no doubt set this whole affair in motion—the affair you've been reading about for more than a few pages now—what no doubt set it all in motion was that Gastinel, fearing he might miss his uncle, left for the Limousin seventy-two hours in advance. As we might well expect, his obesity earned him the coolness, the uncongeniality, and the ostracism of more than a few hotel owners. Having—very politely—inquired at the front desk of the Cuiller d'Or, where his uncle was planning to stay, he was informed that their beds were not stout enough for a man of his bearing, they'd had troubles of that sort just three months before, when a group of sumo wrestlers came to town for a public demonstration of their art. He crisscrossed the region several times at the wheel of his old car, outraged to find the hoteliers turning him away without even a hint of hesitation or regret, his massive bulk—he'd reached nearly 330 pounds—a potential distraction for guests having their lunch or dinner, if only when his astonishingly plump derriere came to rest on the fragile dining-room chair, and what to say when the maître d'hôtel anxiously inquires if Monsieur would like a double or triple portion of ember-cooked truffles or tripoux d'Aurillac? Can you imagine the smiles on the nearby diners' faces? Perhaps even outright titters from the more ill-mannered among them? Was it not in fact out of kindhearted charity that these recalcitrant proprietors refused entrance to one who might well become the laughingstock of an entire dining room?

At long last, the chambermaid of the Sanglier d'Argent in Ussel directed him toward La Halte du Bon Accueil, where Céline Ferdinaud welcomed him with open arms. There was already one fatty staying there—a 350-pound beef-wholesaler from the Boulonnais—and this orotund pair were soon something very like fast friends. Learning that her abnormally bloated guest was a publisher, Céline suddenly seemed to take a most lively interest in him. Gastinel told her he'd be heading to Brive two days later to meet up with his uncle, the owner of the Pernochot cannery, and naturally enough Céline assumed he was one of the Pétainists:

"You're Lulu Pernochot's nephew? You've got to be kidding! Why, he's an old friend of mine! As a matter of fact I'm expecting him here in a day or two. No need to go to Brive."

And indeed, Pernochot appeared at La Halte two days later, on July 22, at around eleven A.M. He emerged from a bus packed with some thirty people, mostly male, clearly old friends, a few of them carrying pennants, all dressed in civilian clothes but sporting the distinctive blue beret of Joseph Darnand's militia. Most were old geezers—former collaborators, escapees from the Purge—but there were younger folk, too: the offspring of Vichyites imprisoned postwar for collaboration or dealings with the enemy, even the child of an auxiliary of the German police who met his end before a firing squad at Fort Montluc in 1946. Many of them, ever faithful to their creed, wore a little Francisque on their vest or lapel. Nearly all came here every year—so Uncle Pernochot explained to Gastinel—one or two days before July 23, the anniversary of Pétain's death, for a pilgrimage to his grave on the Ile d'Yeu. The uncle introduced the blimp to a few of his friends:

"Doctor Crespiaud, Monsieur Petitprêtre, Maître Lacharmerie—he's a *notaire* in Loudun—Madame Valentini-Chapuzot, Monsieur Olivier, Monsieur and Madame Jouffroy, who run a candy store in

Charleville, Monsieur Larmory, the Baron de La Coeuillière, ex-member of the Horsemen of Saumur, who is kind enough to co-finance this excursion with me, and whose generosity is well-known among even the humblest of our escapees from the Gaullo-FFI-ist Terror of Fall 1944. The baron is the founder and endower of the PMNR, the Populist Movement for National Reconciliation."

Gastinel had no choice but to shake the outstretched hands. He felt somewhat ill at ease in this group, fearing he might find himself conscripted in a battle that wasn't his, apolitical as he was. "Whatever it takes to get by," such was his only creed, an anarcho-Machiavellian individualism more or less typical of your average French slob.

With nothing to occupy his time in those two days at La Halte, Gastinel had many occasions to chat with Céline. She took an immediate interest in the adipose gentleman, primarily because he was trying to put together a publishing house. And indeed, no sooner had Lucas Pernochot got off the bus than he promised his nephew a loan, a very tidy little sum, all the blimp would need to make his dream a reality. Nevertheless, this dream deserved to be talked over at greater length, and at leisure.

Gastinel soon understood that this annual pilgrimage was a real drag for the hotelier, and that, though she'd taken part once or twice in her younger days, she'd long since lost interest, and had no plans to accompany the group on their voyage. She'd last set foot on the Ile d'Yeu back in 1956, thirty-two years ago already.

La Halte was the real starting point for this journey. The group stopped by to pick up Odette, a longstanding participant—Odette Pontayrac, once the mistress of an NCO in the Wehrmacht, later paraded through the streets of Limoges with her head shaved—and to greet good old Céline, meanwhile taking on the picnic lunches packed by La Halte's ladyfolk and collecting any comrades who'd come straight to the motel without stopping at Brive, among them Lucien Leblond, a nurseryman from Villefranche-sur-Saône, inevitably accompanied by his orangutan (Céline looked after the animal during the pilgrims' two-day absence), son of a Franc-Garde officer, Hector Leblond, ladies' hairdresser in Roanne from 1922 to 1940, executed at Chambéry in 1945.

"I'm afraid I won't be able to look after your beast this year, my dear Leblond," the Ferdinaud woman informed him.

"There won't be anyone at La Halte to keep an eye on Jojo?"

"Nope. I'm closing for two days. This time, you see, I'm coming along."

"No kidding? What's got into you, Céline? So you want to go snuggle up to little Pépette again?" (Leblond, to the consternation of most of his friends, habitually referred to Pétain as "Pépette.") "Well, if that's how it is, you can count me out. I can't leave Jojo all alone."

"Bring him with us," suggested Doctor Crespiaud. "He'll keep us entertained till we get to the island."

"Out of the question. Poor Jojo would never withstand the boat ride, he gets seasick. No, we'll be on our way. Say good-bye to the nice people, Jojo. No, not the fascist salute, you imbecile. That's all over now."

Why had Céline decided to join the excursion, she who didn't give a good goddamn about this memorial ceremony? Well, it's very simple: in order to deepen and broaden her acquaintance with Charles Gastinel. Two days of travel, two nights at the Hôtel Beau-Rivage in Port-Joinville: a most interesting opportunity to get closer to the fledgling publisher.

And indeed, by the time they returned to La Halte, Céline and Gastinel were thick as thieves. The ex-tripemonger even stayed on for a week longer.

Oh, the things they said to each other! (You'll understand later.)

For the moment, let's see what comes next . . . We're going to talk a bit about Céline, perhaps draw her portrait with a little more detail, this time around.

But before we do, let us return to a remark we made earlier: what no doubt set this whole affair in motion was that Gastinel, fearing he might miss his chance to meet up with his uncle, set out for the Limousin three days early. Had he not been grossly overweight, no doubt the story that concerns us here would never have got underway, or at least wouldn't have unfolded as we've seen. Too fat, too misshapen, bothersome, burdensome, Gastinel ran into closed doors at every hotel he entered. Which brought him to La Halte. Had he been built like anyone else, Gastinel would have been readily accepted in the first hotel he applied at, and there he would have quietly awaited his uncle and the chat concerning his publishing plans. Having received the promise of a loan, he would have found some way to ditch the captain of the canned-food industry, and thus never boarded the Pétainists' bus. He would thus never have met Céline.

And in fact we could go still further back, and say, more simply, this: had he remained svelte, Gastinel would have continued as a puppeteer, from which trade he was earning a perfectly respectable livelihood. He would thus never have thought of re-establishing contact with his uncle Pernochot. Céline and he, let us underscore this point once again, would thus never have met. And that, it must be agreed, would have given our tale a very different turn.

Would Dochin have participated in the murder of a young girl in Carrouges? Very likely not. Which leads us to formulate the following observation: is it not strange that a few surplus pounds of human flesh can be the primary cause of a tragedy such as the story we here recount?

58 Céline's Salad Days

It had all worked like a charm. Nothing you might call a hitch. Just one or two delicate tightrope tricks—unexpected, but in the end not all that difficult, and so the acrobat dropped to earth safe and sound.

A moment had come when Céline could no longer keep silent. She had to make her move. The years were rolling by. She was nearing her seventy-third year when Dochin, snubbed by the local hoteliers, showed up at La Halte. She realized at once that a prize pigeon had fallen into her lap, maybe the pigeon of her dreams. Besides, she'd taken a shine to him right from the start, sweet innocent Dochin, forty years old and still a kid.

"It's weird, how you remind me of a brother of mine."

She never had a brother, of course. The portrait in her room was of Joseph Lévêque, the auxiliary to the French Gestapo. She'd become his mistress in September 1940, not yet twenty-two years of age.

Dochin bore not the slightest resemblance to Lévêque, but that was a way to break the ice, to explain the sudden surge of warmth she'd displayed for this drifter with the beginnings of a novel in his backpack.

Because she was in a hurry. Years before, she'd begun her great novel, a saga provisionally titled *When We Were Twenty*, the story—slightly reworked, of course—of her affair with Lévêque, the one great love of her life. As a backdrop, Paris under the German

Occupation, the arcana of the Vichy régime, the secret lives of the cream of the collaborationist crop. The drawing rooms, the back rooms, the press rooms, the offices, the prisons, the clandestine rendezvous, etc., etc., a universe she knew intimately, since Lévêque—a jealous and untrusting lover—insisted she follow him nearly everywhere he went. For Céline had once been a beautiful woman, a wake of admiring male glances trailing after her like the fiery tail of a comet. Sometimes Lévêque even dragged her into those fearsome, dank cellars where the men and women of the Resistance had their secrets wrung out of them. She stood stranded in a corner, a captive audience as the interrogations ground on. How, in those cramped quarters, to hide herself away? In what tiny mousehole? How not to see everything, hear everything, nausea writhing in her entrails? But Lévêque knew how to keep his hands clean. He asked the questions, nothing more. Would she have left him had he wielded the tools himself, like the three or four brutes—petty hoodlums, for the most part—at his side? She had to face it: the answer was no. Her love was too strong. And it was because Lévêque almost inevitably took her along when he headed to Drancy to question a fresh batch of detainees that, when the Liberation came and she became a wanted criminal, the newspapers stuck her with the cognomen "the Bitch of Drancy." Her, Céline Feuhant, daughter of the far-right bookseller Armand Feuhant, whose shop on the Rue de Tolbiac specialized in political works, screeds, and pamphlets, primarily of a fascistic bent. Armand Feuhant, who from time to time ventured out to rough up the leftist students in the Latin Quarter, who numbered among the mob that attacked Léon Blum during Bainville's funeral procession. She'd grown up with all that. A select clientele, members of the Cagoule . . . thanks to whom, in 1940, she'd made Lévêque's acquaintance.

Joseph Lévêque was a fine figure of a man, ambitious, vigorous, thirty-one years old, a former swimming champion turned owner and manager of a gymnasium at Billancourt. Forceful personality. It was love at first sight.

Little by little, into this novel she was writing—hundreds of pages kept in a cardboard folder in her armoire—she'd begun inserting certain secrets she'd learned from Lévêque. Inside information, unknown to the general public . . . Because Lévêque told her everything. Coming home from a mission—an interrogation she'd been lucky enough to miss out on, a planning meeting with a Lafont, a Bucart, a Doriot, among others—he always brought back a heap of gossip, sometimes things that were more or less well known, sometimes genuine state secrets. Thinking she might be amused, certain she'd keep it strictly to herself, he dished it all up for her, a particularly dark sort of pillow talk. Gradually—a paragraph here, a scene there, sometimes an entire chapter—she'd worked those grim tidbits into her book, doctoring them up just a little. Solely for the purpose of unmasking some of the good citizens who'd muddied their feet in the sewer that was 1940–44 but cleaned themselves up just in time—the old quick-change routine, in the words of a caustic Purge-era judge—to land themselves nice cushy positions in the new-born Republic.

Name after name . . . only half-disguised . . .

Never to appear in print, of course, since her own name was Céline Feuhant.

In 1940, that name was already relatively well known in the Parisian literary world, for in the late thirties Céline had published a handful of poems and several short stories in two or three journals. Her work had not gone unnoticed: two influential critics, now deceased, as well as a great writer—an advisor to a major publishing house—had lauded her remarkable style, hailing the discovery of a new literary voice, of a writer with an undeniable gift.

And then came the war, putting an end to all that.

Back to the white page, soon gone black.

After the debacle of June 1940, she found herself caught up in the maelstrom of the Collaboration. Her long love affair with Lévêque began, and not one more line did she write.

The imperious need to create came roaring back just after the war. A few brief short stories flowed from her pen in 1945, Lévêque having been executed at the Fort de Montrouge, herself having gone into hiding in the Limousin.

In 1950, the postwar upheavals gone calm at last, she returned to Paris and tried to live as discreetly as possible, keeping the lowest of profiles. She was taken in by some old friends: Monsieur and Madame Crespiaud, former collaborators, now real-estate agents with a medical-student son who briefly became her lover. She then set out to publish her recent work. Somewhat dubiously, though, for if a major writer like Jean Giono, who'd never hurt a fly, could be blacklisted for several years by the *Comité National des Écrivains*, what hope was there for the Bitch of Drancy?

The amiable young man at the helm of the journal *L'Artiste*, a certain Urbain Langillier, warmly complimented her on the six stories she'd given him. But he had no choice but to hand them back:

"Don't take it amiss . . . I know who you are . . . It would be dangerous."

She went home with her stories. Into the drawer with them. Forbidden to publish, probably for life. Perhaps worse than the firing squad, for a writer.

Placed on the public-enemies list from late summer 1944 to 1948, she'd managed to escape the Court of Justice, public disgrace, the charge of consorting with the enemy. She'd never even had her head shaved!

But in late 1950 she was caught.

What to do with Lévêque's girl, the Bitch of Drancy? Haul her up before a judge?

"Confidentially, Céline Feuhant," she'd been told by a very courtly commissioner from the Directorate of Territorial Security, "the problem is not that you were Lévêque's mistress. It's that you weren't deaf. Everyone knew it: once he was alone with his lady-friend, he might as well have been in a confessional. Déat himself once remarked on it."

"I've always kept quiet. Céline Feuhant is a vault. And in any case, do you think I gave a damn about all those stories he told me? Politics had no place in my life with Lévêque. I was never a fascist. I couldn't have cared less about that tripe. But if I say so, no one will believe me. So what's the use?"

"We have only one goal at this stage: getting the country back on its feet. The hour of Reconstruction has sounded. An immense task ahead of us. What good would it do to drag you into a courtroom? Six years have passed! We're sure an intelligent woman like you will see to it she's never heard from again."

They'd engineered a dismissal of her case. All very discreet. No public uproar. Six lines in four or five newspapers.

So a few grouches might grumble, "Can you imagine! No trial for an accomplice of the traitor Lévêque! Charges dropped!" Let them: it'll pass. If necessary, the spotlight could be turned toward some nice, grisly crime as a diversion. There's no lack of them. They could even cook one up, if they had to.

She couldn't quite remember what they'd come up with to justify her release . . . "Service to the Resistance," perhaps? Who knows? A deal had been struck. All they asked was that she keep her mouth shut and think of the reconciliation of the French people. They weren't going to go on imprisoning or shooting people for the next twenty-five years! Lévêque had paid the price. Richly deserved. As for her . . . They were willing to shut their eyes. As long as she kept out of sight!

They gave her a new identity, printed up some official fake papers. She wanted Ferdinand for her new surname, first because it went nicely with Céline, and second because she adulated that writer's work. And furthermore, she could keep her initials: C.F. But given that the author of *Death on the Installment Plan* was still alive, the commissioner overseeing her case suggested Ferdinard or Ferdinaud instead. In the end, she chose Ferdinaud, keeping her real date and place of birth: Paris, 13th arrondissement, December 27, 1918.

And then, as requested, she quietly vanished into the scenery.

And so, in March 1951, aged thirty-two, she found herself in the Limousin, managing a sort of motel (in those days they still called it an inn).

Little by little, the people of Térignac adopted her as one of their own, unaware of her past, not knowing quite who she was. A former bookseller, she called herself. (And before that a script girl, no invention there, that had indeed been her job from 1936 to 1940.) She'd even been married! And then divorced. Pure fabrication, of course. A past made to measure, cobbled together for the circumstances.

The multitude of books lining the walls of the former post house came largely from her father's shop, which, alongside the political pamphlets, also sold ordinary novels and all the other wares usually found in such places.

Time went by . . .

But then one day the fever resurfaced, and she started writing again. Alone, undisturbed, tucked away in her big bedroom at La Halte, a soothing curtain of trees outside her window, not a sound to be heard but the murmuring river and the songs of the birds, in summer and winter alike. Pages and pages she filled, piling up as the years went by. Her novel! A major undertaking. A manuscript that might well end up as hefty as *The Brothers Karamazov* or *The Century Was Young*, to cite two works she knew well.

No chance, though, that her work might one day find its way into the shopwindows. And this for reasons that had absolutely nothing to with literature.

So just forget about it? Put it away in the drawer and be done with it?

59 The First Gray Hairs

It was when she found herself growing old that the rage suddenly came over her. Lévêque riddled with bullets, fine, that was all part of the game. He'd chosen the wrong team, it's only right that he pay the price. In time she'd come to accept that, although her fond memories of the former Olympic swimming champion hadn't faded a bit, the Germanophile's portrait never leaving its spot in her room for what would soon be forty-five years. But, she told herself, there were others, others whose consciences weren't exactly clean, others who'd got off scot-free, others who'd even ended up draped with honors for their wartime service, their inevitable, indecent little excuse—"You know, it was all much more complicated than you think"—grating on her like fingernails on a chalkboard.

Unable to forgive and forget, she thought of the police raids, the city buses hauling detainees across Paris, the Vélodrome d'Hiver packed to the rafters and not a cyclist in sight . . . She thought of all that, and began to feel a rancor that some might have considered a tad misplaced.

Yes, it was when the first gray hairs began to gleam at her temples that the idea took hold of her. Stop the music. Off with the masks. Some of the ones who'd remade themselves just in time, at the price of certain complicated, almost comical contortions, were still alive. And for those who might think of writing their memoirs, or of having them written, she might well add a chapter or two to their opuses that they'd surely prefer to see languish at the bottom of her inkwell . . .

Oh, to wipe the smiles off their faces! But for that, *When We Were Twenty*, and the fierce diatribe it contained, would have to be published.

But by whom? What publisher would ever consent . . . ?

Let one single figure from the literary world unmask her, and . . . The Bitch of Drancy has written a novel, a big fat novel! Her sad, cursed youth dragged out into the harsh light of day! Imagine the reaction!

The news would race through the capital like a wildfire. Particularly because the people at Territorial Security were probably still keeping watch on her, if only with one eye.

Should they learn that Mademoiselle Feuhant was planning to renege on her promise to fade into the woodwork, the authorities might be a little annoyed. Steps would be taken to "deal with her," for the sake of the public order. There are ways. For instance, pressure might be placed discreetly on any publisher insane enough to put out a novel by the Bitch of Drancy. And not just any novel, but a roman à clef! About the worst thing she could do. So: pressure on the editor, threats of prosecution, administrative reprisals, etc.

So perhaps she needed some sort of stand-in?

She'd thought of that, but such angels don't exactly grow on trees. Besides, who would ever want to team up with someone so notorious? So compromising? No, that would be strolling into a minefield. The lady has too many enemies.

She tried Gastinel, but no luck. Though on reflection, the former puppeteer wasn't really right for the job anyway. He wasn't a writer, wasn't much of anything, couldn't put together a single sentence that would stand up to scrutiny . . .

424

She needed someone who wrote. Even not very well. An author. That way . . .

Jean-Rémi Dochin was the answer to her prayers. A godsend. And so malleable, so lacking in will . . . Down on his luck, too, which certainly didn't hurt.

He was even writing a book. A book that, once finished, would serve as a vitally important prop in her little charade. But asking him outright to sign his name to someone else's work . . . Presumptuous, to say the least. Hard to believe he wouldn't start asking questions: "But why not just publish the book yourself?" This wasn't the mid-seventeenth century, when Mademoiselle de Scudéry graciously let her brother Georges take credit for the thick novels she'd written. And she couldn't very well tell him who she was—"You see, the thing is, dear friend, you have before you the Bitch of Drancy. Ring any bells?"—when one of Dochin's uncles had died at Mauthausen under torture by thugs of Lévêque's ilk.

No, she'd have to find some other way. Dochin would think he was publishing a book of his own, when in fact it would be someone else's. That was the little trick she'd come up with. Dochin would submit his novel to a publisher, but, unbeknownst to Dochin, that publisher—himself unaware of the novel's true author—would put out a very different book, one by Céline Feuhant. Simple and complicated at the same time. At some point Dochin would find out, but by then it would be too late. The hard part would be finessing the interval between the day he sent off his manuscript and about a month after it went on sale, when all the critics had spoken and eager buyers were crowding the shops. If the book was a hit—and she was assuming it would be, of course—would Dochin, having been sidelined, immobilized, "put to sleep," gagged just before its release and the appearance of the reviews, ever dare, then, on awakening, with the deed already done—and with money, torrents of money, manna from heaven, now pouring in—would he ever dare publicly deny he'd written the thing? Particularly if a secondary means of coercion, far more formidable, could then be used against him?

Hand him a nice, fat fait accompli. A forced stand-in, in short. And without him ever suspecting a thing!

What could Céline possibly care that her name wouldn't show up on the cover? All she really wanted was to see her writing acknowledged, to know she wasn't a complete failure, to be able to tell herself she would have become another Colette or Duras if it weren't for that bastard war. As for the riotous praise her book would undoubtedly reap . . . Dochin or no Dochin, it would go straight to her heart!

And there were the revelations to think of, as well.

Two birds with one stone. On the one hand, find some sort of acclaim as a writer; on the other, blast certain bastards and wise-asses who'd disappeared into the crowd in 1945, slapping a mask on their faces and discreetly tossing their Francisques into the garbage.

She'd turned seventy years old by the time she made up her mind to throw her own personal wrench into the works, to reach into the dark closets of her memory and pull out the spiderweb so patiently woven over so many years: her novel, her life's work. At that age, by God, one doesn't have much left to lose. *Après moi le deluge!*

60   A Tactical Question

But those disclosures raised a tricky tactical question. Should she throw her revelations out all at once, publish one single enormous book stuffed with all the finest flowers of her bouquet of hate? In the end she decided this wasn't the best route: it would have delayed the assault far too long, since her book was nowhere near done. But now she had Dochin close at hand. She'd have to take advantage of that windfall, not let her fish get away. And so she decided to publish Part One long before she'd written "The End" on the last page of her manuscript. There would be three volumes. Volume one: no revelations, just a sprinkling of gossip and the promise of far bigger scoops in the sequel. Volume two: raise the pressure, something a touch more menacing taking shape . . . in bits and pieces . . . "Get ready for some really hot stuff! Wait till you see what comes next!" A volume two that some would already find rather unsettling. And then, in the final volume, now being written, the thunderbolt would finally fall, a great gush of secrets, all the masks torn off at last.

61   Max and Mimile

Needless to say, her book had nothing in common with Dochin's, save that they'd both chosen to set their stories in Occupation-era Paris (which can, after all, be said of a number of novels): in the one case a vibrantly true-to-life portrayal, in the other a stumbling, incoherent attempt, and riddled with plagiarisms to boot, Dochin having drawn his inspiration primarily from movies like *Four Bags Full*, *Army of Shadows*, and so on—borrowings from which were scattered liberally throughout his text.

Two utterly disparate works, then. With one exception: Céline had resigned herself to renaming the two kids who popped up now and then in her novel, a certain Fred and Riri. These two lads—the mischievous, wily offspring of a collaborationist schoolteacher named Carpus—played a far smaller role in her book than Max and Mimile did in Dochin's. It was her fear of giving herself away that forced her into this minor appropriation, which no one could possibly call a "theft." Otherwise, while speaking with Dochin about the novel's two children, her tongue might have played a terrible trick on her, and in place of Max and Mimile, out would come Fred and Riri!

Reluctantly, then, she rechristened the two kids.

The laughable cardboard cutouts concocted by Dochin bore not the slightest resemblance to the vital, complex characters of Feuhant's book. Like day and night. Thanks to Lévêque's insistence that she stay by his side wherever he went, she'd had multiple opportunities to rub elbows with her characters' models, in the flesh and up close. Had she not, alongside her gentleman friend, dined with Bucart? With Doriot (a man who had absolutely no notion of good table manners)? With Costantini? Had she not sometimes accompanied Lévêque on hunting trips alongside Déat and Lafont? And had she not spent hours in a nightclub with an Alain Laubreaux of *Je Suis Partout*, with a Luchaire, with an Epfig?

62   Rumblings in the Ministry of Justice

The people she'd struck a deal with in 1950—or their successors—
soon discovered the origin of the book making headlines all over
the literary pages: *Dancing the Brown Java*. There remained only to
clear up the matter of the two stand-ins: Dochin and Gastinel. So
now the Feuhant woman was back on the scene all of a sudden?
And her seventy-six years old!

Something had to be done. Somehow, they had to convince that
bitch to lay off. They did all they could to make her see sense. Hoping to put a stop to volume three after *Rage Beneath the Cagoule* hit
the shops, they went so far as to plant an unambiguously ominous
little bulletin in all the papers:

> *After a number of complaints from the children of the Vichy
> regime's victims, sources within the Ministry of Justice report
> that new inquiries are planned concerning the wartime ac-
> tivities of Céline Feuhant, also known as the Bitch of Drancy,
> one-time lover of Joseph Lévêque. Although her case was
> shelved following Lévêque's execution in March 1945, the
> Ministry is now said to be considering charges against Ma-
> dame Feuhant for crimes against humanity. We have been
> unable to obtain official confirmation of this rumor, nor any
> further details.*

They're bluffing, she told herself. They had to be: even after all these years, there were some people who wouldn't be overly eager to see Céline Feuhant placed on the stand before an examining magistrate, especially given that judges had been proving somewhat refractory lately, and even rebellious, with respect to admonitions from on high or elsewhere. No, what she feared was incarceration, so-called protective custody. The isolation ward. The hotel with no checkout desk.

Yes, they'd done their best to intimidate her. She simply snapped her fingers in their scowling faces. For just as so many have waited in vain for the trial of Monsieur X, Y, or Z (sometimes secretly hoping the gentleman in question might kick off or go senile before anything unpleasant happened), it could be said without fear of contradiction that Lévêque's confidante wouldn't be asked to give evidence anytime soon. A potentially embarrassing judicial dossier is a lot like a briska:[5] in the right hands, it can be made to drag on and on and on . . .

---

5   A large Russian sledge. (Author's note.)

63   Poor Jean-Rémi!

Céline, you were finishing your book. Hard at work. At the typewriter. An old habit of yours. You spent hours hunched over that
Underwood, an ancient machine filched by Lévêque from the Gestapo offices on the Rue de la Pompe in mid-August 1944. Sometimes that thing frightened you a little, sometimes it sort of turned
your stomach. The scenes it had witnessed! The brutal, blood-
spattered interrogations it had transcribed! And to think: it was on
that very machine that *Dancing the Brown Java* (or rather *When
We Were Twenty*) was written! Is there some sort of curse on that
old Underwood? In the thirties, apparently, it belonged to the real
estate agent Lesobre, later murdered by Eugène Weidmann, and
then, God knows how, it ended up on the Rue de la Pompe. Is it
forever doomed to rattle and clack wherever death lurks?

Far from the brightest bulb in the pack, Dochin assumed it was
his text you were typing. The poor boy handed you his barely-de-
cipherable pages, and then, the moment his back was turned, you
mailed them off to Colette—your daughter, Lévêque's daughter—or
sometimes delivered them in person when you went to Bordeaux.
And then Colette got down to work, painfully decoding Monsieur
Jean-Rémi's microscopic handwriting, laboring to come up with a
presentable typescript.

Naturally, for safety's sake, certain ground rules had to be followed. You always kept a few pages of our friend's work close at

hand, just in case . . . Sometimes you even suggested he change a word here or there, or reconsider a phrase, just to keep up the illusion that it really was you typing his work. Need it be added that Colette had a machine identical to yours, dug up in some local junk shop?

When Jean-Rémi finally learned the truth—after the book had been launched and the money was filling the coffers—he agreed (he was so docile! and, like most men, so spineless), he agreed, for your sake—and for his too, for the cash, yes indeed!—to go along with the game.

You and Gastinel had poor Dochin by the balls. There was that dead girl, back in Normandy . . .

But even with that hanging over him, Dochin could still have caused problems if he saw the novel when it first appeared. All it would have taken was for him to open to the first page—he might have flipped out, might have run amok, might have screamed bloody murder, might have gone public with the whole thing . . . Whereas after four or five weeks, with the novel already a hit . . . everything coming up roses . . . a fat check from the publisher, and the promise of plenty more to come . . . That's enough to keep anyone quiet, livid or not.

For those few weeks, then, he would have to be immobilized, taken out of the picture, set adrift in an unconscious haze. Child's play. An old trailer blocking the road . . . Larmory watching for Dochin from the top of the cliff, then dropping a stone on his head . . . Oh, nothing too big! Knocked cold, Dochin would stay out for . . . what? not even an hour! But, after treating his very minor head wound, dear old Doctor Crespiaud will, with a few well-chosen injections, keep him quiet in the clinic for a good, long time. A month, say. An artificial coma. No big deal, hardly a major offense.

Poor Jean-Rémi!

Later on, he'd taken to working at the typewriter himself. And what was he typing when that paparazzo came along with his telephoto lens? Your words, Céline. Now he was the secretary. The tables had turned! You gave him a handful of pages you'd already typed or written by hand—because sometimes you wrote that way as well—and the poor boy retyped them, transcribed them . . . All for the delectation of the masses! For the photographers' prying eyes! To show everyone he was still hard at work, still productive, to prove that he hadn't quit writing, that he'd buckled down to the next volume—this whole act performed, of course, with Gastinel's blessing.

But it wasn't just your prose he was typing, Céline. Laugh if you must, but poor Jean-Rémi had gone back to . . . the crime novel! It's true! He'd started another one. Another of those dark-as-shoe-polish affairs (as if the world were really so terrible as all that!), obedient as ever to the fashion of the moment: life in the suburban nightmare. *The Viper of Val Fourré* he was calling it. Incorrigible!

"What do you expect me to write, Céline? My *Java*'s all over now, someone's broken the music box . . . the little song in my head's all full of wrong notes . . ."

Poor boy! Don't worry, Céline, in spite of everything you put him through, nobody's questioning the sincerity of your fondness for old Jean-Rémi. A bit like the son you might have had—a not particularly clever son, kind of a dreamer, shall we say, in need of a mommy to watch over him as long as he lived.

64 Like a Line from Baudelaire . . .

Remember . . .

"Look, instead of arguing with me, why don't you just show me my books?" I said to Céline.

"They're out here in the hallway . . ."

Only later did Dochin understand why Céline seemed to be dragging her feet so. Still reluctant to drop the bombshell, apparently, right up to the end.

It's true, even with the books right there at hand, and with Dochin asking to see them, Céline was still hesitating. Up to the very last second, she acted as if her protégé would never know. As if something, some sort of miracle, were going to prevent the truth from emerging. Whence this charade, even when they were standing right there by the books. Until the very last second . . . let Dochin steep in the illusion that he was the writer all of France was abuzz about.

The TV show posed no real danger. Gastinel kept an eye on Dochin, and Eyebrows held the book in his lap the whole time. And Dochin had just got out of the clinic, still groggy, still lost in a fog . . .

■

As for those proofs he'd corrected . . . Dummies, of course, fabricated by a friend of the motel, Louis Petitprêtre, a printer in Saint-

Étienne, child's play for any typographer, simply a matter of setting Dochin's manuscript.

Needless to say, Gastinel saw to it that the real proofs went to Céline. She corrected them in Bordeaux, at her daughter's, then sent them back to the behemoth, who signed his name on the authorization to print form, forging Dochin's signature at the same time. And then off it went to Le Papyrus. That's the hard part about a scheme of this sort: the little things, the endless niggling details . . .

"So they didn't change a thing, eh? Probably would have been for the best if they'd changed everything," I snorted.

"Oh, we're back to that again. Really, now . . . So all these compliments you've been getting from everyone, those are just farts in the wind? You're not just a little bit moved . . ."

"Look, instead of arguing with me, why don't you just show me my books?"

"They're out here in the hallway . . . I got them yesterday morning. Malgodin sent them right away."

We started down the long hallway, the walls lined with columns of books squeezed in so tight they seemed to meld into some weird amalgam, almost right up to the ceiling.

"Here they are."

There was something gloomy and dejected in her voice, like we were standing not by a bookshelf but by a tomb where these "They" were resting . . . like this hallway was some sort of graveyard—and it's true, there were a lot of dead people there . . . I picked up one of my books, opened it, and once again discovered my pointless prose, my thick-headed wordplay, my dialogue straight out of a dimestore novel or a TV series . . . I paged through the volume, the book in my hands making it clear as day: this was the best I could hope for, I'd never do better, never rise above this ocean of blather, this mountain of commonplaces . . .

I put my old crime novel back on the shelf. What the hell was it doing there with those *Brown Java*s? My hands were shaking. And then, all of a sudden, I understood why everyone was so wild about *Dancing the Brown Java*. Because it was a great book, obviously, a real novel, loaded with talent, a rare specimen. Because the book published by Malgodin wasn't mine at all! Not mine, of course— what a joke that would be! So the critics weren't out of their minds after all. I finally got it, mug that I was. And I realized I had only to make one little move, just one little move, to get the truth right in the kisser. But did I dare make that move?

"Well, what's the matter, my fine fellow? Still down on that book of yours? What's wrong with it? All the shopkeepers loved it. The baker was telling me just the day before yesterday, she . . ."

Her mocking smile infuriated me. I almost lost it. I wondered if she was talking about *Dancing the Brown Java* or *Mayhem in Les Minguettes* by Jean Rem, my crime novel. Surely she hadn't hunted down a bunch of copies of *Mayhem* to give out to the shopkeepers, for Christ's sake! What was she talking about? *Brown Java*, then? What was all this supposed to mean?

"What have you got to complain about? Listen . . . There's one thing I have to tell you, though, Jean-Rémi . . ."

Make a move . . . Just one move . . . And then I'll bet everything would be clear.

"What the fuck is my crime novel doing with those *Brown Java*s?"

"I believe you understand at last, my boy."

"Bitch!"

"Shut up . . ."

"What the fuck is that goddamned book doing there?"

"Odette brought it back from the market. Along with a bunch of other trash. Would you look at all the books on these shelves! I swear, they're going to fall on our heads one of these days. Anyway, your book's been sitting there for weeks. I put the *Java*s right next to it, but I swear, it wasn't on purpose."

"Did you read it?"

"I couldn't get past the second page. I'm sorry. You know, I don't care that much for crime novels . . ."

I shrugged and took another of my books down from the shelf. This was the move! The move that would deliver me, give me the truth right in the kisser. Pow! It was a different book I now held in my hands. Still mine, though, since it was *Dancing the Brown Java*.

I opened it.

From the first lines, I realized it was the work of a writer. A real writer, the kind you don't meet every day. Sometimes you can just tell, like when you open the *Journey* or read a line from Baudelaire.

Beside me, poor Céline was looking all shrunken and wizened, just an ordinary little old lady. Deep down, I think, she was ashamed at what she'd done to me. That whole act . . . I almost pitied her.

"I was so scared you were going find out," she murmured.

Watching for my reaction to every word, she revealed her true identity. So that tony bookstore on the Quai des Grands-Augustins was all make-believe. She'd only been a script girl, for four years, from '36 to June 1940, one day in the paws of Duvivier, the next week in Christian-Jacque's. Then came Vichy. The vert-de-gris clad soldiers. The waltz of the Francisques. The brown java. The bastards' ball.

She swore she'd never done anything horrible herself. But she'd fallen in love with a sort of shady character, a traitor, she tagged along almost everywhere he went, even into the jail cells, into little dark corners where love really has no place. More or less arm in arm, and that was one hell of an albatross around her neck.

"You couldn't have known . . . You weren't even in your father's balls yet when the Liberation came . . . If I'd told you, you never would have agreed to stand in for me."

"That's for sure. I would have thought of my poor uncle, dying at the hands of scum like your pal Lévêque."

"But Jean-Rémi, wouldn't it have been a terrible crime just to leave *Brown Java* in the drawer? You saw what the critics thought of it! What does politics have to do with all that? Literature is a great lady, all-powerful, and no narrow-minded twat has any business trying to tell her where she gets off! Isn't a half-century long enough? Am I supposed to hide myself away in this backwater forever?"

Her voice was shaking, she was bleating like a lamb, almost spitting as she spoke. Her eyes were shining. I thought her makeup was going to melt and flow down over her dress, that makeup she'd started plastering on in the fifties for fear of being recognized, because the newspapers had spread her photograph far and wide when Lévêque faced the firing squad.

Back on the shelf went *Dancing the Brown Java* by Céline Feuhant, signed Dochin-Gastinel.

"The revelations, the denunciations, I've got them all written down in black and white. They're as good as published already. I've got three hundred pages waiting up in my armoire."

"Why did your Lévêque tell you all this?"

"I never asked him a thing! And then he had to go trumpeting left and right how I knew all about everything! Almost right up to the firing squad, he kept blabbing that. As if I were his own little book of memories. As if I loved him for his politics! And all the shit that came with it!"

"So there are people you're hoping to piss off . . . But look, you got off scot-free yourself, didn't you?"

"Sure, as long as I agreed to become one of the living dead. Not exactly a nice comfy life with all sorts of honors and rewards . . ."

"And what's Gastinel's part in all this?"

"He's a jerk-off, a loser. But a clever one, and a skillful one. Believe me, surplus flab or no, he's got a head on his shoulders. I used him. He knew it. He even seemed to like the idea. And in the end—anything can happen!—he turned out to be useful."

"So you knew about . . . the girl?"

"I never wanted that kind of monstrosity involved, I think that goes without saying."

"How did you meet that tub of lard?"

She told me about the Pétainists and their little jaunt to the Ile d'Yeu. She'd assumed Gastinel was part of that crowd, so she wasn't shy about saying who she was.

"When I heard he was starting a publishing house with his uncle Pernochot's shekels, I started to find him very interesting."

"You slept with him?"

"A little, now and then . . . There was no other way. Don't ask me to describe it."

"Walking turds really turn you on, don't they? What, do you dredge them up with a scoop or something?"

"But the blimp wasn't really the ideal stand-in. What I really needed was another novelist . . . Someone who hadn't made a name for himself, a young person I could . . . manipulate."

"Me."

"You caught my eye right from the start. I let you write your book. I urged you on and everything . . . I didn't hold back, did I? I needed a manuscript. An author with a manuscript, to approach a publisher in the usual way, leading to a contract made out to Dochin."

"And where does Gastinel come in? What, was he off fishing or something?"

"Well, I'd asked him to find me a pigeon. Good luck locating a rare bird like that around Térignac! A little author of no renown, someone we could rope in. He was a publisher, after all . . . That was a pretty pathetic little joint he ran, but still, he had loads of people bringing him manuscripts . . . He said fine. Thought it would be fun. But he never dreamed I might be a real writer. That made him laugh. He was sure I'd fall flat on my face, no one would publish my book. He never did manage to find me my pigeon. But when I saw you here in front of me, well, I called and asked what he thought."

"And somehow you got me to send him my manuscript . . ."

"Remember that book I threw down on the table? That book he put out? I was hoping it might catch your eye. And so it did."

"Suppose I'd picked somebody else?"

"No big deal. I would have found some other way to make sure you went with the big lug."

"And Gastinel got your manuscript?"

"You brought him yours . . . A half-hour later the mailman gave him mine. He knew it was coming."

"And he read it?"

"Of course. Poor dim Jean-Rémi . . . I told you, we were in cahoots! We had you by the short and curlies. Gastinel gave your book a quick once-over, just out of curiosity . . . Maybe two minutes he spent with it . . ."

■

"*Dancing the Brown Java*. Well, what do you think of that?" He cracked open Dochin's manuscript. "Should I read it?" he asked himself. "Give it a quick look, or not?"

He leafed through it with no great enthusiasm, a dubitative pout on his lips, and came across a page that was all dirty and stained, most likely with coffee. He pulled the fouled sheet out of the manuscript. Set it on one corner of his desk. The doorbell rang. He closed the thick red folder. The front door opened. The mailman came in with the package he'd been expecting. Céline's manuscript.

∎

"But the moment he got his friend Céline's novel, he sat right down to read it."

∎

It was lunchtime. Closing up his shop so as not to be disturbed, he dove into the manuscript that had ended up in his hands late that morning.

The interjections started to fly around page thirty-five, Gastinel's avid eyes never leaving the page:

"Holy cow! Suppurating catfish!"

In his exaltation, he even forgot to go to dinner. He paused in his reading around 9:00, ecstatic, joyous. He sat breathless, his face clammy. Then he looked around for something to mark where he'd stopped. His hand landed on Dochin's coffee-stained page. He slipped it into Céline's manuscript, like a bookmark, and closed up the folder. Back in his humble abode, he reopened the manuscript. A scowl briefly ruffled his features on encountering page 192, covered with brown stains. He gave the filthy thing a quick glance and set it aside. What, did that asshole put his leaky coffee pot down on it or something? He went on reading old lady Feuhant's massive tome, turning the pages one by one with eagerness and curiosity. Still as good as ever. What class!

"Oh! that phenomenon! Oh! that dirty rare bird! Oh! pus-flower! I'm flying! I'm going to scream! With joy! I'm losing it! Such talent, where's it been sleeping all this time?"

■

"In the beginning, Gastinel had his doubts about me. Not for long, though! Just till he got hold of the manuscript. That thing knocked him out . . . the first time he read it, at least. But then—he never tried to hide this—he started to wonder. He wasn't sure if he liked it or not, so he sent it along to Malgodin. Pretty soon he heard back: Malgodin was head over heels, wanted to publish the thing himself, wouldn't take no for an answer . . . And at that point he knew . . . We'd pulled it off."

"And what about my manuscript? What did that fat hog end up doing with it?"

"I picked it up from him, of course. I've got it right here."

We went into her room. I stared at Lévêque's portrait with new eyes. I looked out the window too, and suddenly, for the first time since I'd come to La Halte, the garden outside seemed like a sinister place. Everything had gone gray. From now on, I was living in a black and white world. Or worse: sepia. Like dried blood, blood from long ago.

"Here's your manuscript right here. Nothing's happened to it."

She took it out of the armoire. That fat, bulging folder looked like some dead thing to me. Something hacked off a corpse. Blankly, like I'd just got hit on the head—it was getting to be a habit with me—I paged through it a little, without speaking a word. Four and half years I'd spent writing that book. Four and a half years, and nothing to show for it.

"What, you're not planning to reread it, are you?"

"Why do you talk to me like that? Twisting the knife, is that it?"

"Forget that book, Jean-Rémi."

"Easy for you to say! When I remember how you kept nagging me to work on it! To write! To finish it! All those compliments you kept pouring over my head! Insanity!"

"Well, I was in a hurry, Jean-Rémi. I was eager to send you off to a publisher. Don't tell me you would have gone with an unfinished book under your arm. What are you looking for?"

"A page. Page 192. It's disappeared."

"It must have fallen out somewhere . . ."

She looked on the floor.

"It was all stained . . . I remember. I spilled something on it at the café. Just before I went off to the horse-butcher's to meet my fate."

"So? Gastin' must have seen your dirty page and thrown it away. What do you want with it anyway?"

"Never mind," I snapped, closing the manuscript. "Enough of that."

She took the stack from my hands and put it back in the armoire—almost threw it in, like a bunch of old shoes—next to a pile of sheets.

"You're not going to get all upset about one missing page, are you? You'll just have to write up another one, that's all."

"What—are you pulling my leg again? Leg of lamb's sort of gone out of style now, hasn't it? These days everyone wants a leg off poor little Dochin! It's all the rage!"

"You're upset, Jean-Rémi. Oh, I can imagine! But I hope you're not thinking some publisher's going to take on your own *Java*!"

"You're sure it's not worth anything?"

"Don't you see, the real novel isn't what you wrote, it's all the stuff that was going on around you while you were writing."

"No, but seriously, you're sure it's not . . . ?"

"If you could have heard Colette when she was typing it up! . . . It's worthless, my poor boy. Buck up, though, my dear. It's no crime to write like a pig."

"I get it coming and going in this joint. Six months ago I was Céline. Now I'm not even Georges Ohnet!"

"Oh, my little lamb is making a joke. He must be on the mend."

"In spite of the paving stone I got on my head? Bunch of bastards, you could have killed me!"

"Don't worry, Larmory took great pains to avoid anything unpleasant like that. A most cautious man, Larmory. 'Moderation in all things,' that's his motto!"

"Oh, right! This is all a big joke to you, isn't it? And suppose I decided to talk, Céline?"

65 A Petty Little Crime

"Hmm? Suppose I talked? Suppose I spilled a big, fat, juicy load of beans?"

"Don't be silly, Jean-Rémi. You know perfectly well you're not going to do that."

"You'd tell them everything you know about the girl?"

"Gastinel's still got the video . . . That fat guy's a tough customer, you know. And there's no proof he was holding the camera. You're the one with the poor girl in his arms, Jean-Rémi, staring straight into the lens."

"So you and the turd planned that thing out too, I suppose?"

"No, not exactly. Believe me, not like that. But we had to have something on you, you understand, just in case we screwed up somehow and you stumbled onto the truth . . ."

"Blackmail."

"In a way, yes. I'd asked Gastinel to get you mixed up in a petty little crime of some sort . . . something compromising . . . just to make sure you'd keep quiet . . ."

"A petty little crime that just happened to be murder."

"No, Jean-Rémi! I never wanted that! I was thinking of some minor offense . . . an ordinary little drug deal, that sort of thing . . . Gastinel could have set it up in a second . . . Some little crime like dealers commit every day . . . Just enough to keep you quiet, should you ever feel tempted to rat us out. But that imbecile had to go and cook up a murder, without breathing one word of it to me! I prom-ise you, it would never have happened if he had. Talk about showing initiative! I swear, that guy . . ."

"The shitwad could very well have done without me."

"How do you mean?"

"Well, when he realized your novel was going hit it big . . . He could have just put his own name on it, and left me out of it. That would have brought in more cash, wouldn't it?"

"Out of the question. Oh, it's true, the thought did cross his mind."

"At least that poor girl wouldn't have had to be killed."

"No, Jean-Rémi. For one thing, you could have raised a big ruckus and got us in trouble. But that's not the real reason . . . Like I told Gastinel, I wanted you in on the deal, no matter what. For the royalties, you understand. The cash. So you'd get your share. Sort of repay you for all the trouble I'd put you through, if you like."

"Gee, thanks."

"So you see, there was no way Gastinel could go it alone. He was just there to put my plan into action."

"Where's that tape?"

"I don't have the slightest idea. At his place, I suppose. But what does it matter now? At long last, someone's acknowledged my gifts as a writer. Almost sixty years I've been waiting for that! Mean-while, the money—all the money that book's bringing in and will go on bringing in—it's all yours, every last centime. What have you got to complain about? I'm not pocketing one half sou of your roy-alties. Don't tell me I'm only in this for myself!"

"And that fat hog will be raking it in too, right? Fifty percent! Just for sitting there twiddling his thumbs!"

"There was no other way, Jean-Rémi. You shouldn't have let yourself get mixed up in that idiotic murder. You fool, you just jumped right on board! And, I repeat, that was never part of the plan! But what was I supposed to do? And oh, that guy, what a blessed pain in the ass! Always underfoot! Nagging me all the time, wanting to know how it was coming along . . . What was up with volume two . . . Abetz miraculously escaping assassination . . . Coëdel's claims on the murder of the Rosselli brothers . . . he even blabbed about it on TV, the cretin! As if all that were going to show up in your book. Oh, I swear, what a crew!"

66 The Other Side of the Picture

"I don't care about all that, Céline. I don't give a good goddamn about the money! But you see . . . well, in the end . . . it's stupid, but . . . in the end I'd sort of started to believe in my book in spite of myself . . . just a little, but . . ."

"Dear piglet! And I worked so hard to fill your head with the idea you knew how to write! Oh, what you put me through! After a while I started running out of ideas. By the end I was losing patience. I wasn't going to compare you to Victor Hugo or Shakespeare! Sometimes I had to pinch myself to keep from bursting out laughing."

"When those critics started piling on the praise . . . that incredible ovation . . . almost unanimous . . . I couldn't believe it, I couldn't understand . . . But I never once suspected it wasn't my book they were talking about. On the other hand, there was Langillier's reaction . . ."

"Yes, let's talk about this Langillier of yours. I figured it all out when he called you about the missing page. Intuition, you know. I realized you'd given your book to a journalist when you were in Paris, and didn't want me finding out."

∎

Two days later I got a phone call. It was a little awkward, because Céline was right there in the front office talking with Félibut.

I jumped when I heard Langillier's voice.

"Is that you, Dochin?"

"Yes, I . . . I'm here . . ."

I'd almost added "Monsieur Langillier," but caught myself just in time. Céline was still searching my face.

I stood speechless. No sooner had he told me he was sending the missing page than he hung up the phone. Sort of like somebody running for dear life.

"What was it?" asked Céline.

"Nothing . . . Someone at my parents' house . . ."

We were crossing through the orchard . . .

"What was the missing page? Which one?"

"Oh, nothing . . . Page 111 . . . I noticed it the day before yesterday."

Céline furrowed her brow ever so slightly. She veered back toward the one-time post house.

"Wait a minute! . . . Go to your room and look at the manuscript. I'll be right there."

■

"About Langillier and all that: what do you mean, you figured it out?"

"Your page 111, I mean . . . There I screwed up. I could see it all. You went on through the orchard; meanwhile, I ran up to my room and opened my manuscript. And there, between my page 99 and my page 101 . . . I found your page 111. I'd stuck it in there for some reason after it was typed, I must have been in a hurry, thinking about something else . . . I can't even remember who typed it, me or Colette . . . Anyway, it ended up in my manuscript. Understandable, with all this paper flying around every which way. Meantime, my page 100 must have got stuffed into *your* manuscript somehow. I knew you never really looked over the typescript, just a bit here or there, so I figured you hadn't actually seen it. Lucky for me, huh? Because if you had, you obviously would have seen it wasn't yours, and the whole thing would have come unraveled. Whereas Langillier . . . he must have read that page 111—my page 111! And then he must have known."

"Known what?"

"That it was my work, of course! Langillier read some of my short stories back in 1950, when he was directing a literary journal. He must have recognized my style, nothing far-fetched about that, even after all these years. He was absolutely wild about those stories, said they were brilliant, congratulated me on my exceptional talent. I can still hear his words: 'It's love at first sight! I've fallen in love with your writing!' And he had absolutely no reason to flatter me. Forgive my lack of modesty, Jean-Rémi, but Céline's style doesn't exactly grow on trees. You can't forget it that easily. I'm talking about Céline Feuhant, of course. Although the same goes for the other Céline."

"All right, so suppose he recognized your style . . . So what? I'm sorry, I'm having a hard time following all this."

"Well, he must have wondered what the hell was going on. Here's a man who looks over your manuscript—a text that we might call . . . very average, just to keep you happy—and who then, a little while later, discovers a page that supposedly comes from the same manuscript, only it's filled with a different sort of writing, a bit more distinguished, shall we say. In short, imagine somebody reading a novel by Georges Ohnet and then suddenly coming across a page by . . . well, let's say Céline, since he's there waiting. You follow me? He'd be a bit surprised, to say the least, don't you think?"

"So Langillier's little discovery was kind of inconvenient for you, wasn't it?"

"What do you mean?"

"Well . . . we can assume he isn't going to be digging into that mystery any further, now that he's got himself run over by a speeding van."

"Yes, and? I don't see the connection. Surely you're not thinking . . ."

"What's the matter, Céline? Did I say something wrong?"

"It was an accident . . . fate . . . Just a stroke of bad luck, that's all. I don't see what you . . . Lots of people get killed by bad drivers every year."

■

Having sat by her great-uncle's bedside at Cochin Hospital in his final moments, and having remembered what Titi, the young maid, had told her about the missing page—the page from the manuscript of *Brown Java*—as Langillier was racing across the street toward the bookstore, Tracy Le Cardonnel had finally grasped the connection between those two pronouncements—the Ethiopian maid's and the dying reporter's—and hence now understood the history of that lost page:

With Langillier away, Titi is doing the housework in the apartment, as usual. Seeing Dochin's manuscript on the desk, she opens it and reads a few passages, no doubt less out of curiosity than because she's been going to night school in hopes of improving her French. She's beginning to pick it up quite nicely, in fact. Often she practices by reading a newspaper. *Info-Matin*, *La Croix*, or *Le Figaro*.

Sometimes *Le Nouvel Économiste*. This time it'll be a manuscript for a novel. So she leafs through it at random, reads a half-page here and there. Well, what do you know, there's no page 111 after page 110. Page 100 instead. Page 100 between page 110 and page 112? Got to be a mistake. So Titi takes out that page 100 to put it back where it belongs, which is to say between 99 and 101, but, to her surprise, there's already a page 100 at that spot. A page 100 that is thus precisely where it's supposed to be. So what does Titi do with the page 100 she has in her hands? She sets it aside on the boss's desk.

Two or three days later, Titi is once again at work in the study, vigorously shaking her feather-duster . . . Papers go flying . . . The extraneous page 100 flutters to the carpet . . . Titi picks it up and stuffs it beneath a pile of papers on Langillier's desk.

"Mustn't forget tell Monsieu La Gilié bout that page . . ."

But soon her mind turns to other things—perhaps her boyfriend: at that age fun always comes first. She doesn't even think about the little note she'd begun three days before, alerting Langillier to the superfluous page. The unfinished note is still sitting just where she left it, under a paperweight.

Having abruptly abandoned his reading of Dochin's manuscript well before page 112, Langillier never noticed that one page wasn't where it belonged. Nor did he notice it as he was leafing randomly through the work later on, not really paying attention . . .

And so the reporter returned the text to Dochin without that anomalous page 100, the maid having removed it. And, of course, without page 111.

Two days later, searching for something among the papers on his desk, Langillier comes across the lost page. He reads it. Finding it involves a Max and a Mimile, he understands—besides, he'd already recognized the look of the type, the layout of the text—that it comes from Dochin's manuscript. But the writing seems so very different . . . It reminds him of something . . . why, that's Céline Feuhant's style! Yes, it was all long ago, but how to forget? Dazed, unbelieving, he shakes his head and rereads the page. The most utter bewilderment—stupefaction, even—descends over him. No doubt about it, that's the very distinctive style of the girl who submitted some stories when he was directing *L'Artiste*. Céline Feuhant. He remembers. Disconcerted, he struggles to understand. Nonetheless, aware of Céline Feuhant's Occupation-era activities, he decides to avoid getting involved; he thinks it best simply to call Dochin and send back the page.

■

"I don't know how that page could have slipped out of the manuscript," Céline told me. "But in any case, Langillier sent it back to you. That business was nagging at me something fierce. So I went on the alert. I just had to wait for the mailman. When I saw you'd got a letter with the return address of a well-known journalist . . . Urbain Langillier . . . I understood the whole thing, and realized there wasn't a second to waste. It was an old-fashioned envelope, thank goodness, so it wasn't hard to steam open. Took no time at all. I pulled out my page 100 and put it back in my manuscript. As for your page, page 111, I slipped it into the envelope and resealed it. And Camille brought you the letter. You tore open the envelope and recovered your page 111 . . . which had never left the house. But from that day on I sometimes wondered what might have gone through Langillier's mind when he read it . . . if he hadn't suspected something was up. I thought of him when volume one of *Brown Java* came out, told myself he was probably going to buy it, read it . . . and see it all. That was worrying."

"So admit it, his accident must have come as a great relief . . . very convenient for you . . ."

"That's true. But believe me, I'm not kidding when I say it hit me hard all the same. I thought back to 1950, that charming young man in the offices of *L'Artiste* on the Rue de Seine, the cordial welcome he gave me . . . What went through his mind when he read that page? Assuming he did. After all, I have no way of knowing . . . But he must have at least given it a glance, since he figured out that it came from your manuscript. It had the names Max and Mimile on it. My Max and Mimile, of course."

"Just like my own page 111 . . ."

"My poor Jean-Rémi . . . How strange life can be . . ."

"Langillier didn't like my book at all. If you'd only heard the demoralizing things he said about it!"

"So he didn't like *Brown Java* . . . And he ended up paying for it, didn't he?"

"Exactly. Which makes me think of those dark predictions you made way back when. . . 'I pity anyone who doesn't like *Dancing the Brown Java!*' And all that."

"What of it?"

"Well, I'm thinking of those few critics who didn't like it . . ."

"They had every right."

"You understand what I'm trying to say, Céline? This is serious business I'm talking about!"

■

To my eye all those weird little pictures seemed about as eloquent as hieroglyphs, but just then I spotted one that sent a shiver racing straight down my spine. Upside down, to be sure—its top toward me—but all the same: a human skeleton holding a scythe. Céline noticed the troubled look on my face:

"Don't worry. Death's not in the cards. At least . . . not for you."

∎

Her lips pulled back into a smile, and she stifled a burst of laughter.

"Just like I told you, the tarot never lies."

I felt a chill run down my spine. She shot me a glance that felt like a sharp stone aimed straight at my head, and I concluded she didn't feel like talking about this. But I wouldn't let it drop:

"You really put one over on me."

"Oh, you think so?" she asked sarcastically.

"I mean about the tarot. All that glorious success you were promising me!"

"Just part of the act."

"But . . . forgive me for dwelling on this: people who didn't like it . . ."

"Well, yes, I pitied them. I just wanted you to believe your book was worth something. I wanted you to think it was wonderful. It's all very simple. What more are you looking for? What's so hard to understand?"

"But . . . the tarot cards . . . 'Death's not in the cards. At least . . . not for you.' That wasn't just play-acting, was it?"

She cracked an enigmatic little smile. "You know, the tarot . . . You've got to take it all with a grain of salt. Maybe I was thinking of that dead girl?"

Then I pounced:

"What the hell are you talking about? That was before I went to Gastinel's! I didn't even know him then! We hadn't killed her yet!"

But she kept her cool. "Oh, that's true, you're right. Sometimes I get mixed up. So many dead people . . . Excuse me. I don't know why I said that. But you know, in the tarot, Death . . . Often it doesn't mean anything, or else it's just some sort of metamorphosis, a transformation . . . It's as simple as can be. It all depends on the card's position. Maybe I was thinking . . . about everyone who might be shaken up by the book's revelations . . . If by chance one or two of them were so distraught that they ended up putting a bullet in their brains, that wouldn't be such a bad thing, would it? I would have got some kind of result."

"It's very strange, all the same . . . Cuzenat, La Briançais . . . Was that just an accident, too? Or fate? Like with Langillier?"

"Listen, you're starting to bore me. Let those critics rest in peace, Jean-Rémi. Don't lose your head, my boy. Keep calm."

"Let's just hope no one else decides to turn up his nose when volume two hits the shelves, that's all I can say."

(. . . *end of flashback.*)

67   Tracy's Investigations

"He hung up on me," said Tracy.

She was in the offices of Le Guetteur, the private detective agency on the Rue Delambre, where she worked as an intern. Her boss, ex-commissioner Chignard of Internal Intelligence, answered with a grunt from behind his paper-strewn desk, his nose buried in a file.

"You're wasting your time, my dear Tracy," he said. "Suppose you stop worrying yourself about those two guys . . . I'm going to have to put you on a serious case, that'll give you something useful to do."

For months she'd been after Dochin and Gastinel, ever since the release of *Brown Java* volume one. Her uncle's dying words were still ringing in her ears, and she felt duty-bound to do something, in hopes of untangling this whole troubling affair.

"Look, suppose you do figure it out—where will that get you?" asked Chignard. "If you start sticking your nose into every little literary intrigue that comes along, you'll never find your way out! I've even heard people claim Shakespeare and Molière didn't really write the things their names are on."

She'd had more than her fill of tailing middle-aged ladies who were two-timing their men—Paris is full of them!—or vice versa; of trying to unravel small-time drug-dealing rings; of struggling to figure out where burglars fenced their booty; of delving into the private lives of unemployed executives applying for jobs at big corporations. She was sick of it! Not exactly the Philip Marlowe lifestyle she'd been promised.

The Dochin-Gastinel affair, though—well, that was more like it. She'd read the novel that bore their names. First-rate stuff. A top-of-the-line book. Written by Céline Feuhant, the so-called Bitch of Drancy, that much was obvious. That old scofflaw had the sword of Damocles hanging . . . from the end of her pen! Any child could see the book was her work. For Pete's sake! Dochin had been living with her for close to five years now! Almost certainly her lover in spite of the great age difference, he'd lent his name to her novel, it was as clear as watered-down Chablis! No, the really mysterious thing (and was this not what had so intrigued her uncle Langillier?) was the presence of Charles Gastinel in their weird little partnership. What exactly was the role of the ex-puppeteer in this affair? That she just couldn't figure.

In the end, not knowing where to start with this exceptionally tortuous case—and having finally concluded that her uncle's death was simply a matter of bad luck—she'd come very close to giving up on the whole thing. But she roared back into action on making the acquaintance of Sven Pélissard, that young critic whose wont it was to massacre—in a sudden burst of breathtaking savagery at the very end of his article, after sixty sugary lines of kudos and happy little pats on the back—the book and the author he'd deigned (but at what a terrible price!) to review.

Newcomer that he was, Pélissard had nonetheless already demolished a good dozen novelists deemed promising by some—novelists who, mortally injured, now rang in vain at their publishers' doors with their latest manuscript under their arms. For these publishers knew all too well that the killer was still watching, lying in wait for his prey, determined to finish them off with one final slash. Henceforth, the only door still open to these writers led not into the offices of a Furne or a Gallim's or a Lacroix and Verboeck-hoven, but into the cemetery . . . the suicide section, to be precise; which is, for a rejected and unpublished author, more or less what the file cabinet is for a manuscript nobody wants.

But as fate would have it, this impetuous young critic bore a strik-ing resemblance to René Lefèvre in the role of Monsieur Lange—exactly Tracy Le Cardonnel's sort of man—and so she fell, wholly consenting, into his arms.

The young couple had met at the Maison de la Radio, in the Charles-Trenet studio. Tracy was in the audience for a taping of the literary talk show *Le Masque et la Plume*. Pélissard, who had recently heaped praises on *Brown Java* in *Le Panorama des Lettres, des Sciences, et des Techniques*, confirmed his enthusiasm that eve-ning, something he'd never done before. From her seat, Tracy inter-rupted to raise certain objections with respect to the promised dis-closures concerning the underside of the Vichy regime. A promise unkept, she asserted, for to her mind the novel offered nothing more than idle chatter such as had long been making the rounds, startling only to a few benighted naïfs, at best. There ensued a lively discussion between Tracy and the Critic Sadistic, gradually evolv-ing into a heated debate. The show's host soon put an end to this sharp little exchange—they had other books to dissect, and time was running out—but not before Pélissard had amiably invited his spectator to pursue their quarrelsome conversation after the show, over a drink.

And then, in Le Glamour, a karaoke bar on the Rue du Ranelagh, love abruptly blossomed, the ice cubes melting unnoticed at the bottom of their glasses. Sven and Tracy had fallen for each other, head over heels. The whiskey had not yet entered their entrails, and already they were kissing up a passionate storm, Pélissard's hand as busy as when wielding his pen to write up a column, Tracy's tongue wriggling like an eel, feverishly exploring the far reaches of the Critic Sadistic's throat, as if hoping to dredge up the truth of the *Brown Java* affair.

Over the following few weeks, Pélissard sent three more promising young novelists to the literary potter's field, but then he committed the grave imprudence of blasting the latest novel of a literary luminary. A deplorable gaffe, grievously lacking in tact, a misstep that led to his eviction from *Le Panorama des Lettres, des Sciences, et des Techniques*. Unfortunately for our impetuous young friend, whose sole crime was to like only very good books, the mandarin so cruelly skewered in his column had not long before taken the helm of the editorial board at Marpon, whose director, alas—alas for Sven, but also for literature in general—had, during a dinner out, promised to publish *The Petunia Garden*, the first novel of Oleta Vilmassan, wife of the owner of the journal that Pélissard wrote for. You can guess what happened next. Oleta, an unparalleled harridan—and principal stockholder of the journal—had moved heaven and earth to get "that little cunt Pélissard" fired right then and there, an act of particular cruelty in this age of high unemployment. Her contract with Marpon hadn't yet been drawn up, and the *éminence grise* of the editorial board could still change his mind. The mandarin was thus handed the head of the Critic Sadistic, who now found himself under fire from two sides, the head of the editorial board at Marpon and his boss's wife. Great fun.

And what does our friend come up with to remedy this sad state of affairs? Well, in hopes of extracting himself from that tar pit, he dreams of getting some great literary scoop: if he played his cards right, a coup of that sort might earn him a new column in another journal. *L'Européen du Jeudi*, for instance, where there'd been a vacancy (let's not even mention the fill-in who really isn't up to the job and will soon be sent packing) since the tragic death of Archibald Ranfolin in the Parc des Buttes-Chaumont.

So, a literary scoop . . .

It was thus in hopes of granting her new lover's wish that Tracy Le Cardonnel once more turned her attention to the mysterious *Brown Java* affair. Céline Feuhant is unquestionably the book's author. What, then, is Dochin's role? And what of this Gastinel, the one-time tripemonger and marionettist? A painstaking investigation was called for, an exhaustive search for evidence: Pélissard wanted an airtight case. Jean-Rémi Dochin's ridiculous manuscript, read by Urbain Langillier, would have to be located, and the reasons for the presence of a page by the real author of *Brown Java* in Dochin's grammaticidal oeuvre discovered. The handwritten first draft of Feuhant's own *Brown Java* would have to be dug up. If that first draft was typewritten, same mission: find that typescript number one, including insertions, erasures, additions, etc. Then gather all available information on the enigmatic Gastinel, shed any possible light on his role in what bears all the hallmarks of a literary con game, lift the veil on the behavior of he who seemed to be pulling the strings in this matter . . . Was Gastinel Feuhant's evil mentor? A high-ranking member of the literary Black International? Had he had some hand in the covert manipulation of the Rushdie affair? The apocryphal Stalin-Franco correspondence (as yet unpublished)? Ceaușescu's private notebooks? Dig deep into the erstwhile tripemonger's murky past; discover what lies behind his mask.

Having many times tried and failed to make an appointment with Dochin (he inevitably hung up in her face), Tracy finally went to her boss, begging him to schedule a burglary at La Halte du Bon Accueil—what's known as an investigative burglary, untinged by financial cupidity, a perfectly routine measure for any good detective agency—in hopes of recuperating the manuscript Dochin had given Langillier. What had become of that manuscript? Was it still on the premises?

Chignard dragged his feet for a while, then reluctantly agreed to help out his young colleague. He dealt mostly in cuckolds, con men . . . not writers . . . although sometimes . . . But anyway. He brought in one of his former agents, Clovis Chabut, now retired. Feigning an advanced case of Parkinson's disease, the old man successfully secured a room at La Halte, but once there, he got precisely nowhere. No way to gain entrance to Dochin's little house, nor to the bedroom of Céline Feuhant, aka Ferdinaud. This man had a forty-year career behind him; he'd ransacked a prodigious number of apartments, rented rooms, suburban houses, châteaux, vacation homes, etc.—always careful to put everything back as it was, really top-class work—but now, clearly (perhaps because he'd just celebrated his eighty-fifth birthday), he'd lost his touch at last.

Finding the motel on the banks of the Vézère an apparently impregnable fortress, Tracy decided to pursue the Gastinel angle instead. Time for another burglary. More precisely, the execution of a sort of unofficial nocturnal search warrant, in hopes of locating some sort of lead among the blimp's personal papers. (Gastinel had been a publisher from 1988 to 1995; perhaps that had some bearing on this strange affair?) Tracy had no fear of dirtying her hands, and she was resolved to push her inquiries as far as they'd go—but only to help out poor Svennie, who was so eager to get back on his critical feet, so anxiously awaiting the conclusive evidence he needed in order to drop his bombshell: the real author of *Brown Java* is Céline Feuhant, the Bitch of Drancy: friend and confidante, from fall 1940 to summer 1944, of Joseph Lévêque, this latter having been a major figure in the French Gestapo, intimately acquainted with the secrets of the collaborationist upper crust (often, admittedly, indistinguishable from the dregs). Before his arrest in September 1944, less than a quarter-mile from the Spanish border—Feuhant was to join him in Spain after things had cooled down—he'd found time to squirrel away his highly damning files on the notables of the pro-German regime and other less well-known figures who gravitated around the politicians of the time. These files were never recovered. Ye gods, what a scoop!

Ideally, Sven's explosive exposé would appear just before the release of volume three, *If These Francisques Could Talk*, scheduled for late fall.

Still hesitant—but he was really very fond of his little Tracy, so . . . —Chignard ordered an illegal search and seizure at the home of Gastinel, Charles, 17 Avenue de Suffren, sixth floor right, seven rooms, two balconies, views over the Champ-de-Mars and the Eiffel Tower.

They waited until Gastinel set off on a cruise around the Balearic Islands with a new girlfriend. In spite of the reinforced hardware and electronic security gizmos, the operation's commander, a certain Leduc, one of Chignard's best men, opened the door with little to-do.

But alas, that nocturnal search turned up nothing of interest: only a clutch of insignificant papers from the pachyderm's defunct publishing house, quickly microfilmed and put back in place. It was only as she and Leduc were preparing to leave the premises that Tracy discovered a videocassette that seemed to have some special value, as its owner kept it not with his other cassettes—by his VCR, his TV, etc.—but under a pile of shirts in a dresser.

She hesitated for a moment, then shrugged and slipped the cassette into her bag, without telling Leduc.

After carefully erasing all trace of their presence, they left the building by the service stairs—nothing terribly original there, just one of the standard little tricks to get out unseen, you can even go over the rooftops, it's all so terribly banal . . .—and separated a little further on, at the corner of the Avenue de Suffren and the Rue Jean-Rey. Leduc rushed off toward the Bir-Hakeim station, with luck he'd just make the night's last métro, but don't worry about him, he can always take a taxi.

Carrying the microfilm and the videocassette in her bag, Tracy headed off through the night toward the parking lot on the Place Joffre, where she'd left her Golf.

Two men from the Special Services Squad (SSS)—all sorts of people had taken an interest in Dochin and Gastinel (and in their friends and acquaintances, of course) ever since *Brown Java* came out—emerged from the shadows and began tailing the young woman on foot, a black Audi following at some distance behind them, its lights dimmed, as if in search of a parking place.

It was now nearly one in the morning, and the lot was deserted. The two men tackled Tracy and put her to sleep in four seconds flat, using the venerable but ever-effective chloroform-soaked cloth—that old chestnut, a standby from Arsène Lupin to Fu Manchu. They left her lying outstretched by her car, having confiscated anything interesting they could find in her bag: to wit, the microfilm and the videocassette.

Playing the tape, the SSS men discovered a wild-eyed Jean-Rémi Dochin gaping into the lens and clasping a bloodied human corpse—a female corpse. On the whitish-gray wall behind him, a network of cracks suggested various surrealistic figures. They now set out to determine where this macabre tableau had been filmed. They inspected all Dochin's regular haunts—La Halte du Bon Accueil, his parents' house in the Mayenne—in hopes of locating that wall. They were aware that Dochin's collaborator Gastinel owned a vacation home in the Orne, a little renovated farmhouse outside Carrouges. They examined the premises in midweek, when the house would be empty, and found just the wall they'd been looking for, the telltale wall, on an outbuilding, just like the one in the video. Same patterns in the stone. So it was here, his back to the wall, that Dochin, the pseudo-coauthor of *Brown Java*, had held that girl's body in his arms. The SSS then searched the farmhouse's grounds (having first assured themselves that Gastinel was out of the country: the blimp was off toasting his flab in Hammamet, accompanied by two or three new flames). They searched under cover of darkness, their task simplified by the house's isolation. Soon, in a shallow grave, they discovered the girl's body, almost entirely decomposed, more or less a skeleton, but still identifiable, of course—by the tattered clothes still wrapping the bones, to begin with, but also (a) by the identity papers found in those clothes, and (b) by the recently devised technique of DNA analysis. And then, in a pocket of her moldering dress, they found Dochin's papers (he'd been issued a new set in June 1995, they'd learned from the regional police). Jean-Rémi Dochin was nailed but good.

They took a sample from the remains for examination by Forensics. They covered the grave, carefully smoothing out the dirt. They headed back to Paris with the two sets of papers.

Tracy Le Cardonnel couldn't understand what had happened to her in the parking lot. She awoke at around five in the morning, shivering. Not a soul in sight, just a little herd of cars. Realizing that the cassette and microfilm had disappeared from her bag, she briefly thought she'd been mugged by Gastinel, not out of the country after all. She climbed into her car and drove home. She later described this strange assault to her boss, who, no doubt sensing the heavy hand of some more or less subterranean unit attached to Intelligence Services, or perhaps even Special Services, immediately advised her to let the matter drop there.

Old man Chignard, who, on retiring from the force, had started up a sedate little private detective agency devoted primarily to the service of humble cuckolds—"I avoid big-time capers like the plague: I live and work with the prudence of the man who each morning repeats to himself that sage old adage, 'To live happily, we must live hidden' "—had no desire to ruffle the feathers of some high-placed police official, or to bother his former colleagues by muscling in on what was clearly their turf. Let them sort it out for themselves, that was his motto.

"Believe me, my dear little Tracy. Don't get involved in these things. Too big for us. That's my intuition, at least."

Special Services was a very complicated outfit, he explained—and, having long labored in the ranks of Internal Intelligence, he knew whereof he spoke. She soon realized that this no doubt reductive label—Special Services—could just as well mean black as white. You could get lost trying to figure it all out. All smoke and mirrors, all cloaks and daggers, all very hush-hush, but wasn't that the most elementary prerequisite for any covert organization? Listening to the ex-cop's explanations, Tracy began to understand. She glimpsed, in the structure and nature of those so-called Special Services, a whole world of ramifications and subdivisions, occult and otherwise, some of them encompassing still other networks, even parallel clans undercutting and hindering each other's efforts. She also came to realize that their clientele was not necessarily political. The rules had sometimes been bent—inquiries or interventions by the police or a concomitant police organization, by the secret services, etc.—on behalf of some powerful individual, generally with connections in the parliamentary world, or business, or industry. Not strictly legal, not exactly open and above board, but all the same, it's been known to happen . . . In short, and in conclusion: perhaps the real powers that be—what people call the powers that be—are not necessarily found in the top ranks of government.

All a bit nebulous, no doubt . . . and at the same time perfectly clear.

"In astrology, my dear Tracy—my wife's an astrologer, you know, and a consultant to several ministers—espionage, the secret services, the parallel police, all that good stuff, they all live in the twelfth house of the Zodiac. The house of hidden things, of forces apparently inert but in reality influential and active, a house ruled by Neptune, the planet of ambiguity, mystery, secrets. Anyway, let's change the subject. Hand me the Brétillard file—you remember, he's that cuckold who lives on the Avenue Raphaël: another cheating-wife job. He's coming by this morning, then he's off to go hunting in Finland. Good luck to those poor wild boars, that's all I can say . . ."

68 Three Years Later

Confidential conversation, in a villa on the Basque coast, between an ex-Special Services agent turned macrobiotic restaurateur, and one of his trusted friends, a politician whose name needn't be mentioned here (nor his politics, nor his nationality, nor his age), in October 1999, i.e., some thirty-six months after the resolution of the highly delicate matter—and potential state scandal—that was the *Brown Java* affair:

"We sort of panicked when volume one of *Brown Java* came out. Remember, Malgodin had been promising all sorts of earth-shattering revelations on the subject of you know what. We had our orders. You of all people must know, when we get wind of a potentially subversive book in the works, we go on the alert."[6]

"Internal Intelligence usually deal with that, don't they?"

"Of course. But this one ended up going to us, because it seemed like something much bigger than the usual tabloid gossip. One of the authors, Dochin, lived with Céline Feuhant, who'd been holed up in the Limousin since 1951, politely minding her own goddamn business the whole time, it's true. We didn't know quite what to do when the orders came down, because Malgodin was a well-known drunk and a notorious bigmouth. Absolutely no good using the classic forms of coercion on him. Lush that he was, we knew he'd have blabbed it all to the four winds without a

---

6   Is that right? (Author's note.)

moment's thought. No, this was a delicate matter, and it called for the utmost discretion."

"You got your hands on the manuscript."

"The usual way. The standard method."

"The galleys."

"Right. Malgodin's secretary was a police informer. We put in a call to HQ, and they kindly sent us a set. G. read it. Skimmed it, I should say. Didn't see any real reason for us to get involved."

"So in the end the book came out as planned. Uncut and uncensored. No pressure on the publisher, even indirectly."

"Nope, not a thing. As it turned out, there was nothing too terrible in that first volume. It was the next one that scared us, we'd heard it was going to be brutal, maybe even dangerous. The boss was pissed off, though, because the reviews were all glowing. And the sales were huge. *Papillon* huge. Our little experiment with the critics before volume one hadn't done any good at all. Pointless. A complete waste of time."

"You know, if you want to intimidate those people . . ."

"Even before volume one came out, we knew we had to keep volume two—much more worrisome, or so we'd been promised—from ever hitting the shelves. Let the whole thing just fade quietly away. And for that, all we had to do was make sure volume one was a complete flop. No sales for volume one, no volume two."

"You can't buy off a literary critic."

"But you can make an impression on them. You can try, at least. And thereby—who knows?—maybe shut them up. That was the approach we settled on—far more effective than the old cash-stuffed envelope, we thought—and so we drew up a list of the most important critics, the most influential. I mean the ones who make a book sell, the ones who can send thousands of buyers scurrying out to the bookstores with one single word. Internal Intelligence has its moles in the literary world, of course, in the bistros and all that, so before long we found out that the two critics we had our eye on, Folenfant of *Le Cabinet de Lecture* and La Briançais of *Le Temps*, were madly and passionately in love with the thing. They'd read it in galleys. They were planning to praise it to high heaven, and of course that would have ruined everything: guaranteed success for volume one, the door left wide open for the far more worrisome volume two. So we had a staff meeting and went over the pros and cons, and finally decided we had to stop volume one from becoming a hit—and this when the thing was just about to come out. No way to buy those two off, obviously, but if we could eliminate them in time we'd at least keep their reviews out of the papers. Furthermore—two birds with one stone—the mysterious deaths of two big fans of *Brown Java* might—this was S.'s theory, bunch of crap if you ask me, put he had a lot of pull with the boss—might, as I was saying, send a little shudder running through the ranks of the critics. Sort of them give them pause, you see? Hey, you never know! The other critics who liked the book were also a headache, it's true, although a bit less so, but . . ."

"But you couldn't very well get rid of them all."

"Right. You know, those guys aren't like a soccer team or a theater troupe . . . You almost never see them all together, all taking the same plane . . ."

"Not even for a big book fair?"

"Absolutely not. Very few of them bother getting out of bed for that sort of thing. And the two or three who might end up going tend to do so under their own steam . . . By train, by car . . . In any case, for our purposes, it was only those two that mattered. The others had less of an effect on sales. La Briançais and Folenfant were the only real thorns in our side. Anyway, it was kind of a long shot, but we thought we'd give it a try, see what happened. At the last minute, the boss got cold feet . . . afraid we might screw it up . . . Remember those so-called IRA men we arrested in Vincennes? That sort of thing. Finally, after all that dithering, he decided to go for it."

"But something went wrong with Folenfant?"

"Well, yes. That's where we blew it. We gave the job to some youngsters who'd just joined the service. Real thickheads. They'd just come waltzing in from the antiterrorist squad. They fell all over themselves."

"They screwed up the mission?"

"The plan was for Folenfant to drown accidentally in the Forest of Compiègne or Rambouillet. In the end, we'd settled on Rambouillet, because it's closer to Paris. They botched it completely, the morons."

"Not the first time that's happened, I think."

"No, but it's rare. Thank God."

"Senseless deaths . . . inexplicable . . . illogical, even . . . There've been a few. I'm talking about well-known people. C., B., P. Let's stick to initials."

"Pure hearsay. But back to our little project. So my two ham-handed colleagues are waiting in the parking garage near Folenfant's car, a red Ford Fiesta I think it was. Folenfant's at the Lipp, having dinner with Cuzenat from *Le Francilien Week-End*, who hates *Brown Java*. They talk about the book, things start to get nasty. They almost come to blows. Doret, from Internal Intelligence, was eating a plate of choucroute at a table nearby, and I think it's safe to say Cuzenat was making no attempt to conceal his disagreement with Folenfant. Apparently he was really laying into him."

"So what happened?"

"So Cuzenat walked up to the red Fiesta and pulled out a key, and those two jerks jumped him."

"They thought it was Folenfant."

"Of course. Dumbfucks were only going by the car, you see? They had no idea what Folenfant looked like, never even looked at his picture. And as it happened Folenfant had lent his car to Cuzenat."

"So then what?"

"Well, they chloroform him and dump him into their Volvo, then off they go to Rambouillet. They drowned him, the jackasses. Cuzenat, who hated *Brown Java*! Can you imagine! An enormously influential critic, whose review might have stopped the book in its tracks!"

"I see. So it was the one who didn't like it that died."

"A tragic mistake."

"What about La Briançais? Was that a mistake too?"

"Of a kind. In a way."

"They said he didn't like the book. Or that he did like it at first, then had a complete change of heart."

"His girlfriend was saying that to anyone who would listen. She had a thing for that book, and she was furious to hear him bad-mouthing it."

"What happened?"

"In reality La Briançais hadn't changed his mind at all. He still adored the book. He was just trying to piss off his girl, because she was dumping him. No, he loved it. We know that because when the police looked into his death—as usual, they didn't hear about it till afterwards—they found the beginning of the review in his desk drawer. That thing could have done a great deal of damage. We asked the police to hand it over to us, just for safety's sake, just to be sure those few lines never showed up in *Le Temps*. And that was the end of the sensational review La Briançais never managed to finish."

"So La Briançais was crazy about *Brown Java*, and was going to make it a best seller."

"Exactly. So in that case we hit our mark. We were eliminating someone who really did like the book. Nothing like the tragic accident that did-in poor Cuzenat, whose very welcome loathing for the book should by all rights have earned him a long and happy life."

"I understand."

"So by slipping La Briançais under the wheels of a subway train, we sort of made up for our earlier mistake, if I can put it like that."

"Not that it really accomplished anything, since the book was a huge hit all the same."

"That's true. Too many good reviews. And one of our two targets, Folenfant, managed to publish his piece after all; ergo, fantastic sales. Maybe if we'd been able to deal with him like we did La Briançais . . . Maybe . . . No way to know."

"Couldn't you have tried again? With Folenfant, I mean?"

"We considered that, after a few days. But the bastard had already handed in his article. In any case, a second operation on Folenfant would have had dangers of its own. These things have to be prepared in advance, you know, it's not like popping a TV dinner into the oven. Besides, we were feeling sort of paralyzed after our earlier screw-up . . . We didn't want that happening again."

"In short, Folenfant barely avoided the scythe . . ."

"You can say that again. Some people are just lucky, I guess."

"And so volume two could come out."

"At that point W. stepped in to give it one last shot, one more try at intimidating them. Internal Intelligence had been asking around in the literary cafés, so we knew some of the critics were starting to wonder what the hell was going on . . . Some of them were even hinting at a vague menace hanging over anyone who panned *Rage Beneath the Cagoule*, citing the mysterious deaths of Cuzenat and La Briançais as evidence. And that's enough to inspire certain rebellious thoughts in people like that, who, simply to show their independence, would, in some cases at least—typical Frenchmen— have been perfectly capable of giving *Brown Java* a terrible review, even if they were head over heels in love with it."

"Which would have been pretty damn convenient for you."

"True. But those were just words. Just empty words spouted by journalists who didn't want anyone trying to manipulate them. As expected, that revolutionary impulse died out as quickly as it had come up. Everybody calmed down and decided to write whatever they liked. And the trouble is, they'd almost all gone ape over that goddamn volume two."

"But it turned out there wasn't much more in the second volume than in the first . . . Nothing really to write home about . . . So you could have saved yourselves the trouble, and . . ."

"It's true, we ended up pretty much right where we were with volume one. Except that it was all much trickier this time, with volume one having been such a spectacular success . . ."

"You didn't know whether to step in or not?"

"That's right. But the threat of volume three was still there. Getting clearer all the time. And much more dangerous."

"But suppose that threat, as you call it, was just more hot air? Just another attempt to drum up publicity, who knows . . ."

"We couldn't take that chance. If this were a book by . . . by Jules Dupont or whoever, that'd be different. But we knew Feuhant was behind this whole thing. She was deliberately turning up the heat from one volume to the next, that was clear. Very irritating, from our point of view. Let me tell you, there were some . . . let's call them X., Y., and Z. . . . who were just about wetting their pants. So we took the threat very seriously. Besides, unless you're a complete idiot or pathologically naïve, you only had to read a little between the lines in volume two to see volume three was going to be a bombshell. No, I repeat, we just couldn't take that chance."

"But wasn't it a little late to try putting a stop to the thing?"

"You know, sometimes the sequel to a smash hit ends up a flop. It's been known to happen. Yes, we were very reluctant to act . . . Suppose volume two didn't sell—would that stop the publisher from bringing out volume three? None of us could answer that one. It was pretty much a coin toss. We went on mulling it over, back and forth, and then in the end the boss decided we had to do something. The elimination of a critic with a gift for selling books might just do the trick."

"In short, a carbon copy of the first scenario."

"Yes, but tougher to tackle, and riskier, like I said. We almost ended up letting it drop. But we were too far in to quit now . . . No stopping in mid-stream. One of Internal Intelligence's informers got a look at Ranfolin's review for *L'Européen du Jeudi*. Very positive, dripping with praise, almost over the top. The boss gave us the go-ahead to step in, though he wasn't too happy about it. Ranfolin was a real menace from our point of view. He could fill a bookstore with buyers quick as a November wind covers a sidewalk with dead leaves. So we couldn't just stand around staring at our shoes. A review like that in a journal as widely read as *L'Européen du Jeudi* could make volume two a surefire bestseller. That rag had a circulation of 650,000, and still does today. Of course, the news wasn't slow to spread: 'Have you heard? Ranfolin's written a glowing review on volume two of *Brown Java*,' etc."

"And so?"

"Well, to deal with the most urgent problem first, we destroyed Ranfolin's review. Which we couldn't have done even if we'd wanted to in Folenfant's case, because the editor of *Le Cabinet de Lecture* had taken the article home, and was keeping it under lock and key. Furthermore, we had no one in place at *Le Cabinet*, unlike *L'Européen*, where we had three or four moles. So Ranfolin's text ended up shredded. We did it the day before the next issue was going to be set up. I don't remember the exact date."

"And what came of that?"

"Well, the editors were wondering what the hell had happened to Ranfolin's piece . . . the photocopies, the whole deal . . . There were no duplicates, nothing. A wave of panic swept over the place, because pretty soon Malgodin heard the review had been lost. And what a review it was! An apotheosis! At a dinner party, Diasse's son-in-law heard *L'Européen*'s editor-in-chief saying that Ranfolin's article seemed almost as much to be praising *Brown Java* as . . . Sartre's *Nausea*, one of his favorite books. A very odd review."

"So then what happened?"

"Well, the newspaper called Ranfolin right away, and fell all over themselves apologizing for losing his article. He blew his stack. Particularly because he'd never bothered to make a copy. 'Don't you see the risk I'm running?' he was screaming into the phone. They couldn't understand what he meant. Ranfolin hadn't written a word on volume one. He didn't like it. But he was sure as hell making up for that now!"

"So what did Ranfolin end up doing?"

"As diplomatically as they could, they asked him if he would be so kind and so generous as to rewrite his article. Before the next morning! And mind you, he was a very slow writer. So he bitched for a while, but finally he calmed down and agreed. One of our stoolies let us know, and we stepped in at once. We weren't going to let him make the same mistake twice. Ranfolin always liked to take a little after-lunch walk in the Parc des Buttes-Chaumont."

"I see."

"He never even knew what was happening."

"Why couldn't you have just dealt with Feuhant herself? Wouldn't that have been simpler?"

"That's what we told ourselves later. As you can imagine, it's not an easy decision to make. We couldn't eliminate Feuhant unless we were absolutely sure there'd be no inquest. No way did we want an examining magistrate on our ass! Too many waves. So we needed a 'prêt-à-porter' murderer, if I may."

"A lunatic. A fanatic."

"Exactly. Like with Kennedy. Like with Jaurès . . . or Laval . . . well, that one didn't work out, but . . . And let's not forget Gandhi . . . or Jacques Clément, a little further back . . . And others . . . You've got your motive all wrapped up in a neat little package. Open and shut. No inquest. No investigation. The judges leave us in peace. Perfect."

"I understand. The tried and true methods."

"Never been known to fail!"

"And why not an accident?"

"We weren't using that trick much anymore. At least, that's how it was when I left the force. Again, because of the inquests. Besides, putting someone into a plane that's already loaded with passengers . . . and then bringing down the plane . . . It's a big operation. Too much heavy lifting. And anyway . . . could you see Feuhant taking a plane? To go where? To the Ile d'Yeu to put flowers on the old man's grave? To begin with, she didn't give a flying fuck about any of that stuff. No. Not an option."

"So what then?"

"Well, before long they were saying volume three would be out in October or November '96."

"So clearly your little games with the critics hadn't got you very far."

"An unfortunate initiative. Very badly put together, too. What a waste of time! And as it happens, it was right about then that the service was reorganized from top to bottom."

"So . . . what about volume three? If memory serves—I confess I haven't read *Brown Java*, but if I remember right, it never came out."

"No, but it was a close shave."

A newspaper had been left on a nearby coffee table, next to the glasses, the liqueur bottles, and a small box of cigars. Lying open to pages two and three, the newspaper displayed a brief article, a headline, and a quarter-column of text:

RELEASED

Jean-Rémi Dochin, coauthor of Dancing the Brown Java, *emerged yesterday morning a free man from Limoges district jail, where he was incarcerated in July 1996 following the murder of Céline Feuhant—an "act of justice," in Monsieur Dochin's words, carried out on learning that the woman who had taken him in was none other than the Bitch of Drancy. It must be remembered that an uncle of Dochin's was arrested and tortured by the French Gestapo in 1943 before being deported to Mauthausen, where he died at his captors' hands. Sentenced in June 1997 to four years' imprisonment—his sentence lightened by extenuating circumstances and the improbability that he might pose a danger to others—the writer was given time off for good behavior.*

69   The Panhandler

It happened toward the end of July. There was no one at La Halte but Céline and me. Odette had left for the Ile d'Yeu with her Pétainist friends, Colette was laid off, the place was empty, no guests since the day before and none expected for two or three days.

The guy showed up around two in the afternoon. I recognized him right off. It was that panhandler who'd stayed here a few times before, the one with the straw hat, always complaining about being driven out of downtown La Rochelle.

Céline and I had just finished lunch. We were out in the garden, enjoying the sunshine on our chaises longues.

He was looking even grimier than the last time, and now he had a scruffy beard half-hiding that Mongol face of his. He'd driven up in a ratty old car, and parked it by the front gate.

"Well, look who's here, it's our old friend from La Rochelle," said Céline, a bit surprised, but still sociable. "Passing through our pretty little corner of France?"

She barely had time to stand up. Wearing gloves, the drifter pulled out a huge automatic handgun, a .38 I think, and started to fire, emptying the whole barrel into Céline's chest. It made one hell of a noise. Céline collapsed without so much as an "oof." It looked like someone had thrown a ladleful of crushed cherries on her dress. I'm sure she didn't even have time to realize what was happening. I looked at the blood. She'd taken a load of the high-caliber stuff. Like a wild boar.

"My turn now?" I said, jumping up.

"No, we're going to spare you, Dochin."

Slipping his weapon into his battered old shoulder-bag, he added:

"But remember this, and remember it well: you've just shot the Bitch of Drancy."

I didn't get it at first, but then it all started to make sense. The whole thing had been planned out in advance. The guy knew Céline and I were alone in the house. How? I figured that out later, when I realized he was working for . . . I heard somebody call them the Special Services Squad. That could mean anything at all. At the service of who, exactly? No one knows much about them, but they exist all the same. So clearly this guy had been keeping an eye on Céline. He showed up at the motel now and then, did his little act . . . They never let Céline alone. Same deal for the two or three ordinary-looking guys in three-piece suits, those traveling-sales-man types who sometimes came looking for a room at La Halte. Internal Intelligence. Céline always turned them away, told them to try at a normal hotel. She was always polite about it, told them somewhere else would be more to their liking.

Céline's killer confiscated some papers from the house, search-ing the place without a care in the world, knowing there was no one around. What was I supposed to do? The man was armed, and all I had was my bare hands. Besides which, I'm not very brave.

Of course, the SSS guy took the final draft of volume three, *If These Francisques Could Talk*, practically done, maybe ten pages left to type. He also went through Céline's armoire and took the first drafts of volumes one and two, the outlines and sketches, a big load of paper, reams of notes and notebooks, then went out and dumped it all into his car. Malgodin was expecting volume three in mid-August, and he'd promised to send the proofs by the end of September. The book was supposed to be out in November, the galleys sent off to the major critics around the tenth of October. It was going to be a big deal, make a whole lot of noise, give a nice case of cold sweats to two or three traitors who'd got themselves rehabilitated after the war.

The guy also made off with the manuscripts of my own *Java*, the typescript I'd given to Gastinel as well as the handwritten one, pounds and pounds of my chicken-scratch, and even the draft of the crime novel I'd started—a real clean sweep.

He didn't leave me waiting there long. In a few words, he re-capped all my filthy little secrets, dragged them out into the daz-zling light of day. I realized he knew everything. The cops had got their hands on the videocassette. The murder in Carrouges had been discovered. He spilled all that out in a sentence that wouldn't have taken up two lines in a book. How had they figured it out? Had Gastinel double-crossed me and handed that goddamn video over to the police? I never did figure that out. One way or another, they held in their hands the proof, more or less, that I'd murdered Maryvonne Le Goff, who vanished on June 3, 1995, never to be seen again (damn right!), not even by the hosts of the TV show *Missing Person*, who her parents had gone to in December '95.

"So we know you killed that girl, Dochin."

"Gastinel was with me!" I shouted, enraged.

"We don't care about that. You're the one who interests us. No-body else. You've got a life sentence coming for sure. But we're pre-pared to let that whole thing slide if you'll agree to be the murderer of Céline Feuhant. The public won't see the execution of the Bitch of Drancy as an unpardonable crime. Just give them the 'act of jus-tice' routine . . . You might even be interviewed on TV. 'I killed her to show that, however devious they may be, those who commit crimes against humanity will never escape, as long as there are people like me who have the courage to let justice be done . . .' That sort of thing, shouldn't be hard to come up with. You could even go further, maybe say you were seriously thinking of heading to Sarajevo to deal with one of the masterminds of the massacres there, something like that. They'll eat it up. As for Feuhant, all you have to do is mention your uncle who died at Mauthausen . . . His arrest by the French Gestapo . . . His unspeakably cruel interrogation . . . You weren't even born yet, it's true, but you saw your parents' grief clearly enough! Throw all that out, and you've got some lovely hand-embroidered extenuating circumstances in your pocket. Understand? Might make people think . . . Lay it on as thick as you like. Give it some thought. If you had a prior record, the jury might worry you could kill again . . . But in your case . . . They should go easy on you. Ten years max, that's the going rate for crimes of passion. But don't worry, you won't even get that. Whereas if we're talking about an innocent fourteen-year-old girl . . . And besides, you're not just anybody, you're a well-known writer, a celebrity. If they stick you with five years, I'll eat my hat. In Paris or Versailles you might end up with a vaguely Pétainist jury . . . or just a nostalgic one. But not in the Corrèze. So, Dochin? Thinking it over? OK, but make it quick."

"But you've got it all wrong! Céline Feuhant never killed anyone."

"No, but she looked on as more than one Gaullist or communist died at the hands of their torturers. . . and she never made a move. Never put up a fight. That's pretty much as good as a special show at the Vélodrome d'Hiver with free admission for women, children, and old men, wouldn't you say?"

"She never killed anyone . . ." I murmured again.

"Listen, we're not going to reopen the case . . . Make up your mind, Dochin. Five years or life in the pen. Take your pick. But make it fast. The clock's ticking. Three P.M. already. I believe your handyman Monsieur Félibut's supposed to come by this afternoon to pick up some tools and a ladder . . . Make your choice, if you'd be so kind. Do it fast."

"And if I say no?"

"I suppose we might still be able to spare you a life sentence."

The man in the straw hat laid his hand on his dingy old bag for a moment.

"What does that mean?"

"We'll deal with it in our own way . . ."

We waited a while. The guy understood that my answer was yes. He ordered me to take the corpse by the ankles. He grabbed her arms, and we carried her into the little front office. Poor Céline was already stiff as a board.

He kicked up the bloodstained sand around the chaises longues.

"You know what to do next," he said.

Still holding his pistol, he went to his clunker and got behind the wheel. He started her up and drove off who knows where. Probably a ways down the road, behind some trees. Then he walked back to the motel's front door and stood there looking toward the Térignac road. As for me, I was waiting on the threshold of the front office, with Céline lying dead just behind me, almost touching my heels. Then came the sound of an engine, getting louder. The Mongol hurried over to me:

"That's your handyman . . ."

Félibut coming to pick up his gear. I knew he'd been doing some work back at his place.

"Hurry!"

The fake vagrant shoved me into the office. My feet got tangled up in the corpse, and I almost went flying. The door to the garden was still open. The guy slipped outside . . . The old sedan pulled into the yard. Félibut opened the driver's side door. A couple of gunshots rang out. Out of sight of Félibut, the ersatz panhandler tossed the pistol through the open office window. I picked it up. My spineless way of accepting his offer. The murderer had already taken off through the back, disappearing into the undergrowth. It wasn't hard to guess what would come next: he'd race toward the Vézère and leave the grounds a little further along, jump back into his jalopy and vanish for good . . . And that would be that.

Félibut came into the office and found me with the gun in my hand. Speechless, he looked at Céline's body on the floor. Then all of a sudden he lunged at me, reaching for the weapon. Before long he realized I wasn't going to put up a fight. He picked up the automatic, using his handkerchief because of the fingerprints. Hick that he was, he still knew the drill.

"What have you done, Monsieur Jean-Rémi?"

What was I supposed to tell him? I must have been white as a sheet. He was staring at me with eyes wide. He picked up the phone in his big callused paw and called the police.

A half-hour later, at the police station in Térignac, I made my confession. Yes, I'd killed Céline Feuhant. Because . . . In short, I laid it out just like the guy in the straw hat said I should.

70 On the Banks of the Vézère

*You know, when Justice absolutely must
have a guilty party, she always
finds one in the end . . .*

Marcel Aymé
La Tête des Autres

It's true, I didn't do too badly out of that deal. Three or four years
sitting on my ass in a jail cell, that's a hell of a lot better than life
behind bars, let me tell you.

That dimwit who wasted I can't remember who in '93 or '94 got
to go on TV. I'm not sure how he swung that, because I myself got
nothing, not even the local radio.

I don't know how it was for that guy, how he felt about his victim,
I mean, but in my case, when the sun went down and I sat in my
cell thinking of the woman I'd supposedly killed, I bawled like a
little baby.

The trial was in June '97. They gave me a lawyer, a young guy,
Peyrebeilh was his name. Did a great job. Four years. Just like they
promised.

"You'll be out in two, Dochin."

Some reporters came around after I got out, wondering if volume three of *Brown Java* would still be published someday. I told
them my co-author had been away for a while—the blimp thought

it might be nice to take a round-the-world trip, just for a change of scenery, he said, and to flee the "wearisome spotlight" of success—so now the manuscript was stalled out.

A few weeks later I heard Gastinel had met his end in an alleyway in São Paulo. Stabbed in the heart by a mugger, they told me. No suspects, no arrests.

The day after my sentencing, the papers printed a little article:

> *According to a statement by Monsieur Euloge Malgodin, CEO of Le Papyrus Editions, the lucky publishers of* Brown Java, *it may be true that (to take a well-known example) Mademoiselle de Scudéry was the real author of the thick novels published under the name of her brother Georges, but there is absolutely no truth to the persistent rumor that Céline Feuhant, shot to death by Jean-Rémi Dochin, was the true author of the literary monument that is* Dancing the Brown Java, *volumes one and two. To be sure, as a young woman, the Bitch of Drancy produced a number of poems and short stories much admired by several eminent literary figures of the prewar years, but it is well known that she had long since abandoned all pretensions to a literary career.*

I got out of the joint in fall '99, and Malgodin was the first person to take me in his arms. (A quick remark, in passing: his breath reeked of Pernod.) He immediately dragged me into the nearest café. Half sloshed, of course.

"So, how about *Brown Java*? You'll be getting back to it now, I hope? How's volume three coming along? What's it been up to all this time? Wandering around in the cellars of the Bibliothèque de France?"

"First we'll have to find out where Gastinel's got to," I objected.

"He's traveling . . . . All over the world . . . Not a word from him. The rat! What a thing to do to us!"

"We'll have to wait till he comes back, then."

"You wouldn't happen to have anything else for me in the meantime, would you, my dear Dochin?"

Before Céline died I'd started a crime novel, an S-H-A novel (suburbs-hash-AIDS), that sort of thing still hadn't gone out of fashion, no one had come up with anything better. I knew I'd never finish it. Or more precisely, that I'd never start it all over again, since the Mongol had made off with it. Malgodin was beginning to get on my nerves. I didn't even suggest he republish my crime novel *Mayhem in Les Minguettes*, this time under my real name, Jean-Rémi Dochin.

I hung around Paris for a few weeks, sick at heart, staying in that same old hotel by the Gare d'Austerlitz. Pretty soon I had more than my fill of the capital. By chance, I heard that La Halte du Bon Accueil had been put up for sale. With each passing day, the memory of Céline grew inside me. I couldn't get her out of my head.

And it was the banks of the Vézère, at the dawn of the third millennium, back behind the motel—all closed up now, shut down, dead, even the birds had gone silent—that her little lamb chose as the place to put a bullet in his brain.

PIERRE SINIAC (1928–2002) received the Grand Prix de Littérature Policière in 1981 for three of his works, including *Aime le Maudit*. Under the title *Ferdinaud Céline*, *The Collaborators* was published in French in 1997 to great acclaim.

JORDAN STUMP is the noted translator of numerous modern French novelists, including Nobel prize winner Claude Simon. His translation of Simon's *Le Jardin des Plantes* won the French American Foundation's Translation Prize.

JANICE GALLOWAY, *Foreign Parts*.
   The Trick Is to Keep Breathing.
WILLIAM H. GASS, *Cartesian Sonata
   and Other Novellas*.
   Finding a Form.
   A Temple of Texts.
   The Tunnel.
   Willie Masters' Lonesome Wife.
GÉRARD GAVARRY, *Hoppla! 1 2 3*.
ETIENNE GILSON,
   The Arts of the Beautiful.
   Forms and Substances in the Arts.
C. S. GISCOMBE, *Giscome Road*.
   Here.
   Prairie Style.
DOUGLAS GLOVER, *Bad News of the Heart*.
   The Enamoured Knight.
WITOLD GOMBROWICZ,
   A Kind of Testament.
KAREN ELIZABETH GORDON, *The Red Shoes*.
GEORGI GOSPODINOV, *Natural Novel*.
JUAN GOYTISOLO, *Count Julian*.
   Juan the Landless.
   Makbara.
   Marks of Identity.
PATRICK GRAINVILLE, *The Cave of Heaven*.
HENRY GREEN, *Back*.
   Blindness.
   Concluding.
   Doting.
   Nothing.
JIŘÍ GRUŠA, *The Questionnaire*.
GABRIEL GUDDING,
   Rhode Island Notebook.
MELA HARTWIG, *Am I a Redundant
   Human Being?*
JOHN HAWKES, *The Passion Artist*.
   Whistlejacket.
ALEKSANDAR HEMON, ED.,
   Best European Fiction 2010.
AIDAN HIGGINS, *A Bestiary*.
   Balcony of Europe.
   Bornholm Night-Ferry.
   Darkling Plain: Texts for the Air.
   Flotsam and Jetsam.
   Langrishe, Go Down.
   Scenes from a Receding Past.
   Windy Arbours.
ALDOUS HUXLEY, *Antic Hay*.
   Crome Yellow.
   Point Counter Point.
   Those Barren Leaves.
   Time Must Have a Stop.
MIKHAIL IOSSEL AND JEFF PARKER, EDS.,
   *Amerika: Russian Writers View the
   United States*.
GERT JONKE, *The Distant Sound*.
   Geometric Regional Novel.
   Homage to Czerny.
   The System of Vienna.
JACQUES JOUET, *Mountain R*.
   Savage.
CHARLES JULIET, *Conversations with
   Samuel Beckett and Bram van
   Velde*.
MIEKO KANAI, *The Word Book*.

HUGH KENNER, *The Counterfeiters*.
   *Flaubert, Joyce and Beckett:
   The Stoic Comedians*.
   Joyce's Voices.
DANILO KIŠ, *Garden, Ashes*.
   A Tomb for Boris Davidovich.
ANITA KONKKA, *A Fool's Paradise*.
GEORGE KONRÁD, *The City Builder*.
TADEUSZ KONWICKI, *A Minor Apocalypse*.
   The Polish Complex.
MENIS KOUMANDAREAS, *Koula*.
ELAINE KRAF, *The Princess of 72nd Street*.
JIM KRUSOE, *Iceland*.
EWA KURYLUK, *Century 21*.
ERIC LAURRENT, *Do Not Touch*.
VIOLETTE LEDUC, *La Bâtarde*.
SUZANNE JILL LEVINE, *The Subversive
   Scribe: Translating Latin
   American Fiction*.
DEBORAH LEVY, *Billy and Girl*.
   *Pillow Talk in Europe and Other
   Places*.
JOSÉ LEZAMA LIMA, *Paradiso*.
ROSA LIKSOM, *Dark Paradise*.
OSMAN LINS, *Avalovara*.
   The Queen of the Prisons of Greece.
ALF MAC LOCHLAINN,
   The Corpus in the Library.
   Out of Focus.
RON LOEWINSOHN, *Magnetic Field(s)*.
BRIAN LYNCH, *The Winner of Sorrow*.
D. KEITH MANO, *Take Five*.
MICHELINE AHARONIAN MARCOM,
   The Mirror in the Well.
BEN MARCUS,
   The Age of Wire and String.
WALLACE MARKFIELD,
   Teitlebaum's Window.
   To an Early Grave.
DAVID MARKSON, *Reader's Block*.
   Springer's Progress.
   Wittgenstein's Mistress.
CAROLE MASO, *AVA*.
LADISLAV MATEJKA AND KRYSTYNA
   POMORSKA, EDS.,
   *Readings in Russian Poetics:
   Formalist and Structuralist Views*.
HARRY MATHEWS,
   *The Case of the Persevering Maltese:
   Collected Essays*.
   Cigarettes.
   The Conversions.
   *The Human Country: New and
   Collected Stories*.
   The Journalist.
   My Life in CIA.
   Singular Pleasures.
   *The Sinking of the Odradek
   Stadium*.
   Tlooth.
   20 Lines a Day.
ROBERT L. MCLAUGHLIN, ED.,
   *Innovations: An Anthology of
   Modern & Contemporary Fiction*.
HERMAN MELVILLE, *The Confidence-Man*.
AMANDA MICHALOPOULOU, *I'd Like*.

FOR A FULL LIST OF PUBLICATIONS, VISIT:
www.dalkeyarchive.com

STEVEN MILLHAUSER,
  The Barnum Museum.
  In the Penny Arcade.
RALPH J. MILLS, JR.,
  Essays on Poetry.
MOMUS, *The Book of Jokes.*
CHRISTINE MONTALBETTI, *Western.*
OLIVE MOORE, *Spleen.*
NICHOLAS MOSLEY, *Accident.*
  Assassins.
  Catastrophe Practice.
  Children of Darkness and Light.
  Experience and Religion.
  God's Hazard.
  The Hesperides Tree.
  Hopeful Monsters.
  Imago Bird.
  Impossible Object.
  Inventing God.
  Judith.
  Look at the Dark.
  Natalie Natalia.
  Paradoxes of Peace.
  Serpent.
  Time at War.
  The Uses of Slime Mould:
    Essays of Four Decades.
WARREN MOTTE,
  Fables of the Novel: French Fiction
    since 1990.
  Fiction Now: The French Novel in
    the 21st Century.
  Oulipo: A Primer of Potential
    Literature.
YVES NAVARRE, *Our Share of Time.*
  Sweet Tooth.
DOROTHY NELSON, *In Night's City.*
  Tar and Feathers.
ESHKOL NEVO, *Homesick.*
WILFRIDO D. NOLLEDO,
  But for the Lovers.
FLANN O'BRIEN,
  At Swim-Two-Birds.
  At War.
  The Best of Myles.
  The Dalkey Archive.
  Further Cuttings.
  The Hard Life.
  The Poor Mouth.
  The Third Policeman.
CLAUDE OLLIER, *The Mise-en-Scène.*
PATRIK OUŘEDNÍK, *Europeana.*
FERNANDO DEL PASO,
  News from the Empire.
  Palinuro of Mexico.
ROBERT PINGET, *The Inquisitory.*
  Mahu or The Material.
  Trio.
MANUEL PUIG,
  Betrayed by Rita Hayworth.
  The Buenos Aires Affair.
  Heartbreak Tango.
RAYMOND QUENEAU, *The Last Days.*
  Odile.
  Pierrot Mon Ami.
  Saint Glinglin.

ANN QUIN, *Berg.*
  Passages.
  Three.
  Tripticks.
ISHMAEL REED,
  The Free-Lance Pallbearers.
  The Last Days of Louisiana Red.
  Ishmael Reed: The Plays.
  Reckless Eyeballing.
  The Terrible Threes.
  The Terrible Twos.
  Yellow Back Radio Broke-Down.
JEAN RICARDOU, *Place Names.*
RAINER MARIA RILKE,
  The Notebooks of Malte Laurids
    Brigge.
JULIÁN RÍOS, *Larva: A Midsummer*
    Night's Babel.
  Poundemonium.
AUGUSTO ROA BASTOS, *I the Supreme.*
OLIVIER ROLIN, *Hotel Crystal.*
ALIX CLEO ROUBAUD, *Alix's Journal.*
JACQUES ROUBAUD, *The Form of a*
    City Changes Faster, Alas, Than
    the Human Heart.
  The Great Fire of London.
  Hortense in Exile.
  Hortense Is Abducted.
  The Loop.
  The Plurality of Worlds of Lewis.
  The Princess Hoppy.
  Some Thing Black.
LEON S. ROUDIEZ,
  French Fiction Revisited.
VEDRANA RUDAN, *Night.*
STIG SÆTERBAKKEN, *Siamese.*
LYDIE SALVAYRE, *The Company of Ghosts.*
  Everyday Life.
  The Lecture.
  Portrait of the Writer as a
    Domesticated Animal.
  The Power of Flies.
LUIS RAFAEL SÁNCHEZ,
  Macho Camacho's Beat.
SEVERO SARDUY, *Cobra & Maitreya.*
NATHALIE SARRAUTE,
  Do You Hear Them?
  Martereau.
  The Planetarium.
ARNO SCHMIDT, *Collected Stories.*
  Nobodaddy's Children.
CHRISTINE SCHUTT, *Nightwork.*
GAIL SCOTT, *My Paris.*
DAMION SEARLS, *What We Were Doing*
    and Where We Were Going.
JUNE AKERS SEESE,
  Is This What Other Women Feel Too?
  What Waiting Really Means.
BERNARD SHARE, *Inish.*
  Transit.
AURELIE SHEEHAN,
  Jack Kerouac Is Pregnant.
VIKTOR SHKLOVSKY, *Knight's Move.*
  A Sentimental Journey:
    Memoirs 1917–1922.
  Energy of Delusion: A Book on Plot.

FOR A FULL LIST OF PUBLICATIONS, VISIT:
www.dalkeyarchive.com